Infinity's Child

Also by Harry Stein:

THE MAGIC BULLET
ETHICS (AND OTHER LIABILITIES)
HOOPLA
ONE OF THE GUYS

Infinity's Child

HARRY STEIN

Delacorte  Press

Published by
Delacorte Press
Bantam Doubleday Dell Publishing Group, Inc.
1540 Broadway
New York, New York 10036

The trademark Delacorte Press® is registered in the U.S. Patent and
Trademark Office.

ISBN 0-385-31476-0

Manufactured in the United States of America

For Priscilla
For everything

ACKNOWLEDGMENTS

In all the time we've been together, as confidants and helpmates, never has my wife Priscilla been a greater source of inspiration and support than in the creation of this book. Her input is to be found on almost every page.

I also owe particular thanks to my friends Mark Allen Smith and Dr. Cy Stein, both of whom gave unstintingly of their time and talent. I hope they know what it means to me.

Among the many others who, in various ways, contributed their thoughts and expertise are: Ken Rotner, Lucy Schneider, Lary Greiner, Kevin Dawkins, Myra Stein, Steven Clarke, Zach Berke, Dr. Leonard Lustgarten, Steve Michaud, David Black, Martha Malave, Dr. Stephen Dolgin, Annie Rotner, Rich Sauerhaft, Mike Winkelman, Dr. Alvin Berman, Sybil Adelman, Martin Sage, Ed Golson, Susan Soriano; and most especially, Cherise Grant. To each and all, I am profoundly grateful.

Finally, I've been blessed with the wondrous Joy Harris as agent and friend. And with an extraordinary editor, Leslie Schnur, whose talent, warmth, commitment, and sheer enthusiasm make the act of writing—and even rewriting—very nearly pleasurable.

Infinity's Child

Sally Benedict didn't know how much longer she could keep up appearances. Never much at lighthearted party chatter to begin with, playing hostess this evening for the *Edwardstown Weekly*'s annual Halloween open house left her mouth dry and her head throbbing.

It was incredible, some kind of grotesque joke—this year there were babies *everywhere*. Where had they all come from? As editor of the *Weekly*, how could she have not known about so dramatic a rise in the local newborn population?

But, no, of course it wasn't that. Probably there had been just as many at last year's party, and the one the year before. She'd just never noticed before.

The change was in her.

Now, turning the corner on her way to the kitchen for another bottle of cider, she stopped in midstride. This one was the most achingly appealing yet. Asleep in his mother's arms, all pink cheeks and blond fuzz, he was a vision out of a Renaissance painting.

For a long moment she just stared.

"He's two months, this is his very first party," announced the mother, beaming. "His name's Charlie."

"He's beautiful."

Though Sally had known the woman vaguely since high school, her name always seemed to escape her.

"I'm really lucky. I never thought it would happen, I just about gave up hope. . . ."

Tentatively, Sally reached out and brushed his cheek with her thumb; as always, surprised at the extraordinary softness.

"What about you, Sally? Think you might still take the plunge?"

She quickly withdrew her hand. "Uhh . . . I can't say."

"Of course," said the mother coolly, defensive. "To each her own, I guess. Not everyone's a baby person."

Jeannie Porter, Sally realized through her pain, that was her name—and she'd never much liked her. But she resisted the impulse to answer in kind. After all, the feeling was probably shared by most in the room. Sally Benedict's driving passion was her work, that's what everyone around here thought.

And how, really, could she even blame them? Not so long ago she'd have said the same thing herself.

"Does he have a costume?" asked Sally. "I'd love to get a shot of him for the paper. . . ."

Generating goodwill for the *Weekly* was, after all, the purpose of this gathering. Kids had been trooping to the makeshift photo studio in the den all evening long to be snapped for the paper's annual "Edwardstown's Kids Do Halloween!" feature.

Instantly, Jeannie was smiling again. "I tried to make him a pirate, but he wouldn't take the eye patch."

"Next year, then," offered Sally, starting to disengage. "We'll save the front page."

Distractedly greeting people as she went, she made her way through the crowded dining room to what was left of the six-foot-long super hero and sliced off a piece.

Then, pouring herself a plastic cup of red wine—her fourth—she retreated to a corner.

"You okay?" asked her husband, Mark, appearing beside her.

"I gotta get out of here."

He nodded meaningfully. "Jeannie Porter's immaculate conception, right?"

"What?"

"Oh, you're lucky, you were spared the full story." He took her hand and squeezed. "Don't let it get to you, she's resented you since high school—ever since you whipped her in the finals of the four forty."

"Thanks, that helps." She gave a wistful smile. "It beats thinking of *myself* as bitter and petty."

In fact, he'd loved her just as long. Even back then, she was more complicated than she showed; a lithe blonde with an athlete's grace, inquisitive and full of humor, her deep brown eyes reflecting her quicksilver moods. Something of a star himself in high school—rhythm guitar in the area's best novice rock band—like everyone else he recognized Sally Benedict as a supernova, operating at a level of competency and confidence that had nothing to do with normal adolescence. Already the future she'd been plotting since elementary school seemed to be unfolding. Who else in this rural New Hampshire town had ever won *Mademoiselle* magazine's annual essay contest, with its prize of a summer internship in New York City? Who else had even thought to enter?

Four years ago, when she returned to town after her father's death in a car accident, it was as a big-deal reporter with *The Philadelphia Inquirer;* while he was still going off every day to their former alma mater, teaching science. So he was startled the first time they ran into one another by her offer to buy him dinner—and nothing short of floored by her admission that she'd had a secret crush on him also. Steeling himself for her departure three weeks later, he scarcely dared believe it when she announced her intention to stay.

"What about your job?" was the obvious question.

"My mother needs me a lot more. I hear they're looking for

someone to run the *Weekly*." She paused, then, with such conviction, it was as if the words had never been spoken before, "This is home, this is where I'm happiest."

As literal about these things as most guys, Mark understood only much later that, on some level, her return had at least as much to do with starting a family of her own. Even now, just thirty-six, she could probably have her pick of high-profile jobs in Boston or New York. But what she wouldn't have was this rambling Victorian with its immense front yard, and relatives close at hand, and the ability to bend a work schedule around the demands of motherhood.

To Mark, an easygoing sort, the idea of kids was fine. Why not? In a vague sort of way he'd always figured it would someday happen. But not having kids would be okay too. It was this helpless in-between state that was so hard to take; the maelstrom of anxiety and doubt into which Sally had been thrown after more than a year of trying.

Now, at the party, he spotted a pair of sullen sixteen-year-olds with pierced noses and dyed pink hair lounging in a nearby corner. "Hey, guys," he called out, for Sally's benefit. "Terrific costumes."

"You know them?"

"Former students of mine." He dropped his voice. "Look at the bright side—*that's* what babies turn into."

She smiled weakly, appreciating the effort. "I'll take my chances."

"Look," he offered, "you really look like you can use a break. Why don't you duck out for a while? Your mom and I will handle things here." He nodded toward Sally's mother in the next room, shepherding a half dozen kids into line beneath a jack-o'-lantern piñata.

She hesitated, then nodded. "Just for a little while."

Slowly she made her way upstairs and into the spare room Mark had turned into a home office.

Taking a couple of Tylenol, she clicked on the TV and collapsed onto the couch. Arm flung across her face, watching through one heavily lidded eye, she flashed by the channels.

Abruptly, she sat up, and flipped back a couple of spots.

Yes, there he was—R. Paul Holland! Slightly grayer than when she had last seen him, back when they were working together in Philadelphia, but wearing precisely the same thoughtful expression he always used for public appearances.

America's greatest science reporter—a man of unsurpassed integrity and acumen. And the single most cynical person she had ever known.

The program was on the cable station CNBC. Holland and another guest flanked the host, who was speaking directly into the camera.

". . . challenging the belief that aging is inevitable. Could science really make the age-old dream of eternal youth a reality? Tonight: the exciting new field of longevity research. Our guests: Dr. Jaroslav Dusek, a pioneer in such research in his native Slovakia. And prize-winning reporter R. Paul Holland of the *New York Herald*, who has recently written a series on . . ."

She noted the host's deference and, in reaction, Holland's warm smile.

Though the pounding in her head was worse than ever, the feeling that swept over her was remarkably like relief. God, to think of all the months and years she had spent among acclaimed journalists whose egos, up close and personal, never stopped needing shoring up! For all the frustrations of the life she was living, how lucky she was to have left her old one behind!

Still, she couldn't bring herself to switch it off.

R. Paul Holland liked to tell people he'd learned from one of the masters. Just before his first appearance on the *Donahue* show, Phil himself had taken him aside and offered his patented pep talk: *Open strong, grab the audience in the first two minutes, or they're gone!*

Now, in the cozy Fort Lee, New Jersey, studio, the adrenaline was already pumping as the host read the last words of his introduction off the monitor and turned his way.

"So, Mr. Holland, you've been looking into this. Any truth to the claims by some scientists they're going to stretch the human life span far beyond present limits?"

"I always like to start with good news." Holland smiled broadly. "What once would have been regarded as close to miraculous is now about to become routine. It looks like millions of us now in our thirties, forties, and fifties will live past one hundred."

"*Millions* of us?" He looked surprised, delighted.

"With a little care and self-restraint. Our understanding of the human body and its needs is expanding at an astonishing rate. With improved diet and proper conditioning, plus early detection and treatment of a few key diseases, we should be able to add years to the average life span."

The host turned to his other guest, an intense, florid-faced man. "Is that a fair estimate, Dr. Dusek?"

"I would go *much* farther," he replied, in heavily accented English. "Much! One hundred twenty years will be standard. Some will live to two hundred, even more. There is no limit."

"Two hundred years?!"

"These are the findings not just from my own laboratory, but of colleagues from around the world. In perhaps thirty to fifty years everyone will accept these things."

"That's the bad news . . ." cut in Holland.

The others turned his way. "What?" asked the host.

"The irresponsibility of so many in this field. The extent to which their wild claims prey on people's hope."

"Excuse me, sir," shot back Dusek, starting to redden. "*You* are not a doctor, I believe!"

"No. Nor do I play one on TV."

Holland gave a small smile; he'd used the line before.

"What are your credentials?"

"My master's is in biochemistry. But, for our purposes, my press card. Unlike you, I have no ax to grind—I'm just interested in the truth."

"I, too, am interested in the truth, sir!"

Holland cast a quick glance at the show's producer, off camera, and nodded blandly. More than once he'd been advised he came across on the tube as smug, and he was working hard to overcome it. "Of course, Doctor, this isn't personal."

In fact, while others in his circle of respected print journalists and editors regularly disparaged TV as the province of the illiterate (and he was known to disparage with the best of them), Holland seized almost every opportunity to appear on screen that came his way.

The colossal power of the thing, its stark appeal to his vanity, was simply irresistible. Half an hour on even a modest show like this would bring Holland to the attention of tens of thousands who'd never before heard his name.

Nonsense, as Holland had assured the producer apologetic about the timing of tonight's show, he didn't mind at all working on Halloween; adding with a laugh, "Hey, I'm recently separated, it gives me somewhere to go."

"Well, Dr. Dusek," asked the host, "can you tell us something about your own research?"

"In my work"—he reached for the briefcase at his side and withdrew a sheaf of paper—"we are demonstrating the antiaging properties of proprietary extracts from the tissues of fetal monkeys rich in thymosins, superoxide dismutases—"

"I'm afraid you're losing a lot of us."

"These are proteins produced by the juvenile thymus gland."

"Can you tell us where this research was conducted?" cut in Holland.

"In my own laboratory," he replied warily. "In the Czech Republic—at the University of Brno."

"Ahhh. I see." Holland paused meaningfully. Though he was scoring points here, he knew he had to watch himself; respect for other cultures and all that. "Excuse me, Doctor—what is it, exactly, that brings you to our country?"

"To lecture. Not everyone is so close minded as yourself."

"Nothing else? No fund raising?"

"Naturally. Research demands money, who can deny it?"

He nodded. "Viewers should just keep that in mind when they hear these claims."

"You do not know the details of this work. I have many testimonials here from patients."

"With all due respect, Doctor, I could show you alchemists with persuasive testimonials—guys who claim they can change lead to gold! There are some who say testimonials are the last refuge of the crank."

"Are you accusing Dr. Dusek of being a fraud?" cut in the host with unseemly eagerness.

Holland shook his head no. "I prefer to deal in precision. Frauds don't believe their theories, cranks do."

As the host tried to suppress a smile, Holland turned back to Dusek, continuing calmly. "What are you going to tell us next? How the medical establishment's always trying to hold people like you back for its own nefarious purposes? Isn't that the standard line?"

"This is not right! This man is not qualified!"

"If you'll allow me," continued Holland, "I've brought some documents also. Affidavits, signed and notarized, from some of your former patients who were less than entirely satisfied."

Dusek appeared about to lose it. "What is even the bearing of this on our discussion?!"

"Any reputable physician will tell you the first law of medicine is *Primum non nocere*—First, do no harm. Apparently you've got a real problem in that area." Holland knew to look directly into the camera. "Read these—or, better yet, go to the assembled case histories in the *Index Medicus International,* as I have—and you'll find that a number of Dr. Dusek's patients have experienced anaphylactic shock." He paused. "But, again, this isn't a personal fight. The real issue in any discussion of life extension is about the distinction between wishful thinking and the search for objective truth."

"You're saying there's absolutely nothing to all this research we keep hearing about?"

Holland hesitated. "Look, this is a booming area. Obviously there's some serious work being done by gerontologists, molecular biologists, and the like. Some of the data on vitamin C and melatonin is interesting. But I'm afraid claims like these"—he nodded amiably at Dusek and shrugged—"it just ain't so."

"Impossible?" asked the host deferentially.

"That's a word I don't use." He smiled. "But you figure the odds. Of the seventy billion or so people who've inhabited the earth since the appearance of Homo sapiens as a distinct species, we know of only two that have made it even to 120—a Japanese man and a Frenchwoman. Make that three, if you include Methuselah—but he's on faith." He paused. "There just are limits to what science can achieve. The human body is a machine; eventually its parts simply wear out."

"This is an incorrect analogy," muttered Dusek, shaking his head.

"No," came back Holland, "it is a very precise analogy. Cells stop reproducing and die. Free radicals—the byproduct of breathing and other critical life processes—begin to overwhelm our natural defenses and disrupt cell function. When an autopsy is conducted on an exceptionally old person, they'll often find a seeming irony: everything wrong but nothing in particular. These processes are irreversible. They can't be wished away."

It went on for another fifteen minutes, but for practical purposes it was over.

Afterward, Holland shook Dusek's hand and expressed the hope that there were no hard feelings. The host, brimming with good feeling, followed the journalist down the long corridor that led to the elevator.

"Your series on the antiaging industry has been terrific," he enthused. "You deserve a Pulitzer!"

Holland pushed the elevator button. "Thanks. Here's hoping the Pulitzer committee shares your enthusiasm."

"But there is something I want to ask you—I didn't think I should say it on the air."

Holland looked at him curiously. "What?"

"It's surprising. You've done all this work in this area, and over and over you find the claims are wildly exaggerated. Yet you keep on it. It's—I don't know—almost like you're on a personal mission of some kind. . . ."

Realizing his expression betrayed his dismay, Holland was grateful they were no longer on camera.

"You couldn't give me a higher compliment," he said after a moment.

The elevator doors slid open and he stepped in.

"I'm a reporter. With me the truth *is* personal."

Sally was dead to the world when the phone rang. The room was black, for a long moment she was disoriented. Then she realized: she'd fallen asleep on the office couch, missing the end of her own party! Though Mark had removed her shoes before lovingly tucking a blanket beneath her chin, she was otherwise still fully dressed.

It rang again. Raising herself up on one elbow, she was aware that the throbbing in her head was still there.

"Christ," she muttered. Then, in self-recrimination: "What an idiot!"

She let it ring once more before reaching for the receiver.

"Sally? It's Jack Stebben." The local chief of police. "Don't tell me I woke you."

"Uh-uh," she replied reflexively. "Just a little groggy."

In the dimness she had to bring her wrist within an inch of her face to read her watch. Five forty!

"I'm up here at Grace Church. Got something for you, missy."

*   *   *

Twenty-five minutes later Sally followed the beam of Stebben's flash-light down into the empty pit, then up to the weathered slate slab still embedded in the ground at the head of the empty grave.

"Pretty kinky, wouldn't you say?"

The flashlight was no longer necessary. Though the sky was still alive with stars, dawn was breaking; she could see his breath. But, for Stebben, it made a nice, dramatic touch.

She nodded at the chief, in uniform and heavy leather jacket, sitting on the mound of dirt alongside. "Who in the world would do something like this?!"

"Ah, shit, on Halloween night . . . ?"

In his late fifties, tall and lean, Stebben bore a faint resemblance to the actor Jack Nicholson—slit eyes and leering grin beneath a receding hairline—and he had the same disconcerting habit of making even chitchat sound insincere.

"When did you hear about this?" she asked, pulling a notebook from the parka she'd thrown on over sweat clothes.

"That's our Sally, right down to business. Maybe an hour ago. Got a call from Davis in the office. Someone phoned it in." He smiled. "Going jogging after?"

"You know who was buried here?"

He returned his beam to the slate slab, the words upon it long since obliterated by weather. "Make up a name, no one'll care." He laughed. "Guess some idiots figured it beat bobbing for apples. . . ."

Sally managed a smile. She dealt with Stebben on a regular basis. Putting up with his sense of humor came with the territory. "Which idiots do you suppose that might be, Chief?"

He laughed again. "Young ones. With big brass balls."

"So there are no suspects in particular?"

"*Suspects?* That's a pretty rough word, missy. We're talking about some local kids pulling a prank."

She wiped a stray blond hair from her face. "You have any actual *evidence* it was kids?"

"Sure, I do—I used to be a teenager around here myself. I'm just grateful no one made too much of the crazy stunts I pulled."

"I see."

Sally took a deep breath, and gazed about her. In northeastern New Hampshire winter comes early, and a few large snowflakes drifted lazily down. The churchyard was at the crest of a rise at the far north end of town. Even in the faint light she could make out everything that had long made this community of fifty-five hundred souls so irresistible in postcards: the nineteenth-century buildings of wood and brick along Main Street; the broad porches and steep gables of so many of the houses; deep, placid Edwardstown Lake looming beyond, mirroring the brilliant reds and oranges of the surrounding hills. From here even the two abandoned factory buildings beyond the tracks—evidence of the town's recent economic decline— looked picturesque.

Yet all Sally felt at this moment was the insularity of the place, its astonishing protectiveness of its own. Local boosterism was one thing—this guy was in denial.

"You know how difficult you make my job sometimes, Chief?"

"Right back at you."

"You think this is cute? A law has been broken here. I'd like to know what you plan to do about it."

"Which law is that, exactly, Lois Lane . . . petty larceny?"

"Worse than that . . . It's a . . . sacrilege."

"Is that the end of the lecture part of the program?" He rose to his feet. "Because I figure I've done my duty by the local press."

Turning, he began striding down the hill. She watched him a moment, then had no choice but to follow.

"Where's your car?" he asked in the church lot.

"In the shop," she mumbled, and realized he must have known; the garage was owned by his brother-in-law.

"Real sorry about that—transmissions can be a bitch." Not un-expectedly, he laughed. "Want a ride back to that cozy bed of yours?"

She clenched her fists inside her parka pockets. "Don't bother, the walk'll do me good." *You sonovabitch, like I'd give you the satisfaction. . . .*

"Suit yourself. . . ." He opened the cruiser door and slid inside. "Anything more I can help you with, you know where to reach me. . . ."

Leaning nonchalantly against the churchyard wall, she waited until the cruiser had disappeared round a bend before beginning to trudge home.

The deterioration was even worse than the scientists had feared. It was to be expected that after more than two hundred years in the ground, in such a climate, there would likely remain no trace of flesh or marrow. What they hadn't anticipated was that the bones themselves would be in such lamentable condition. Most were decalcinated—soft and badly eroded.

That noted, they plunged ahead.

Time was at a premium. Recent events had put the very future of this research in doubt. According to their best estimate there remained enough funding for only another seven or eight months. If they were to maintain momentum, several million dollars had to be raised in the immediate short term, with tens of millions more to see the project through to completion.

And the biotech venture capitalists from whom it would have to be raised were as coolly pragmatic as mob hit men. Impressed as they might be that a pair of unheralded scientists in the wilds of New Hampshire had isolated a protein that helped lab rats live longer, in practical terms the achievement was close to worthless. Lacking persuasive evidence that the remarkable protein functioned also in humans, they knew no one would fork over a dime.

On the basis of exhaustive research the scientists had no doubt such evidence existed. Their data, genealogical as well as biological, indicated it was already working its magic in a tiny subset of human beings, encoded in their DNA as the result of a long-ago mutation. The problem was demonstrating it. For the mutation was remarkably elusive, confined to a select few extended families; and even then, it appeared, was not present in all members.

It was this that had led them to the graveyard in Edwardstown.

"They did quite a nice job," ventured one of the men. "I understand there's been no outcry in the town at all."

"Not *now*, Lynch," said the other sharply. "Don't talk cops and robbers while we're doing science."

At the rebuke Lynch fell silent. Though he was far more physically imposing than his colleague, Foster—and, at forty-eight, almost a decade older—five years of working together had left them equals in name only. Lynch was the project's public face, but Foster was its heart and soul; a creative force far beyond any his associate had ever known. If the younger man was demanding and imperious, even if he was sometimes openly derisive, the other accepted even this as part of the price of keeping the project moving forward. There was no room for ego—not with the goal in sight.

Now Foster surveyed the several dozen bones and large bone fragments arrayed before them, his small, dark eyes moving left to right above his surgical mask and back again.

"We'll start with the right talus," he abruptly decided, focusing on its color and relative absence of erosion. With a gloved hand he reached for the small, intact anklebone.

In theory all it would take was one cell. If they could salvage the DNA from that single cell, they could conclusively establish that this was the family that held the key to the project's success.

The immediate task was locating a pure sample. The genetic material at hand was sure to be randomly mixed with that of worms and moles and other subterranean organisms; and, quite possibly, given the cemetery's layout, with that of other corpses. Then, too, the most glancing contact carried the risk of further contamination.

Taking extreme care, over the next forty-five minutes Foster worked at the bone with a balpeen hammer; then, when the fragments were small enough, using a mortar and pestle, reduced them to fine powder. This he passed along to Lynch, who placed it in a buffer—an aqueous solution of hydroxymethyaminomethane, pH 7.4—and bombarded it with ultrasonic waves.

Nothing. The red needle on the spectrophotometer remained resolutely fixed on zero.

They began again, this time with a lumbar vertebra. Then tried again. And again.

Each such repetition took more than an hour, the work made all the more grueling by the fact of having to labor in a small interior room, without the assistance of technicians.

There was no conversation except that involving the task immediately at hand. Foster had no interests at all beyond this project. Indeed, he had taken up residence in this building, in one of the spare rooms a floor above. Lynch, formerly married and the father of two, likewise had come to have almost no life beyond these walls; arriving each morning from his sparsely furnished apartment before seven, usually staying past midnight. Like Foster, he took most of his meals here.

Though occasionally Lynch did think of his family with sorrow and regret, he kept it to himself. He was keenly aware that his colleague regarded such sentimentality with searing contempt.

It took thirty-two tries. The third day, when they returned to the lab in the early morning after a short break, Foster chose a metatarsal bone from the right foot, his interest drawn by a patch of black residue at the narrow end where once the bone had met a phalanx; possibly the remains of a ligament.

For all their fatigue they worked quickly, the procedure having by now become routine. Only, this time, at the end, when Lynch

placed the sample in the machine and pressed the button that acti-
vated the light source and photomultiplier tube, the needle at once
began to waver; then, after a few seconds, it jumped.

"There it is," enthused Lynch, watching the needle settle between
.7 and .8. "We're in business."

But, as always focused on what came next, his colleague would
not even permit himself a smile. "We're still going to need an intact
sample," he said sharply. "*Living* cells."

"**I**'m really not sure I understand, Sally," said Father Morse, rector of Grace Episcopal Church. He dropped his voice. "Really, just between you and me, what difference does it make, anyway?"

For a moment she just stared at him, dumbfounded. "What difference does it make who was in that grave?"

He smiled. "I don't mean that the way it sounds. But think about it—is that piece of information going to *help* anyone?"

"It's a big part of the story, Father—people have a *right* to know." She paused, reining in her frustration. "You're telling me there are no burial records prior to 1815? They've *completely* disappeared?"

"Now, Sally, don't take that tone. . . ." He nodded vaguely at the rectory building behind him. "What I'm telling you is that we haven't been able to locate them just yet. They'll probably turn up one of these days."

"Our perspectives seem to be a little different, Father. In the news business we don't think in terms of eternity." She managed a tight smile. "It's been almost a week since that grave was violated and as far as I can tell, the police have done *nothing* to solve this case."

"I agree it was a malicious little prank. But it's over and done with—why not let it rest?"

Sally and the minister had always enjoyed a pleasant relationship. Only a few years older than she was, good humored and involved in all aspects of town life, Father Morse was always good for a quote in a pinch. More than that, he was close to her mother, who, since her father's death, had been a regular volunteer at the church.

Yet at the moment he seemed to represent the aspect of Edwardstown life that drove Sally most absolutely bonkers: the complacency of the place.

"Are you really telling me you don't *want* this case solved, Father?"

He spread his hands in a gesture meant to take in all of humankind. "Sally, I'm in the compassion business. As Chief Stebben says, do we really want to drag any of this community's young people through the muck?"

"Look. . . ." She took a deep breath. "Aside from Stebben's say-so, what evidence do we have that it even *was* a prank?"

"Sally, he's right. This is a tight-knit community. I'm sure that in due course, this will be handled the right way—quietly."

The truth was, she was hearing the same thing even from her own staff. In a town where it was hard to find anyone who wasn't at least a friend of a friend, almost no one wanted to risk giving offense to anyone.

Abruptly, unexpectedly, Father Morse laughed. "I'll bet at times like this, there are things you miss about big-city newspapers."

"Which things would those be, Father? The rotten hours or the vicious political infighting?"

He smiled. "Just don't forget why you came back here, Sally. This is a special town. There's no better place to raise a family."

"Even if it happens to include a vandal or two. . . ."

"Maybe even then." He chuckled. "Speaking of which . . . do you have any plans in that direction?"

Caught by surprise, she hesitated.

"I don't mean to pry, but I'm sure you know how happy it would make your mother."

Sally continued to stare, scarcely believing the conversation had taken THIS turn. "Don't forget my grandmother," she offered finally, trying to sound breezy. "She loves babies too."

Only now, reading her face, was he aware of the magnitude of the gaffe. "I'm sorry, I guess that was out of line."

"No problem," she said coolly, making it clear it was. She glanced at her watch. "Actually, I have to be someplace anyway. . . ."

"Come on, Sally, don't we have more to talk about?"

She couldn't help noticing the new eagerness to please—and instinctively, despite herself, moved to press the advantage. "Not if the subject is how not to do my job . . ."

He looked at her thoughtfully, then indicated the rectory door. "Come with me."

He led her down a flight of stairs and through a mystifying array of corridors until they reached the oak door of his office. "You see what we're up against," he said, taking a seat behind his desk and inviting her into the straight-back wooden chair facing it. "To paraphrase Winston Churchill, Grace Church is a mystery wrapped in a question mark. In the attic alone there are a dozen crawl spaces no one's been in for a century. It would take four or five days to thoroughly search them all."

"Let me do it."

"Be reasonable. Who's to say those records *ever* existed? This church is over two hundred years old; Edwardstown was hardly a speck on the map. Surely back then people knew where their loved ones were interred without having to look it up on a chart."

"Let me try."

He hesitated. "Tell me again why the name is so important."

"*You* of all people?" Her exasperation was only partly for effect.

"That poor soul once lived in this town, walked these streets—who are we to decide that who he was no longer matters?"

She paused meaningfully. "How do we know—maybe the family still lives around here. . . ."

Slumped in a plastic chair, Mark flipped through a four-month-old copy of *Ladies' Home Journal*. He paused briefly at an article on Katie Couric's home life, then tossed it aside and picked up an even older copy of *Family Circle*.

At her desk across the waiting room in Edwardstown Hospital's Department of OB/GYN, Nurse Barbara Walker smiled. "You know, Mark, there's probably an *Esquire* or two at the bottom of the pile."

He looked up. "Oh?"

"You're not the first guy that ever stumbled in here, you know." The nurse paused, then tapped a desk drawer. "Treat me right and I might even give you the good stuff—what we refer to around here as 'the sperm-count material.'"

"Actually, I already gave—at home."

"I remember. Sally brought it in."

"But that's all right—toss one over anyway."

"Calling my bluff, huh? Not many do."

Mark laughed—which was precisely the point. Having been with Dr. Lee Malen, head of OB/GYN at the hospital, for nearly a decade, among her many talents, Barbara had a gift for putting people at ease. Mark had been here a quarter hour, waiting for this consultation with Malen, his body language a dead giveaway.

"So," she asked now, "what's keeping Sally?"

"That's what I want to know," echoed Malen, appearing at his office door.

In his early sixties, he had the look of a faded matinee idol—rugged features set off by a preternatural tan and slate-gray hair.

Mark stiffened. Though the doctor had been among Sally's father's closest friends—and since Paul Benedict's death had shown an almost paternal interest in his wife—he'd never liked him. Twice married and estranged from his only child, too readily dazzled by wealth and celebrity, Malen had girlfriends, as even Sally liked to joke, younger than some of her clothes.

The feeling was more than returned in kind, the doctor leaving little doubt that he viewed Mark's marriage to Sally as an unfortunate accident; as if vivacious, snappy Murphy Brown had thrown away everything for a New Hampshire version of John-Boy Walton. When they met socially, he sometimes treated the younger man with an indifference that bordered on rudeness.

On the other hand, Mark had been reassuring himself, maybe today would be different. This was the first time he was seeing the doctor in his professional role.

"She said something about stopping by Grace Church . . ." he observed now.

"Ah . . ." Malen paused, glancing in annoyance at the clock on the wall, and Mark understood things between them would be the same as always. "Maybe you ought to remind her to do it on her own time. She's really going way too far with this."

Under other circumstances Mark might have agreed; he, too, was starting to regard her fixation on the grave robbing as wildly over the top. "Isn't that what we love about Sally," he asked instead, bemused, "—that everything she does is all out?"

At her desk Barbara smiled. "Give her a break, Lee. She doesn't find many stories she can sink her teeth into around here."

"No," he agreed curtly, "not around here."

Mark was at a loss. How to even begin to respond to the insinuation that somehow *he* was responsible for having derailed Sally's career?

Pushing open the office door, Sally immediately sensed the tension.

"Hey, Sal," called Mark. "I'm supposed to remind you you're late."

"Sorry, I got a little hung up." She looked at Malen. "C'mon, Lee, after all the times I've had to cool my heels waiting for you?"

But suddenly, in her presence, Malen's mood, too, was lighter. "I didn't realize you were keeping a running tally."

"Lee, with you any edge I can get. So what's the story, Barbara—testosterone flowing like water?"

"No more than usual." The nurse smiled. "You know, it can get a little weird with husbands in this office. . . ."

"Thanks for that analysis, Barbara," said Malen dryly. He began ushering Sally and Mark into his office. "Why don't we get to it?"

"Look, it's hard on me too," Malen was saying, five minutes later. "I can't pretend this is just an ordinary case."

He leaned forward slightly. Though both faced him from a pair of leather chairs flanking his desk, he addressed himself to Sally, shooting Mark only an occasional glance. "Sixteen months—that's a long time to have been trying."

Sally nodded. "For the last eight or nine I've been pretty careful about the timing."

"Still, I really don't think there's any reason to panic. The sperm count and motility are both good. The only obvious problem, based on the hysterosalpinogram, is the partial blockage in one of the tubes."

Sally's anxiety was not allayed by so casual a reassurance. "That doesn't *sound* minor."

"I don't think that's key. Obviously, you might want to have it taken care of—it can probably be handled through laparoscopy. But the truth is, that condition's probably existed for a long time, maybe since childhood."

She nodded uneasily. "I see."

"And after all, Sally, you got pregnant once before."

From the way Mark's head whipped her way, the doctor abruptly realized: she'd never told him.

She hesitated, avoiding her husband's gaze. "That was quite a while ago."

Malen looked from one to the other, quietly relishing the moment. "That's true, you're right. Which of course leads us to the most likely possibility—that it might be age related." He paused. "There's a clinic down in Manchester that offers an excellent series of diagnostic tests and corrective measures, up to and including *in vitro*. A lot better than anything this old country doctor can do for you."

"You're recommending we go this route immediately?"

"It doesn't have to be today." He smiled at Mark. "Look at your calendar, see where you can fit it into the school year."

"We'll consider it," he allowed. "Money might be an issue."

Instantly, knowing the remark had been at least partly prompted by his distress over what he'd just learned, he wished he could take it back.

"I already looked into this a few months ago," he added quickly, digging himself in even deeper. "Each IV treatment costs roughly ten thousand dollars, and our insurance doesn't cover it."

He could feel Sally's eyes boring into him. "That's our problem," she hissed, defensive and angry. "We'll discuss it later."

As soon as they stepped outside, he wheeled on her.

"Why didn't you tell me?"

"What's this sudden BS about money? Money is NOT the issue!"

"Why didn't you tell me?"

"If it comes to that, I'll take on freelance work. There are still plenty of places that I can sell my stuff."

He said nothing, just looked at her.

"Mark," she said more softly, "it was a long time ago. I had to tell Malen as part of my medical history."

"That's not an answer."

"Has it occurred to you that maybe it's because I'm ashamed?" She looked away briefly, then back at him. "I miscarried, I can't say if I'd even have kept it. It was the most miserable part of an awful relationship."

"Right," he said, "I understand," and turned away, striding toward his car.

He had his answer: Paul Holland.

Holland didn't come by the Herald Building much anymore. Like other luminaries at the paper—columnists, critics, a couple of other star reporters with highly defined areas of expertise—he had the option of working at home: selecting his own stories, reporting them on his own schedule, dealing with editors and researchers by phone, fax, and modem.

So he was surprised and rattled by the summons to a meeting with Executive Editor Dennis Boyles.

Boyles knew it—and made a point of greeting him with his most reassuring smile. "Well, well, Mr. Wizard in the flesh."

"Not exactly, Dennis," said Holland, going for the banter that seemed to mark them as equals. "He's on TV, he gets paid a helluva lot more than I do."

Boyles guffawed, pulling out a cigarette and Dunhill lighter. A crusty Irishman of the old school who'd made his stripes as a police reporter, he was built like a boxer, with piercing blue eyes beneath thick, snow-white hair. Even now, five years after his elevation into the ranks of senior management, he seemed out of place in his tailored suit and elegant paneled office.

"This okay?" he asked, holding up the cigarette. "See what the world's coming to—I have to ask in my own damn office!"

"Go ahead. You read my stuff, you know the risk of secondhand smoke's been highly exaggerated."

He lit up and inhaled deeply. "Yeah, right, it eased my wife's mind considerably. Now I wanna read one telling me a bottle of Johnnie Walker a day's good for you."

"But I gotta say, Dennis, there's still no good news on *first*hand smoke. Someone actually did the math: each puff of a cigarette costs seven minutes in life expectancy."

"Hey, Holland, what *do* you want me to die of?" He paused. "Then, again, maybe you're still thinking we don't have to die at all."

"Wouldn't it be nice . . . ?"

"Would it? Putting up with the same old assholes *forever?*" He leaned forward, eyes narrowing, and got to the point. "What is it with you and this goddamn longevity crap anyway, Holland? You've been riding that broken-down nag of a story for a year!"

The reporter was caught short. "Dennis, antiaging is a hot field. It's not just all these wild-eyed entrepreneurs with their little start-up companies. Some of the most prestigious universities in the country are starting to look into—"

"But that's not what you're writing about, Holland. Every time I turn on the fucking tube, I see you with some wacko planning to live to a thousand!"

"Because I think it's important to debunk some of the—"

"Goddamn it, we're not the fucking *National Enquirer*! We pay you to write about science, not quackery!" He slammed his hand down on the desk. "I'm sick to death of it. Wrap up whatever you're doing and move on!"

Holland nodded. "Yessir . . . . there are just a couple of odds and ends—"

"Good." The executive editor leaned back in his chair, congenial again. "You know, you and me really oughta talk religion sometime.

Your problem's that you don't believe in anything. My problem too."

"I couldn't keep up with you, Dennis. I don't have your religious background."

"I'm a lapsed Catholic, Holland—that's not a religious background, it's a prescription for cynicism." He smiled. "And you know what? That's the disease that's *really* gonna get us both."

Sally looked from the proposed editorial written by her managing editor, Florence Davis—a polite appeal to anyone with information on the grave robbing to consider coming forward—and into the woman's hopeful eyes.

Christ, why was she so rotten at this office diplomacy stuff?

"Look, Florence," she began. "Don't take this personally, but I'm afraid this needs a lot more muscle. Our concern has to be what the cops are doing to solve this thing—or, rather, *not* doing."

No good—Florence looked like she might actually start to cry. In her early sixties, she dated back to the paper's previous regime, and any semblance of conflict upset her. "I'm so sorry, Sally," she said softly. "I did my best."

"Of course you did," Sally agreed, "and I appreciate it. We've never had a story like this before. It requires a new set of skills."

Collecting herself, Sally gazed about her sorry excuse for an office: two rooms, four steel-gray desks, two Mac computers, a single light-table. She had accepted the job in the optimistic expectation, in the words of the chairman of the *Weekly*'s parent company, that she would raise the paper to her own high standards of professionalism. But by now, for all the improvements in the paper's style and design, she'd stopped kidding herself. The limitations of budget—and what a small town liked to read about itself—were all but impossible to overcome.

Still, it wasn't in her nature to stop trying.

She smiled at the older woman, moving to safer ground. "So what do you see as the best prospect for next week's lead story?"

"The new steamroller?"

That was another thing that drove Sally crazy—this tendency of Florence's to make statements that sounded like questions. "Great, what's our angle?"

"Well, no final decision has been made. The trustees are planning to discuss it again next month?"

"So the headline would be something like"—Sally made quote marks with her fingers—"'New Steamroller *Likely*'?"

The older woman hesitated. "Well, maybe we shouldn't be quite so bold. Perhaps 'New Steamroller *Possible*'?"

Sally caught herself. Some days she just didn't have the patience to deal with this kind of thing. "Well, let's look at the issues. How much would a piece of equipment like that *cost*? After all, Edwardstown's hurting economically. There are people who don't think we can afford a garden hoe, let alone a steamroller."

"Oh, dear, quite a great deal, I'd imagine."

"Do we have anything more precise than that?"

"Well, I'm not actually working on the story myself. . . ." She nodded across the room toward the extremely attractive young woman poised before her computer.

"Hey, Lisa!" called Sally.

Lisa wheeled in her swivel chair to face her boss.

"We're talking steamrollers. How much do those things cost?"

"Figure forty-five thousand, with maybe a ten percent negotiated discount."

"Good. I want to see that within the first two graphs of your piece."

"I'm way ahead of you, it's already in the lead."

Sally nodded. Lisa, whom she'd hired right out of the University of New Hampshire, at least gave her hope. Raw as she was, she was far more ambitious than any of the four reporters she'd had during her tenure here, and eager to learn; more than that, she had about her a sassiness that reflected a genuine independence of spirit.

"Sally . . . ?"

She turned back to Florence.

"I'm sorry, I was just wondering if I might take just a little bit of time off now? My sister Jane, over in Union? She's not well."

"Why not—things seem under control."

"It's only a flu." Already, Florence was edging toward the door. "But, you know, at her age . . . ?"

As she left, she passed Sally's mother, on the way in. "Where was Florence going in such a rush?" she asked, glancing around. "And where's Mr. Keeton?"—the business manager.

"Out visiting her sick sister. And sick himself."

"Oh, dear. I wonder if I can help either of them out with grocery shopping." Mrs. Benedict's tirelessness was legendary; in addition to her work here, she spent a good twenty hours a week volunteering at the church, all the while keeping an immaculate home and caring for her own elderly mother. Yet she was always instantly up for whatever random do-gooding passed her way.

By what aberration of genetics, Sally sometimes wondered, had she and this vision out of Norman Rockwell ended up related? As an adolescent she used to get so irked by her mother's unfailing good nature that once, on a bet with a pal, she smashed a teapot against the kitchen counter just to see if she'd lose her temper. Sally won: Mrs. Benedict only stared at her, wide eyed, "Goodness, gracious, honey, what's gotten into you today?"

"I don't know about them," said Lisa, "but as long as you're at it, pick me up a Yoo-Hoo."

"A what?"

"The finest chocolate blended with the finest water—I've loved it since I was three."

"Oh, Lisa, it sounds absolutely vile."

Sally stared balefully at the prim seventy-one-year-old—white haired, dressed in a floral print dress and sensible shoes. Though her mother was only a part-timer—Mondays and Tuesdays, helping out with classifieds—her presence often contributed to a pleasant sense of extended family. Yet today it served only as a further reminder of the job's frustrations.

"Forget that," she abruptly announced. "We're going to talk grave robbing."

She caught the others exchanging a glance.

"I don't care how many times I have to repeat this—we're staying with this thing till we get some answers. If people around here have a problem with that, so be it."

"But there's no *news*," ventured Lisa.

Sally nodded. "Maybe we'll luck out and find the church records. Until then we're going to keep pounding away in editorials. . . ." She paused. "And maybe create some news on our own."

She held up a vintage leather-bound volume, its title, *Rituals of Death in Eighteenth Century America*, so faded it was barely perceptible. "For starters, did you know our body was probably wrapped in a shroud soaked in pitch? Until the nineteenth century almost no one around here was buried in a coffin."

"Where did you find that book?" said Mrs. Benedict.

"In the library, Mother," she replied evenly, though from anyone else such a question would have invited sarcasm.

"There's more. Chief Stebben wants us to believe this is completely harmless. He can't even say for sure that any law's been broken." Carefully she opened the book to the page she'd marked. "New Hampshire enacted its first statute pertaining to disinterring the dead in June of 1796, with penalties of up to three years imprisonment, a thousand-dollar fine, plus a public whipping, and I quote, 'not to exceed thirty-nine stripes.' " Sally tapped the page. "In other words, back then people knew what was what. By the way, it's been amended a few times, but that statute is still on the books."

"Why was it such an issue?" asked Lisa, her interest aroused. "Who was after those bodies?"

"That'll be part two in our series. Often it was medical schools after anatomical samples. And when the heat was on, they could usually afford to buy off the authorities."

Gingerly, she displayed the nineteenth-century lithograph illustrating the point: a pair of shadowy figures going about their grisly work, while a policeman stood by, arms folded. "We can use this; the copyright's expired." Studying the cop in the picture, she laughed. "Even looks sort've like Stebben, doesn't he?"

"Will there really be enough for a series?"

"Let's think short term—parts one and two." She snapped the book shut and extended it to Lisa.

The young woman didn't try to hide her excitement. "You want me to write it?"

"It'll look good on your resume—it shows initiative." She glanced at her mother. "I've got a lot on my mind these days. I can't do this alone."

Even by the lofty standards of top New York investment-banking firms, Rotner and Noble's waiting room was impressive: antique oriental carpet, hunting scenes in oil on burnished walls, the works. Looking about him, Dr. Raymond Lynch realized that, as much as any stage setting, it was designed for effect—to reassure or, just as often, intimidate.

It had done its job on Lynch. On his last visit here eight years ago, as an executive with a leading pharmaceuticals firm, he'd been received with an almost fawning cordiality. But now, as director of the Manchester, New Hampshire, based Life Services Institute, he'd never been more of an outsider.

At last a side door opened and the firm's managing director, Kenneth Rotner, stepped into the room.

"Dr. Lynch?" he inquired, looking from Lynch to the two other men in the waiting room, both younger and expensively pinstriped.

Lynch stood. Though he'd steeled himself for the possibility of not being recognized, this was another sharp blow to his confidence. Extending his hand, he tried to smile. "Actually, we've met."

"Oh?" said Rotner, leading him through a paneled door. "When was that?"

"Seven or eight years ago, I was VP of research development at Stafford-Barnes."

"Of course, I saw that on your resume. Forgive me."

But Lynch found no more reassurance in this than in the prominent display of family photos in his immense office. He already knew Rotner was a nice guy—that didn't cost him anything. It was his firm's $700 million in investment capital that interested him.

"So how long a trip is this for you?"

"The flight to New York's only about an hour and a half from Manchester."

"Just come in this morning?"

"Last night."

He was not about to mention the hotel where he had stayed; a ninety-five-dollar-a-night place called the Aldine.

"I suppose after Stafford-Barnes you sometimes feel like you've dropped off the face of the earth. . . ."

"By choice."

That isn't what Rotner's people had told him, but he didn't press it. Nor was he so indiscreet as to ask why an institute bankrolled by Clifford Stagg, with his reputedly bottomless pockets, would be so eager for additional funding.

In fact, Rotner knew Lynch had contacted several other high-caliber firms also, and none had so much as granted the director of this unknown facility a meeting.

"Well, then," said Rotner, ushering him into a chair, "let's talk longevity. That's an attention-getting proposal you've put together."

Lynch nodded uncertainly. "Thank you."

"This fellow you're working with . . . Foster? All the data are his? And the projections?"

"He's the chief research scientist on the project, yes. A very gifted man."

He paused. "I've shown the proposal to our science people—our due-diligence committee. I hope you don't have a problem with that."

"Not as long as they're covered by the confidentiality agreement."

But inwardly he shuddered: *their science people!* These prissy academics hired by money people *never* stuck their necks out; not when being wrong could cost them their fat retainers!

"They find it quite intriguing."

"Oh, yes?"

"A drug able to appreciably delay the onset of Alzheimer's would be a godsend! The publicity bonanza alone would be unbelievable!" He smiled. "For a little while the press might actually make us heroes again, instead of rapacious exploiters."

Lynch actually allowed himself a glimmer of hope.

"Of course, as I'm sure you know, you're not the first research team to come to us with such a proposal. At least three drug candidates aimed at roughly the same result are already in development. You're talking how long before you'll have anything ready to be tested—a couple of years? And then it would be a minimum of seven or eight years more before FDA approval. We're talking a price tag of fifty to eighty million, with no guarantees."

Lynch nodded evenly. *What did he think—in science there are NEVER guarantees. Just possibilities—and this was a dazzling one!*

"The development time can be cut down," he said intently. "We've made great progress already, we have a cohesive and highly motivated team in place. And given the character of this disease, pressure can be brought to speed up the approval process."

"Then there's cost of treatment. I frankly have trouble imagining many HMOs sitting still for monthly bills in the fifteen-hundred-dollar neighborhood."

"Mr. Rotner, those numbers are preliminary."

Rotner leaned forward. "I understand. On the other hand, I was looking at your projected costs for . . ."

But already Lynch was tuning him out. He should have known, it was *always* this way with these guys! Not even putting the most appealing spin on the research—focusing on Alzheimer's, its flashiest potential by-product, instead of on the final goal; sugarcoating the research to make it palatable to the terminally timid—would do the trick!

He should have known!!

"I'm not saying this is definitive," Rotner was saying. "I assume you're going to forge ahead on this no matter what obstacles we naysayers throw your way."

"Absolutely. We're very high on this project."

"Good—that's what it takes." He smiled; then, as if it was an act of generosity: "Tell you what—let me know where you stand in six or eight months. Maybe we'll have more interest then."

You smug sonovabitch! Why not make it six or eight decades?!!

Rising to his feet, gut churning, Lynch extended his hand. "Thanks, I'll do that."

It took four afternoons and an entire Saturday morning, but at last Sally was almost ready to acknowledge Father Morse might have a point. For all the pristine elegance of Grace Church, with its soaring arches and stunning Tiffany windows, beneath the surface the confusion and disorder was overwhelming; an endless array of tiny rooms, hallways leading in circles or ending abruptly at bricked-up walls. Indeed, only one section, once used as office space and comprising less than a third of the basement area, was electrified.

She found caches of old documents stored in several rooms—more than two dozen wooden boxes in all. All manner of local records were there, seemingly thrown together at random: marriage and baptismal certificates, property taxes and estate settlements, real estate transactions and births. They spanned almost two hundred years, the oldest dating from the church's earliest years in the mid-eighteenth century, the most recent from the 1950s, with many gaps in between. Most merited only a cursory glance by flashlight; others, faded or water stained, she set aside for more careful examination.

But increasingly the conclusion loomed as inescapable: the record she sought, documenting the early grave sites, was absent—if it had ever existed at all. In fact, she discovered only a single document pertaining to the churchyard, and it was useless—a 1738 deed for the original purchase of the land.

As she hurried to her mother's house after this latest futile effort, the heavy early-December sky seemed to match her mood. She wanted nothing more than to crawl beneath a soft comforter and feel sorry for herself. Unfortunately, Saturday afternoons with the family had evolved into a kind of ritual.

"Uh-oh . . ." observed Mark, from a living-room chair, catching her look as soon as she walked through the door. "Came up empty, huh?"

Something about the way he said it bugged her—or maybe it was just that he read her so well.

Wordlessly, she removed her coat and sat down on the couch opposite him, between her mother and grandmother. "I'm not done," she said. "I'll go back."

Gazing at the three generations of Benedict women—clear skinned, high cheekboned, strong jawed—Mark was reminded of photographs he'd seen of flinty, indomitable pioneer women.

For his part, he loved these visits. These people were his only real family now. His own parents' marriage had come apart when Mark was in college. His father left Edwardstown when the Applejack plant's closing cost him his foreman's job; and within three years his mother and younger sister were also gone, one to southern California, the other to St. Louis.

"Mark been treating you all right, Gram?" asked Sally provocatively.

"Not bad."

"He been telling you his jokes?"

"*Repeating* them. They're not exactly new."

Sally laughed. No one who knew them had ever wondered where her mordant wit came from; only why it had skipped a generation. Though now, at ninety-two, she was increasingly in and out—talking lucidly one moment, off on some odd tangent the next—her grandmother remained a vital presence, not far removed in spirit from the beaming teenager in a vintage family photo who'd traveled all the way to New York City for a women's suffrage march.

"I like Mark's jokes," said Mrs. Benedict quickly.

"We all do, Mother. It's just the material gets a little stale. Back in Philly, if there was a big tragedy in the news before lunch"—she snapped her fingers—"by day's end you'd already heard a dozen jokes about it."

"While out here we clods all sat around telling our knock-knock jokes."

"She didn't say that, Mark. . . ." Mrs. Benedict rose to her feet. "Sally, I can use some help in the kitchen."

"All right, Mother, I know it wasn't *nice*. I've just been a little upset lately."

"Listen to you, Sally—someone who didn't know you might think you were awfully self-centered."

"Mother, I *am* self-centered."

She considered a moment. "Well, as long as you realize it yourself . . ."

Despite herself Sally smiled. *How would she have turned out with a mother who* wasn't *supportive?*

Mrs. Benedict turned away to check the roast in the oven of the vintage Hotpoint.

"Sit down, Mother, I'll take care of that."

"Just relax, I'm fine."

"Mother, I'm thirty-six years old and healthy as an ox. *You're* seventy-one with a bad gallbladder."

"Don't concern yourself about that, I don't."

It was an argument they'd had a dozen times before. "Malen's been after you for years to have it taken care of. If it gets infected, it could be dangerous."

"Sally, we're talking about you. Why can't you ever just stop and count your blessings? A wonderful marriage, lots of people who love you, a fine job . . ."

"I *know,* Mother! I know love makes the world go around. I know good things come in little packages. I know every one of the clichés!" She paused and came out with it. "Mark's dragging his feet about seeing a specialist. Who knows, maybe he doesn't even *want* a baby."

"Give him time."

"That's what I don't have, Mother!"

"I know him, Sally. He's hurting too." She paused. "Why don't you try separating your anger toward him from your anger at yourself?"

Sally avoided her mother's gaze. Why was she always underestimating this woman, mistaking gentleness for weakness, quietness for having nothing to say?

"You made choices in your life, Sally. Probably they were the right choices at the time. But you waited a very long time."

"I know that," she conceded softly.

"What, now you're feeling sorry for yourself? *That* isn't going to help." Wheeling, Mrs. Benedict walked across the room and withdrew a small newspaper clipping from a drawer. "Here," she said, handing it over, "—just to get some perspective."

Sally studied it—a death notice from a local paper in Wilbur, South Carolina: an infant named Brian Craig, only five weeks, son of one Charlotte Craig. Born prematurely and still in the hospital, he had been found dead in his crib, apparently a victim of sudden infant death syndrome.

She looked at her mother, perplexed.

"Aunt Mary sent it." Her father's Florida-based sister was the family historian. "Charlotte Craig is a distant relative of ours, a second cousin twice removed. She's now lost two children this way in two years."

"Oh, my God! How awful."

"Exactly," she said. "There are women who have it a lot tougher than you." She paused. "I know you'll get through this all right, Sal. You've always been a fighter."

"Yeah," she said, the facade beginning to crack. "Only, it was never my own body I was fighting."

Mrs. Benedict held out her arms, and slowly, Sally allowed herself to be drawn in. "Just remember, I was thirty-five when you were born. Gram's mother, my grandmother, was forty-four when she had the last of hers."

"Really?"

"Didn't you know that?" She laughed, then, with uncharacteristic pride. "We Benedicts have great genes out the wazoo."

The invitation to visit the Life Services Institute outside Manchester, New Hampshire, arriving a few days before Boyles's order that he drop the story, had caught Holland by surprise. Given his known hostility to nontraditional antiaging research, institutions involved in such work rarely courted his journalistic attention. To the contrary, most went to great lengths to avoid it.

But the main reason he'd agreed to visit the place was the signature at the bottom of the letter: Clifford Stagg. Responsible for the transcom microchip widely used in portable radios in the fifties, wealthy beyond rational measure, Stagg had long ago dropped from sight. Holland hadn't heard his name in years—in fact, had assumed he was dead.

What the hell, he figured. *If nothing else he'd end the series with a bang.*

Rounding a curve in his rented Chrysler, Holland saw the brick rectangle that housed the Life Services Institute in the middle distance, set back several hundred yards from the main road. Evidently a converted factory of some kind, it was larger than most of the facilities he'd visited. Otherwise, it appeared altogether unremarkable.

At Holland's knock the metal door fronting the reception area immediately swung open. Facing him was a tiny, wizened figure. Well into his eighties, the man was dressed in a Green Day T-shirt and jeans.

For a moment the journalist couldn't help but stare. "Would this be the Life Services Institute?"

Squinting, the old man leaned forward slightly, as if trying to make sense of some foreign tongue, but he said nothing.

"I said I'm looking for the Life Services Institute," said Holland, louder.

Though his eyes appeared alert, almost youthful, he still gave no sign of comprehending.

"Thank you, Clark," said another man, appearing behind him. Middle aged, bespectacled, and balding, he might have stepped directly from a university faculty lounge.

When the old man again failed to respond, the other touched him lightly on the shoulder.

"Thank you, Clark," he repeated when the old man turned toward him, enunciating clearly so he could read his lips. "I'll see to this."

"Yessir," said Clark, and began shuffling off.

"Mr. Holland," he said, addressing the visitor. "Thank you so much for coming."

"And you are?"

"My name is Raymond Lynch. I'm chief of research development here."

Holland nodded and set to work. "Very pretty area. How long have you been here?"

"Four and a half years and counting."

"I gather this is a converted factory of some kind?"

"It was a bottling plant. We were lucky to get it." He moved aside. "Please come in, this is a real honor."

Accepting the obsequiousness as his due, Holland stepped into the reception area—and was taken by surprise. On the wall to his right hung the chassis of a DeLorean automobile, evidently intended as an art object; on the one opposite, an immense inflated question mark in soft yellow plastic.

"Mr. Stagg," explained Lynch, smiling. "You should know not all of us share his taste."

"Stagg oversaw the renovation of the place?"

"The public rooms, the library, the living quarters, of course."

"He *lives* here?"

"You'll find Mr. Stagg doesn't believe in halfway measures of any kind. But, come, he's waiting in the library."

Lynch led him down a long, fluorescent-lit corridor, then down another, before stopping at a paneled door and knocking once.

"Enter."

"I'll see you afterward," whispered Lynch, pushing open the door.

Stepping into the room, fitted with Oriental carpets and Victorian upholstery, Holland was again taken aback. The painfully thin old man in the armchair at the far end of the room was draped in an extravagant Hawaiian shirt. A carefully trimmed jet-black beard—an obvious dye job—and the jaunty little sailor cap perched on his head completed the bizarre portrait.

"Stop staring!" he said, not unpleasantly. "Come over here and take a load off."

"It's a pleasure, Mr. Stagg," said Holland, heading toward him.

With some effort the old man struggled from his chair and extended a bony hand. In the other hand he held the book he'd been reading.

From the clips Holland knew Stagg to be seventy-six years old; but up close, for all the attention devoted to obscuring the fact, he could have easily passed for ten years older. The tightness of the skin around his thin mouth and watery blue eyes suggested repeated cosmetic surgeries. The skin itself was rough and a deep red-brown, the kind commonly found among day laborers and the very wealthy.

"I wanted to see you for myself," said Stagg, gingerly sitting back in his chair. "You have an amazing gift, sir."

Holland took a seat in an armchair a few feet away. "Thank you, that's nice of you to say."

"No, it's *easy* for me to say." He laughed again, "I once had a gift myself, but I let it get rusty. So now I try to surround myself with people who do."

"I see that I've interrupted your reading."

"Ah, yes." He held up the book. "Quite a nice little life of George Washington."

"You're interested in history?"

"In the lives of the great, yes, very much so. And lately, of course, in their deaths."

Holland cocked his head slightly. "How exactly do you mean?"

"The specific circumstances. In hindsight, whether those deaths might have been preventable." His gesture took in not just this room but the entire building. "Obviously, the subject has been on my mind. You probably know that Washington was bled heavily on his deathbed. It was the prescribed treatment of the day for throat infection."

Holland nodded. "It's a gruesome story."

"Do you think so?" Stagg seemed disappointed by the reaction. "Well, maybe we modernists shouldn't be so sure of ourselves. Maybe there was more to the old methods than we allow."

"It didn't seem to do Washington much good."

He snorted. "Really, Holland, I'm surprised to hear you, of all people, talk this way. I don't think of you as someone boxed in by conventional thinking."

Holland felt unaccountably defensive. "You're saying you think bloodletting *has* therapeutic value?"

"I'm saying it's always a mistake to be hard-line doctrinaire.

About anything! If I'd listened to conventional thinking as a young
man, do you think there's a chance in hell I'd have got rich enough to
spend the rest of my life on vacation? The world is full of people
who're scared off of good ideas because they're afraid other idiots
will laugh at them. When I hear the word *impossible, that's* when I
get interested." He tapped the book. "Know what they'd use to re-
vive him between bleedings?"

"No, I don't."

"A whiff of vinegar and a stiff glass of diluted urine. Don't look
so alarmed, Mr. Holland, I've tried it myself—it delivers quite a
kick."

Holland just stared at him. The vague possibility of a moment
before was beginning to crystallize as a distinct possibility: *This guy
wasn't merely eccentric, he was out of his fucking mind!*

Still, Holland realized he'd have no regrets about having made
the trip. He'd get a terrific piece out of it—and dine out on the scene
for months.

"Do you mind if I use a tape recorder?"

"Whatever for?"

"I want to be sure I get down what you say accurately."

"Why in heaven's name would you want to write about *me?*"

"That's why I'm here, Mr. Stagg. I've come all the way from
New York."

He shrugged this away. "Nonsense, what I say doesn't matter."

"Then," said Holland, exasperated, "I'm really not sure why
we're talking."

The old man motioned him closer. "I want to show you something." He picked up a manila envelope on the table beside him and
withdrew a couple of eight-by-ten photographs. The first was of a
man, perhaps thirty-five, sunbathing on what appeared to be the
deck of a yacht; having been caught by surprise, he wore an expression of amused insouciance. He was movie-star handsome.

"Is it you?"

"It used to be. I spent quite a while in southern France, you know, giving myself over to life's pleasures."

The other photo was of his former self at a premiere of some kind, with a devastatingly beautiful young woman in an evening gown on his arm. "This was my second wife. A model—Monique Mariani was her professional name."

"You've obviously been a very lucky man."

"As Goethe said, do you really think I'd have been such a fool as to be born unlucky? I'm sure it applies to you also." He offered a thin smile. "Only, I haven't been very lucky lately."

Abruptly he shot out his left arm, revealing a shunt—the artery fused with the vein to provide easy access for an outside line. "Chronic kidney failure. I have to undergo dialysis three times a week. I've also had two heart attacks." He paused, then matter-of-factly added, "I'm dying, Mr. Holland. Unfortunately, I won't be able to take advantage of the work that will make mortality obsolete."

Holland, uncomfortable, made no response, but it didn't matter. For the old man was looking off into space, actually *seeing* it. "Someday soon people will be able to walk into a hospital and walk out just days later with a new heart and lungs. We'll have so thorough an understanding of the immune system that any chance of breakdown will be eliminated! Imagine a world—can you even conceive of it?—where no one younger than a hundred will be considered mature enough to be a leader!"

"I wish I could," Holland answered honestly. "I'm more of a skeptic."

"Oh, you will."

There was a soft knock at the door, and the old man from the front door shuffled into the room with a tray.

"Ah," said Stagg brightly, as Clark moved laboriously toward him, "my afternoon tea and drug overdose. I'd ask you to join me, but I see Mr. Speedy here's only brought one cup and I don't think we want to wait while he fetches another." He laughed. "Don't look so mortified, Mr. Holland, he can't hear anything."

Holland nodded noncommittally.

"I suppose you're thinking I'm no one to talk. But at least I have the excuse of age. Clark's just a kid."

"Excuse me?"

"He's only twenty-two years old, Mr. Holland. I've got the birth certificate right here in the drawer."

Astonished, Holland turned from the man with the tray, to Stagg, and back again. It couldn't be! Though small boned and otherwise thin, he had an old man's potbelly; the muscles in his arms had already gone to flab and his skin was waxy and almost translucent.

"I'm sure you've heard of adult progeria, Mr. Holland. . . ."

"Of course. But never a case so . . . *extreme.*"

Also known as Werner's syndrome, the disease remains little understood. Conventional science offers no explanation as to why, whereas human beings normally move toward old age slowly, their cells replicating themselves fifty or more times, progeria patients rush toward advanced biological age in a mere seven or eight cell generations.

"Well, naturally, the extreme nature of his disease is what aroused interest here."

"He's a research subject?"

Stagg nodded. By now Clark Warren was at his side. Gingerly, Stagg removed from the tray a teacup and a plate bearing a vast array of capsules. "Herbal tea," he noted. "They take good care of us here, don't they, Clark? More wheat germ, oat bran, sweet potatoes, and cruciferous vegetables than you can shake a stick at. God, what I'd do for a cheeseburger!"

"Also, I see, megadose vitamin therapy."

"Antioxidant supplements, E, C, A, beta carotene, whole vitamin B-complex, zinc, selenium, you name it." He paused, watching Warren begin to shuffle away. "We keep him around now as a sort of mascot. Dr. Lynch is extremely fond of him. He's taught him to play checkers."

Nodding, Holland couldn't help wondering: *How much had that particular stab in the dark cost them? How many other half-assed research projects did they have going here?* "Tell me, what's been your total investment in the Institute?"

"We set aside seventeen million when we began," he answered blithely. "More since then."

"How much more?"

"I haven't kept track."

"You don't *know?*"

He laughed. "You sound like one of my accountants. I've never been a dollars-and-cents man, Mr. Holland. That's not how I look at the world."

Holland said nothing. The figure was far greater than he'd anticipated. It was almost beyond comprehension: the guy was an endless supply of cash, and *no one* ever asked questions. Of the many bogus operations he'd looked at, suddenly this one loomed as potentially the most outrageous of all.

"Whatever the sum," picked up the old man, "I consider it a bargain. The work being performed here is absolutely revolutionary!"

"I'd appreciate the chance to look over the facility."

Indeed, he realized, between the Stagg factor and the sums involved, this could be huge. Even Dennis Boyles wouldn't be able to resist giving it front-page play.

"Absolutely." The old man paused, eyes bright. "We're on the edge of humankind's last, greatest frontier. I'm happy to invite you along on the journey. How about tomorrow morning?"

For an instant he almost felt sorry for this sweet, deluded old man. But the feeling quickly passed. After all, when it came to it, the guy was trying to use him also, angling for some favorable press.

"Tomorrow morning's fine," he agreed. Then, with calculated enthusiasm: "I can't wait to hear more."

"Of course not, Mr. Holland. You're in the same boat I am."

It took him a moment to respond. "How's that?"

"You're dying also—just a little more slowly. You may have— what?—another eight or ten years."

Already the color was going from Holland's face.

"Both your parents died of early-onset Alzheimer's, and three of your four grandparents. Isn't that what drew you to this research in the first place?"

Stunned, Holland was unable even to get out the question: *How could he know?!*

"Genealogical research is key to what we do here," Stagg said evenly, nodding at the door through which the progeria patient had disappeared. "That's how we found Clark Warren. If one has the right connections, Mr. Holland, it isn't all that hard to isolate the genetic populations of particular interest."

"I see," managed Holland.

"We're also often able to obtain relevant tissue samples. If you like, I'll have Dr. Lynch take you through the report on yours."

After the working-over Stebben had been getting in the *Weekly,* Sally decided to see him at home, on his day off, rather than at the two-room suite in city hall that served as police headquarters. There was little enough chance he'd come forth with anything useful; none at all if approached in front of his men.

"Want me to wait for you?" asked Lisa hesitantly, as they pulled up before the little house in her VW.

If it wasn't apparent before, the young woman's tone made clear how intimidated she was by the chief. "No way," said Sally blithely. "It's about time you learned how to deal with guys like this." She flashed a grin. "Don't worry—if he turns violent, just call the cops."

As they made their way up the walkway toward the tidy white clapboard jewel Stebben shared with his wife, Sally was struck by how inviting the place looked. Teardrop lights twinkled on the twin fir trees flanking the front porch, brightening this dreary December morning; and, beyond, poking above the snow cover, neat rows of stakes marked an immense vegetable garden.

No one answered the door, but they found the chief in back, in the section of garage converted to a makeshift greenhouse. On his hands and knees over a sorry-looking primrose, he glanced up, squinted, and spoke loud enough to make himself heard over a pair of space heaters. "Well, well . . . my poison pen pals from the press!"

Surprised by so unexpectedly mild a reaction, Sally replied cautiously. "Nice setup you've got here."

"Right. I'll bet you know people who'd see it and start thinking marijuana."

She smiled. "As a matter of fact, I probably do."

"Well, I'd be happy to put 'em away in the clink for you."

"Good. Glad to hear you haven't totally lost the instinct. . . ."

So they were on to it already. Sally waited, steeling herself for his reaction.

But Stebben only shook his head slowly, a wise old soul dismayed by the incorrigible behavior of a child. "When the hell are you gonna get down off that high horse? What are you trying to do now, ruin pretty little Lisa here too?"

"No, just make her a reporter—you'd rather she was a stenographer."

He slowly rose to his feet, towering over them. "I hear you hit a dry well up at the church."

Sally wondered from whom. "I wouldn't say that. I'm not done yet."

"Riiight." He paused. "So I guess you're getting pretty desperate. And maybe hoping against hope I'll give you something to help keep your little story alive."

"What we were hoping, Chief," said Sally, with an edge, "was that maybe you were ready to start doing your job."

"Now, take Lisa here," he replied coolly. "It seems to me, *she* might be able to get a red-blooded heterosexual male to tell her what she wanted to know."

"What is this, Chief, some lame attempt at divide and conquer?"

"Say, Lisa . . ."

She blanched, trying to maintain her composure. "Yes . . ."

"Think you can knock it into your boss's thick skull to stop expecting big-city results in a little town?"

"She's right," said Lisa. "There's no evidence at all it was kids!"

"As a matter of fact, there is."

The response was so unexpected, for a moment neither of the women reacted. "What kind of evidence?" asked Sally, with deep skepticism.

He slowly removed one gardening glove, then the other. "First, some ground rules. This has to be totally off the record."

"I can't agree to that sight unseen."

He shrugged. "Your call."

Sally looked at Lisa, then back at the chief. "I don't believe you."

"You know the way out."

For a long moment she stood there, mute. Then she nodded. "Okay, off the record. And this better be good."

"Those are the magic words. Wait here," he said, turning away. "No need for us all to track dirt into the house—my wife would give me hell."

When he reappeared a few minutes later, it was with a large manila envelope. Slowly, almost seductively, he removed the contents: a number of eight-by-ten black-and-white shots showing the dirt surrounding the empty grave. Taken with a flash, they were of near-professional quality.

"These were taken just afterward."

"Who by?"

"Sergeant Wilson." He pointed. "See that?"

Sally looked closely. A half-dozen footprints could be clearly discerned.

"See these two?" He indicated. "Air Thrill by Nike, almost brand new. Size nine and a half."

"What about the others?"

"Converse Run 'N Slam, size ten. Both models are real big right now—all the kids are wearing 'em."

"How'd you figure that out?" asked Lisa, impressed.

"I took the shots over to Smart's"—the shoe store in nearby Union—"and started looking at sneakers. The conclusion's pretty clear, don't you think?"

Lisa nodded slowly. "Kids. Two of 'em."

"Like I've been telling you all along."

"Nice work, Chief," offered Sally pleasantly. "You're right up there with some big-city cops I know."

"Spare me the compliments," he spat, the contempt he'd kept in check finally surging forth. He jabbed a finger her way. "All I want is for you to leave me the hell alone!"

Sleep well, Mr. Holland?" asked Lynch.

He shrugged, wary. "The motel up the road isn't exactly the Plaza."

In fact, he had slept surprisingly well. Once the shock faded, it was simply a matter of thinking things through. All right, so someone at this place had discovered he carried the gene for Apo E, the marker for incipient Alzheimer's. That was no trick; all it took was a tissue sample, some technical expertise, and a suitably equipped lab.

The question was how they planned to use it—for to Holland it was inconceivable that anyone would go to the trouble of finding someone's weakness otherwise. And that one seemed a no-brainer. These yokels actually thought they could blackmail him! They'd offer silence about his condition in exchange for their half-assed little institute getting a big buildup in the lofty *Herald*.

Well, fuck them! Already he was ready with his response, had been replaying it in his mind all morning. *Shit, did they really expect him to be rattled by such a threat?! That just proved how long they'd been buried away in the sticks! In today's social climate, word that he was doomed to an early death would elicit only sympathy and support. It would send his stock soaring higher than ever!*

Still, it was a delicate matter. For all the conviction he'd bring to the performance, there was always the chance they'd guessed at the larger truth: he couldn't bear being pitied.

"So," he asked Lynch, "what do you want me to see first?"

"The animal lab," said Lynch. "Follow me."

Moments later, turning a corner, Holland picked up the faint, familiar rustle of rodents on newspaper.

It was an impressive facility, long rows of cages stacked floor to ceiling on shelves the running length of the room. Lynch proceeded immediately to a large cage directly across the room and plucked out a white mouse. He held it aloft for the visitor's inspection, its tiny head protruding from his encircling fingers.

"Turn off the lights, will you, Greg?"

Only now, as the room went dark, was Holland aware of the man with a wispy beard watching in the corner.

"Please hold out your hand, Mr. Holland," said Lynch. "I want to give you something."

Holland played along—but instead of the mouse he felt in his palm a narrow metal cylinder.

"It's a fluorescent light pen, the kind ophthalmologists use. Turn it on."

He did so, producing a narrow beam of intensely blue light.

"Hold it steady," said Lynch, and he slowly lifted the mouse into the beam.

Normally bloodred, the animal's eyes shone bright green!

Momentarily startled, Holland said nothing.

"Hit the lights, please."

Lynch stroked the mouse with his index finger. "Aequorin—the same protein that causes jellyfish to glow."

"Ah," nodded Holland, dismissive, "you've injected it into the eyeballs of the mice. A neat little scientific parlor trick."

Lynch glanced at his colleague, then back at Holland. "We're not in show business, Mr. Holland, our interest is longevity. Shall we proceed?"

Only now, back in the brightly lit corridor, was the reporter suddenly aware of how empty the place seemed to be. Doors to several labs and offices stood open, but they were deserted. Midway into a weekday morning, in a large and well-equipped facility, he'd seen but a half dozen souls.

"You think we're quacks here, don't you?" picked up Lynch out of the blue.

The reporter tensed. "I'd never say that. I think we disagree on the question of longevity."

"Tell me, are you aware that the European larch survives up to twenty-three hundred years? The bristlecone pine, five *thousand*?"

"You want to talk to me about *trees*?"

"No, the mechanics of aging. You recall the Norwegian study on Pacific salmon?"

"Yes," said Holland, "I wrote a piece on it."

Though back on familiar ground, he was confused. Why would Lynch raise a study that had been widely blasted by the longevity crowd; aiming as it did to prove that the deterioration and death of almost the entire salmon population upon spawning is, in fact, an accelerated and highly dramatic model of human aging?

"I know," said Lynch dryly, "I read it. I was surprised by your rigidity, a man in your position." The reporter watched Lynch glance at his colleague, and steeled himself for what seemed certain to come next: a threat, dressed up as a plea that he cover the work being done here with greater "balance."

But instead, after a pause, the scientist continued to press his case on its alleged merits. "My question is this, Mr. Holland. Why even bother with the ninety-nine point nine percent of cases where salmon die after spawning? What about the tenth of a percent where they *don't*! *That's* the question—why is it that a select few members of the species escape what seems a preordained fate? *Why?*"

This actually gave Holland a moment's pause. "There are probably thousands of factors—a huge number of random genetic tendencies that come together in just the right way to produce exceptional hardiness."

"Why are you so certain? Why couldn't a single genetic mechanism trigger all the biological processes associated with aging?"

"Excuse me . . ."

It was the first time Foster had spoken, and they simultaneously turned to him in surprise.

"If I could have a word with you, Dr. Lynch," he asked tentatively. "Just for a moment . . . ?"

"Oh, Christ!" said Lynch, throwing up his hands as he started from the room. "Please bear with us, Mr. Holland."

Once they were alone, two doors down, roles abruptly reversed.

"Did I say something wrong?" asked Lynch sheepishly.

"What the hell's the matter with you?! Why don't you just grab your ankles and bend over for the sonovabitch?!"

"I'm trying to engage him on the issues."

"*I'm trying to engage him on the issues,*" mocked Foster. "We've got him by the balls—you'll engage him when you squeeze!" He shook his head bitterly. "What do you want, his *respect*?"

From Foster's point of view this had long been the drawback in allowing Lynch to front for the operation, the price paid for the critical layer of protection he was afforded by remaining in the shadows. Strongly committed to the project as he was, Lynch was weak; and, worse, still susceptible to the naive idealism he had picked up back in his graduate school days. Only just recently, when it became a priority to obtain samples from the newborn in South Carolina, Foster had had to beat back his colleague's squeamishness, driving home the realization that his primary—his *only*—responsibility was to the project.

In fact, the South Carolina experience had been a wrenching disappointment. Every scrap of genetic research at their disposal indicated the child should have carried the mutation; indeed, since cells replicate themselves most furiously in infancy, its cells should have expressed the protein in particularly concentrated and accessible form. Yet after all the trouble and risk—the meticulously planned infiltration of the rural hospital, the carefully negotiated arrangement with the local coroner—the autopsy samples had indicated nothing of the sort. Grasping for a plausible explanation, they could only surmise that, since this branch of the family was nearly two centuries removed from the primary line, at some point the genetic link must have been severed. Until recently, after all, illegitimacy routinely went unrecorded for posterity.

But afterward, too, so tantalizingly close to their goal yet more desperate than ever about time and money, they had moved to revise a key element of their strategy. The idea of bringing in a well-connected outsider could no longer be dismissed as unthinkable—even if it was this one.

Still, there were limits. Watching Lynch in action today, seeking to ingratiate himself with the number-one critic of antiaging research, a man for whom Foster had a deeply personal loathing, was more than the scientist could bear.

"He is NOT your friend, Lynch," he spat now. "Give him half a chance and he'll destroy us." He paused. "Do you UNDERSTAND what I'm telling you?"

He nodded hesitantly.

"Then get back in there and close this deal!"

"**T**ake a seat, Mr. Holland," said Lynch, back in the lab, indicating the chair before an oversized fluorescent microscope in the corner. "There's something we want you to see."

Holland did so, sighing softly, to make clear he was indulging them.

The scientist produced a wooden slide box. "These are tissue samples from one of the aequorin-treated mice." He slid off the top. Each of the thirty or so slides within was neatly labeled: brain, pancreas, spleen, liver, lung, prostate, and so on. Lynch held up five or six, as if performing a card trick. "Pick one."

Holland chose the one labeled LARGE INTESTINE.

"Tell me what you see," said Lynch, placing it beneath the lens.

Holland peered down. "Specks of green. Thousands of them."

"That's the aequorin. You can pick out any slide, any organ, it will be the same!"

The reporter was momentarily confused.

"We didn't *inject* it into the animal's eyes. It's everywhere in its body—in every cell! We've succeeded in packaging the gene responsible for aequorin with a retroviral vector and transferring it between species."

Holland looked up and stared at him. "To what end? What does that have to do with antiaging research?"

"When it is further refined, the same mechanism should allow us to transfer *any* gene from one living organism to another." He paused meaningfully. "And we have already isolated the gene for the protein that plays the key role in human cellular immortalization."

Holland was thunderstruck. "A protein that allows cells to live forever?!"

"Forever's a long time, Mr. Holland. For the moment we're prepared to settle for—what, Foster?—three hundred years? Let's just say we're confident we will shortly have a drug that allows human beings to override their genetic limitations. An antiaging drug, if you will."

Abruptly, Holland had to consider the possibility that these people were mad. Even if not, their sheer presumption was beyond anything he'd ever experienced.

Yet, glancing again at the microscope, he couldn't afford to dismiss them out of hand.

Could it be? Was it even remotely possible that here, in this unlikeliest of places, he'd stumbled on what he'd been so feverishly seeking all along?

A drug that would keep HIM alive?

"You've done all this yourself?" he pulled back, looking for maneuvering room. "The two of you are the only principals?"

"Basic research doesn't have to be as cumbersome as some make it," replied Lynch. "Fleming discovered penicillin in a one-man lab, Einstein developed the special theory of relativity as a clerk in the Swiss Patent Office."

"That's pretty fast company you put yourself in."

"Not me personally. Dr. Foster is the chief researcher on the project."

Holland turned to Foster in surprise. Scientists with major league talent invariably flashed major league egos; this guy was so nondescript, he all but faded from view. "May I ask your background?"

"Molecular biology," he allowed, though the scrutiny appeared to make him even more uncomfortable. "I'm a molecular biologist."

"Dr. Foster trained at the Whitehead Institute at MIT under D. L. Cohen."

"Really?" said Holland. "I interviewed Dr. Cohen after he won his Nobel on the genetic analysis of blood cells. It was quite an honor."

Lynch eyed him levelly. "That was Dr. Foster's work. He was a postdoc under Cohen. But his name wasn't even listed on the paper as a contributor. . . ."

Holland nodded, uncertain. Absurd as the claim seemed, he knew too much of the cutthroat business of high-stakes science to dismiss it out of hand. "You have proof of that? Maybe I could write something on it."

"I tried," said Foster mildly.

Lynch could only marvel at his colleague's restraint; he knew that after the appearance of the laudatory piece on Cohen, the young scientist had written the journalist a series of long, impassioned letters and, getting no response, even tried phoning him. Holland never bothered to reply—and now he didn't even remember!

"Because he wouldn't go quietly, there wasn't a quality university in the country that would touch him," added Lynch, his indignation seeming to rise on his associate's behalf. "He ended up at Barnett College in Salt Lake City. That's where we met and began working together."

Barnett College? Holland had only dimly even heard of the place.

He nodded with evident understanding. "I see."

"Before that, I was at Stafford-Barnes for eight years, the last two as associate research director. Until I was fired."

Holland nodded, hiding his surprise. The pharmaceuticals firm was among the most prestigious in the Northeast.

"I pushed too hard, Mr. Holland, I got sick of watching good drugs killed by rules and committees and petty bureaucrats. Like everywhere else in this business, the guiding principle at Stafford-Barnes was: Don't make waves, keep the FDA off your ass!"

All at once Holland understood the relationship between these two; an alliance of resentful souls, each convinced he'd been denied his fair share of glory. Still, that did not necessarily reflect on the quality of their research. Almost all of the most successful people he knew were driven by bitterness.

"Tell me more about this project of yours," he returned to it, his tone carefully neutral. "That's why I'm here."

"Actually, Mr. Holland," said Lynch, "you're here because we told you to be." With a cool smile he turned to Foster. "Greg, Mr. Holland and I need a few minutes alone."

Confident now, Foster quickly walked from the room.

"Dr. Foster doesn't always understand what's necessary to achieve important ends," said Lynch. "He's not as practical as we are."

Holland nodded and crossed his arms. So, here, finally, it came.

"We need to raise a great deal of money. Very quickly. We want your help to do it."

"Money?" asked Holland. "What about Stagg?"

"Mr. Stagg is nearly tapped out—he's only recently learned himself how desperate the situation is. If we're careful, we might have enough to see us through another six months."

Holland looked at him intently. "You've spent millions already. How much more funding could you possibly require? This seems like a very lean operation."

"Leaner than it was. We've cut way back. A year ago we had seventeen scientists here, looking into a wide variety of antiaging therapies, plus full support staff. Now, besides Dr. Foster and myself, we're down to a secretary/nutritionist and"—he paused—"a few others who help keep up appearances. I won't even insult your intelligence by showing you their work. Virtually all resources are now focused on *this* research. But it is enormously costly."

Holland was silent, waiting for him to elaborate.

"There are quite a number of individuals on the payroll who"—he hesitated—"have no formal affiliation with the Institute. People who assist us in various ways." He stopped again; then added, obliquely, "We find, Mr. Holland, that those on the local scene are usually better positioned to obtain the materials our work demands than we are as outsiders."

Holland didn't need to have it spelled out. Clearly, they were paying off individuals—in data banks, governmental agencies, hospitals, God knows where else—to supply them with confidential information; as well, quite possibly, as law enforcement, senior medical personnel, maybe even ordinary citizens. After all, if they could get to *him,* seemingly no one was beyond reach.

"You should know," added the scientist suddenly, "that we intend to personally be the first beneficiaries of this work."

Lynch watched the journalist closely. His reaction—suddenly alive, hopeful as a child early Christmas morning—was exactly what he'd been looking for.

Across the room the door began slowly to open. They watched Clark Warren enter, holding a tray bearing ginger snaps and two cups of tea, the cups rattling with each laborious step.

"Dr. Foster must have sent him," observed Lynch. "He's very considerate that way."

Twenty feet away, behind a two-way mirror, Foster smiled: that was a nice touch.

"I understand he was obtained for research purposes," said Holland.

The scientist nodded, smiling warmly at Warren. "He's helped establish the overriding importance of our target protein—since skin biopsies indicate its total *absence* in his cells."

"You mean," said Holland, beginning to understand, "the genetic component he lacks . . ."

"Exactly, would logically be the very one that functions especially *well* in human beings who live to be abnormally old. Accelerated progeria appears to be the exact inverse of the condition we're trying to foster. This confirms the experience we've had with lab animals."

Warren had still only made it halfway across the room. As Holland studied him, another question, related but far more troubling, came to mind. He hesitated, knowing that to even speak it aloud would be to edge across an ethical line. For all his private lapses, after all, he'd always been—*prided* himself on being—a public man of conscience. He was known for his thoughtfulness in grappling with such thorny moral issues as euthanasia and late-term abortion. More to the point, he'd written with searing eloquence about the Nazi pseudoexperiments with eugenics.

But this, he was suddenly certain, was different. This single, small sacrifice stood as a potential boon to all humanity. That it might benefit him personally was beside the point.

In any case, surely, Clark had only months to live anyway.

"But why only *skin* biopsies?" asked Holland evenly.

Catching the scientist's stricken look, he paused, but only for half a second. "Can you really get everything you need through skin biopsies? Wouldn't the finding be tissue-specific?"

"We've been quite satisfied with the results," said Lynch. He paused, wondering that someone who seemed to get so little joy from life would cling to it so tenaciously. But, glancing toward the mirror behind which his colleague watched, he realized that suddenly he was being tested as much as this complete stranger.

"To really nail down the case," pressed Holland, "wouldn't you need samples from a wide variety of organs? Like with the aequorin-treated mice?"

Lynch paused. "Interesting thought . . ."

By now Clark Warren was beside them, and the scientist took a ginger snap from the plate on the tray. "Thank you, Clark," he mouthed the words, "we're not very hungry now."

As Warren turned and began moving off, Lynch picked up the phone. Dialing three numbers, he listened for a moment, then nodded. "I'd like you to get Mr. Van Ost down here, please. Lab three."

Holland looked at him curiously.

"Someone else I think you should meet."

The man who entered the room moments later was unlike anyone Holland had ever before encountered in such a facility. Powerfully built, his bulging chest and biceps barely contained by the fifties-era white shirt he wore, jacketless, with a clip-on tie, he was surely a weight lifter. But he was short, no more than five five, and had fine, almost feminine features.

"Mr. Van Ost is our director of security. He comes to us from the former South African Bureau of Internal Affairs."

Holland nodded uneasily. "Nice to meet you." If the introduction was intended to intimidate, it had served its purpose.

"The pleasure is entirely mine," he offered, excessively polite, in an odd, lilting accent the reporter guessed to be Afrikaans.

"It appears Mr. Holland will be working with us."

Holland hoped his smile was ingratiating. "Of course, we still need to talk more about my role. Basically, you'll just want me to point you toward some money people?"

"Perhaps a few other small things. This is a . . . *delicate* project, it can make unorthodox demands." He paused, nodded meaningfully at Van Ost. "That's a responsibility we have to share."

In an instant Van Ost had bounded behind Clark Warren and tapped him on the shoulder. "Let me get that for you, Clark," he said gently, easing the tray from his grasp and setting it on a nearby table.

As Clark gazed at him, confused, he placed a comforting hand on his shoulder; then, abruptly, shifted it to the back of his neck. With a single, violent move, he jerked the head back and his thumb down. The snap of the cervical vertebrae made no more sound than that produced by a very dry twig.

Holland blanched as Van Ost held up the lifeless form. With the clothes pitifully loose around the emaciated body and the slack skin sagging, he looked like an oversized rag doll.

"Too bad," offered Van Ost, "he was a sweet fellow. Where would you like him?"

"Ask Mr. Holland—it was his idea."

Light-headed and slightly sick to the stomach, only by sheer will did Holland seem to take the question in stride. "I assume you have a room where you do your cutting."

Arriving at the office before 7:30, Sally was startled to find the door unlocked. She hesitated before very gently pushing it open and peering inside.

"Hey," called out Lisa, glancing over her shoulder from her computer.

"Christ, Lisa!" Sally strode into the office. "What are you *doing* here?"

Lisa had already turned back to the machine. "Trying to get down something Stebben can live with. *Suggest* that the cops have proof without violating our agreement."

"I like the instinct," said Sally with a smile.

Lisa returned it. "That's what I'm here for."

"But, sorry, forget it."

"You mean because it's off the record?" asked Lisa. She nodded at the story on her monitor. "You've said yourself that's why terms like *reportedly* and *according to sources* were invented."

"Because I think Stebben's full of crap. Rule one in this business is never trust anyone with an agenda—and his is to get us off his back." She paused. "If those shots are legit, let him release them. We'll be happy to splash them all over the front page for him!"

"He won't do that."

"Then the question we have to ask is why not!" She paused. "It's possible he leaked this to us so we'd embarrass ourselves. What proof do we have they're genuine?"

Lisa looked at her doubtfully. "Sally, I really don't think that—"

"You don't have to. *I'm* the one paid to think about it."

"I mean, look, maybe cops fake photos in L.A. or New York. This is Edwardstown."

"Fine—go back and ask if he measured the prints for depth."

"How would that—"

"It would give some idea of their weight—if, that is, if he's sincerely interested in putting together a profile of these guys." She paused. "But don't bother—I already called and asked. *Nada.*"

Lisa fell silent.

"I'll tell you something else—I sure as hell didn't notice any prints that night."

"So all we've got to run on the case this week is more ancient history?" She indicated the latest volume unearthed by Sally, on her desk beneath a stack of papers; entitled *A Brief History of the Late Conflict with Our English Cousins,* it dealt with the War of 1812. The section that had caught Sally's eye recounted the fears of New Englanders, after the British burned Washington and desecrated Revolutionary soldiers' graves in Maryland, of an impending invasion of their region from Canada.

"Listen, Lisa, at least it provides a plausible explanation about why those burial records might be missing. It describes how grave markings were disguised and church records hidden for safekeeping."

The younger woman shook her head, deeply skeptical. "Even I'm starting to feel like we're just wasting time."

"No," she shot back, "we're *buying* time. Maybe Stebben's right, maybe it was just a stupid prank. But we'll never know for sure unless we find out for ourselves."

"What do you mean?"

"If the cops won't do the legwork, we'll have to do it for them. It's about time the concept of investigative reporting got introduced to this part of the world."

Abruptly, the phone rang. Sally snatched it up. "Sally Benedict, *Weekly*."

She listened a moment, then seemed to freeze. "How did you find me here?"

Lisa stared, perplexed. She'd never seen Sally so rattled.

"No," said Sally, "believe it or not, we sometimes put in long days here too."

Lisa pushed her chair from her desk, eavesdropping unabashedly.

"Oh, yeah?" said Sally. "It's really been that long?"

She listened a moment, then, with obvious hesitance, asked, "You are? When?"

The call lasted another minute or so, with Sally doing far more listening than talking.

"What's going on?" asked Lisa cheerily, when Sally hung up.

"Just someone I used to know."

"Who?" She grinned. "You're the one who's always telling me to be persistent."

She hesitated. "His name is Paul Holland."

"Paul Holland?" she asked, awestruck. "Of the *New York Herald*?"

Sally saw, with ambivalence, that the fact was enough to instantly restore her standing in the younger woman's estimation. "We used to work together in Philadelphia."

"Paul Holland of the *Herald*," she repeated, as if talking of a rock star. "It's my dream to work at that place."

Sally turned away to make a notation on her calendar.

"What did he want?"

"Who the hell knows?" She paused. "He wants to get together. He'll be in the area next week."

Five days later Mark was staring into his bloodshot eyes in the men's room off the faculty lounge. Leaning down, he splashed cold water into his face.

Christ, how in the world would he make it through this day? Through five of the quasi-performances it took to keep twenty-five to thirty teens focused for forty-five minutes on science instead of themselves?

"What the hell's with you?"

He looked up at his friend Steve Montera, from the history department.

"Something you ate? You look terrible."

"Just trying to get my game face in place before first period."

"Screw it, it's the last day before vacation. Give 'em a study hall."

Though they'd known each other forever—since Montera replaced the original drummer in Mark's old band—Mark couldn't bring himself to come clean. How to explain his stomach was in knots because his wife was having a drink with an old boyfriend? That the very thought of being measured against this hugely successful other guy and all he represented sent his anxiety level soaring? He was supposed to be way beyond this sort of thing. He was a teacher at this place—hell, chairman of the science department—not some insecure kid!

"Can't, we're starting a new unit—genetics. There's a lot of material to cover."

"Today?!"

"I want to get a head start. There'll be questions on the statewide exam."

"I swear, Bowman," said Montera, smiling, "you'd do this for free, wouldn't you?"

Mark ripped a handful of paper towels from a dispenser and mopped his face. "Not a chance, Steve, not today."

But as usual, Mark had underestimated himself. Once in front of the class, by far his most stimulating group, everything but the challenge before him was forgotten. Sally might be a whiz on the printed page, but this was *his* stage.

80,000

"Okay," he said, whipping around after scrawling the number a foot high on the blackboard, "make my day—what's the significance?"

In most of his classes he could expect such a question to be met only with glazed looks. But now several hands went up.

"And, no, it's definitely NOT what I get paid around here. . . . Paul?"

"It's the total number of human genes. The things that pass on things from one generation to the next."

"The *things* that pass on *things*? Like what, dirty socks? Back issues of *National Geographic*? A bad temper?"

The kid gave a sheepish smile; he should have known better. Mr.

Bowman was forever bugging them about clarity and specificity. "Traits—how you look and how you act, stuff like that."

"Good—I didn't throw in the bad temper for nothing. Genes contain all the millions of bits of information we've inherited from all the countless generations that preceded us. And which will be found in our own descendants centuries after we're gone and forgotten."

"Jeez," murmured the boy sitting directly in front of him, "you don't have to make it sound so depressing."

"Depressing?" Mark seemed genuinely surprised. "It's miraculous. You hate your eye color, or the size of your backside, or the fact that you can't throw a baseball more than twenty-five miles an hour? Well, you really *can* pin it on your parents. . . ." There was laughter. "But if you get into the blame game, don't have kids of your own, because they'll nail you in turn. Each of us is inextricably linked to ancestors a million years before the dawn of recorded time."

A girl in the back of the room raised her hand. "How about genetic engineering? Won't it change that?"

He smiled, more relaxed than he'd been all day. This was a terrific group! "You think so? Theoretically, rewriting the genetic code to dictate new or different cell behaviors—to help delay the onset of certain diseases, for instance—may sound easy. But we're dealing with something of almost unimaginable complexity. When you start tinkering with six hundred million years of evolution, you never know what sorts of unforeseen results you might get. Even God is hit and miss when He starts playing with genetics, right?"

He waited a moment to see if anyone would pick up the cue.

"I'm talking mutations—the kind that occur naturally in nature. The fact that very occasionally, for no apparent reason, at the moment an individual is conceived, there's a tiny change in the composition of a gene, fundamentally altering its behavior. And that change may then be passed on to future generations." He paused. "We've actually been able to follow a mutation back in time to its origin. For instance, the BRCA-one mutation, which puts certain Jewish women of Eastern European origin at risk for breast and ovarian cancer, has been traced to one village in sixteenth-century Russia."

"So mutations are bad?"

"Usually. But what makes this so fascinating is that once in a blue moon a genetic accident does great good. There's a tiny isolated Italian village called Limone where cardiovascular disease is almost completely unknown. It seems to be the result of a chance genetic mutation in a single man about two hundred years ago."

A hand shot up in back. "What about reproduction? I heard genetic engineering could make that a lot more fair?"

"Fair?"

"For women. I mean, you see an eighty-year-old guy and he looks totally decrepit, right? But his sperm can still make a baby? While a woman of forty-eight or fifty who's in terrific shape can't."

He suppressed a smile. "I've got to tell you, Kate, biology isn't about fairness. But if it makes you feel better, on average men actually live about seven years less."

Mark glanced at the clock; he still had a lot of material to cover. "Let's put it this way: It would be one unbelievable whopper of a mutation that'd allow women to start conceiving at eighty. Even *mad* scientists don't go around trying to change the fundamental nature of life itself."

Sally emerged from the numbing cold of the late December afternoon into the Clover Patch, Edwardstown's best bar/café, nearly empty at this hour but ablaze with holiday cheer.

Spotting Paul Holland at a corner table, she quickly turned away to hang up her coat.

Already, she was starting to regret she'd come; indeed, had only agreed to the meeting for the most pragmatic of reasons. Prominent and well connected, Holland could help get her the kind of freelance assignments that would make a real dent in the cost of fertility treatments.

By the time she turned back, he was on his feet.

"Sally!"

There was a brief, awkward moment when it was unclear whether they would shake hands or embrace. He ended it with a quick peck on her cheek. "You look fabulous."

She was wearing a short black skirt to go with her green, form-fitting jacket; the one that so vividly brought out her eyes.

She pointedly ignored the compliment. "Hope I didn't keep you waiting."

"No, you know me—compulsively early." He smiled as he pulled out her chair. "All those years of having to make the seven-eleven."

"Right, I forgot you live in the suburbs. So how is Elaine?"

"*Used to live* in burbs. We were divorced last year."

So that was it! His sham of a marriage was finally over and the bastard wanted her back in his life!

"Sorry to hear it," she said.

"Don't be. It's really for the best."

"How's your little boy taking it?"

"No problem, Scotty's fine."

"He's how old now, seven?"

She saw he actually had to think about it. "Right, in April. He's in second grade."

"What's his favorite toy?"

He shrugged. "I don't know, the usual. Cars, trucks, various weapons of destruction."

"And what's his teacher's name?"

"What, you're *testing* me?" He shook his head at the realization. "You haven't changed, Benedict."

In fact, Holland had dreaded this encounter even more than she had. As a journalist, artifice came to him virtually as second nature. He was used to subtly shifting conversations to suit his needs and pretending interest, or warmth, he did not feel to elicit confidences. But Sally Benedict knew all that about him. Worse, he had genuinely cared for her.

Then, again, it looked like she was going to make it easier on him than he'd expected.

"Looks like you haven't changed, either, Holland," she shot back now, "—giving yourself so much attention, there's none left over for anyone else."

He responded only with a weak smile. "It's great to see you again too."

"Hey, just think of me as the conscience of relationships past."

"Something to drink, Sally?"

She looked up at the waitress who'd materialized on her left. "Just a coffee, Paula. You, Dick?"

He shot her a look—he detested his never-used first name, the short version even more. "I'll have a beer. Any microbreweries around here?"

The waitress looked at him blankly.

"You have Harp?" He paused. "Beck's?"

"Paula," said Sally dryly, "bring the man a Bud."

"So," she said a moment later, "it still bugs you to be called Dick?"

"It's fine—from you."

"How's Elaine holding up? Not that you care."

He leaned forward earnestly. "It wasn't like what happened between us, Sally. She wanted it over too."

"*What happened between us!* We had a sleazy affair, that's what happened between us! You cheated on your wife and child and I was an accomplice. And I felt like shit every second of every day for a year and a half. And then you dumped me!"

She hadn't planned to sound so bitter. But she couldn't help it; the very sight of this guy pushed her buttons.

"Has it occurred to you that people change? Maybe I'm no longer the person you think I am." He tried a smile. "Probably even you've changed a little."

"It's the small-town lifestyle—high on fiber, low on bullshit."

"The truth is, a lot of people thought you were crazy for leaving. But personally, I admired it. It took guts. Who doesn't dream about dropping out?"

She felt herself flushing. "Oh, come on! *You* know damn well what I wanted to get away from. And I succeeded!"

"Me?"

"Don't flatter yourself. *All* the self-important, opportunistic jerks who have no clue what really matters. And, by the way, I haven't dropped out. I like what I'm doing."

"I can see." He reached into his jacket pocket and pulled out a rolled-up newspaper—the *Weekly*. "Very impressive."

"You always were a bullshitter, Holland."

"You can't have very much in the way of resources, but it's a nice little publication. Extremely readable."

She nodded. "Take some copies home with you, I'm sure it'll impress all your pals at the *Herald*."

"You got it—I'll give a copy to Dennis Boyles personally."

"You do that," she answered self-mockingly. But secretly she hoped he would—no one was in a better position than the *Herald*'s executive editor to throw work her way. "You said you were up this way on a story," she said, shifting the subject. "More on this longevity business?"

He looked at her in surprise. "You've been reading my stuff?"

"Occasionally. What's this all about, fear of getting older yourself?"

Seeing how unexpectedly hard the remark seemed to hit home, she felt a twinge of regret—but also some pleasure.

"I'm visiting some institute down in Manchester," he said soberly. "But it's just spinning my wheels. The whole project's been a bust."

"In all that time you've come up with nothing?"

"Not unless you count a lot of frauds and wackos making plans for their three hundredth birthdays. This'll be the end of it—Boyles's orders." He shrugged. "Can't complain, I gave it a shot."

Sally had never seen Holland so muted, and it was a revelation. *He really WAS hurting, his personal life shot, even his work life was going to hell!*

She watched as he picked up his beer. But instead of sipping, he held it suspended in midair. "I hear you're still married to the teacher. . . ."

"For better or worse. Some people still do it that way, you know." She stopped. "For future reference, his name is Mark."

"Mark, that's right." He paused. "Well, tell him for me he's a lucky guy."

Never could she have dreamed up such a moment. Were it anyone else facing her, so obviously vulnerable, she'd have resisted saying it, but now the words came with quiet relish.

"Just for the record, I'm even luckier. . . ."

Ten minutes after his last class Mark watched the two boys shuffle into the room.

This was the part of the job he liked least, the flip side of teaching alert, engaged kids. He wasn't cut out to be a disciplinarian. Why were so many kids these days so openly contemptuous of authority?

Just yesterday these two had been caught, only several hundred yards off school grounds, in a bit of malicious mischief touching directly on his department. They'd blown to smithereens the beaver lodge at Payne Creek—the one over the years he'd taken countless interested students to see.

At least he'd had a few hours to cool down. His first impulse, on surveying the remains during his lunch hour with the school principal, had been to hand these two directly to the cops.

Even now, the sight of them—laconic, arrogant, already on the edge of insolence—challenged his self-control.

"Ah, Sutter and Boyd." He assumed the upbeat mode he so often used with difficult kids. "So what're you guys expecting, a couple of weeks of detention? A lecture? What?"

They deposited themselves into adjacent desks in the front row and stared up at him. Even seated, they seemed oddly matched, one gaunt with shoulder-length blond hair and vacant eyes—the sort teenage girls thought of as ethereal; his friend, dark, wiry, purple haired, full of nervous energy. Both wore multiple ear studs—still a rarity in Edwardstown.

"Whatever," shrugged the vacant one, Pete Boyd.

Mark fixed him with a hard look. "Let me put it this way: What do you think you *deserve*?"

"You know, Mr. Bowman," spoke up the other, Terry Sutter, the very picture of sweet reason, "I don't think we really did anything *wrong*. I was thinking about it—was it really illegal? And, I mean, it wasn't on school property, so it wasn't against *school* rules."

Mark was caught short. He'd had this kid the year before in his "slow" class in earth sciences. He'd never so much as spoken up in class.

"Anyway," the boy added, "the thing was deserted."

Mark moved around to the front of the desk and sat on its edge, looking down on him from a distance of only a few feet. "You thinking of being a lawyer, Terry?"

"Yeah, right." He smirked. "My mom'll be happy if I just end up not needing one."

His friend laughed loudly.

"Quiet!" Mark shut him up. "What the hell's wrong with you?! That lodge has been there as long as anyone can remember and now it's *gone*! It's irreplaceable!" He stopped. "Why? Because a couple of standard-issue morons wanted a cheap thrill! Just a point of curiosity—what makes someone do something like that?"

Terry rolled his eyes. "C'mon, don't tell us you didn't pull the same sort of crap when you were a kid."

"I did my share of firecrackers, cherry bombs, ash cans—the whole arsenal. But I sure as hell never did anyone any harm."

"Neither did we," shot back Terry.

"How do you *know* that lodge was deserted?"

"Because *I'd* been watching it for a while too. You think we would've done it otherwise?"

"That's exactly what I think. I don't think you gave a damn one way or the other."

"No way. I like beavers."

His friend looked at him, ready to laugh—but, realizing he might be serious, thought better of it.

Mark shook his head, thinking the remark might be intended as crude. "We're talking the *mammal* here, Terry. . . . Big teeth? Webbed feet?"

"Yeah," he answered earnestly. "I like 'em."

For argument's sake, he took him at his word. "That lodge was still habitable, did you think of that? They might've returned."

Terry shook his head vigorously. "They don't do that. Once they leave they don't come back."

Mark looked at him closely; either he'd totally misjudged this kid or he was one of the most masterful bullshit artists he'd ever run across. "Oh, yes?"

"Yeah. I know this stuff."

"Fine. Tell me something about"—Mark mentally groped for a pertinent beaver factoid of his own—"their mating habits."

"They mate for life."

He nodded slowly. "You're right, they do."

"Of course." Unexpectedly, Terry erupted in a smile. "Maybe not the ones there. Probably they got divorced, like everyone else around here."

Mark hesitated; vaguely he recalled that Terry's parents' split had been a particularly nasty one. "Listen . . ." he picked up, only slightly mollified, "over the years I took a lot of my kids over to see that lodge. Whole classes sometimes."

"Not ours," said Terry sharply.

"What, you're looking for sympathy points because you're not in one of the high-achievement classes? Well, sorry, it doesn't work that way. Earn it and maybe it'll be there for you."

There was a long silence, each fixing the other with an unwavering stare.

"Watch it," said Terry finally, smiling faintly, "people get sued these days for messing with kids' self-esteem. So what's our punishment?"

"How about if you tell me?"

He considered. "How's this? We promise to pull B's in science next term."

"Come again?" said Mark, surprised.

"Write IOUs or something."

"And if you don't?"

"I don't know"—he shrugged, smiled—"make us pay. Stick us with six months' detention."

"Whoa!" cut in his friend. "What are you saying, man . . . ?"

Mark gazed at him impassively. "Boyd, your friend here's actually trying to be a *good* influence on you. Why don't you take him up on it?"

"Gimme a break, will you?" Distractedly, he picked at a bit of dried gum on the bottom of his sneaker. "I mean, the thing wasn't even on school grounds!"

"Okay," said Mark, turning back to Terry, "you're on. Starting after vacation. We'll see if I'm a complete idiot to trust you."

They'd been sitting in the Clover Patch over an hour now, and the place was starting to fill up. To Sally's discomfort the couple who ran the hardware store next to the *Weekly* had just sat down a few tables away; and now she spotted her colleague Florence's son-in-law at the bar.

But even more awkward than the thought of having to explain herself was the conversation at hand. Stripped of his old cockiness, Holland seemed to have nothing left but self-absorbed earnestness. All at once she couldn't help wonder: *How in the world could she ever have been so infatuated with this guy? What was HER problem?*

"I'm in therapy, you know," he was saying now. "I really am trying to change. I don't want to keep hurting people I care about—the way I hurt you."

"Forget it. Water under the bridge . . ." She paused. "Look, Dick, it's getting late, I'm due at a party."

"I don't want to forget," he said. "I want to make it up to you."

She hesitated. On the jukebox in the corner Judy Garland started singing "Have Yourself a Merry Little Christmas." "Actually, there is something I wanted to tell you. I'm keeping my eyes open for some freelance work."

"Oh?"

"If you're comfortable, maybe you could say something to Boyles. Who knows, maybe the *Herald* can use a stringer in this area."

She saw on his face a familiar expression, something between concern and calculation.

"I just, you know, want to keep a hand in," she added quickly, then realized how lame that sounded. "Not that the money wouldn't be okay too."

Leaning across the table, he looked at her intently. "Sally, can I ask you something?"

"Shoot."

"Is this because you're trying to start a family?"

Stunned, for several seconds she said nothing. "Just a lucky guess?" she asked finally.

"Call it a semieducated one. I know you, I kind've expected you'd have kids already."

Then, too, she realized, it was also possible he'd picked up something from one of the several friends from the old days with whom she was still in contact. "It's not always that simple."

He paused, seeming to think it over. "You know, Sally, I'm close to some of the top fertility specialists in the country."

"Thanks," she shot back, "but we're already looking into a clinic in Manchester—"

"I'm talking about the most advanced methods, technologies not yet available to the public. Some of these people owe me. I'm sure I can arrange it free of charge."

She hesitated, as the import of the proposal hit home. She looked away, then back at him; her eyes locking on his. "That's quite an offer."

"It's nothing, just a small favor. I owe you."

"You're wrong as usual—it's a huge favor." Heart pumping, she pushed her chair from the table. "I'll get back to you."

The party, at the home of Marcia Pulley, Edwardstown High's unassuming principal, was in full swing when Sally walked in. Gazing anxiously about, she spotted Mark in a corner of the crowded living room. He was wearing the collarless shirt with mattresslike stripes she had ordered, against his protests, from the J. Crew catalogue. Looking a little lost, he also had never looked so appealing.

She made her way to him and took his hand. "We have to talk."

"How'd it go with Holland?" he asked apprehensively, as she led him down the hallway.

Finding the bedroom, she removed her coat and tossed it on top of the pile on the bed.

"It went okay with Holland?" he repeated.

"Yeah, fine." Suddenly she reached out, drew him close, and kissed him. "God, Mark, don't ever let me forget how much I love you."

He looked startled, then smiled. "Go ahead, see the guy as often as you want."

She began to unbutton his shirt, then stopped to lock the door.

"Sally, what are you doing?"

But already she was leading him back toward the bed. "What do you think?" she said, laughing softly.

Pushing him onto a pile of coats, she gently fell on top of him and reached down to unbutton his jeans.

"C'mon, Sal," he said weakly, "this is my boss's home. . . ."

"Shhh," she soothed, pulling off her sweater, then undoing her bra.

"You're out of your mind," he said, but reached out to gently touch one of her breasts.

Slowly, she lowered herself over him, pushing her breast close to his mouth. "I know," she said, then gasped as he took it between his lips.

Her breasts were small, and at first he'd been surprised by how unbelievably sensitive they were. Now, gently sucking a nipple, he slowly moved his hands behind to grip her ass beneath her skirt.

"Wait a minute," she said, "let me take off my panty hose."

He watched as with astonishing speed she pulled off her boots and yanked off her underclothes. "Sally, this is so irrespon—"

"Oh, God," she cut him off, lying beside him on the bed and hitching up her skirt. "Who brought a mink coat, it feels so good."

She took his head in her hands and raised herself up to kiss him on the lips. "Take off your pants," she whispered urgently. "Now."

Almost as soon as he entered her, Sally was at the edge. He felt her ass muscles tighten in his hands and her entire body start to arch.

The doorknob turned as someone tried to enter the room.

"Hello . . . ?" came a tentative voice.

Mark started to pull back, but Sally wrapped her legs even tighter around him. "Don't even think about it."

"Just a minute," she called out, in an amazingly natural voice.

"Uh . . . okay," they heard, then retreating footsteps.

The near discovery seemed to excite her even more. In a moment she was thrashing wildly, eyes closed tight, a hand in her mouth to stifle the sounds of pleasure. Mark, increasingly oblivious, stayed with her stroke for stroke.

They held each other for a long time. When they pulled apart, they smiled, then, together, started laughing.

"Jesus, Sally . . . !"

"Next time, doors open, everyone invited!"

"Can we *please* get out of here?" he asked.

Moments later they rejoined the party, flushed; but no more obviously so, Sally thought, than some who'd been dancing or lingering around the punch bowl.

A slow song was playing now, the only kind Mark would agree to dance to—Johnny Mathis singing "Misty"—and she led him onto the floor.

"We have to talk," she said, holding him tight.

"Isn't this where I came in?"

"About something that came up with Holland. It changes everything."

Lisa, I really need you to run with this. There are too many other things going on in my life right now."

The younger woman looked at her, reluctant. "I'm just not sure I'm comfortable with this. Isn't there another approach?" She paused. "I'm interested in serious reporting, not . . . *flirting.*"

"What we're both interested in is *results.*"

Sally paused, reining in her impatience. As one of those young women who drew men effortlessly, Lisa often made much of resenting being judged by her looks—or claiming to. "I'll let you in on what shouldn't be a secret," added Sally, "—a reporter uses *everything* she has. You say it's your dream to work at the *New York Herald*? What, you don't think guys at that place loosen up sources by talking sports? Or women?" Sally smiled. "Believe me, if I could still get teenage boys panting after me . . ."

In fact, Sally was not surprised at how readily the doubts were overcome—or that once they were, at how fully Lisa launched herself into the assignment.

Edwardstown High was closed for Christmas vacation, but the wrestling team was still practicing three mornings a week and Lisa's timing was perfect. Her VW bug pulled into the lot by the school

gym just as three boys in letterman's jackets walked from the building.

They'd chosen today based on the weather—unusually mild for
this time of year, a few degrees above freezing; warm enough for Lisa
to plausibly ditch her bulky down jacket in favor of a light blue
parka that matched her eyes and set off her thick black hair.

The targeting of wrestlers was not random either. As a former
athlete herself Sally vividly recalled the hierarchy of male athletes.
Wrestlers were a distinctive breed; involved in an intensely demanding yet low-status sport, macho types who were also good citizens,
they were high school's version of career military men.

What caught the boys' attention first were the long legs in calf-
skin boots and tight jeans emerging from the car. Lisa actually saw
one elbow another, then watched, bemused, as they continued to
saunter her way, pretending to be oblivious.

"Excuse me, guys . . ." she called anxiously.

They stopped in their tracks.

"Don't tell me I missed practice!?"

The oldest of the three, a tall redhead, looked at her curiously.
"We're on the wrestling team . . ." he answered vaguely.

"I know, I was supposed to be there for it!"

"It just ended, we get out at noon."

"Oh, no, I thought that's when you *started*." She shook her head
miserably. "My editor's gonna have my ass."

"What," he asked incredulously, "are you a reporter or something?"

"If you can call it that—it's my first job. She wants something
about, you know, how dedicated you guys are, working so hard
during vacation and all."

"If you're a reporter," asked one of the other two, "how come
there's no camera?"

"Maybe she's a *writing* reporter, stupid," hissed his older friend.

"Yeah," she said, "for the *Weekly*."

Awed by so worldly a creature, the older boy found himself with nothing more to say. "Well, good meeting you. Try again tomorrow."

"Yeah," said the second boy. "Good meeting you . . ."

They began moving on.

"Hey, guys . . . ?"

They turned.

She hesitated. "Oh, never mind, it's stupid."

"What?" The second boy snapped at the bait.

"As long as I'm here, something else my pain-in-the-ass editor is making me ask about."

"What?"

"She's really giving me a hard time on this one—I just got here and my job's already on the line."

"What?" he pressed, his protective instinct engaged.

"It's about something that happened a couple of months ago. Some cemetery that got robbed."

"Oh, right! Grace churchyard."

"You *know* about it?" she asked, brightening.

"Sure, everybody does. We even talked about it in school."

"Really? What'd you say?"

"My English teacher thought it was pretty sad."

"And you?"

"I thought it was cool," volunteered the second kid. "Lots of people did."

"Who do you think did it?"

"It's pretty old—how come they're still even interested in that?"

She shrugged. "Who knows? I guess nothing else ever happens around here. . . ."

"How do you get to be a reporter?"

It was the smallest of the trio, a towhead whose voice had not yet changed—the first time he'd spoken.

"I just wrote a bunch of letters."

"Is it fun?"

"I don't know, ask me in six months."

"Think you'll ever get to be on TV?"

"Shut up, dorky, that's stupid."

"Yeah, I'd like that a lot. But not much chance I'm gonna get there at this rate." She paused, looked back at the first kid. "C'mon, guys, any theories about who could've done it? I gotta bring back *something*."

"How would we know?"

"No one had any ideas? People didn't say stuff . . . ?"

The two older boys exchanged a look. "Sorry," said the leader, "I really don't know what to tell you. Anyway, we gotta get going. C'mon, you guys."

They resumed walking.

"How about you?"

"Me?" The towheaded kid slowed his pace.

"What's your name?"

He reddened slightly, but answered boldly. "Brian. What's yours?"

"Lisa. How old are you?"

"Fourteen." He grinned. "How old are you?"

"Twenty-two."

He tried to think of a clever comeback, but settled for "Oh."

"Too old for you by about fifteen years," smirked the older boy. "C'mon, Bri, let's go."

"So, Brian," she repeated, lowering her voice conspiratorially, "how about you? Heard anything?"

"Oh, you know, nothing special. I guess there were some rumors and stuff. . . ."

"That's it? Just a few rumors?" She sighed and shook her head again. "Oh, well, I guess a good rumor's better than nothing. You up for a Coke?"

"**W**ho else have you seen?"

Lynch hesitated, caught off guard by the question's bluntness. He'd only been ushered into the presence of the young husband/wife venture-capitalist team of Craig McIntyre and Melissa Reed a moment before.

"I really can't get into that," he replied, hoping the discretion would be taken as laudable. "A couple of places."

McIntyre fixed him with a hard stare. "Cut the crap, Lynch, we *know* you've already been shot down by both Rotner-Noble and Allen Capital Ventures. Who else?"

"Reber-Coates. Just those three."

"*Just?*" McIntyre smiled. "You been turned down by *all* the heavyweights. So now you come to us."

"That's not why—"

"We're not insulted, Mr. Lynch, we're nobody's first choice." His glance around the room took in the fluorescent lighting, no-nonsense carpeting, and battleship-gray steel desks that made the place look more like a low-level accountant's office than what Lynch had come to expect from high-flying venture capitalists; even more telling, the view from the room's single window was not of gleaming Manhattan towers but of a neighboring office complex here in suburban White Plains. "You can't blame people for being seduced by image."

"I'm not interested in superficials."

"Right," spoke up Melissa Reed for the first time, "that's what everyone says." In her early thirties, a few years younger than her husband, she exuded the same confidence, their polished nails and tailored suits a stark contrast to the visitor's cut-rate stab at style.

"I'm here because, from all I've seen and heard, we'd make a good match."

"And what have you seen and heard?"

"As a scientist I've been impressed by the *character* of the work you've supported. You seem to appreciate far better than most that there are new ways to look at old questions."

He was startled when Reed responded by making "jerk off" motions with her hand. "Try again."

"I'm just saying I want to be in business with people who aren't afraid to make things happen. Fast."

"Good, better."

In fact, in the increasingly timid world of venture capital, these people were known as riverboat gamblers, always on the lookout for the big score that would yield several hundred times' return on investment. Though only a handful of the fledgling biotech companies they'd backed had panned out, the returns were such that they'd always managed to avert the sort of full-scale disaster that had sunk similar enterprises.

"I need capital. I think you'll be excited by the work we're doing."

"Which of our deals have you so impressed?" asked McIntyre evenly.

He shifted uneasily, wondering if they were ever going to ask him to sit down.

"Applivax, for one—you obviously saw that their work toward

an AIDS vaccine was as potentially exciting as it was risky. Also Anionix—their approach to generating new compounds is—"

"No!" cut in Reed. "What was exciting about those companies from *our* perspective was their marketplace potential."

"Of course, but—"

"We are interested in profit, Dr. Lynch, period! We don't mind helping humanity, it's a nice bonus, and I'm glad if it makes you more comfortable being in a room with us—but that is not our business."

Lynch nodded. If anything, this woman was an even stronger personality than her husband. "I understand."

"Both the companies you cited were major disappointments. We were lucky to get out in time. As you surely know, the quick kills in biotech these days are few and far between. Like everyone else we've had to become far more cautious in who we back."

"Also Retinex."

The two of them exchanged a quick glance. The company, manufacturer of an experimental antiwrinkle cream, was almost completely unknown. Since the product lacked FDA approval, it was being produced in Matamoros, Mexico, and distributed only in Latin America. But for M & R it was a cash cow, a prime example of the sort of audacity—and moral flexibility—that had kept them a player in the field.

"Won't you have a seat, Mr. Lynch?" said Reed, ushering him toward the chairs arrayed around a coffee table in the corner.

"Retinex," she picked up, with amazing aplomb. "I'm glad you brought that up. Retinex gets us right into the area of equity."

He nodded. "I'm listening."

"Usually, for instance in the cases of both Anionix and Applivax, our policy is to provide first-tier financing only—the five to ten million it takes to get a company rolling. In return we and our investors assume upwards of fifty percent of equity."

"That sounds reasonable."

"On riskier enterprises—like Retinex—our percentage of equity runs considerably higher, in the neighborhood of eighty or even more." She paused. "We set the terms for our participation. If you can't live with it, let's end this now."

"That's not a problem," said Lynch, then realized that to their ears such ready acquiescence might sound naive. "Please understand," he added quickly, "I'm not in this just for the money. But when we're done, there'll be more than enough of that to go around."

When there was no reaction to this, he was reminded of something else: these people spent their entire lives listening to bullshit. In the last month alone they'd probably seen fifty entrepreneurial types like him, including a good dozen in the antiaging field.

"What about Clifford Stagg?" said Reed. "Hasn't he bankrolled your work to date?"

"I'm afraid his wealth is not inexhaustible."

"He knows you're here?"

"Of course. I'd *never* do something like this behind his back."

"How very nice and old fashioned." McIntyre smiled. "But what my wife is asking is whether he is prepared to surrender most of his interest in this venture."

Lynch nodded, feeling slightly foolish for having even momentarily confused a personal matter with business around such people. "His interest is in the success of this project. He understands we need more financing to see it through."

"How much financing?"

"A minimum of ten million dollars for each of the next several years."

Reed smiled at his obvious inexperience. "*Several* years?—do you think you could be any less precise . . . ?"

"Four years, to be on the safe side. I've brought a proposed funding schedule."

"And at the end of that time you expect to have what, exactly?"

Lynch paused, dropped his voice for maximum impact. "We expect to all but eliminate Alzheimer's disease."

The reaction was not what he had hoped. Both nodded politely.

"Well, then," said McIntyre, slapping the arm of his chair and rising to his feet, "why don't you leave whatever material you have for our science people to look over?"

"Actually," he said hurriedly, "I've brought along a brief presentation. May I use the slide projector?"

"Dr. Lynch, we've got other people to see."

But already he was moving toward it, pulling a plastic box of slides from his briefcase. "This will only take a few minutes. Will someone please kill the lights?"

After a moment Reed rose and did so. Reluctantly, her husband resumed his seat.

Lynch had planned this carefully, anticipating tough questions from science advisory types. His first slide showed a human chromosome: its deceptively simple appearance, two *U*'s joined at the base, belying its almost unimaginable complexity. "Let's start with the basics. What you see here is chromosome number twenty-two, magnified eighteen thousand times by electron microscopy. It harbors the gene we are in the process of sequencing."

There was no reaction.

"Think of it as the Infinity gene."

"The 'Infinity gene'?" asked McIntyre.

Instantly, Lynch regretted it. "I realize the term has no scientific credibility, it was dreamed up by the popular-science press to describe an entire constellation of genes."

"No, no," cut in McIntyre, waving away the objection, "that's what makes it *appealing*—it would make it an easier sell."

"I see what you mean."

Rifling through his slide box, Lynch made a snap decision to skip those illustrating the intricate process of sequencing the gene responsible for the remarkable antiaging protein. Then, after a moment, he also set aside the ones that showed the protein was absent in Clark Warren's vital organs.

Instead, the next slide he brought up showed three faces, side by side: a fourteen-year-old boy, a middle-aged woman, and an elderly man, rheumy eyed and enfeebled. "This is what we see with our eyes," he said.

He brought up the next slide, the same chromosome as earlier, only this time with a bright red arrow directing the viewer's attention to one of its four tips. "This is what's happening genetically. This chromosome is from the healthy young boy we just saw. The arrow indicates the distance between the center of the chromosome—the centromere, it's called—and its tip, the telomere."

He replaced the slide with another showing a chromosome that, to the untrained eye, seemed nearly identical. "This is the same chromosome, only this time it's from the forty-six-year-old woman."

He allowed them a moment to study it before moving on to the next.

"Again, the same chromosome, but now from our old man, who happens to have advanced Alzheimer's."

He waited a full fifteen seconds before bringing up a slide showing all three. Side by side the difference was unmistakable.

"You can see that the distance between the centromere and the telomere gets progressively shorter with age—and by the time of the onset of the disease, they are nearly touching. What's happening is the tip of the chromosome is literally falling away. Its genetic blueprint is eroding, vital information is being lost. The result is that the surrounding cell becomes vulnerable to toxins and free radicals that earlier it would have easily defended itself against." He looked at McIntyre. "Are you following?"

"More or less."

"Think of the chromosome as a boxer. At twenty he's fast with his fists and able to absorb a punch; by forty, even under ideal circumstances, his reaction time is slower and it takes him longer to recover every time he's hit. By eighty, if he's unlucky, the very memory of what he was once capable of is gone." He paused. "But the protein we've discovered—Terminase, we call it—has a dramatic impact on the erosion of genetic information. It prevents the deterioration and restores the telomeres. It actually makes the chromosomes of an old cell resemble those of a young cell!"

"I gotta tell you," said Reed, breaking the spell, "it's all Greek to me."

Lynch snapped off the projector, momentarily leaving the room nearly dark; fortunately, for his face mirrored the deep anxiety he managed to keep from his tone. "We have a great deal of supporting data."

"Good, that's where we started. Leave it with us."

"Also," he said quickly, in mounting desperation, "we have a working animal model."

"Don't tell me . . ." guessed McIntyre. "Mice!"

Lynch's silence made clear he'd hit on it.

"Isn't it amazing, Melissa?—how many of these brilliant ideas end up helping rodents?"

Laughing, Reed snapped on the light. "I don't think there's much demand for a product like that—the *opposite* of a better mousetrap."

"In just a matter of months I'll be able to produce evidence this protein works in human beings—"

"Unfortunately, Dr. Lynch," said Reed with finality, "in this business time really is money."

Lynch's eyes moved from one to the other, calculating. "Will you excuse me for just one moment . . . ?"

They were still in place, perplexed, when the scientist hurried back into the room. "I'm not saying your skepticism isn't warranted. . . . But I hope I can offer you at least some reassurance. Have you met Paul Holland?"

Lynch held the door open and Holland, in casual slacks and a tweed jacket, walked in.

The effect was everything Lynch could have hoped. Instantly the balance of power in the room was changed; it was as if a movie star were suddenly in their midst.

"No," spoke up Holland, "I don't believe I've had the pleasure."

"You're involved with this project?" asked McIntyre, incredulous.

"On an informal basis. I suppose you could call me a kind of advisor."

"Actually," said Lynch, "it was Mr. Holland who recommended you people to me."

"Ah," said Reed, flattered. "I see—and that's also how you knew about Retinex. . . ."

"That's how I knew we might get along, yes."

McIntyre edged closer to Holland. "Dr. Lynch has made some rather spectacular claims today."

"To my mind he's earned that right."

"You've examined the work?"

"Closely. I consider this a breakthrough of almost incalculable significance, potentially the greatest I've run across in my career. I want to do what I can to see it realized."

The words hung in the air.

"We have a private dining room downstairs," said Reed. "Any chance we could pick your brain over lunch? I've been reading you since high school."

"My pleasure." Holland smiled. "As long as you don't say anything else that'll make me feel ancient."

Taking his arm, she looked over at Lynch. "I'll alert our science people. I think it's time to start talking business."

Rushing into the sedate hotel lobby, Sally was painfully aware she looked like hell. Never mind New York's Plaza Hotel, she wouldn't even show up at a meeting of the Edwardstown Chamber of Commerce in a bulky down jacket and baggy corduroys, with windblown hair and no makeup!

She'd planned to change, of course; had brought along her best business suit and a pair of heels. But between the storm that slowed their departure from New Hampshire and the New York traffic, they hadn't even had time to check into their own hotel. Already, they were twenty minutes late.

"My God," she said, "how can I even face the guy?!"

"Relax," reassured Mark, squeezing her hand, "you look fine. Wonderful."

She stopped, and looked at him tenderly, realizing he meant it. Mark's own down jacket, worn with an old pair of jeans and work boots, was even rattier than hers. "Thanks for that, Mr. Fashion. But I don't think the good doctor will also be blinded by love." She sighed. "Come on, I think the Oak Room's this way."

Dr. Carl Keller, director of the Dallas-based Keller Institute for Reproductive Services, was the only person in the room late this wintry Saturday afternoon. A thin, middle-aged man in a three-piece suit, he was on his feet the moment they appeared, hand extended, a delighted smile creasing his bearded face.

"Ms. Benedict and Mr. Bowman?"

Sally nodded uncertainly.

"I have heard *so* much about you. You've just arrived?"

"It was one helluva trip," observed Sally. "Our famous New Hampshire weather."

"I'll wait, if you want to run up to your room and freshen up."

Sally hesitated. "Actually, we're not staying here."

"Our reservation's at the Howard Johnson Motor Lodge," said Mark.

"Ahh." He indicated his table. "Please, join me."

"The convention is going well?" asked Sally, by way of small talk. Keller's secretary had told her this is what had brought the doctor to New York.

"Oh, I showed my face, that's all that matters." He laughed. "I was on a couple of panels."

"It's over?" she asked, only now aware of the possibility he'd stayed behind to see *them.*

"Yesterday." Then, by way of explanation: "Don't think anything of it. Paul Holland has been exceedingly kind to us. . . ."

For a moment neither responded. When the doctor turned his way, Mark hoped his expression mirrored something like gratitude—not the resentment of Holland's astonishing largesse he was feeling. "So," he said, "here we are. What can we do for you?"

"Well," said the doctor, with a brisk nod, "why don't we just think of this as a preliminary consultation. I've studied the material sent me by your hometown doctor. . . ." He looked down at an open notebook.

"Dr. Malen," prompted Sally.

"On the basis of what I see, one tube is partially blocked by adhesions, probably the result of some condition you weren't even aware of—maybe a minor bout of pelvic inflammatory disease. Which means we have to examine the possibility the other tube might be damaged too."

This came as a complete shock. "Malen never told us that."

"What I'm suggesting is a full round of diagnostic tests. We'll make our treatment decisions on that basis." He paused. "The good news is that you're both relatively young. In this business time is our greatest enemy."

"We're told you offer a broad range of treatments," Mark bored in, brushing aside the feel-good talk. "What do you see as the most likely scenario here?"

"That would be highly speculative, I'd hesitate to—"

"Because, frankly, we're feeling a little whipsawed here. Give us a worst-case scenario—just so we'll be prepared."

He smiled his best doctor's smile. "We do a number of procedures involving implantation of fertilized eggs. Perhaps GIFT—it's one of those intimidating acronyms standing for—"

"Gametic Intrafallopian Transfer," cut in Mark.

"Very *good*, Mr. Bowman, you've been doing your homework. Or ZIFT."

"Zygote Intrafallopian Transfer," noted Mark quickly.

". . . But there are other options also. We've enjoyed some success promoting superovulation by medication, producing as many as fifteen eggs per cycle. And in producing what we call 'kamikaze sperm' "—he smiled—"the name should be self-explanatory. And also with what's known as zona drilling, where we literally drill microscopic holes in eggs to facilitate penetration."

Mark nodded, satisfied—and overmatched.

"The first thing is to get you down to Dallas for tests. Can you block out ten days or so in the next couple of months?"

"How about early April?" Sally looked at her husband. "Easter vacation."

"Okay," he said softly.

"Good." Keller leaned forward, hands cupped on the table before him; and though Sally knew he'd spoken the words hundreds of times before, that made them no less reassuring. "If it's humanly possible, we will see to it that you conceive a healthy baby."

"Thank you," she said—and gave in, this once, to sentimentality. "We promise, if it's a boy, we'll name it Carl."

"Don't—I didn't even burden my own son." He laughed. "How about Paul, for Holland . . . ?"

Three hundred fifty miles away, in the town of Union, ten minutes down Route 11A from Edwardstown, Lisa stood outside Smart's, the only shoe store of any size in the area. The storm had slackened into intermittent flurries, but the temperature was brutal, just a few degrees above zero, and there was no street traffic in either direction. Peering into the well-lit store, she saw there were no customers.

Good.

The storm was a lucky break; she'd have come today anyway. Saturday was the manager's day off—and on an earlier visit she and Sally had found him uncooperative

In her pocket was the list they'd compiled over the last month, bearing seven names: kids with a history of antisocial behavior and a penchant for petty mischief. Each name had surfaced three or four times in a casual conversation struck up with one of their classmates.

Walking in, she smiled at the one employee—a teenage boy behind the counter.

"Hi," he said matter-of-factly. "Can I help you?"

"I sure hope so, after going out on a day like this. I need to get my cousin some sneakers for his birthday. . . ."

"Do you know his size?"

"I'm not sure. But I'm pretty sure he shops here." She shook off her coat and, tossing it on a chair, joined him at the counter. "His name's Brian Keane—he's fourteen."

A nice touch, she thought—the kid on the wrestling team, the first who'd named names.

As the clerk punched the name into his computer, Lisa wandered around the counter to join him. "Oh, that's fantastic!"

"Sorry, you're not allowed back here."

"Oh, c'mon . . ." She gave her most winning smile; already Brian's sales record had appeared. "I'm curious. . . ."

"I can't, it's not authorized."

Just her luck to hit on a by-the-book geek. "I just want to see, you know, the kind of thing he likes."

"I am very sorry, miss," he said, summoning up all the adolescent authority he could muster. "I can give you a printout!"

Sighing dramatically, she moved to the other side of the counter. In a moment the machine was churning out a page.

"Now, then," he said, handing it to her. "I can see he prefers Nikes. But that depends on how much you have to spend."

She scanned it indifferently. "Oh, that's not a problem. Let me see a selection in his size."

"A selection in size eight?" he asked uncertainly. "Well, we have all sorts of things."

"I want to get an idea of what's available," she said, conveying no sense of the malicious pleasure she was feeling. "How about—I don't know—let me see eight or nine pairs? A variety of makes and styles and colors . . ."

"It'll take a little time."

"No problem."

"Well," he said, indicating the displays as he headed toward the storage room, "I guess you should take a look around. Maybe you'll find something for yourself too."

In seconds she was behind the counter punching in the first name on her list. Robert Baldwin. Almost instantaneously, there he was. She smiled—*like candy from a teenage baby*. She looked first for the shoe size—nine and a half. Then searched the sales record, checking out recent purchases. No good: no mention of either Air Thrill or Run 'N Slam.

The next was one David Caine. She quickly noted the shoe size was right—nine and a half—and now her eye began moving down the screen. . . .

"Excuse me?!"

Startled, she looked up. The manager!

"What do you think you're doing?!"

She shrugged and smiled, hitting the button that cleared the screen. "I'm getting a pair of sneakers for my cousin, I was just looking at his record to see—"

"Wait a minute," he cut her off, thrusting a gloved finger her way like some misanthrope out of Dickens. "You're the one who was in here before, wanting to look at the records!"

She edged away from the counter and picked up her coat. "All right, let's forget it."

"I told you before, young lady, these records are private and confidential."

"I'm just trying to do my job."

"Your *job*?"

"I'm a reporter. For the *Edwardstown Weekly*. We've been trying to track down who was responsible for that grave robbing at Grace Church."

"I see," he replied, stone faced, and whipped off his gloves to reach for the phone. "Well, we'll just see about that!"

Sally's impulse was to be understanding. After all, it took balls—and at that age she might have done the same thing.

"Look, Lisa," she offered, "the main thing is you've learned your lesson."

"And what lesson is that?" she said, all innocence.

"Simple—you're a journalist, not a con artist. I mean, c'mon, it's not exactly a great idea to get caught rifling the files of a local store!"

Lisa nodded. "How about if you *don't* get caught?"

The observation stopped Sally short. "No, Lisa," she said, firmly now. "There are lines you don't cross. Ever."

"I always thought the *bottom* line was getting the story." She smiled. "I hear lots of big-time editors are ready to overlook almost anything if you do that."

Sally looked at her closely. Ambitious as she knew Lisa to be, never had the young woman revealed herself so fully. "I guess you don't see yourself staying here in Edwardstown very long, do you?"

"Would you if you were me? Sure, I'm trying to make a name for myself—what's wrong with that?"

"What kind of name, Lisa? That matters too." The phone rang on her desk. "What?" she said, snatching it up.

"Now, now, Lois Lane, I wouldn't be taking that tone with me."

Sally blanched. "We're kind of busy right now, Chief."

"I'd think your first task would be making some serious amends." He paused, the very essence of put-upon. "Do you know I had to convince that man personally not to press charges?"

"We appreciate that, Chief. Lisa knows she overdid it."

"Well, I also understand you've been sneaking around talking to all sorts of high school boys. I want this witch-hunt stopped! Now!"

The threat didn't have to be made any more explicit. Sally knew how this community would react to word of their investigation.

"Get it through your head—this is *police* business."

Sally managed to keep an even tone. "Look, Chief, we don't have to be adversaries here. We both know it was kids—I'd be glad to pass on what we've got."

On the other end there was a burst of laughter. "You really think I'm gonna make a suspect out of every goddamn kid in Clark County with a new pair of sneakers?"

Hanging up a moment later, Sally sighed. "Nice guy. Velvet touch."

"So . . . ?" asked Lisa. "What about the story? What do we do next?"

Sally stared at her a moment, incredulous. "Don't you have any idea what's going on? Stebben has us—we're going to let it slide."

Though it was a snap decision, Sally knew it was the right one.

"We don't have to do that, Sally," said the younger woman, shaking her head adamantly. "I can work around him. Let me stay on it."

Sally was startled by the vehemence. She'd seen that look in the eyes of reporters before—not ones she admired. "You want the best advice I can give you? Trust me, no story's worth even a tiny piece of your soul."

But even as she said it, she knew Lisa wasn't listening.

O
n the screen a bright yellow cartoon bird flitted happily from orange tree to orange tree, while in the background a chorus of dancing cows, horses, and pigs sang the product's catchy jingle.

Hap-hap-py morn to you. . . .
Sunny days and healthy too
Get your start the natural way
With laughter, fun, and Happy Day

"Remember," chirped the bird in conclusion, "just a glass a day of delicious Happy Day Farms OJ concentrate gives you one hundred and TEN percent of your daily requirement of vitamins C, D, and A!! Best of health to you and then some!!"

Food and Drug Administration Deputy Commissioner Kennally snapped off the videotape machine and the screen went black.

"How long have the bastards been running this thing, Porter?" he asked, turning to the FDA staff investigator sitting in his office, a thin, weary-looking young man in tortoiseshell glasses.

"About ten weeks. In markets all over the Southwest."

He shook his head. "Jesus, the *cajones* on these people! You'll get one hundred and ten percent of your daily requirement, all right—if you inject the stuff into your veins with a syringe? How can they think they'll get away with crap like this!?"

"They know we're understaffed, Commissioner," said Porter. "And that Congress isn't done cutting us yet."

"Well, if they think we're just gonna roll over . . ." His voice trailed off. "Their corporate headquarters are where?"

"Indianapolis."

"Interested in delivering the bad news personally?"

The commissioner was pleased to see the other break out in a smile—a rare sight in this office. "Simple message: They pull that ad immediately. Otherwise we're talking a major financial hit."

"That's it? The *threat* of a fine?"

"I have to deal with reality here, Porter. We don't need to get ourselves tied up in court. If they want to peddle orange *water,* that's their business. Ours is making sure they don't pass it off as nectar of the gods." He paused. "What's next on that list of yours?"

"That festering sore," said the younger man. "McIntyre and Reed."

"What about them?"

"Actually, good news for a change. Potentially *very* good. It looks like we might finally be able to squeeze them."

He leaned forward. "Tell me."

"Retinex—the company that makes the phony antiwrinkle stuff?—it's been their major source of revenue the past three years. It's what's kept them in business."

"But it's a Mexican company, we have no jurisdiction."

"That operation looks to be in serious trouble."

"The problems with the peso?"

Porter nodded. "And it gets better. Word is that some of their workers have come down with acute leukemia."

"Chemically induced?"

"Tough to prove conclusively, but public perception's another story. Wait'll we tip off the network news magazines. These guys've turned that whole section of Matamoros into a toxic waste dump. We have reason to hope they'll get nailed on criminal negligence and have to shut down the company." He smiled. "Translation: we've finally located a few honest regulators down there."

The deputy commissioner was skeptical. "What about their investments in the U.S.?"

He glanced down at his notes. "They're backing a start-up company in Cincinnati doing HIV work . . . and one in Houston looking to manufacture a more efficient artificial heart." He paused. "Then there's a new one we don't know much about—a place in New Hampshire that's supposed to be going after some kind of Alzheimer's preventative."

The commissioner snorted. "Welcome to the club—my family doctor's probably working up one of those in his garage."

"But you know their MO with these start-up types—promise them the world, but hold back serious money till they're sure the product's for real. The only exception has been Cytometrics, a midwestern company working on a drug to counter septic shock. M & R has sunk forty-five million in R & D into this sucker."

"Forty-five million!"

"And not pesos. They were encouraged by strong preliminary results."

"What's its status now?"

"They're winding up phase-three clinical trials at the University of Iowa. They should have final results in six months, by September or October at the latest."

His boss nodded. "Far be it from me to wish ill on any medical advance—but do we have any sense of what those results might be?"

"Officially? Of course not—that's privileged information." The investigator smiled. "But if I were you, I sure as hell wouldn't be advising my friends or family to put their life savings in Cytometrics."

Stepping into the Delta lounge at Dallas–Ft. Worth International Airport after their flight from Boston, Sally and Mark spotted the limo driver with the placard bearing their names, at the same instant.

They exchanged a look, and Mark approached the man. "Would that be *Sally* Benedict and *Mark* Bowman?"

"For the Keller Clinic?"

He nodded.

The driver reached for their overnight bags. "Would you like to go there directly, or should I take you to your hotel first?"

"We don't have one. We're thinking *motel*."

"I have you booked at the Royal."

It took a moment for this to sink in. "The clinic, please," said Sally. "Let's just take it from there."

The Keller Clinic for Reproductive Services was actually located in the wealthy northwestern suburb of Highland Park, in a three-story modernistic structure of black glass and steel.

Pulling up in the white stretch limo, sipping an orange juice from the small refrigerator they'd found along with a TV and VCR, Sally noted a similar vehicle waiting at curbside. "Infertility, the Great Leveler," she said with a wistful smile, eyeing a woman in a Chanel suit emerging from the other car. "That woman actually *envies* single moms on welfare."

"Please don't misunderstand," said Mark, half an hour later, "but we really can't accept all this."

"It's no big deal," said Dr. Keller, with a wave of his hand, "just a little something we sometimes do for special friends. We get a special rate on the hotel."

"Still, you're doing more than enough already."

He leaned forward, his smile somewhere between solicitous and condescending. "I respect that, Mr. Bowman, but I promised Paul Holland you would be provided with the very best—"

"Forget that," he cut him off. "This is none of Holland's business!" But he caught himself, knowing that in the impossibly awkward situation in which they'd placed themselves, that's exactly what it was. "Thanks, but we'll take care of our own accommodations."

"Mr. Bowman, I shouldn't have to tell you that this will be a long and arduous process. Your wife has more than enough to worry about. A little comfort at the end of the day can only help her chances."

Mark considered a long moment. "All right," he conceded. "We'll go to the hotel."

"Good. I think that's wise."

"Only, we'll pay for it ourselves."

"I see. Well, maybe you should discuss it first with—"

"I don't have to, Doctor. She feels the same way."

*   *   *

A floor below, Sally was already on an examining table.

"So," she asked the attractive young black woman conducting the examination, "do they give out medical degrees down here in *high school*?"

She smiled as she slipped on a pair of latex gloves. "I'm twenty-eight. I've been here at the clinic almost two years. I was blessed with good genes. You should see my mother." She paused. "All set?"

Sally slipped her bare feet into the stirrups. "So what drew you to this field—the opportunity to work with terminally desperate neurotics like me?"

She laughed. "Actually, the thought that you're doing some good."

Sally was always chatty during gynecological exams, as if willing one of life's more awkward processes into a routine social interaction. Yet today the pretense of normalcy was more strained than usual. After more than two months of anticipation this journey to the Keller Clinic had taken on the dimensions of a pilgrimage.

But a secret one. Aside from Malen no one in Edwardstown knew they were here, not even her mother; *especially* not her mother. Difficult as it was for Sally herself to accept the likelihood of failure, her mother's disappointment would be even harder to bear.

Instead, they'd put out the story that they were staying with her college roommate in Ft. Lauderdale; she'd call the office regularly during their ten-day stay to keep abreast of business and maintain the ruse; her ex-roommate would relay any messages that landed in Ft. Lauderdale.

"I guess I was also drawn by the excitement of discovery," added Dr. Carson, beginning to probe with the speculum. Still a junior staffer here, she'd been instructed this patient was due special handling—and that meant partly being very careful about what she said. "Dr. Keller is doing cutting-edge work. It's a privilege to train under him, an adventure."

"Right," answered Sally, staring up at the overhead light. An *adventure*.

This preliminary exam was the first of countless procedures she'd be undergoing here in the next ten days. This afternoon she'd be passed on to Keller himself, to begin the real work of high-tech baby-making.

"Well," said Sally, pretending a nonchalance she feared she'd never again feel, "if it happens, it happens. My mother would say it's God's will."

"Mine too." *Funny*, thought Carson, *there seems to be a slight bluish discoloration to the cervix. Could that be Chadwick's sign?—it was something she'd only read about in the texts.*

"But that's her way of protecting herself. This is a woman who was *born* to be a grandmother. . . ."

"Uh-huh." She began gently palpating the area with thumb and forefinger.

Sally caught her shift in tone. "Something wrong?"

"I'm sorry, just give me a moment." No question about it, there was a softening of the cervix and the uterus.

"What's going on?" she asked, her panic rising.

"It's nothing to worry about, it's just . . ."

The doctor was suddenly on her feet, reaching for the phone. "This is Dr. Carson in Examining Room B, I was wondering if I could get Dr. Keller down here?"

"Doctor, I'm a big girl."

"Really, don't be alarmed. I just think it's best to have Dr. Keller take a look."

"Please, *I have a right to know!*"

But when Dr. Carson turned to face her, Sally was surprised to see the look on her pretty face was one of wonderment. "We'll need a sonogram, and probably a blood test. But you seem to be pregnant."

Two days later Mark pushed open the front door of the Florida condo they'd taken for the week, loaded down with groceries.

The condo was an indulgence, two rooms plus kitchenette with a spectacular ocean view. Then, again, when would they ever have another chance?—and given what they'd have had to pay for the hotel in Dallas, it felt like a bargain.

"Hey," he called out, "I've got a surprise. I picked up some champagne in town." He waited a moment. "Don't worry, nonalcoholic. I'll have to use my *charm* to seduce you."

Only now was he aware she was on the kitchen phone.

From one of the shopping bags he pulled a container of raspberries—her favorite—and headed for the kitchen. "My charm AND raspberries."

"No," she was saying, "its just Mark back from the market. . . ."

She silently laughed when she saw the raspberries, and blew him a kiss. In a black one-piece bathing suit she'd never looked more achingly appealing. Could it be her breasts were already slightly larger? Already, to his delight, he'd learned they were more sensitive.

"Who are you talking to?" he asked softly.

She mouthed the words. *"My mother."*

Mark moved beside her. She shifted the phone to the other ear so he could nuzzle her cheek, then elbowed him away. "Not now," she whispered. "Jeez!"

He took a seat on a stool by the counter to eavesdrop.

"Oh, by the way, Mother, are you sitting down?"

She caught her husband's eye.

"I didn't mean it literally, Mother," she continued evenly, "it just means I've got big news." She paused, no longer able to contain herself. "I'm going to have a baby!"

There was a moment of silence. Then, from the other end of the line, came a sound neither of them had ever imagined they'd hear from her mother: a shriek of pure joy.

"I know, Mother," she exclaimed, "that's how we feel! I'm due the first week in December."

Mark got to his feet. "Let me talk to her. . . ."

Sally waved him away.

"Tell her I love her."

"Mark says he loves you."

Listening, she rolled her eyes. "I know that, Mother, I know how lucky I am. . . ."

"Damn right," laughed Mark. "Let me talk to her."

But Sally held tight to the phone and turned into the corner. "You know what I've been thinking about a lot since I found out?" she said, her tone suddenly intimate. "The way you were with me when I was little. Just now I was looking through some old pictures, and there was one of you and me and Benjy."

She laughed. "Right, my stuffed lamb. But the thing was, I must've been six or seven in the picture. And I was thinking how you never tried to tell me I was too old to be carrying around a stuffed animal. Or pointed out how ratty he was. You can see that even in the picture."

Mark was more than a little surprised; this sort of thing was completely out of character. More often than not Sally spoke of—and to—her mother with bemusement or gentle annoyance.

"You *do*?!" Sally was saying. "You still *have* Benjy?!" She looked at her husband, eyes glistening. "Of *course* I would, we'll keep him in the baby's room!"

Mark suddenly felt like an intruder. "I'm beat," he said. "I'm gonna go, you know, lie down."

But she seemed not even to hear, and he quietly walked from the room.

Touching as the scene was, to the ever-practical Mark there was also something about it vaguely disconcerting. He'd heard that the hormone rush of pregnancy could turn even women who were normally highly disciplined and composed into quivering masses of emotion for months on end. Only now, for the first time, was he struck by the thought: could Sally be a candidate?

This time even less was left to chance.

The heavy cloud cover left the night virtually black, and in early April the ground was ideal for the purpose—yielding, after weeks of intermittent drizzle following a month of melting snow, but not yet muddy. They'd brought along two tarpaulins; one pitched like a tent to eliminate any possibility the flashlight beams might be detected, the other covering the ground alongside the grave so there would be no prints. The pickax was the same one they'd used before, but they also now had a shovel of solid wood to avoid the clink of steel striking stone.

Given the magnitude of the task, speed was all. Over the past weeks they'd practiced feverishly, as if for an athletic competition, timing themselves, reducing the elapsed time from start to finish to under an hour, and it showed. They worked with startling efficiency, alternating implements every few minutes; the ax slicing easily into the soft ground, chewing it up; the shovel casting off the loose dirt with the rhythm of seconds ticking off a clock. Though there was a chill in the air, neither felt it, just the clamminess of sweat-soaked clothes on skin.

Less than a foot down the damp earth began giving off the pungent odor of rotting vegetation. By the time they hit wood, at four feet, it was so all encompassing, they literally could taste it.

The casket was walnut and of superior quality; even as the dirt was brushed aside, it held its sheen in the artificial light. Clearing several inches beyond either end and a foot at the front, they found it lifted open with ease.

They had no interest in examining the remains, merely in removing them. In less than a minute they'd maneuvered a sheet beneath them and over, and were gingerly lifting them to the surface.

Only when this task was completed, surveying the scene, did they allow themselves a moment of satisfaction.

Neither liked the term *grave robbers*. The romantic image they carried of themselves was conveyed far better by the one they'd run across in an old book: *resurrection men*.

But the respite was brief. It was only a couple of hours till dawn and there remained more to do.

"**O**h, it's such wonderful news!" exclaimed Florence Davis, as Sally walked through the door her first morning back.

Though she smiled with genuine pleasure, she could not wholly shake her old, cynical self; in her flower print dress and matching hat, hands clasped to her breast, Florence bore an unmistakable resemblance to Aunt Bee on the old *Andy Griffith Show*.

"Thanks," said Sally, taking off her coat. "It makes us pretty happy too."

"Now if you ever need a sitter, you'll know who to call?"

"Her mother," chimed in Mrs. Benedict. "You'll have to wait on line, Florence."

"Don't you both think it's kind've early for that sort of talk?"

"Oh, no! You have to start planning now, every detail!" Florence threw up her hands in dismay. "The time will *fly* by. You must start thinking about things you've never thought about before in your life, asking all sorts of *new* questions: Who's the best pediatrician? Who might have some quality hand-me-downs? Heavens, even how to use a breast pump."

Sally could only nod mutely. Why, she couldn't help wonder, had this woman never gotten nearly so excited over anything that had to do with journalism?

"Actually"—Sally smiled at Florence—"Mother's planning a trip to the hospital herself."

"That's not final, darling," cautioned Mrs. Benedict. "You just raised it last night."

"Uh-uh, you *promised*!" Then, to the others: "She's finally having that gallbladder thing taken care of."

"Sally insists there's nothing more boring to a small child than a sick old grandma. I still say I can put up with a little pain."

"You hoping for a boy or girl?" called out Ed Keeton, the retired insurance salesman who served, part-time, as the *Weekly*'s business manager.

"Oh, really, Mr. Keeton," her mother answered for her, "every child's a miracle."

"The important thing is that it's healthy," added Florence, with a depth of sincerity that suggested the words had never been spoken before.

Mrs. Benedict nodded. "That we have to leave in God's hands."

"Lee Malen'll probably be insulted," chuckled Keeton. "He likes to work alone."

Sally held up her hands. "Look, this is great, but we've got a paper to put out here. Unfortunately, this doesn't qualify as news."

"Yes, it does," said Florence adamantly. "It's the best kind of news."

"Fine, Florence, but it's not *news* news."

"Why couldn't it go in the paper, darling?" asked Mrs. Benedict. "Everyone who knows you will be delighted."

"Startled, you mean. 'Sally Benedict Does Motherhood'—it almost qualifies as one of those 'Man Bites Dog' stories."

"You could put it in one of those little boxes on the front page," suggested her mother.

"I was kidding, Mother. Nobody—not even the *Weekly*—runs a *pregnancy* announcement." This time she clapped her hands for emphasis. "All right, everybody, let's get to work!"

Only Lisa, working away at her computer, had remained aloof from the conversation. Now Sally wandered over to her desk. "No congrats from you, Ace Reporter?"

"Sure. I just can't get into all this goo-goo stuff."

"I hear you—I was the same way." She smiled. "Still am. Mark and I have promised ourselves we won't turn into the sort of parents who run around boring people about our kid."

Lisa nodded. "I guess I just don't see it as some kind of big accomplishment."

"Let's give them a break, they're a different generation. . . ." She paused. "How about stepping into my office?"

"So," she asked a moment later, settling in behind her desk, "how's 'Kids in Crisis' coming?"

The story, on the dramatic rise in the number of abused and neglected kids in what had only recently been a region of stable homes and families, was an ambitious one. Begun as a result of their reporting on the grave-robbing case, it was a real shot, thought Sally, for Lisa to strut her stuff.

"It's coming," said Lisa coolly.

"I want to make it a two-parter—how does that sound? Part one, the stuff you're getting from cops and teachers on the impact these kids are having on their communities. Vandalism, shoplifting, break-downs in school discipline, all the rest. Part two—causes and possible remedies. That's where you'll get into latch-key kids, single-parent families, and the mumbo-jumbo from psychologists and social workers. Think you can have the first part ready next week?"

She hesitated. "I'm not sure."

"Lisa, I gave you this assignment six weeks ago."

"I've still got a lot of reporting to do."

"Then do it! I want to see an outline for part one by Friday."

She shrugged—"Whatever, you're the boss"—and turned to walk from the room.

"Lisa," said the editor sharply, "I don't want to have to say this again—get over it. Pulling the plug on the grave-robbing story was the right call. This story may not be as flashy, but ultimately it's more important. It could make a real difference."

"To who?" she asked evenly.

"To this community!" Sally paused, realizing. "But maybe that's not your concern. Maybe you're more interested in impressing editors out there in Chicago and New York."

Lisa hesitated. "Nothing wrong with that. You know I don't plan to stay in Edwardstown forever."

"As long as you're working here, you will give the *Weekly* one hundred percent!"

Through the open door she could see that both Florence and Mrs. Benedict had turned their way. Only Mr. Keeton, slightly deaf, was unaware of the conflict.

In the room outside, the phone began jangling.

"I've heard you say yourself that a good reporter makes waves—that's part of the job."

"Christ," said Sally sternly, "if that's *all* I've taught you, I'm not doing *my* job!"

But before matters could escalate further, Florence appeared at the door. "Excuse me, Sally, I think you'd better take this."

"Get a number," she said. "I'll call back."

"He says it's urgent."

Shooting Lisa a look, she snatched up the phone. "Sally Benedict."

She listened a moment.

"Oh, my God!"

Hanging up, she looked at the younger woman, momentarily speechless.

"What's going on?"

"That was Father Morse. There's been another grave robbing!"

This time two graves had been violated—and there was no question about the identity of either of the missing bodies.

One of the grave sites, out of view in the back, was marked not by a headstone but by an eight-foot odalisque in black marble.

CARLTON L. GILES
APRIL 4, 1911–JULY 12, 1944
WITH THE LOVE OF HIS FAMILY
AND
THE GRATITUDE OF HIS COUNTRY

The other was off to the left, between the church and the rectory. When Sally came to the simple white stone lying faceup next to the desecrated grave, she let out an involuntary gasp.

MARTHA WHITSON AVERY, 1834–1936

"I know," agreed Lisa beside her, staring down at the coffin lying open at the bottom of the hole. "Pretty gruesome."

But Sally just continued to stare.

Lisa noticed. "Is something wrong?"

"It's Gram's grandmother," she said softly.

"You're kidding me!"

Sally shook her head. "My great-great-grandmother. I've heard stories about her all my life."

"Hey, real sorry about that," spoke up Chief Stebben, standing on the other side of the hole with another officer. "My condolences. Or whatever."

Sally looked up at him, stung.

"Well, you didn't *know* the woman, did you?"

"The first question, Chief, is why *you* didn't call us."

"Maybe I learned my lesson the last time." He shot Sally a mirthless smile. "You ladies notice how nice and soft the ground is? The first one must've been so easy, they decided to just keep on going. There, you got your quote."

"Question two. When do you expect to make an arrest? Or is that the lesson I should learn from last time—never?"

"We're pretty busy just now, ladies, so if you'll kindly excuse us . . ."

"Chief Stebben," spoke up Lisa deferentially, "are you at least able to tell us when you first heard about this?"

"Oh, maybe five A.M. Simmons here called me from the night desk." Though he nodded at the younger woman, the comment was aimed at Sally. "Honey always beats vinegar with this old fly. . . ."

"You're saying you knew *for over five hours* and didn't let us know?!" demanded Sally.

Stebben flashed the same smile. "Ooops. Sorry."

Sally turned to the other officer. "How did you learn about it?"

"He got a phone call," answered Stebben.

"Who from?"

"We don't know, it was anonymous."

Sally glared at the chief. "Forgotten how to speak for yourself, Officer Simmons?"

Simmons looked imploringly at Stebben, who nodded his approval. "The guy didn't say who he was. He just sorta laughed and said I better get my ass down to the cemetery."

"He laughed?"

"Like it was a big joke or something."

"I've been dealing with pranksters since you were just a little girl," cut in Stebben. "That's always the attitude."

"How old would you say he sounded?"

"Pretty young."

"How young? Teens? Twenties?"

He shrugged. "Coulda been either."

Stebben held up his hand. "Enough!"

"Let's get down to cases," said Sally, ignoring him. "Do you have any witnesses? Anything solid at all?"

"I said that's *all*, ladies. This little press conference is *over*."

"What are you afraid of, Chief? That you'll start looking so incompetent, people won't buy your act anymore?"

He stared at her, the color rising in his cheeks, and jerked his thumb toward the front gate. *"Now."*

Forbidding as he was, momentarily she held her ground. "This isn't just professional, Stebben. I've got a family interest here."

He cast her a withering glance. "You're even sicker than I realized, Benedict. You'll say *anything!*"

"That was bad," said Sally softly, half an hour later at the Clover Patch. "This time I went *way* too far."

Not at all displeased to find herself cast in the unfamiliar role of confessor, Lisa tried to make it sound sympathetic. "It was like you were talking to *me*."

"What was I thinking? For Chrissakes, that's one of the things I've been trying to drum into you for a year: you can't lose your cool." Sally lifted her glass of orange juice but didn't drink.

"You were pretty shaken up. If it was me, looking into the grave of my relative . . ."

"I have to break the news to my mother and Gram. That won't be easy."

"No, I guess not. . . ." Lisa sipped. "Well, I gotta get back—I know you want me hard at work on 'Kids in Crisis.' "

"Think you can be a little less subtle, Lisa?" She smiled. "We're back on this case big time—and just let Stebben dare to try and scare us off it! I'll want to go over that list of names, it's a good beginning."

"A *beginning*?"

"Maybe more. But, I don't know . . . there's just something about the way Stebben refuses to go after this . . ."

She stopped. "I know what every smart cop I've ever met would be asking about now—and smart reporters too: 'What the hell is going on here? Who would be interested in doing this? What could they be looking for?' "

"**W**onderful!" exclaimed Foster, surveying the corpse laid out on the autopsy table before him, illuminated by a fluorescent operating-room lamp. "Now, here's something we can work with!"

"It was the lead-lined coffin," observed Lynch blandly. "It kept out all the moisture."

"Look at her, fresh as a daisy. She might have died yesterday!"

This was a considerable exaggeration, of course. The corpse's face was skeletal, the old woman's cheeks and eye sockets sunken beneath bone-level, the skin chalky white. The effect was otherworldly; she was something between the human being she had been and the featureless skull she would soon become.

Still, the evidence of her life, even her personality, was unmistakable. Her silk dress, navy blue with delicate pearl buttons up the front, was of an age even earlier than the one she'd departed; as was the style of her white hair, in a turn-of-the-century knot. On one bony finger she wore a plain gold band and beneath her throat a delicate, inlaid pearl cameo brooch.

"This will answer most of the questions," observed Foster. "Every organ should be intact."

Lynch nodded. "Let's hope it's enough to satisfy them."

In fact, in the ten weeks since the meeting with McIntyre and Reed in New York, though terms of a proposed deal had been accepted by both sides, the scientists had yet to see even the fifty thousand dollars promised as a good-faith gesture. The hitch seemed to be M & R's chief scientific advisor, Dr. Eric Cooper, who evidently had persuaded his bosses to withhold final approval until the scientists produced clear evidence that the protein in which they placed such hope expressed itself in every part of a subject's body.

"After all," as Reed repeated to them the advisor's admonition, set forth in terms lay people could readily grasp, "the chain is only as strong as its weakest link."

To such an argument the frustrated scientists had no definitive answer—at least not yet. Cooper's observation was as technically accurate as it was shortsighted. True enough, if the gene failed to generate the antiaging protein in even one of the vital organs, the therapy would be ineffective. What would be the use of the liver and spleen remaining robust for two hundred years if the heart gave out after seventy-five?

The scientists knew that such an eventuality was highly unlikely. Cooper was looking at it backward—he was summoning up a worst-case scenario and challenging them to disprove it.

Still, infuriatingly, his seemed to be the paramount influence.

That's why they'd needed this body on such short notice. In just a couple of weeks Cooper would be coming to Manchester to evaluate their operation firsthand.

Now, standing over the cadaver, the scientists hesitated a moment; then Foster unclasped the brooch and set it aside.

"Careful," he said softly, to himself, "let's not do any unnecessary harm."

It was only after he'd unfastened the first three buttons that it became apparent something might be wrong. There was an ugly gash in the upper chest—and it appeared to have been haphazardly closed by heavy black thread.

"Oh, God!" said Foster, and elbowing his colleague aside, he hastily undid the last four buttons. "No!!!"

When he spread open the delicate material, all doubt was gone. She'd been slit open not only across the upper chest cavity, but downward from the xiphoid process—the flap of cartilage beneath the sternum from which the abdominal muscles are suspended—all the way to the pubis.

"Damn you! You goddamn do-gooder!!" Foster slammed down his hand on the edge of the autopsy table "She willed her body to science!" For, indeed, the crudeness of the job marked it almost beyond question as a medical-school class dissection. "There's nothing useful *left* in there!"

"There's muscle," observed Lynch. "And tendons."

That was true, it might not be a total loss. It was possible the muscles and tendons would provide a partial sequence of the mutated gene, enabling them to confirm key aspects of the research conducted on mice.

"And there's the other specimen."

Foster nodded. The decision to take a second body had been initially designed merely to ensure the appearance of randomness should this latest episode prompt closer scrutiny than the first; they'd come to the idea of locating one that might itself have some research value almost as an afterthought.

But Lynch didn't have to say the obvious: it wouldn't have what they needed. Indeed, they'd been drawn to this subject not by any illusion that it would present the gene but in hopes of finding evidence that it was absent for other than the usual reasons.

Staring down at the open, decaying cavity, Foster could almost see Cooper smugly posing the question: *What good does it do you if your muscles age slowly while your heart and lungs continue to age at a normal rate?*

There was an unaccustomed edge of desperation in his voice as he handed his colleague a scalpel. "Let's make the best of it. Might as well have a look."

Stebben didn't seem surprised in the least when Lisa appeared in his office that afternoon—just that she'd changed from the work shirt and jeans she was wearing earlier to a blouse, short skirt, and more makeup than usual.

"All right," he observed coolly. "You've got my attention. Now what?"

She retreated behind a coy smile. "It's common courtesy. This is an office, not a graveyard."

"I didn't notice much concern with courtesy before."

"C'mon, Chief, don't lump me in with her, I've got my own problems there. May I at least sit down?"

Wordlessly, he motioned her into the metal folding chair by his desk.

"I've got a confession. . . ." She hesitated. "She's the one who suggested I dress this way. She thought it might make you more talkative."

"Well, I'll be damned!"

"You know, you really get under her skin like no one else around here."

He couldn't help smiling. "Missy, I'm not sure you're as buffaloed by her as you let on."

"I try. Tell me, Chief, have you notified the other family yet?"

"The Gileses?" He shook his head.

She paused, then plunged ahead. "Who are they? It seemed from the inscription on the grave he was some kind of war hero."

"Killed at Normandy," he replied evenly. "The family left town maybe thirty years ago. I remember 'em from when I was a kid. The father was some bigwig lawyer."

"Have any idea where they are now?"

"I got Simmons working on it"—he smiled—"so we should know in six or eight years." Lacing his hands behind his head, he leaned back in his chair. "Not that probably we should even bother. It's just buying trouble—none of them's been back here in years."

"It's not gonna get you any closer to finding out who did it, right?"

He returned her smile, completely at ease now.

"So I guess you've got nothing to go on? No witnesses . . . ?"

"At four-thirty in the morning? Use that pretty head. Most everyone in this town's been dead to the world six hours by then." He paused. "See that—look how you get me to talk. Why don't we just leave it at that?"

"Can't I just—"

He wagged a finger her way. "See, your boss's problems, she badgers people. When you're dealing with me, it's the fastest way to get nothing."

"Sorry." She looked suitably contrite. "I don't want to spoil this nice thing we've got going."

"You think we've got a nice thing going?"

"Don't you?"

"Ah, shit, I'm too old to flirt." He laughed. "Better get the hell out of here before I do something that lands *me* in trouble."

* * *

Lisa changed back to the clothes she'd been wearing earlier before returning to the office.

"Where've you been?" asked Sally, glancing up from the news clipping she'd been reading.

"Out and about." She flashed the kind of grin Sally associated with the kids who used to cut English class to catch a smoke. "I've come up with some information on the other family—the Gileses. Apparently they were pretty big stuff around here."

"Right, the father was a prominent lawyer." Noting Lisa's consternation, she glanced at Florence and old Mr. Keeton in the next room. "Journalism's not rocket science. I asked."

"So," she recovered quickly, "I guess the question becomes how to track them down."

Sally looked through some papers on her desk and located one that she handed to her colleague. It bore a name and two phone numbers.

"Wilson Giles . . ." read Lisa, then, looking up at Sally, asked, "Who's this, his son?"

She nodded and held the clipping aloft. "The guy's obit—the names of survivors included—is right in our files. After that all it took was two phone calls. To the Veterans Administration and Pittsburgh information."

Lisa thought of Stebben's man Simmons and his apparently fruitless efforts to locate the family. "You got home *and* office numbers?"

"The grandfather was a lawyer—something like that sometimes runs in the family. This time it checked out." She picked up the receiver. "Would you like to do the honors?"

Lisa shook her head and handed back the slip of paper. "Show me how it's done."

In thirty seconds Sally had Wilson Giles's secretary on the line. "Yes, I understand he's busy," she was saying. "but I think he'll want this brought to his attention. Tell him I'm calling from Edwardstown, New Hampshire. Tell him it's about his father."

A couple of minutes later she hung up the phone. "He was pretty upset—who wouldn't be?"

"And?"

"He'll be here in a few days—he has to clear his schedule." She smiled faintly. "He wants to know what the police are doing about it."

"**W**hat is it with you, Holland," asked Sally, mock-conspiratorially, leaning across the table in the Clover Patch. "Keeping tabs on me?"

This time he'd shown up in town on only a day's notice. Just down the way in Boston, he explained.

Sally was surprised the lighthearted remark seemed to leave him momentarily stricken. "No, no. I just wanted to tell you in person how happy I am for you."

Sally could only nod and answer in kind: "Well, believe me, I'm plenty grateful to you. Mark too." She'd never get used to this impossibly sincere version of the man she once knew.

"No, it turns out it was nothing at all."

She smiled blandly. "What can I say? We got real lucky."

How long, she wondered, would she have to spend with him this time?

"But I also came for another reason. I've got news that I think may please you almost as much." He took a sip of beer, letting the drama build before delivering it. "I've lined up something for you at the *Herald*!"

"The *Herald*? What are you talking about?"

"I told Dennis Boyles you were the sharpest underemployed reporter out there. And that he should grab you!"

"Listen, Dick—"

"Not that it was a tough sell, he remembered your stuff." He blossomed in a smile. "I guarantee you two'll get along. You'll start on the metro desk, doing features."

"Whoa, Holland, don't jump to conclusions here."

"You *belong* in the big leagues, Sally." From his jacket pocket he pulled out a copy of the *Weekly* with its report on the latest grave robbings. "It's painful seeing you wasting talent on stuff like this. In New York you'll have something more exciting to chase after every day—and the resources to get to the bottom of it."

"Look, this is real flattering. A few weeks ago I might have jumped at it. . . ."

He looked at her closely.

"What's the problem? I thought this is what you were looking for."

"I was looking for *freelance* work. And now I don't even want that." She paused, amazed it even had to be said. "I'm having a *baby,* Dick! My life is here. My mother and grandmother. Mark's job. Even my doctor."

"I've taken care of that. I already have you set up with one of the top obstetricians in town! Rich Sauerhaft—he's a friend of mine."

"I'm happy with my doctor here—he's a friend of *mine.*"

"Look," he pressed, "what kind of money are you making?"

"That's not the issue," she said, taken aback by his mounting sense of urgency.

"Boyles'll start you at ninety-five."

"Sally!"

She looked up, startled. There stood, of all people, Lee Malen, an attractive young woman at his side.

"Lee!" She knew she was blushing, as if caught in something illicit. "This is an old friend. Paul Holland."

Now it was Malen who was caught short. "Lee Malen," he said, extending a hand. "I practice medicine here in town. This is Jennifer Downs, a colleague of mine."

Sally had never seen the young woman before. Possibly she was a nurse trainee at the hospital—Malen had dated a number of those.

"So," asked Malen, "what brings you to our little burg?"

Agitated as he was, Holland reflexively responded to the admiring tone with a smile. "Just happened to be in the area."

"Well, anything you want to know about the lay of the land, medically or otherwise, I'm the guy. Right, Sal?"

"That's right, Lee."

He took Jennifer's arm and began moving away. "See you around, Sal."

Sally watched as they took a table in the corner. "Well, speak of the devil."

"You mean," he said with sudden understanding, "*he's* the one who'll be delivering your baby?"

"Right down the street at Edwardstown Community Hospital. Believe it or not, they've got all the high-tech stuff up here you've got in New York. Plus something else. Lee's practice—he and his two predecessors—has been serving this community continuously for more than a hundred years. That matters, at least to me."

"That *is* interesting." She watched as he looked over at Malen a long moment, thoughtful, before turning back her way. "So tell me"—he got right back to it—"what's the real problem—your husband doesn't want to move to the big city?"

"Nooo. . . ."

He smiled coolly. "Tell him we have high schools in New York too."

The sneering remark was so unexpected, it took her an instant to react. Here, out of the blue, was the old Holland—poisonous, wearing his contempt for others like a badge.

"You don't even have the faintest idea how you sound, do you?" she said, in a quiet rage.

"Or maybe you're worried about *me*? Don't be—nothing's going to happen between us."

"You're right about that!"

The waitress placed the check before Sally, but Holland grabbed it. "I'm on an expense account, remember those?"

Whipping open his wallet, he displayed a blinding array of credit cards in platinum and gold; Mark carried only one, in green, but preferred using cash.

"Look," he tried again, "I'm just asking you to think it over. I'm sure you'll come to your senses."

"That's what I'm telling you, Holland—I *have*!"

Abruptly, startlingly, he gave a hollow laugh.

"You think that's funny?"

"I think it's the greatest negotiating ploy I ever heard in my life! We both know you're going to take that job."

As she stood up, she snatched the check from his grasp. "Don't worry about it, Holland, you've paid back whatever debt you thought you owed me and then some." She turned away. "So good-bye."

An hour and a half later Holland walked into Lee Malen's waiting room and asked to see the doctor.

"He's with a patient," said Barbara Walker, eyeing him curiously. There were no husbands of patients due for a consultation; and, in any case, she knew almost everyone in the area. "Would you like to wait?"

He hesitated, then shook his head. Withdrawing a business card from his wallet, he jotted down a phone number. "Just make sure he gets this."

The sight of a stretch limo on Main Street this glorious, late-spring afternoon made people literally stop in their tracks.

Moving slowly past the Independence Pharmacy and Seggerman's Hardware & Farm Exchange, the black Lincoln drew to a stop outside the brick two-story building at 16 Main. Watching from the window of the *Weekly* office on the ground floor, Sally was struck by the sense of command of the man who emerged from the car. Square jawed and trim in a tailored pinstriped suit, he was a gracefully aging Marine poster boy; in his sixties showing no suggestion of tentativeness, let alone frailty.

She opened the door before he reached it. "Mr. Giles, I'm Sally Benedict."

He nodded briskly.

"This is Lisa Mitchell, who's also been working on the story for us."

"I'd appreciate any details you have."

Leading the way into her office, she closed the door behind them.

"You were born in Edwardstown, Mr. Giles?"

"I was."

"Have you been back here much?"

"I don't mean to be rude, Ms. Benedict. But I've come a long way—what I would like is an update."

"Of course." She motioned him to the folding chair beside her desk and nodded at her associate. "You're on, Lisa. The man wants an update."

Lisa took a deep breath. "The police are working on the premise that it was kids on a lark."

"Why?"

"They claim they have some sneaker prints."

"There was a similar incident a while back," noted Sally.

"*Similar?* I'm told *exactly* the same thing happened recently in the same cemetery and *nothing* came of it." His hard look moved from one to the other. "What the hell goes on around here?"

"This is a small town, Mr. Giles. Things don't always work as efficiently as they probably do in your law firm."

"They proceed as efficiently as those in power want them to— and I assume in a town like this, that includes the editor of the newspaper. I want you to know I intend to see to it these ghouls are found and prosecuted to the full extent of the law! It should be a simple enough matter—unless you people make it complicated."

"That's not fair," shot back Lisa. "We're as personally affected by this as you are."

"I doubt that."

"The other grave was her grandmother's."

Giles turned to Sally in surprise.

"Thanks, Lisa," she said, "but I've dealt with bullies before. No need to exaggerate—my great-great-grandmother."

"Oh." Giles looked genuinely contrite. "I didn't know that. You'll understand I've been quite upset since I heard."

Sally nodded. "We're at least as aware as you are of how badly it reflects on our town. Just so you know, the *Weekly*'s been trying to get the police to move on this from the beginning."

"All right," he said crisply. "What about these high school kids? Are they doing everything now that can be done?"

"That isn't their style. We feel they could still use some encouragement."

Giles fell silent a moment, gazing out the window at Main Street. "Yes, as a matter of fact, I've been back to Edwardstown a number of times. Seven or eight."

"You still have family in the area?"

He nodded toward the churchyard. "Only my father." He paused, uneasy at the lapse into sentimentality. "I've paid a lot of money over the years to make sure his resting place is properly maintained."

"Did you know him?" asked Lisa.

"I was nine when he died. But we have lots of photographs and letters. One retains a very strong sense of him." He paused. "I'd like to visit the cemetery now to see the damage for myself."

Don't give me that, Mark, you talk about your students all the time—sometimes I can't get you to shut up."

"Stop it, Sally! I have an obligation to those kids."

"Not to talk with your wife? It's an innocent enough question—what kind of kids are they?"

"You come to me with a list of names and call it innocent?" Shaking his head, he reached into the KFC box for another piece of chicken.

"I'm asking off the record."

"*Off the record*—so now I'm a *source*? Eat your dinner, Sally."

"Some dinner." She cast a disdainful glance at the mashed potatoes, green peas, and lightly cooked carrots on her plate. "That chicken as good as it looks?"

"It'll taste even better if we can get through one meal without talking about the damn grave robbing!"

"It's my job, Mark," she shot back, then paused, smiling. "The chicken was a bribe."

Despite himself he smiled back. "Would you really want to be married to a guy who ratted on kids for a box of fried chicken?"

"Look, next week's issue of the paper locks tomorrow at noon.

Which means"—she glanced at her watch—I've got something less than sixteen hours to decide what to do with the information we've got on those kids."

"What information? You have a list."

"A short one." She pulled it from her pocket and tossed it onto the table—facing Mark. "It's a small town, with a very limited vandal population."

"I thought you were the one refusing to leap to that conclusion."

"Circumstances change. That's a luxury I can't afford now—not with Giles in the picture."

He looked at her meaningfully. "Fairness is a luxury?"

"The story doesn't have to be airtight; a newspaper's not a courtroom. It's certainly fair to report the police have *certain unspecified* evidence leading them to suspect *certain unnamed* minors."

He slammed down the chicken piece and got to his feet. "I never expected to hear you talk this way."

"Like someone with a tough decision on her hands? Sorry, that's how an editor-in-chief has to be."

"Like a bully. You're talking about fifteen- and sixteen-year-olds. You shouldn't even *consider* spreading this kind of maliciousness."

There was a long silence.

"Sit down, Mark," she said finally, her tone conciliatory.

Warily, he did so.

"I don't want to hurt them," she said, leaning across the table, "that's not what this is about. But Giles is out of patience. He's talking about a reward to help things along."

"A reward?"

"Twenty thousand for information leading to capture and conviction."

"Christ Almighty!" Mark just shook his head. In a town where so many were hurting, such a thing could provoke an avalanche of unsubstantiated accusations.

He took a deep breath and let his eye wander to the list. "A couple of them I don't even know."

"That's all right."

"Robert Butler . . ." he said, referring to the first name on the list. "See, that's just what I'm talking about. The kid spray-paints a few walls, so what?"

She poked at her food, averting her eyes. "I hear you."

"And this kid—Garry Apgar—I mean, c'mon. The worst I ever heard of him doing was taping a bar code to a piece of cardboard to trick the returnable can machine at the A & P in Union into giving him a few bucks' worth of nickels."

"It's petty larceny, Mark."

"It's also a helluva jump from there to swiping bodies."

There was a long silence.

"How about these?" She pointed at the next pair of names, which Lisa had circled and starred: Pete Boyd and Terry Sutter.

Mark hesitated.

"I understand there's a lot more history there. Breaking and entering. Joyriding in a car that happened to belong to someone else. Lisa had an interesting conversation with one of the county youth counselors about these two."

"Look, I've gotten to know Terry pretty well. He's got tremendous potential. Just this semester his grades have started to pick up. . . ."

"You're telling me with absolute certainty that they're not capable of something like this?"

"All I'm saying"—he dodged the question, shaking his head—"is don't put them in a box. How'd you like it if someone did that to *our* kid?"

This gave her serious pause. "You're a good guy, Mark, you know that?"

"Yeah, right."

"Learn to take a compliment." She stopped. "We'll hold the story for a week. After that I can't make any promises."

Dr. Eric Cooper deeply resented the assumption, so common even in academic circles, that he owed his success to affirmative action. That was one reason why Cooper, an associate professor of biochemistry at Rockefeller University, liked working for McIntyre and Reed—they cared only that he was good, seeming to not even notice he was black.

The other reason was money. Pulling down $93,000 a year at his job, with a mortgage and two kids in private school, Cooper had come to look at the $50,000-plus per year the venture capitalists paid him as found money; and the trips he took around the country evaluating biomedical start-up operations as minivacations.

On the face of it this latest assignment from Reed had seemed routine: spend a couple of days up in New Hampshire assessing the work at the Life Services Institute. In five years none of a dozen similar journeys had come to anything.

That was why, waiting in the entryway of the venture capitalists' Fifth Avenue apartment to report on his trip, Cooper was so uncharacteristically agitated. Though he'd rushed here directly from the airport, he still hadn't decided how to present what he'd seen.

How far should he stick his neck out? The greatest sin in this racket, maybe the *only* one, was being wrong. M & R could come up with a dozen equally credentialed academics to take his place in an hour.

"Will you follow me, please?"

Cooper felt more than a little embarrassed being ushered into his boss's presence by a black maid in uniform; a reminder, if he needed one, that their color blindness merely qualified these people as equal opportunity assholes.

"Professor Cooper," announced the maid, and withdrew.

McIntyre and Reed were sitting at opposite ends of a dining-room table, sipping soup from large bowls. Both appeared engrossed in the financial reports they were reading.

Cooper shifted uncomfortably, glancing at his surroundings. The room was done in Deco. He was surprised to note photographs of children on a gleaming black-and-silver side table, an unexpectedly warm touch—until he realized the photos were of *them.*

"Well, Cooper," said McIntyre, looking up suddenly, "we weren't expecting to see you till tomorrow morning."

"I thought it would be a good idea to talk tonight."

"We're listening. . . ."

"This was far more than just the usual dog-and-pony show. I was quite impressed."

"Good," nodded Reed, "right to the chase. What we need to know is if this Alzheimer's treatment of theirs will really be markedly more effective than the others now in development."

Knowing them, Cooper wasn't surprised he hadn't been invited to sit down. "It's hard to say that with complete certainty," he began, equivocating by habit.

"Then what *are* you saying?"

He paused, began again, wanting to get this exactly right. "You're familiar with the work identifying the E-four gene as a primary risk factor for Alzheimer's?"

Reed nodded impatiently. Who in their business didn't know about research that stood to be worth tens of millions of dollars?

"I believe that what Lynch and Foster are up to could carry it several steps farther."

McIntyre set aside his financial report and leaned forward. "Oh?"

"This research potentially has *far* broader applications! Their therapy appears to actually impede immune-system decline." He looked from one to the other. "In fact, effectively, *biologically*, people will not grow older."

But instead of the enthusiasm he had expected, there was silence.

"So I gather you would recommend that M & R fully fund this project?" asked Reed after a moment.

"I would, yes."

"Let's come down from the clouds, Cooper. This is still basically just speculation, isn't it?"

"No!" he countered emphatically. "As far as I'm concerned, the principle is proven! What they must do now is aggressively move up to primate research. But that's where their money problems come in."

Reed smiled coldly. "Let's not forget our priorities, Dr. Cooper. Their money problems are not M & R's responsibility."

Only now was the tenor of this gathering beginning to make sense to Cooper. It wasn't that the venture capitalists preferred bad news to good, just that they were staking out a negotiating position. The weaker the Institute's finances, the more leverage they would enjoy.

"In this case," replied the scientist, caution to the winds, "their money problems *are* M & R's problem. Without an assured cash flow, covering both their research needs and personnel, they won't be able to continue functioning. I believe it's a mistake to distract these men from their work: they are visionaries."

"We're not in the visionary business," snapped Reed, "we're interested in drugs for *human beings*."

"Fine. Imagine what a successful preventative of osteoarthritis could be worth. Or an over-the-counter product that reversed skin damage!"

Both gazed at him with eyes that were suddenly larger.

"We are talking about stopping the aging process!" he drove the point home. "What's that worth? Think about it—hair dyes alone are a two-billion-dollar industry in this country!"

Reed smiled. "You're not on their payroll, are you?"

"I assume that's a joke. They have no inkling of what I'm telling you."

"Why would they require so much funding?" wondered McIntyre. "They're a very small outfit."

"They're apparently operating a fairly wide network for the procurement of essential genetic material."

"Meaning?"

"Darling"—Reed shot her husband a look—"that's one thing we don't *want* to know. . . ." She turned back to Cooper. "You must be tired. Shouldn't you be getting home?"

He nodded. "What I'm telling you is that you should not risk losing them!"

"Oh, we won't," said Reed. "Because they've nowhere else to go. Thank you, Dr. Cooper."

Nodding, he started for the door.

"Oh, Dr. Cooper . . . ?"

He turned.

"I don't want you to have any further contact with these people. We'll take it from here."

"**I** really have to wonder if we should be doing this," said Mark. Shaking his head, he read aloud from the consent form. " 'Spontaneous abortion. Punctured placenta. Vaginal bleeding. Injury to the fetus . . .' "

"I understand how it sounds," said Malen evenly, "but amnio's completely routine." He smiled, masking his irritation that this should arise now, minutes before he was to perform the procedure. "You and I both know lawyers for insurance companies write those things."

Sally looked uncertain. "Still, Lee, it makes it sound like they *expect* a calamity."

The doctor gave her shoulder a reassuring squeeze. "Sally, I am *not* going to take any chances with your baby."

Malen paused, realizing even that didn't precisely address the issue Mark had raised. For, in fact, they intended to keep their child no matter what the test showed. Why, then, take it at all?

"Look, Sally," he added, "a few years ago I might have agreed with you. But if, God forbid, there is a problem, it's best to know and prepare for it—medically as well as emotionally. These days a number of conditions can even be successfully treated *in utero*." He paused. "I would really appreciate a little confidence in my judgment. At your age it just makes sense."

Fifteen minutes later she was on the examining table, Barbara Walker gently swabbing her midsection with antiseptic solution.

Alert, as always, to a patient's mood, the nurse sought to ease Sally's anxiety. "Easy as pie," she assured her, "never had the slightest problem. The boys"—she nodded at the austere portraits of Malen's predecessors hanging on the wall—"watch our every move."

She barely cracked a smile. "Good."

"So," Barbara tried again, "planning to take some time off this summer?"

"I don't know. Depends on work."

"Right, right." Walker laughed. "Call me crazy, but I just *love* that story."

"Do you?" she asked, surprised. "Not many people have told me that."

"Barbara's a sucker for true crime," noted Malen with a smile. "Even the kind that never gets solved."

"This one will be, count on it! We're starting to make some real progress."

All at once she was fully engaged, the jumpiness gone; seemingly unaware of the prick as Barbara expertly injected the local anesthetic.

"Oh?" he asked. "You mean because of this Giles fellow?"

"Absolutely. I know the way these things work. Sometimes a little pressure is all it takes to start someone talking, and—"

She stopped, aware of the door opening behind her. Craning her neck, she was startled to see the young woman with whom she'd seen Malen at the Clover Patch.

"If it's okay with you, I've invited our new anesthesiologist, Dr. Downs, to join us," observed Malen. "She tells me she's never seen one of these."

Mark nodded.

"We've met," said Sally.

The young woman smiled uncomfortably, reminding Sally of the way she used to feel as a college student when presented to her parents' friends as an equal, at once honored and vaguely fraudulent.

"Nice to see you again," she said, and wordlessly moved several feet beyond Sally to observe the procedure.

"Okay," said Malen, "let's get going. Sally, watch that monitor over there."

He switched on the ultrasound machine and began slowly moving the transducer over her belly. Shadowy forms, like some blurry moonscape, materialized on the screen. The head, the body, the hands, were all where they were supposed to be; the tiny heart was pumping.

"Look at that!"

Mark squeezed her hand. "Unbelievable."

"I think we might have some other news here," observed Malen. He paused. "Unless you want the sex to be a surprise."

They exchanged a look.

"No," said Sally, shakily, "go ahead."

"Barbara, would you like to do the honors?"

The nurse grinned. "From the way it looks . . . Hope you guys like pink."

"Really!!!"

"A girl," exclaimed Mark, stroking her hair. "My God."

"It's what I was hoping for. . . ."

The needle used to withdraw the amniotic fluid from her uterus was fearsome—seven inches long and uncommonly thick.

"Me too," said Malen, who, while she was distracted, seized the moment to begin inserting it into her abdomen.

She's obsessing on this story, Steve, she can't talk about anything else. I swear, even during the amnio!"

"She's not due for, what, another six months?" asked his friend Montera, behind the wheel of his Taurus wagon.

"December."

"Well, pal, it's only gonna get worse." Shaking his head in mock sorrow, he picked up the *Weekly*, folded back to the Garage Sales classifieds, and glanced at it as he drove. "Hey, this next sale's supposed to have old records—that'll cheer you up!"

Mark had seen Montera in this mode a lot lately; speaking, as the father of two young sons, with absolute authority on all matters involving pregnancy and its impact on male life. Usually he found it amusing, sometimes galling. But this glorious Saturday morning in June he had actually invited it, jumping at Montera's suggestion that they relive their college days and hit some garage sales.

"It's just panic," Montera went on now. "She's worried about throwing away everything she's worked for. Half the time during her first pregnancy Cheryl could only talk about how fulfilled she was—and the other half she spent crying about giving up her independence!"

Mark shook his head. "I don't buy it, that's not Sally."

"Christ, Bowman, don't you ever read the women's magazines at the checkout counter? This is it, the dreaded balancing act, the mother of all modern female dilemmas!"

He spotted the house he was looking for, years of junk on display in the driveway, and eased the car to a stop. "Later. This one looks like it's loaded!"

"Whoa!" he exclaimed a moment later, kneeling on the ground before a boxful of 45's, holding up the record he'd just found, "Supertramp's 'Dreamer.' A & M Records, mint condition, still in its original dust jacket! Exceptional acoustics and harmonies!"

"Nice song," agreed Mark.

"*Nice song?* Hell, man, one of our *inspirations*!"

Mark smiled wistfully. "Almost feels like another lifetime, doesn't it?"

"Right. . . ." Montera ran a hand over his receding hairline. "A lifetime with hair."

"You ever think maybe we oughta start playing music again?" Mark picked up as they set off for the next sale.

Montera smiled. "Do you know I actually *still* dream sometimes that we're playing gigs?"

"Oh, yeah? Me too."

"Unlike the real thing, they usually end up involving groupies and sex."

"I've still got my guitar and amps up in the attic. And this time we wouldn't have to ask permission to use the garage. . . ." He paused. "Or does all this sound just too pathetic?"

"Not to me—I'm your therapist here, remember? The only one you can afford."

"And worth every cent."

But Mark wasn't in the mood for their usual give-and-take. Falling silent, he stared out the window at the passing landscape "It's no joke, Steve, I don't like what's going on. When Sally's going full blast on this grave-robbing thing, it's almost like part of herself gets turned off." He chuckled mirthlessly. "Her humanity."

Montera briefly took his eyes from the road to cast him a questioning glance.

"She's been zeroing in on a couple of kids as suspects."

"Ah." Montera nodded. "I didn't know."

"Maybe I shouldn't be so hard on her. I mean, she's been under incredible pressure lately."

"Oh, now he's trying to be supportive. See, you do read those magazines." He paused. "You want some advice?—the grade-A stuff, not the bullshit."

"You can always give it a shot."

"Keep it in perspective. She's at war with herself right now. But she'll work it out, people always do."

Mark thought it over a moment, then nodded slowly. "I'm just hoping no one gets caught first in the crossfire."

Sally hadn't known what to expect, but it certainly wasn't this. Located on the far north end of a town of white-picket-fence orderliness, Terry Sutter's home was a ramshackle wooden structure badly in need of a paint job. Instead of a front lawn there was an expanse of crabgrass-pocked dirt.

Finding the bell didn't work, Sally knocked; then, after a few moments, knocked again, more forcefully. She was just turning to leave when she heard footfalls on the stairs.

She instantly recognized the boy from the photo she'd found in the yearbook. "Hello, Terry, I'm—"

"I know, you're Mrs. Bowman!"

She smiled—no one ever called her that. "Right."

"What are you doing here?"

"I was wondering if we could talk?"

He didn't move from the doorway. "What about?"

"A story I'm working on for the *Weekly*. Can I come in?"

"I guess," he said, and reluctantly let her pass.

The carpet in the entryway was badly stained and Sally noticed empty soda cans and ashtrays full of cigarette butts in the living room off to the left.

"My mom usually doesn't like people coming over without warning," offered Terry, his offhand manner failing to conceal his embarrassment.

"No problem. Maybe we should go to your room."

"I don't think so," he said too quickly. "Here's fine."

Instantly her curiosity was engaged. "How come?"

"Or maybe my sister's room . . ."

"Oh, you have a sister . . . ?"

"Wait here."

He turned and dashed up the stairs. "No!" he heard an adolescent girl's voice shout a moment later. "I'm busy. Go someplace else!!"

"Maybe we can go out," he said, coming down the stairs.

She grinned. "Terry, I don't mind if your room's messy, you should see mine."

Reluctantly, he turned back up the stairs. "All right, come on."

The room was indeed in disarray, the bed unmade, clothes spilling out of half-open dresser drawers. But just as clearly it was a refuge from the drabber and more random disorder of the rest of the house; a showcase for his private and surprisingly idiosyncratic passions, the desk in the corner piled high with magazines and CDs, the walls adorned by weird phantasmagorical drawings he'd done himself.

"You interested in World War II airplanes?" asked Sally, noting the dogfight being played out between plastic models of Spitfires and Messerschmitts suspended by threads from the ceiling above the bed.

He shrugged. "I used to be. My dad put that up before he left."

"It's really terrific."

"I should take it down. I'm too old for that stuff now."

Sally turned to the fish tank in the corner. It was an unusual one, octagonal in shape and set in a polished oak stand.

"Impressive. How big is that thing?"

"Fifty-five gallons. It's salt water."

"What kind of fish?" Not that she could tell one from the other.

He pointed at a flat one a couple of inches in diameter, brilliant orange with white squiggles. "That's a clown anemone, from the Indian Ocean. The long ones are green bird fish. Then I've got a few scissor-tail gobies and a couple of zebra fish. . . ." She looked closely, making mental notes. *The filter was made by a company called Fluval, the heater was the Ibojager brand.*

"They mainly eat shrimp," he volunteered, "same as the zebra morays. See, there's one back there, behind the castle."

"Wow." She turned to him. "My husband's right, you're an interesting kid, Terry."

"Mr. Bowman said that?" he asked; then, to hide his pleasure: "He probably also told you I don't live up to my potential."

"No, actually, that you've turned a corner. Tell me, would you like to go to college?"

"I don't know."

"Well, it's up to you. You're plenty bright enough." She took a seat on the unmade bed. "Which gets to what I want to ask you about."

He looked at her evenly.

"I'm wondering if you might have done something that could screw up your life."

Terry showed nothing.

"Because if you have, it'd be a helluva lot better to come clean now."

"I don't know what you're talking about."

"Really? I have the idea you do."

He shrugged. "You're gonna believe what you want anyhow! People always do."

"Fine, Terry," she said soothingly. "I'm not here to grill you."

He seemed to hesitate, then thought better of it. "So, anything else?"

Reluctantly, she rose to her feet. "Maybe something will occur to you. If you want to reach me, I'm at the *Weekly* office."

"I won't."

But by now, as far as Sally was concerned, it almost didn't matter. Already, she'd spotted above the bed the drawing of two spectral figures in black capes, arms spread ominously as in a gothic novel. Beneath, in ornate letters, was the chilling term she'd only recently stumbled upon in the course of her research: RESURRECTION MEN.

Holland was struck by the change the instant he entered the room. Stagg looked awful—far worse, even, than he'd expected. Propped up on a gurney with throw pillows, the color gone from his cheeks, his eyes half closed and breathing labored, it was as if the mere act of being awake required Herculean effort.

Located in the Institute's basement, the room was a standard operating facility of the sort found in a thousand community hospitals: white tile walls, an operating table and overhead lamp, tanks of anesthesia, and an EKG machine. Except there was another piece of equipment the reporter had never seen before: a gleaming silver cylinder, approximately five by eight feet, with a variety of dials and gauges in the front.

A space-age coffin.

"Who's this?" spoke up Stagg suddenly, in a surprisingly strong voice, pointing a bony finger Holland's way.

Holland started—then realized that in his surgical mask, gown, and cap, there was no way to know. "Paul Holland."

"Ah, good. Now we can get started."

Holland cast a glance at Lynch across the room, alongside Foster and several men in surgical whites—all, presumably, with experience in the procedure.

"Mr. Holland," confirmed Lynch, nodding at the shortest of the three, "this is Dr. Unger, and his team. Dr. Unger is the director of Cryolabs in Santa Fe, New Mexico."

"Pretty part of the country" was all Holland could think to say. On the basis of everything he knew cryonics—the notion that the dead could be frozen and later restored to life—was utterly fraudulent.

"Yes, it is. We're very happy out there."

"Forget him," snapped Stagg, "*I'm* the one you're here to see. I gather you're pretty dubious about all of this."

Behind his mask Holland bit his lip. This was hardly the time or place for such a conversation—or the person to have it with. "Frankly," he hedged, "I've had to examine a lot of my preconceptions lately."

"Don't BS me, Holland, I've read you on the subject." He gave a thin smile. "Relax—Lynch here agrees with you. So does Foster. They think it's a colossal waste of money."

The scientists, looking on, confirmed the assertion by their silence. Money was tight. No matter the rationale, to them the idea of eating up a big chunk of it on an exercise grounded more in hope than hard science was grossly irresponsible.

"In any case," added Holland, "I'm grateful for the chance to . . ." He paused—how to put this? "The *operation* interests me a great deal."

"Good, I thought it would. Look over there, in that briefcase."

Holland retrieved it. Inside was a notebook, one of the old-fashioned kind with a marbled cover. "A few notes and philosophical speculations I set down as this event drew closer. Keep 'em. Or should I say, hold 'em for me. I expect you to write about this sometime."

"Can I say, Mr. Stagg . . . ?" What he wanted to express to the old man was not just gratitude but something akin to admiration. His own life had always been lived secondhand; he and his colleagues were professional *observers*. Yet here was someone who'd had the guts to bet literally everything on a fantastic leap into the unknown. "I just want to wish you luck."

Unnoticed, Foster stared at Holland with naked hatred; the miserable bastard couldn't help himself, even *here* he played to the power in the room.

"Save it," replied Stagg. "You'll get your own chance soon enough."

Shaking the old man's hand, Holland was surprised to find it ice cold; then realized this was another symptom of his advanced atherosclerotic disease—poor circulation to the extremities.

"All this equipment has been thoroughly tested?"

Unger nodded. "Just yesterday. As you may know, cryopreservation is already being performed in half a dozen facilities around the country."

"Generally, though, *after* death," observed Stagg blithely. "Which is probably a little too late."

"Ready to get going, Mr. Stagg?" asked Unger.

"Time is money."

"We'll need you on the table. Would you like some help?"

"I can do it."

They watched the old man slowly drag himself from the gurney onto the adjacent operating table.

"You want me to take this off?" he asked, indicating the smoking jacket he'd donned for the occasion.

"We can do that afterward."

"Well, make sure you leave it where I can find it. I'm figuring on making an impression. . . ."

Five minutes after administration of the anesthetic, nude and strapped spread eagle on the table, the old man appeared to be sleeping peacefully, the tracer line on the EKG machine registering a near normal heartbeat, his breathing shallow but steady.

Having, of course, read up on the procedure, Holland knew exactly what he would see. Still, what he witnessed over the next three and a half hours was riveting, as, step by step, the vital figure on the table was reduced to a meticulously frozen mass of meat; his heart slowed from sixty beats a minute to fewer than fifteen by means of steadily mounting doses of the curariform agent Pavulon, and finally stopped altogether; his blood drawn out by pumps and replaced by crystalloid solution; while simultaneously his brain was frozen solid by a "helmet" bearing liquid nitrogen at minus 196 degrees Celsius.

But what left him most shaken at the end was the old man's color. As he was lifted onto the gurney and wheeled to the silver cylinder, his rigid face was the startling white of fresh snow.

The unit's top unlatched and lifted like that of a conventional meat freezer. Gingerly, he was placed inside.

"Quite a character," observed Holland, casting a glance at Lynch. "Will you miss him?"

"Miss him? I *envy* him. We're the ones left behind high and dry."

They watched as Unger rechecked the settings on the dials and, after a long look at Stagg, slammed the top shut.

"Come upstairs to my office, Holland," added Lynch. "There's something we're going to need you to do."

What is this?!" Lisa wanted to know, entering into Sally's tiny office without knocking.

Sally lowered the newspaper she'd been reading and gazed at her blankly.

"I thought this was supposed to be BOTH our story." Lisa waved the pages she'd just retrieved from her computer.

"It's an *editorial*, Lisa. Last time I looked, I was still top editor around here."

The piece, which she'd composed the night before, implied, without citing specifics, that there existed evidence confirming that local teens indeed bore responsibility for the grave robbings. Its tone was sorrowful, even apologetic, but the message was clear: the time had come for the police to make arrests.

"Goddammit, Sally, I've been on this for months!"

"If I may say so, Lisa, your concern's a little misplaced—how about saving some for those boys we're doing in?"

"What, I'm supposed to be broken up about this? It's about time!"

"We're part of this community, too, Lisa—and what happens next isn't going to be pleasant."

"So why are we running it at all? I mean, we had the same

information months ago, but all I kept hearing was 'Let's not go overboard.' " She paused. "Or does that only apply to me?"

"What's wrong with you?" snapped Sally. "Circumstances change—that was before Wilson Giles and his money were on the scene. And, yes, before *I* got convinced by my visit to Terry's."

Lisa was momentarily silent. "You're not trying very hard to keep me here at the *Weekly,* are you?"

"I'm trying to tell you the way it is."

She paused. "What about when the baby comes?"

"Excuse me?"

"What are you going to do then?"

She sighed. "I don't know, Lisa, I really haven't made any plans."

"Let's talk about it. I have to make some of my own."

Sally stood up, indicating the meeting was over. "You don't know when to stop, do you?! You just push and push and push!"

"That's what makes me a good reporter," said Lisa, holding her ground.

"But also a pain in the ass." She shook her head, but even in her exasperation couldn't help but feel a certain grudging respect for the other's doggedness. "All right," she decided, "you really want the *credit* for this?"

"I only want what I've earned."

"I don't—but I suppose I have to take the responsibility. We'll make it a *signed* editorial, both of our names. Will that do it for you?"

"Yes, it will!" said Lisa, delighted. "Good. Great!"

Sally smiled wistfully. "Just shut the door behind you."

When she was gone, Sally leaned back in her chair, momentarily lost in thought. Then she snatched up the paper she'd set aside—the national edition of the *New York Herald.*

The lead story in the weekly Science section was bylined R. Paul Holland: NEW ENGLAND LAB IN MAJOR DNA GAIN.

She read it through again, this time more carefully.

Apparently, if the story was to be believed, scientists at the Life Services Institute down in Manchester had located a gene that showed promise of having a dramatic impact on a wide range of age-related maladies.

Never much at science, Sally didn't get into the technical detail. But what she couldn't get past was the tenor of the piece. Never, not in life and certainly not in print, had she seen Paul Holland so enthusiastic about anything. Never even close.

And after he'd expressed such outright contempt for this place to her!

What, she couldn't help but wonder, was *this* all about?

Dennis Boyles was thinking the same thing.

"I thought you were done with this longevity crap, Holland," he snapped in greeting, when the reporter responded to his summons.

Holland managed to convey every appearance of calm. "I told you I had some odds and ends to finish up, Dennis. They're doing some fascinating work at this place, it deserves notice."

"*Notice?!* That's a goddamn wet dream you wrote, I had to wash my hands afterward!"

"That's pretty harsh, sir. The science is for real."

"It's not harsh enough—not unless they've got the fucking Fountain of Youth bubbling out of the ground up there!"

Never before had Holland personally experienced the full force of the executive editor's legendary derision. He managed a smile, dying inside, and nodded. "From now on I'm off the topic."

"What's the name of this place again?"

"The Life Services Institute. In Manchester, New Hampshire."

"Right, right. . . ." Boyles took a drag on his cigarette. "Then how come I see on the story sheet you're planning *another* trip up there?"

Holland felt himself flushing. *Why had he been so stupid as to list the trip for reimbursement?!* "I'll cancel it. It's just that they've produced some new research data and—"

"Sure, and they figure they've got a patsy at the *Herald*! When their stock goes public, all their press clips'll be in order!"

"—I'll just have to tell them I'm done, not interested," he concluded lamely.

"How long have you been around this business, Holland? Don't you have the least goddamn concern about appearances?" He took another drag on his cigarette. "Now, get the fuck out of here. I'm busy, I've got enough on my plate without having to worry about you!"

The realization passed over Holland like a cleansing wind—*he was going to get out of this!* "Yessir."

Gratefully, he turned to go.

"Of course, you know why I'm cutting you slack, Holland. . . ."

He turned to see him stub out the cigarette.

"Bees to honey and all that. What's her name again, your little reporter friend?"

"Sally Benedict?" Caught off guard, he was momentarily at a loss. "Mr. Boyles, this has nothing to do with . . . She's a terrific journalist. You wanted to hire her yourself."

"Sure, *you* try to satisfy all those damn diversity guidelines around here. C'mon, Holland, it doesn't take a rocket scientist to figure it out." Abruptly his manner turned warmer, almost confidential. "This would be—what?—your *third* visit to the Granite State?"

Holland knew opportunity when he saw it—there was no rationale more persuasive to someone asking tough questions than the one he comes up with himself. "Mr. Boyles," he said, with a slow smile, "she's a happily married woman. . . ." No need to mention the more telling bit of personal data, her pregnancy.

"Tell me about it—I've had a few of those in my time too."

Holland paused, the smile wider. "Actually, I've got another pretty good story cooking up there. About an honest-to-God old-fashioned country doctor, still rushes out at night to make house calls, the whole bit." He shrugged. "I'm thinking it might even end up being a *series*."

"Let me guess—he's in the same general region as your friend."

He laughed. "The same town."

Boyles walked to the other side of the desk, shaking his head and chuckling. "Just a word of warning, Holland, be discreet. Where you stick your pecker's your own business. But don't fuck with the paper's good name—or someone might just have to cut it off for you."

It was Father Morse himself, arriving at the church a little past seven o'clock the morning after Independence Day, who found the cadavers.

They had been laid out on the patch of grass by the entrance with care, and on this brilliant, early summer day, they looked almost serene. There was no apparent evidence that either had been defiled.

Alongside, in a canvas sack, were the much older bones taken from the first grave.

Within an hour Sally was in Stebben's office, her spirits buoyant.

"Well," she observed, "it looks like applying a little pressure paid off."

"You're trying to take credit for this?" he said sourly. "You think that pissant little editorial of yours—"

"Hey," she cut him off, smiling, "how about a truce? We're prepared to let sleeping dogs lie if you are."

"Why in hell would I do that now," he shot back, "after all the grief you people have given me?"

Sally stared back at him in surprise. "I thought that's what you wanted—to avoid something that might rip apart the community.

Fine, I'm convinced. Clearly, those kids have learned their lesson, let's leave them alone."

"Sure, when it turns out it was a couple of your precious hubby's students!"

"Chief, this has nothing to do with you and me."

"Little lady, the way I look at it, it's been about you from the beginning—you and that paper of yours."

"That's crazy."

"What industrious little reporters you are. How tough you could make yourselves look. How much you could embarrass me and the force." He leaned intently forward. "You wanted us to take this to the limit? Fine—I'm having Simmons bring in those boys this afternoon. Keep your front page open."

"Look, you want me to say it?—maybe we pressed a little too hard."

"Uh-uh, no." He shook his head. "Not good enough. You were *wrong,* is what you were. You took a third-rate little prank by some bored small town kids and used it to make yourself feel important. You took the screwed-up ethics of big city journalism and tried to impose 'em on this town!"

"I admit I come from a different tradition. Sometimes people do play rough—"

"In the gutter is where they play. I don't want to see that tradition get started here."

Seeing how much he was beginning to enjoy this, she summoned all her self-control to keep from lashing back.

"And in the process you took that nice kid Lisa and turned her into a damn conniver also."

"Into a *reporter.*"

He leaned back. "What I want, Ms. Editor, is another editorial—this time a nice, big, fat, wet kiss apology to Edwardstown's finest."

"Chief, we both know it was a legitimate story—"

"I want to see that crow you eat cooked golden brown—*braised,* isn't that what you'd call it? Maybe, when you're mentioning the fine job we've done, you could use the word 'restraint.' ''

"You're not serious."

"It's your call, missy. I'll go right on ahead and arrest 'em, if that's what you want. Then, again, if I do, I hope we can expect some nice words from you anyway—about how we stuck with this thing and finally cracked it. . . ."

She looked at him evenly. "You'll get your editorial."

"Always a pleasure doing business with you." Smiling, he reached his hand across the desk and she shook it. "Now, you be sure to talk to your pal Giles about canning that damn reward of his."

"You weren't going to pursue this anyway, were you?" she asked, with all the dignity she could muster. "This whole thing was just a show for my benefit."

"I dare you NOT to run that apology," he shot back, more pleased than she'd ever seen him, "—then we'll find out, won't we?"

Wilson Giles returned to Edwardstown two days later for the reinterment of his father, this time accompanied by his wife and grown daughter. Among the dozen or so others who joined them at the brief graveside ceremony presided over by Father Morse were Sally and Lisa.

It was as she walked Giles from the cemetery that Sally decided to broach it. "Are you still planning to offer that reward?"

Stopping, he looked at her in surprise. "Don't you think I should?"

She hesitated. "You'd probably like to be done with all this."

"I would, yes." He looked back toward the looming odalisque. "But I'm afraid I've got obligations beyond my own preferences. My father was a very special man. I'm not sure *he* would understand."

She nodded. "I know what you're saying. I loved my own father just as dearly. But maybe under these circumstances—"

"He was adopted, did you know that?"

"Actually, no, I didn't," she answered.

"I've always believed that's why he gave so much to his own children. Over the years some people have been surprised by my devotion to his memory. But I haven't done a thing he wouldn't have done a thousand times over for either of us."

They resumed walking. "Look," ventured Sally, "from the perspective of the paper, a reward would be terrific, it would keep the story alive. But it's clear whoever did it apparently already got the message. I'd hate to see a couple of kids' futures ruined by—"

"Miss Benedict," he cut her off, his look as sharp as his tone, "the subject is closed. I expect the details of my offer to be reported in full. Twenty thousand dollars for information leading to the arrest and conviction of the social misfits who perpetrated this monstrosity!" He paused. "If your conscience precludes your doing your job properly, I'm prepared to purchase the back page of your newspaper and print those details myself. Now, enough of this!"

He stared at her a moment longer, his eyes bright with anger, awaiting a response. When there was none, he strode out the cemetery gate, trailed by his loved ones.

Within seconds of entering Lynch's office Foster knew who was on the other end of the line. His colleague's body language and deferential tone were a dead giveaway.

"Dr. Cooper told you that?" he was saying, hunched over his desk, eyes closed, forehead in his hand. "Frankly, I'm surprised. He left us with an entirely different impression."

Glancing up to see Foster only increased his discomfort.

"No, no, no, Ms. Reed, we're absolutely on the same page, I understand your concern. I'm just asking you to understand ours. We'd like to close this deal as soon as possible."

There was a pause. "Of course not, I never said that proposal was written in stone—just come back to me with what you think would be appropriate adjustments."

Foster slouched into a chair. "Tell her to go fuck herself," he said, loud enough that Lynch felt compelled to cover the mouthpiece. "Tell her we don't need this crap now!"

This was a considerable understatement. Although, thankfully, the woman on the other end of the line had no way of knowing it, another problem had arisen that overshadowed even the funding crisis. Up north in Edwardstown the entire operation suddenly seemed threatened with exposure.

"You should know, Ms. Reed, we've obtained vital new evidence that we're on the right track—a sample of amniotic fluid proving definitively that the family we're tracking—"

As she cut him off again, he was reminded that discussing anything with this woman but the bottom line was useless.

"Actually," he began again after a moment, glancing over at Foster, "you should know that since the appearance of the article we've had other inquiries. . . ."

But when she called his bluff, he visibly sagged. "I assume that's a joke. Of *course* Holland's not on the payroll."

A moment later he slammed down the phone. "That bastard Cooper! After the sweetness-and-light routine he cut us to pieces!"

"She's using his report to demand even *better* terms?!" Foster laughed mirthlessly "They're already looking at eighty percent of the company for their lousy twenty-eight million! Why don't we just sign over the whole thing and be done with it?!"

"The problem was not getting what we needed from that last cadaver. It gave Cooper an opening."

"Actually," said Foster, "I've been giving that some thought. There's a chance the organs from that specimen still exist."

Lynch looked at him for a long moment; he'd long since learned that, with Foster, it was a mistake to dismiss out of hand even the most outlandish suggestion. "Greg, it was more than sixty years ago."

"Have you ever visited the specimen room at Bellevue or Cornell? These places have preserved thousands of organ samples, dating back a hundred years. Anything that seemed of potential value."

"You mean because she lived to be so old . . ." he said, with sudden understanding.

"Which was far rarer then than it is now. I was thinking that if we could locate those samples . . ."

Lynch's spirits, as always, were quick to rebound. "It's definitely an avenue to pursue."

Foster nodded. "While we continue to pursue others." He paused meaningfully. "The immediate priority is this difficulty in Edwardstown. . . ."

"Yes?" said Terry Sutter, surprised to find a stranger at his door late on a suffocatingly muggy summer morning. Terry wore only shorts and a T-shirt; the knock on the kitchen door had roused him from a deeply satisfying sleep.

"I presume you're Terry Sutter?" The man's voice—lilting, almost soothing—was at odds with his powerful appearance.

"Why? What's this about?"

"I've brought a card."

He handed it to him. Terry looked down—at a photograph of the face of the old woman from the grave—then quickly, in horror, at the man.

"I thought that might be familiar," he said pleasantly, brushing past him. "May I come in?"

"What do you want?" demanded Terry, leaving the door open. "Where did you get that?"

He laughed. "Forgive me, that little maneuver really was uncalled for. But we do need to talk."

"About what?"

He reached out a meaty hand and, reluctantly, Terry shook it. "Herman Van Ost. Please close the door."

"About what?" he repeated, not moving.

"Oh, as you please." He paused. "About those favors you and your friend did for Chief Stebben. You see, the chief in turn was doing a favor for us."

"I don't understand."

"Of course not, that's for everyone's protection. I'm just here to let you know we're keenly aware how much heat you've been getting. If it helps, it's been in a good cause—vital scientific research."

"Really?" he asked, intrigued.

"More to the point, that we appreciate your standing up to it. And shall continue to make it worth your while."

"Oh, yeah?" he said, cautious.

"To date you've received a total of seventeen hundred dollars, is that correct?"

"Yeah. . . ."

"How does an additional fifteen thousand dollars sound?"

"Just for not saying anything?"

"Just to continue as you've been doing."

The boy laughed. "Sure, I could do that!"

"Good. My job will be getting it to you. I'd prefer to pass it along in increments. I understand a young man's temptation to spend large sums in one place, but that could arouse suspicion."

"Not me. The only thing I buy is tropical fish."

He nodded, pleased. "An excellent vice. I shared it at your age. Have you any dragonets? They were my favorite."

"No, but I'm planning to."

"What about tangs?"

"I just got a pair of powder-blues!"

"Wonderful. But be careful, watch out for lateral-line disease.

"Do you name them?" asked Van Ost, a few minutes later, up in his room. "Foolish, I know, but I always did."

"Just the morays. That's Kurt and that's Hootie."

Already, the visitor had out the gun. As the boy pointed, he fired directly into the temple, from an inch away.

By the time Donald Cornelius arrived at the University of Iowa Medical Center in Cedar Rapids, the sixty-three-year-old farmer's temperature was approaching 105 and his blood pressure had plummeted to eighty-five over sixty. A busy man, he'd allowed the ugly gash on his forearm, sustained unclogging a combine, to go untreated for eight days.

A cursory examination sent the veteran emergency-room doctor into crisis mode. He first tried lactated Ringer's solution, designed to mimic the electrolyte concentration of blood; then administered the powerful antibiotics ceftazidime and vancomycin to counter anaerobic and staph infection. But after two hours Cornelius's blood pressure still had not begun to rise. By now his extremities were cool and mottled, his breathing increasingly labored.

In desperation the ER physician consulted a colleague, then rejoined the patient and his wife.

"Look," he said, calm only by experience, "what we've been trying is not working. I'm afraid that you've got bacteria in your bloodstream. When a condition like that is severe enough, sometimes antibiotics don't help."

The question came without hesitation. "Am I dying?"

"It is essential, Mr. Cornelius, to clear your bloodstream."

"Oh, my God!" whispered Mrs. Cornelius.

"We do have an experimental treatment designed for exactly this situation. The drug is called Alcumine."

Within five minutes the appropriate informed consent forms had been signed and he was wheeled into the section of the intensive care unit set aside for the Alcumine protocol. The nurse on duty was an employee not of the hospital, but of the drug's manufacturer, Cytometrics, Inc. In the two and a half years since the program's start, she had received an average of one patient every several days— a total, all told, of slightly more than two hundred. Today was busier than usual; another of the four patient rooms was already occupied by a comatose thirty-eight-year-old woman who had been undergoing chemotherapy at the hospital for ovarian cancer.

For her, too, Alcumine was a desperation roll of the dice.

"All right now," said the nurse, easing Donald Cornelius's large frame onto the bed and starting to hook up the IV line through which the drug would be administered, "we'll have you back on your feet in no time."

But the words were by rote. She was a practical woman and, based on what she'd seen, she no longer believed them herself.

When she arrived at the Sutter home, Sally's defense mechanism was in overdrive. Opening her notebook, she focused on the details. The several dozen stricken young people milling about the moonscape of a front yard, several of them crying. The Union-based psychologist dispatched to the scene by the school district, absurdly overdressed this muggy evening in a jacket and tie. The coroner's car, an immaculate white Buick LeSabre, in the weed-choked driveway.

Too, she noted the characteristically ineffectual manner the site had been "secured." Always, in Sally's experience of similar crime or accident scenes, even in small cities, the police would cordon off the entire building, often the whole block. Here there was but a single strip of bright yellow tape across the entryway to the house.

Stebben stood off to the side, looking, she thought, almost as shaken as some of the kids; features rigidly set, jaw muscle working. When she approached, notebook open, he acknowledged her with a crisp nod, avoiding her eyes.

"Did he leave a note?" she asked after a moment.

"Did he have to?"

"How's the family taking it?"

"Bad. You'll be a mom soon yourself"—he nodded at her bulging midsection—"maybe then you'll understand."

"What the hell's that supposed to mean?!"

"His sister found him. She's been in hysterics ever since."

"Cut me some slack, Stebben," she said, still bristling, "I was as afraid of something like this as you were. You know damn well I tried to get Giles to back off the reward." She paused. "How long's the coroner been here?"

"About twenty minutes."

"You're sure there's no note?"

"What do you want, lady, *blood*?"

"Just the facts, same as always." No way she was going to let him get to her; all she'd done was her job. "Have you talked to the other boy?"

Stebben snorted, but the derision lacked his usual conviction. "*You* try and find him."

"What, he took off?"

"As soon as he heard"—he nodded vaguely at the house—"with a change of clothes and all the cash in his mom's bedroom drawer."

"Just today? He can't be far."

"It's her problem now." He shrugged. "Lots of kids in trouble run away. Some turn up, some don't. What you need to know is he left behind a note owning up to everything. So the chase is done."

"Saying what?"

"That he and Terry did it, they're sorry, they didn't mean no harm. Just what you'd think."

"I'd like a copy," said Sally coolly. "We want to get the story right."

"I'll have to see about that. You just make damn sure everyone knows it's *over*."

She nodded. "Gotta run, Chief. Time to crash that barrier of yours and bug the coroner."

Still on emotional automatic pilot, Sally breezed past Officer

Simmons, manning the door, and into the Sutter home. It wasn't until she was climbing the steps toward Terry's room that she realized the depth of her apprehension.

The boy lay faceup in almost the exact center of the room, eyes wide open, wearing sneakers, jeans, a Nine Inch Nails T-shirt. There was very little blood; just a small sticky pool perhaps six inches in diameter by the exit wound. At first glance, from ten feet, he might have been daydreaming while listening to music.

But moving closer, she saw a film had settled over his gray eyes, turning them opaque. The gun lay a few inches from his right hand.

God, he was so young!

"When are you due?"

She looked up at the coroner. Sally recognized the camera with flash attachment around his neck as a vintage Pentax—the very one she'd owned back in college.

"Four months."

"We just had our second." He thrust out his hand. In his early thirties, bespectacled and neatly groomed, he had the aggressive amiability of a student government type. "Ed Clarke—that's with an *e*. You're with the press."

She nodded. "Sally Benedict. I'm with the *Edwardstown Weekly*."

"The notebook's a dead giveaway. A little coroner humor there."

She smiled weakly. "I see the county really goes all out on equipment."

"Yes"—he accepted this at face value—"I get everything I need."

"Well, don't let me interrupt you."

"No problem, I'm almost done here. Just need some souvenirs for the old family album . . ." he said, and she had the idea the line was probably borrowed from some hard-bitten coroner in a movie.

She took a few steps back and watched as he took shots of the body from assorted angles, then moved in for close-ups of the wound.

He looked up suddenly from his camera. "Don't let me stop you from doing *your* job. Anything you want to know"—he paused and winked—"just shoot."

She nodded, not bothering to pretend even mild amusement. Maybe she didn't know much about forensic science, just the little she'd picked up as a street reporter in Philly, but she sure as hell knew a nincompoop when she saw one. "I knew Terry," she observed sharply. "He was quite a kid."

To her surprise he was equally ready to play that game. "Yes," he replied sorrowfully, "it's a terrible waste. Teen suicide's become a national epidemic, more than five thousand a year."

"You've done a lot of these?"

"Oh, sure, at least a dozen. As an instructor of mine once put it, a suicide investigation can be simple or as complicated as life itself. Fortunately, this is the former."

"Oh, yes? Why's that?"

"There are three basic things you look at in cases like this: the position of the gun when it was fired, whether there's evidence anyone but the victim might have been present, and, of course, the person's psychological state of mind."

Nodding, she made a note she knew she'd never use—this was kindergarten-level stuff—and glanced idly around the room. Everything was pretty much as before: the model planes above the bed, the clutter on the desk, the array of posters on the wall, including the one that in her mind had so conclusively linked him to the crimes. . . .

"I've been told the young man had extremely serious problems, he expected to be arrested." He shrugged. "Open and shut."

"Jesus!"

Only just now had she noticed the shards of glass beneath the fish tank in the corner. The bullet had shattered the heat lamp, leaving the tank dark. Even from here she could see a dozen lifeless forms floating on the surface.

"Yes," he noted, "that's very helpful. It establishes angle and bullet track with absolute certitude."

She nodded.

"Look here." Showing off now, he pointed at the wound. "See the abrasion collar and smudge ring around the entry wound? That's consistent with a shot fired from a distance of between two and five inches. Classic."

"What kind of gun is it?"

"A Ruger twenty-two, unregistered. They're easy to get on the street in Manchester."

"Have you examined his hand? I understand there's sometimes a bruise from the recoil of the weapon."

"Who told you that?"

"A deputy ME in Philadelphia."

"Interesting," he said, dismissive. "I'll have to remember that."

Sally glanced down at Terry, almost forgotten in the exchange, and felt a sudden, sharp sense of shame. "He was a nice kid," she said again.

"I'm sure he was. So . . ." He clapped his hands together. "I'm just about finished here if you are. I'll have the body removed for autopsy."

"So tell me," he asked a moment later in the hall, "are you expecting a boy or a girl?"

"It's a girl."

"Good, good, I approve, I've got two myself. In the end boys are a lot harder."

"You think so?"

"I *know* it. Even something like this . . ." His smile was intended to be wistful, conveying understanding and sensitivity. "I'm told girls *attempt* suicide more often. But, I tell you"—he nodded at the closed door to Terry's room—"five out of six times when I get a call that someone's *succeeded* . . ."

I don't want you to beat yourself up over this," said Mark, as beside him in the car his wife once again lapsed into sober silence. "It's not your fault."

"Of course it's not," she said, surprised. "I was thinking about that fish tank."

"The fish tank?"

"It just seems to me he would've been more careful."

Mark said nothing, but inwardly he shuddered. *What now?* For almost ten months they'd lived with this damn story. If nothing else, this overwhelming tragedy had seemed to end it.

"I know it's crazy. . . ." She paused. "But the way he felt about those fish, it doesn't make sense."

"Sally," he said, trying to mute his exasperation, "*suicide is not a rational act!* What in the world are you suggesting? What's the alternative?"

"I don't know, it's just a . . . feeling."

This time he couldn't stop himself. "There's a cure for that—*thinking*. The boy's dead, let him rest in peace."

Beside him, she bristled. This was the quality in Mark she'd always found most galling, this smug . . . *rationality*. Worse, lately, she'd detected in him something infuriatingly like condescension: as if her interest in the case, waxing and waning as it did in intensity, was little more than a matter of surging hormones.

What he couldn't grasp was that she trusted her instincts. Some things were simply beyond logic. This she had learned at her mother's knee, and the lesson had always served her well.

Still, for once she had no ready comeback. This time he not only had the facts, but the moral high ground.

"Well, then, think about *this*," she came back anyway. "I checked with an exotic fish store down in Manchester. That tank retails for almost eight hundred and fifty dollars. Zebra fish alone go for fifty bucks apiece!"

"So?"

"In all, that setup cost more than fifteen hundred bucks! Where would this kid have gotten that kind of money?"

He slapped his forehead. "You're making my head spin, you know that?—and God only knows what it's doing to the baby!"

"Don't you dare bring the baby into this!"

He waited a moment. "All right, Sal, enough—we're trying to have a relaxing day."

Abruptly they hit a dip in the road and the nine-year-old Chevy Impala came down hard.

"Sonovabitch!" exclaimed Mark. "When're they going to fix that thing?"

"Relax," she replied dryly, "don't lose that famous cool."

"I'm writing a letter tonight to the county Public Works Department!"

"You do that, hon," pleased to momentarily regain the upper hand. "You tell them how upsetting their dip is to the Bowman baby."

Even Mark had to smile—realizing that on the subject of the baby's well-being, *he* was the one who'd gone overboard. Home on summer hiatus, he had been obsessively building baby furniture—a cradle and a playpen already, with a pair of Shaker-style rockers to come; this when he wasn't going through obstetrical texts in search of potential problems. Though she was just barely into her sixth month, in his wallet, just in case, he was already carrying the phone numbers of a private ambulance service and the hospital's labor, delivery, and emergency rooms.

The moment seemed to clear the air. He reached over for her hand. "All I mean," he said, "is let's not keep going on about Terry's death. That won't do anyone any good."

"I know that," she conceded. "Maybe you're right, I am feeling guilty. . . ."

"Don't," he said firmly. "It's not your fault. End of subject."

They drove in silence for a while.

"Think maybe we should get a Volvo?" he picked up suddenly. "It's the safest car on the road."

She smiled at him. Awkward as the shift in subject was, she appreciated the effort. "Good thinking, Mr. Rational. Except we can't afford one." She paused. "How about if I just sign into the hospital now?—that way I'm set for *any* emergency."

She was gratified to see him laugh. "It's just a *feeling*," he said, "all right?"

Twenty minutes later she looked up from her Power Book. "Mark, what's an antigen?"

The temperature hovered in the mid-eighties, the setting was out of an Impressionist painting: a small, secluded beach on Edwards-town Lake, dotted this brilliant afternoon with sailboats.

Flat on a beach towel in his bathing suit, Mark raised himself on an elbow. "An antigen?"

"Just something I'm looking into. You know me and science."

"Sal, we're here to relax. Come for a swim with me."

She indicated the billowy blue shift she wore over her one-piece "pregnant lady" bathing suit. "Not if there's anyone else within five hundred yards. You want the world to see you're stuck with a wife the size of Godzilla?"

He squinted at her. In fact, she was not nearly as large as she imagined herself to be. "I love the way you look. You've never looked more radiant."

"*Radiant*—a word that appears only in romance novels and pregnancy books! Don't tell me any normal, healthy man sees someone he wants to sleep with and thinks 'radiant'!"

"It's called biology, Sal. It gets us all in the end." He smiled. "Don't worry, I have it on good authority."

"Yeah, right, Montera's."

"Remember—no one's *ever* really prepared for a first baby."

Terrific, she thought, *he thinks it's funny.* That was something else he'd never understand.

"Ah, well," she said melodramatically, "I guess it's my arrogance catching up with me. I used to look at women who went on about this stuff as ridiculous, pathetic even. Having a baby was something *anyone* could do." She stopped. "Now I catch Lisa looking at *me* that way."

"Right, right," he said, trying to sound sympathetic.

"I was asking you the definition of an antigen."

"Why? What's this story about?"

She slipped her hand into the side pocket of her computer cover and produced a folded newspaper clipping. "This is by Paul Holland. He visited a longevity place down in Manchester, but it sounds like he went to Lourdes."

"Ah," he said noncommittally.

"That place is in our backyard. I think we should look into it." She stopped. "There's something there, I can smell it. It's not like Holland to turn himself into a shill for anyone."

Smelling now? the thought leapt to mind—but he resisted saying it. "Sal, I really don't think you could be objective about Holland even if you wanted to."

"Please, spare me another critique. It's hard enough to ask for your help."

He sighed. "Antigens are simply proteins that help cells function. Since these people are in antiaging research, they're probably working with something related to declining immune function."

"Good, thanks." She hesitated. "I've put in a request to visit this place. I'd like you to come."

"Are you kidding me? If you need company, take Lisa."

"I intend to—but that just gives us ignorance squared."

He smiled, knowing it was true.

"C'mon, Mark, don't make me beg. I don't know a thing about this stuff." She took his hand and placed it on her belly. "Never mind me—you really gonna let your daughter make a fool of herself in front of those scientists?"

It's not right," said Sally. "I shouldn't leave you alone."

"Please, darling, it's fine. I wouldn't say so otherwise."

"Yes, you would."

Mrs. Benedict smiled faintly, realizing it was true. "Anyway, I won't be alone. Lee Malen will be close by."

Sally nodded uneasily. This dilemma had come at her out of nowhere. Her mother's gallbladder surgery had been set nearly a month; the call from the director of the Life Services Institute came only yesterday.

"It's just that I'm totally at the mercy of their schedule," she explained, mostly to persuade herself. "If we miss this opportunity, there's no telling when we'll get another chance."

"Really, darling, all you'd be doing is sitting in the waiting room twiddling your fingers."

"I guess."

"So it's settled. Drink your milk."

"*Drink my milk.* My God, Mother, no wonder I still feel like a six-year-old around you." But she picked up the glass and raised it to her lips. "Why can't you worry about yourself for once?"

"Because you're the one having the baby. You'll find out yourself—a mother never *stops* being protective." Mrs. Benedict smiled across the kitchen table. "It's simple. You can drop me off at the hospital in the morning, do what you have to do, and come back afterward. Really, I'd feel guilty otherwise."

"Heaven forbid *you* should ever feel guilty."

"It's settled, then."

There was a long silence.

"Sally . . ."

"Uh-huh."

"Just in case—you do remember I want my body to go to medical science?"

"Mother!"

"I don't mean anything by it. But it's foolish not to make arrangements ahead of time. This is what we do in our family."

Sally looked away in consternation, then back across the table into her mother's placid eyes. "I swear, it's beyond me how you can be so casual about something like that."

"I'm not eager to die, but there's nothing terrifying about it. I saw my father die very peacefully when I was a little girl. I haven't been scared of it since."

"Well, forgive me, but I am." Sally put down her milk. "Mother, can I ask you something else? As long as we're on the Big Questions? Did you ever want to do . . . *other things* in your life?"

Mrs. Benedict got a wistful look.

"I don't mean that the way it sounds. It's just, I don't know, there's so much—you're a good writer, a talented artist. . . ."

"I also danced as a young girl, did you know that? That was my first ambition, to be a ballerina. I was quite good."

"No, I didn't."

"In those years there was a lady right here in Edwardstown who gave lessons to all the little girls—Mrs. Conley. But, no, I've always just been the girl with potential." Catching Sally's sympathetic look, she smiled. "Don't misunderstand, Sally, I'm not sorry. I'm not you, I don't think the same way."

"You really have no regrets at all?" The idea seemed almost beyond comprehension.

"Just one—that I didn't have more children."

Touched and a little embarrassed, Sally wasn't sure how to respond. "Is that a compliment? Or maybe I'm the reason you stopped after just one."

"Not everything revolves around you, darling, maybe someday you'll learn that. But, yes, you've made my life very rich."

"Thank you," she said simply.

"But you know something? Now even that regret is gone." She beamed, as radiant as Sally had ever seen her. "Now that you're making me a grandmother."

They reported to Edwardstown General a little after 7:00, three and a half hours before the scheduled surgery.

One of the advantages of the small community hospital was its relative informality. Malen had arranged to have Barbara Walker handle the preliminary screening—chest X-ray, cardiogram, and blood work—and the nurse happily bent the rules, allowing Sally inside the examining room. "After all"—she laughed—"it's never a bad idea having the editor of the newspaper owe you one." She winked. "You just be sure and let me know in advance if someone puts up a foldout couch for sale cheap."

Though Sally sometimes found the nurse's relentless good cheer hard to take, this anxious early morning it was just what she needed.

"How long will she actually be in the operating room?" she asked, while her mother changed into a hospital gown.

"Oh, no more than an hour and a quarter."

"I might not make it back in time."

"Don't worry about that, she won't miss you. The anesthetic

won't wear off for a few hours more." She smiled sympathetically. "Relax, this is basic meat-and-potatoes surgery."

"You know Dr. Crocker pretty well, I suppose?"

"Sure thing. He's real good in there." She paused meaningfully. "So don't you worry about that bedside manner of his. . . ."

She might have been reading Sally's mind. At their preliminary meeting the hospital's young chief of general surgery had been curt, answering their questions with little evident empathy.

"I guess Crocker's just not the kind of guy you expect to find in a place like this," as Sally carefully put it now.

"That's true. He's really just one of those yuppies. The man cares more about that little Mercedes sports car of his than I do about my kids." She laughed. "But I suppose not everyone can be in the business for the humanity of it."

Sure enough, when Crocker showed up a little after eight, he initially failed even to recognize Sally. His surgeon's game face in place, his only pressing concern seemed to be that things were running on schedule. She actually caught him checking over her mother's insurance forms before looking in on the patient herself.

Immediately, Sally made for Lee Malen's office. Her friend was at his desk, just settling in, a steaming coffee cup before him.

"Lee, I'm thinking maybe I shouldn't leave."

"Sally . . ." His tone was one of almost paternal bemusement. "I promise you, I'll stay on top of things. Frankly, at this point, I'd be more worried about the stress you're putting on yourself."

She considered that. "I'll leave you a number. You'll let me know if there's any problem?"

"If someone *farts* in that operating room, I'll see there's hell to pay!"

"Thanks, Lee. You're a better friend than I am a daughter."

He cupped his hands together, like the guy in the "good hands" insurance commercial. "Beat it, Sally. Go do your number on those longevity guys."

Opening the door, Ray Lynch showed his surprise. "Well, I didn't expect quite such a crowd."

"I hope that's not a problem," said Sally, who hadn't forewarned him for precisely that reason.

"Not at all, we're always ready to help out the press. You're Ms. Benedict?"

Initially caught short by her call, Lynch and Foster had quickly decided that denying her request for such a visit could only needlessly invite suspicion.

Indeed, given its timing, it might actually be turned into an opportunity.

"Yes. Lisa here works with me, and I asked Mark along to help us out."

"I'm the interpreter," he offered. "The science guy."

"You're in the field?"

"Not exactly. I teach science at our local high school." He stopped, then, in the interest of full disclosure, nodded at Sally, "I'm also married to the editor."

"Very nice. Keeping it in the family"—he smiled, ushering them inside—"which is obviously about to get larger. Sorry we had to do this on such short notice."

"Don't be silly, we appreciate your making the time."

He nodded. "Well, then, I thought we might start at our operational nerve center."

He led them through a hall and down a flight of stairs to a windowless, neon-lit room of perhaps forty square feet. Its sole occupant was a middle-aged woman in sweat clothes, busying herself with some incoming data from a fax machine.

"Mrs. Russo, these people are from a newspaper upstate. I'm sure Mrs. Russo will be pleased to answer your questions."

"Well," said Sally, "why don't you tell us what you do?"

"My training is as a nutritionist—and that's part of it. But as you see"—she indicated a table stacked high with periodicals and a half dozen filing cabinets against the back wall—"basically what I do down here is collect data. Research developments from elsewhere in the world, abstracts from industry and university sources, material from the literature or the Internet. If something catches my eye I pass it on to Dr. Lynch."

"You might be interested in knowing we also run across some very useful information in the popular press," noted Lynch. "Even— isn't this right, Mrs. Russo?—in the supermarket tabloids."

"Really?" said Lisa, surprised.

"For instance, the tabloids were onto DHEA *years* before it was taken seriously by so-called 'legitimate' researchers."

"What's DHEA?"

"A natural steroid secreted by the adrenal glands," said Mark who, as always, had done his homework. "There seems to be a link between falling DHEA levels and immune-system decline."

Lynch turned to him, ostentatiously impressed. "*Very* good."

"I have a question for you, Mrs. Russo—in your nutritionist's hat," he said, not wanting to show he was flattered. "What would be the ideal diet for my pregnant wife here?"

Sally flushed; for her the line between the personal and the professional was sacrosanct.

But Mrs. Russo answered without hesitation. "How far along are you?"

"Five and a half months," Mark answered for her.

"I'd recommend wheat germ, oat bran, and sweet potatoes on a daily basis, as well as cruciferous vegetables for glutathione."

"What about antioxidants and megadose vitamin supplements?"

Behind her placid smile Sally silently smoldered. Now it was just showing off; he knew damn well she'd sooner cash it all in than go on a diet of pills and rabbit food.

"Obviously," said the nutritionist. "Also E, C, A, beta carotene, whole vitamin B-complex, zinc, and selenium."

"Gonna remember all this, Sal?"

She nodded pleasantly, turning to Lynch. "But we don't want to keep Mrs. Russo from her work. Perhaps we could move on to some of the original research we've heard about . . . ?"

"You're the boss."

Several minutes later he led them into a large, well-equipped chemistry lab, dominated by a state-of-the-art rotary evaporator. Though there was work space for half a dozen, only one scientist was in view—a sallow young man with prominent cheekbones sitting at a lab bench across the room

"Do you like red peppers, Ms. Benedict?" asked Lynch.

"Yes . . ." she replied, wondering where this could be heading.

"Dr. Chugayev here comes to us from the St. Petersburg Institute of Advanced Chemical Studies. He's discovered some wonderful properties in red peppers. Tell our visitors."

Deliberately, the young man withdrew from his work station and got to his feet. "Two compounds I have isolated from this plant," he said soberly, his accent so thick they could scarcely make out the words, "both wonderful at scavenging free radicals. Already it leads to big increase of life expectancy. . . ."

Sally noted Mark's skepticism, which encouraged her own. A research chemist who gets his supplies at the supermarket is not what

Holland's piece had led either of them to expect! "How do you gauge that?" she asked.

"The animal model Dr. Chugayev has been using is lab mice," noted Lynch pleasantly. "I'm sure you'd like to see."

Mark nodded, his expectations aroused; he knew that if there is original research being done at such a facility, invariably it will be found in the animal lab. "That's what we're here for."

Surgery was delayed half an hour. A little past 11:00, Mrs. Benedict was wheeled into the hospital's main operating room. Within minutes young Dr. Downs was administering sodium pentothal by intravenous to induce unconsciousness; she followed this almost immediately with an injection of the paralyzing agent pancuronium, to relax the muscles during surgery. Now a mask was fitted to the sleeping woman's face. Throughout the procedure, in addition to oxygen, this would be a conduit for nitrous oxide and isoflurane to keep her resting comfortably.

It took less than ten minutes. Now, scrubbed and prepped, Crocker approached the patient, the target area isolated by sterile drapes on her skin, the skin itself treated by iodine antiseptic.

Since the young surgeon's arrival at the hospital a year and a half ago, traditional, slice 'n' dice gallbladder surgery was a thing of the past, replaced by the far less invasive laparoscopic cholecystectomy—using a miniature camera to operate within. In at least this one respect Edwardstown Community was proudly up with the times.

Momentarily, Crocker took stock, scalpel in hand, glancing around at the others in the room, the anesthesiologist, a scrub tech, and Barbara Walker, serving as the circulating nurse; then, with sudden decisiveness, made a one-inch incision directly beneath the umbilicus—belly button. Within seconds, through this he had poked a needle, not unlike that used to inflate footballs, feeling the accustomed pop as it pierced the abdominal wall. The needle was attached to a tube, the tube to a cylinder of CO_2. In short order, pumped full of gas, the cavity had expanded to create working room.

With great care, through the same incision, he now inserted the camera, affixed to the end of a rod and a mere centimeter in diameter. As he began manipulating it, sharp images appeared on the screen over the patient's shoulder, the liver, the large intestine, the gallbladder, all in extreme close-up. Brilliant deep red, pink, and aquamarine, to the untrained eye they might have called to mind slimy creatures in a fifties science fiction flick.

But to the surgeon this was territory as familiar as the room in which he worked. The camera guiding him from within to ensure he avoided vital organs, he now made three more small cuts along a line that would formerly have been the surgery incision. Through these he'd be able to introduce and extricate the camera and assorted instruments at will.

Everything was going beautifully, the very definition of routine.

"I could use a stretch," announced Dr. Downs, moving toward the door. "If I'm needed, someone just give a holler."

Mark found the animal lab disappointing. Aside from the mad Russian's red pepper research, the work done here seemed to consist of little more than replicating successful experiments conducted elsewhere. Impressive as it might strike a novice that finches fed a diet lacking the common amino acid L-methonine lived an average of sixty days longer than normal, or that hamsters raised on coenzyme Q showed heightened alertness in old age, he recognized it as old news.

Nor was Mark surprised to see that Sally, too, was growing impatient—and not only because she was so keenly aware of having to get back to Edwardstown. "This is all great," she finally put it to

Lynch, "but what we were hoping for was a look at the research Paul Holland wrote about. He certainly seemed impressed."

"Yes, well, no more than we were by him. Mr. Holland is a remarkable individual."

"We'd also love to meet Mr. Stagg," added Sally.

He shook his head regretfully. "I'm afraid not. As you know, Mr. Stagg's no youngster. He's allowed very few visitors."

"Tell me, what sort of repercussions have there been to Holland's article?"

"Repercussions?"

"No, no, that's the wrong word." She smiled sheepishly, an amateur in way over her head. "I mean, has it been helpful to you? Offers of government grants, anything like that?"

"I only wish it worked that way. No, I'm afraid not. Just a few calls from the media—but you people are the only ones we're cooperating with. Since you're in the area."

"If I may ask, what *is* the Institute's financial condition?"

"My goodness," he said, turning to Mark, "she does come right at you, doesn't she? Even Paul Holland didn't ask me questions like that."

"I'm sorry," seemingly ill at ease at having to ask, "I certainly understand if you choose not to answer."

"No, no, not at all. Thanks to Mr. Stagg we are very comfortably funded. Does that answer the question?"

"It does. Thank you." *Right,* she reflected, *and that's why the place is nearly empty. What kind of idiot does he take me for?*

"Okay," he said, "you asked for it. Next stop, the lab where we do some of our most advanced work."

The procedure continued to be entirely uneventful. Less than an hour into it Crocker clipped and secured the cystic artery, then the cystic duct. All that remained now was to sever and cauterize the connection with the liver, and the inflamed gallbladder would be literally suspended and ready for removal.

At this moment, in the recovery room, a vial of bupivacaine was being withdrawn into a syringe. A potent local anesthetic, with far longer duration than the more commonly used lidocaine, it would almost surely trigger arrhythmia leading to cardiac arrest.

The bags of normal saline solution, essential to the maintenance of fluids during the operative and immediate postoperative stages, were kept in a plastic container on a shelf near the bed. It was a simple enough matter, using the "port" at the lower left, to inject the colorless liquid directly into the top bag.

When healthy, the gallbladder is pear shaped and small, generally about four by six centimeters. But Mrs. Benedict's was grossly distended, and so unable to fit readily through the central incision. It was necessary to first cut it open and draw out more than a pint of golden-green bile with an aspirating catheter. When the organ finally emerged, it looked like a deflated balloon, a number of stones still loose at the bottom.

Checking and rechecking with the camera to ensure there was no internal bleeding, Crocker at last withdrew that too.

"I think we're about done here," he pronounced. "Let's bandage her up and get her to the recovery room."

When Lynch led them into the sprawling second-floor lab Sally no longer had to *play* dumb. Arrayed before them in the center of the room were a pair of machines so intimidatingly complex, she was momentarily left speechless.

But the sight brought Mark to life. "My God," he said, with a low whistle, "look at that!"

"Right," said Lynch, smiling, "this is the heart and soul of our operation." He nodded at the eight-foot column rising out of the floor, delicate silver tubing threading in an intricate spiral over its entire length. "We're especially proud of our high-pressure liquid chromatography unit. The design is unique—we're able to isolate the protein fragments we're after with complete precision. It's one of the things that most excited Mr. Holland."

"What about this other one? What does it do?"

"This spectrophotometer determines which wavelengths of light are absorbed by an object and in what quantity."

"Basically," volunteered Mark, "it 'reads' colors."

Sally shot him an exasperated look. "Any way you could put that into English?"

Lynch explained, "We use dyes to help us to identify DNA components that wouldn't otherwise be visible."

"Should I be writing this down?" piped up Lisa, assigned the task of taking notes.

"Go ahead." Lynch smiled at the attractive young woman. "Just warn me if I say something that makes me sound foolish."

"I will—if I understand it."

"I'd love to see this machine in action," observed Sally.

"Sure, why not?" Glancing around, Lynch spotted a beer bottle on the desk, then smiled at Lisa. "This part is definitely *off* the record—beer in the lab is a no-no."

He poured the dregs into a beaker. "Now, then, here we have approximately five cc's of beer. It's yellow, right? What the spectrometer will tell us is *how* yellow and clear. Watch. . . ."

Already Lisa's interest was flagging. Alert for something, anything, that might prove of interest, she allowed her eyes to casually wander from the messy desktop to the bulletin board above it, and back again. No good: everything was in the indecipherable foreign language of advanced scientific calculation, long and seemingly random assortments of numbers and letters.

But now she spotted something scrawled on a yellow legal pad—what appeared to be a list of phone numbers. Immediately, one of them leapt out at her. Chief Stebben's office number! It was at the very bottom, separated from the others by a blank space, accompanied by a notation—*Ck. locally.*

Excited but apprehensive, Lisa looked up quickly. Lynch was still busy with his demonstration, the others watching intently as he poured beer from the beaker into a thin plastic cylinder. "Now look what happens when I place this cuvette in the spectrophotometer. . . ."

Hurriedly, she began copying the numbers.

There were nine in all. She'd gotten down five when Lynch pushed the start button and the machine started to grind like a kitchen disposal unit. "Now, come closer, all of you, watch what happens to the light spectrum on the screen. . . ."

Flipping the page of her notebook, Lisa joined the others.

"So," asked Sally, forty minutes later, following similar demonstrations of two other equally baffling pieces of highly technical machinery, "all this will produce a cure for Alzheimer's?"

"I don't think Dr. Lynch intended it to sound so simple," said Mark. "We're talking about things no one has come close to understanding before."

"One hopes," said Lynch modestly. "But I'm afraid even that's still a long ways off. For now, the point is the knowledge itself. To most of us here this work is above all a quest to unravel the secrets of our environment. That's what makes it such an *adventure*."

"I see. So in a way you're sort of doing God's work."

"Oh, no," said Lynch, "I'd *never* presume to make such a claim. If you have to say anything, make it that we're trying to *understand* His work. For us that's more than satisfaction enough."

Sally didn't make it back to the hospital until past 3:30, a good hour and a half after she'd hoped to. As soon as she stepped off the second-floor elevator, she spotted young Jennifer Downs heading briskly down the hall.

"Dr. Downs," she called, and the anesthesiologist turned.

"The operation went well? Everything's all right?"

She seemed to hesitate, then nodded. "But you should talk to the surgeon"—and continued on her way.

Sally stood there a moment, confused and suddenly uncertain, then heard the familiar voice. "Just get back?"

"She's okay?" she asked, wheeling to face Barbara Walker.

"Perfect, she came through like gangbusters. C'mon, she's still in the recovery room."

"Jeez," muttered Sally, as they moved down the hall, "why couldn't Dr. Downs just tell me that? She gives me the creeps."

Knowing what she meant, Barbara laughed. "She's shy. I guess if you look like she does, you don't have to work real hard on charm."

Her mother lay in bed in the dimly lit room, sleeping peacefully, the only evidence of what she'd just been through was the IV pole hanging over the bed. Sally approached, leaned close, and whispered. "Mother, I'm here. . . ."

To her surprise Mrs. Benedict's eyes fluttered open and she smiled broadly. "Sally." Then, "I'm so tired," and her eyes closed again.

"She'll be groggy a couple of hours more," said the nurse, "but she did just great."

"You get some sleep now, Mother, I'll be here."

"Oh, she'll sleep, all right. That anesthetic leaves one heckuva hangover."

Sally looked down at her mother. "Actually, I should probably go talk to the doctor anyway."

"Crocker? Good luck—he finished and beat it out of here for a golf game."

"Well, I guess that means he's satisfied."

"Seems so."

"Was Dr. Malen in for the operation?"

"In and out, same as me. Don't worry, Crocker knew he was under surveillance."

"Maybe I'll go see him."

"He's out too. One of his patients is spotting, he didn't want her to move—you know how cautious he is."

Nodding, Sally glanced around the room. "I can wait in here with her?"

"Sure, we've got no other customers. Just put on one of these"— she offered her a mask from a tray. "But I can't tell you when she'll come to. Could be quite a while."

"No problem." She patted the bag that held her portable computer. "I've got work to do anyway."

As she headed from the room, the nurse glanced up at the bag hanging from the IV pole and noted it was still a third full. "Just ring me when she starts to wake up. She might be in some pain."

Over the next couple of hours Sally managed what would have been a full day's work at the office: editing two pieces and getting six hundred words into a draft of her story on the Life Services Institute.

Noting up top the favorable notice the facility had lately received from the respected Paul Holland of the *New York Herald,* the piece was a straightforward account of the day's visit; nowhere suggesting that Sally remained as baffled as ever by Holland's remarkable ardor.

"Ms. Benedict?"

Startled, she looked up. "Dr. Crocker. I was told you were out."

"Yes, I had a pressing engagement."

"So I gather everything went smoothly?"

"Very much so. But I'm sorry, Ms. Benedict, I've got to ask you to leave the recovery room."

"The nurse told me I could stay here, Doctor."

"I mean for just a few minutes." The upturned corners of his eyes over the mask suggested a thin smile. "I need to examine your mother."

Ten minutes later he approached her in the hall. "You may go back in. She seems to be doing fine."

By the time Mrs. Benedict awoke, the room was starting to go dark.

"Mother?"

"Sally . . ." she said groggily, scarcely above a whisper. "You've been here all this time?"

"What's a dutiful daughter for?"

"What time is it?"

She glanced at her watch. "A quarter of eight. You had a nice long sleep."

Taking off her mask, she kissed her on the forehead. "I'm supposed to call the nurse. I think she'll give you something to ease the pain."

"That would be nice."

From her mother this was like a primal scream for help.

"So you finally decided to wake up for us," said Nurse Walker, breezing into the room a moment later. "You caught me just in time. I was about to leave for the day."

"She says she's in some pain," said Sally.

"Well, we'll have to take care of that, won't we?"

Walker began to set up a morphine drip on the IV pole, then noticed that the bag of normal saline solution was nearly empty. Plucking up a fresh one from the container on the shelf, she put that in place first. "Say, miss," she said to Sally, "how long's it been since you ate?"

"A while," she answered vaguely.

"Nothing for you to do here for now—why don't you take a cafeteria break?"

"You haven't eaten?" asked her mother, as if this was cause for alarm. "What's the matter with you?"

"Mother . . ."

"Go right now—I won't be able to relax until you do."

Down in the cafeteria, Sally was pleasantly surprised by the quality of the roast chicken and peas that had been sitting for hours beneath a heat lamp. Except for the woman doing the serving and the one behind the register, plus a pair of doctors nursing coffees at a corner table, the place was deserted.

After a long, anxiety-filled day the interlude was unexpectedly soothing.

That could be why, picking at a plate of Jell-O half an hour later, she failed to immediately react when the words came crackling over the loudspeaker:

EMERGENCY TEAM, RECOVERY ROOM—STAT! EMERGENCY TEAM, RECOVERY ROOM—STAT!!

Only when the doctors across the way leapt to their feet and ran from the room did the realization hit—and then with chilling clarity.

She was actually aware of her heart starting to pound as she lurched out the door after them!

"I don't know what to say to you, Sally," said Lee Malen. "I don't have the words."

She looked at her friend, outwardly even more shaken than she. Though it had been more than an hour, she hadn't yet cried. Partly it was her innate stoicism, partly her reporter's training. But she also realized, her mind working overtime, that it could be shock.

Arriving on the heels of the emergency team, standing in the doorway as they'd worked frantically over her mother's prostrate form, a couple desperately administering drugs even as others tried to jolt her back by electric shock, she'd kept her eyes on the EKG monitor over the bed. Flat line. They were unable to even momentarily reclaim a heartbeat.

"Give me *something*, Lee," she said with sudden intensity. "What do you normally say? How do you help people through it?"

"I tell them not to be afraid to grieve." He searched her face. "But I can't pretend this is a normal situation, Sally. I loved her too."

"What about when it happens this way? So unexpectedly? Because I *need* an explanation." She paused, hardly able to get out the words. "I'm the one who made her have the operation!"

"No!" he said firmly. "Don't even think that! The operation was necessary!" He swallowed hard and blinked a couple of times. "Medicine is far from a perfect science."

"I need to know it wasn't just a matter of complete randomness." She hesitated. "Or negligence."

"Sally, honey . . ." His voice momentarily trailed off. "A woman this age . . ." He stopped again. "*You* saw her, she seemed fine."

"Everyone kept telling me she was!"

He held out his hands imploringly. "I thought so, too, Sally, otherwise I'd never have left. . . . She'd just undergone major surgery. It could've been any number of things."

"*What* things? Give me the possibilities!"

"A pulmonary embolism, that's the most likely explanation—a blood clot that dislodged from a lower extremity and lodged in the lung. Or a stroke—a blood vessel rupturing in the brain stem. That can be brought on by stressful surgery." He shook his head. "I suppose cardiac arrhythmia's a possibility. She'd been unhooked from the EKG, so that wouldn't have been picked up."

"You're saying this had nothing to do with the operation itself?"

"You know better than that, Sal," he said sadly. "Don't make it worse by looking to assign blame."

"I just wanted to hear you say it."

"I understand." He paused. "The only way to know for sure is if there's an autopsy."

"*If?*"

"That's your call, Sally. Your mother made quite a point of wishing to donate her organs. You can't have it both ways."

This hadn't occurred to her. "How useful would her organs be, anyway, a woman of her age?"

"That's not necessarily a problem. As you say, she was in generally excellent health. She didn't drink or smoke. The kidneys and liver should be fine, the corneas also."

"I'll need to discuss it with Mark." She hesitated and suddenly was choking back emotion. "I haven't been able to reach him, he doesn't even know."

Her friend took her hands in his. "Unfortunately, you're going to have to decide quickly. Organs for transplant are highly perishable."

She looked at him imploringly.

"You want to know what I would do?"

She nodded. "Please . . ."

"I don't think the details of how it happened would be very important to her; helping others would be."

She looked at him, reassured.

"You know what else? She'd tell us it was God's will."

"Thanks, Lee." She paused only momentarily. "What's the procedure? Are there papers I have to sign?"

Over two hundred people showed up at the Wednesday morning memorial service in Grace Church; almost everyone, Sally began to think, who had known Helen Benedict more than fleetingly. No fewer than a dozen approached her with stories about something her mother had once done for them. Many others, including some from whom she'd have never expected it, wept openly.

Then again, Father Morse was never better. Speaking without notes, the very size of the throng lending his words weight, he drew a contrast between this woman's impact on others and that of individuals who, in a status-obsessed culture, are so much more widely celebrated. "When we search for the definition of a successful life," he said softly, as Sally's own tears at last began to well, "God help any of us who look to Hollywood or Wall Street or Washington before we think of the woman we honor today."

"You okay, Gram?" asked Sally, in the backseat of the Impala as they pulled away from the church.

"It was very nice," came the even reply.

"There have been too many of these events lately," said Sally, looking back toward the cemetery. "Grandmother Avery, Mr. Giles, now Mother."

"Our relations. Our loved ones . . ."

Sally took the old woman's hand. She couldn't help but worry. Since the tragedy she'd been more disoriented than ever. "Gram . . ."

"Hmmm," she said, as if in a reverie.

No sense putting it off. She looked into her watery blue eyes, trying to get her to focus. "There's something we have to talk about."

Sally caught her husband, behind the wheel, looking in the rear-view mirror. "Mark and I would like you to stay with us. In our home."

For a long moment her grandmother continued to stare straight ahead and Sally wasn't sure she'd understood.

"Stay with you?" she asked finally.

"Permanently. We'd like that very, very much."

Sally was motivated by more than just a sense of obligation. She needed this frail, ninety-two-year-old woman at least as much as the other way around. She represented continuity, she was all the family she had left.

"I'll have to think about it," she said, suddenly all there. "I'm a big bother, you know."

"No, you're not"—she smiled—"just a small bother."

"I can still take care of myself."

"Gram, I'd like the baby to know you. It's important to me."

"To both of us," spoke up Mark.

The old woman considered for only a moment. "All right," she decided, and turned to stare out the window.

The task was more draining than any Foster had ever undertaken, six days of highly technical, demandingly precise grunt work. Even the most minute inadvertent slip would skew the results. Each step along the way had to be checked and rechecked before he could move on to the next.

But finally, by the end, he had what they'd so avidly sought for so long: a skin sample from this latest specimen had yielded the elusive gene's complete sequence, all 4,627 letters.

Studying it on the broad, translucent sheets disgorged by the X-ray developer, he and Lynch actually allowed themselves a celebratory hour or so, quietly sharing a split of champagne.

But in less than a day that moment of exultation was forgotten. For they discovered that this sample would NOT yield the other, equally vital data they had fully expected: that which would establish, even to the satisfaction of the venture capitalists, that the wondrous protein was active throughout the body.

Bent over the light table, Foster could only stare helplessly at the X-ray that told the baffling story. The film was segmented into fourteen distinct rows of colorful bands, running lengthwise like lanes in a bowling alley, each representing a different tissue sample: liver, kidney, lymph node, pancreas, bone marrow, peripheral nerve, ovary, lung, small intestine, large intestine, coronary artery, carotid artery, cerebrum, and cerebellum. Not even one of the bands showed the bright yellow streak consistent with the anticipated activity.

"It just can't be," said Lynch disconsolately. "We *know* she's got the ability to produce it, she's got the gene! Maybe if we run the test again . . ."

"That's not the problem," snapped Foster. "I've run it half a dozen times already." He paused. "The *ability* to produce a protein does not necessarily mean it always *is* produced, that's been Cooper's point all along."

"Then, that's it, we're screwed!!"

The younger man eyed him coolly, repelled by this new evidence of weakness. "Has it ever occurred to you the protein could be present in those tissue samples but somehow not active?"

"Do you think so?"

"That there could be some unusual genetic regulatory mechanism involved?"

"Ahh." There was some solace in this, but not much. At the very least it would mean a great deal more research, as they sought to unravel yet another mystery. "Ahh."

"But my strong suspicion is that it's something else. Certain genes are routinely repressed by other, more dominant genetic processes. If not, we'd have biological chaos." He paused, reaching for an example. "Hair being manufactured in the stomach lining, mucus being secreted from the fingertips. After all, *genetically* those cells possess the same potentialities as the ones that actually perform those functions."

Lynch shook his head. "Unfortunately, McIntyre and Reed want results, not an explanation."

"Let me finish! How long had the subject been dead before we started?"

"She died at about eight-thirty in the evening."

"And we didn't get the body till after three in the morning, correct? So these samples"—he indicated the film—"were obtained more than six hours postmortem. Think about it, Lynch—some human proteins are so unstable, they break down almost immediately. In *less* than an hour."

He looked at him hopefully. "You think so?"

"This possibility had been in the back of my mind for a while. That's always the problem, human biology is so much more complex than that of even closely related species. There's only one way to know for sure. . . ." He paused. "How close are we now?"

Lynch at him with sudden understanding. "Mid-December."

"Talk to our friends on the scene. Maybe we can even help nature expedite the process."

Lee Malen had been in Boston innumerable times, of course; most recently, just this past June for a convention at the Sheraton. But he'd been in the city's best hotel, the Ritz-Carlton, only once before, and then just for lunch.

Now, wandering through the lobby, all understated elegance, he felt a sudden, familiar wistfulness. Though practicing in Edwardstown had its compensations, at moments like this they were easy to forget. He was painfully aware that, had he chosen a career in Boston, or New York, or Chicago, he'd be a regular at places like this. Several of his classmates from med school, men with infinitely less skill and polish, had actually become known as pioneers in their fields. Others were minting money in bells-and-whistles oncology practices or big-ticket surgery. They owned country homes and regularly vacationed in Europe.

Well, he thought, maybe this was finally his shot.

Having arrived early, he wandered into the bar, paneled in dark oak. Though not much of a drinker, he ordered a Scotch and soda, and slowly leafed through the *Globe*. The drink failed to calm his nerves.

At last he walked to the elevator and rose in silence to the club level on the sixteenth floor. From up here the view of the Commons had to be spectacular.

When he knocked, the door swung open immediately.

Extending his hand, Paul Holland smiled. "Right on time. I always appreciate that in a colleague."

For nearly six months Sally had made almost no allowances for her condition. She maintained her normal pace, routinely staying up past midnight, ignoring the morning sickness and creeping fatigue.

But no more, not after all she'd endured lately. For the first time in her life she found herself constantly beat.

The sticky, end-of-summer heat didn't help. The week before Labor Day she was out each evening by nine; and even then had to shut down several times for a midday nap. Worse, her concentration was off, her mind wandering in all kinds of new directions.

But for the first time in her adult life, work now was secondary. Owed vacation time, she cut back her office hours to deal with the painful task most immediately at hand: clearing out her mother's home.

A week into the process she maneuvered herself to the top step of a stepladder, holding tight to the adjacent bookshelf for support.

"Lucky Mark's not here to see this," she called down to her grandmother, in an armchair across the room. "I hate to see a grown man in hysterics."

"Do be careful, Sally."

"I was an athlete, remember?"

She began moving books from the uppermost shelf to the now-empty one below.

"Hey, look at that!" Lying flat on its side was the family Bible. "I haven't seen this since I was a little girl."

Her grandmother squinted up at her.

Gingerly she lifted it—more than a foot across and eighteen inches high, a good four inches thick, it was heavier than she'd expected—and began carefully climbing down.

"It was probably the only spot Mother had where it fit," she mused, moving beside the old woman. "Want to look with me, Gram?"

"Not right now, I'm a little tired."

Sally wasn't surprised by the response; the depth of the old woman's continuing malaise was unsettling. Nodding, she placed a comforting hand on her shoulder. "That's us, fatigue central."

Acknowledging the little joke with the faintest of smiles, her grandmother struggled to her feet. "I'll just take my nap now. . . ."

As she shuffled from the room, Sally took her place in the chair and flicked on a reading light.

The volume gave off a musty odor. Studying its black leather cover, worn smooth with years of handling, Sally noticed that the spaces between the faded gold letters in the words HOLY BIBLE were slightly irregular and that the O was higher than the letters on either side; indicating they had been individually stamped in.

Carefully she opened it and found what she remembered. The notations began on the first flyleaf and continued, roughly in chronological order, over the three pages that followed: a record of individuals long gone and otherwise forgotten. Her forebears.

Once, with the smug certainty of adolescence, she'd thrown her mother's interest in family history up at her—*ancestor worship*, she called it, the province of those who looked backward because they didn't want to face the future. She herself didn't have to rely on inherited glory, she would achieve things on her own.

She smiled at the thought of all her mother had had to put up with.

Now, so many years later, she realized these people were as distinctly a part of herself as her fingerprints; they had shaped her grandmother, her mother, herself—and the being who would be her own daughter.

There were fifty or sixty entries in all. In some of the earliest the writing was faded and had turned reddish-brown, the iron that lent body to the primitive black ink having oxidized over time.

John Willson, read the very first, in a neat, highly formal hand. *Arrived Upon this Earth in Mildenhall Parish, Suffolk, England, 20 May, 1637. Gone to his Glory this Fourth Day of November, 1726, in Edwardstown Village. Amiable, Obliging, and Affectionate. Now he Dwells with Kindred Souls.*

Sally had heard of John Willson, of course: her first ancestor in the New World. A farmer who, after settling in what is now Massachusetts, was somehow led, through adversity or opportunity or happenstance long ago lost to family memory, to migrate to the wilds of New Hampshire.

Sarah Willson was the sum total of the next. *She Departed this Life on the Ninth Day of August, 1731, olde and full of Dayes.*

Now the name Willson disappeared; only one of John and Sarah's five children, a daughter, Sally, her long-ago namesake, survived to adulthood and she wed a certain William Hubbard. This was the surname listed most frequently over the next century.

In an era cruel beyond contemporary understanding Sally and William also lost most of their children early. These were listed together, without comment.

Jonathan, 1689
Abigail, 1693

Silence and Submit, 1699
Rachel, 1703
James, 1706

Reading down the grim list, composed in a female hand, gave her the creeps. She could only imagine the depth of despair the writer must have felt—or was it just fatalism?

No matter, this was not the time to dwell on such a thing. She flipped forward and read of an ancestor who'd taken part in the French and Indian Wars; then ahead to one whose fierce commitment to the antislavery cause had helped make Edwardstown a way station to Canada along the Underground Railroad; then on to her great-great-aunt Susan McKinney, once regarded as the family bohemian but now a source of pride. Though she never married, she became a leading suffragist.

The very last listing in the book was dated 1936. Her great-great-grandmother, Martha W. Avery.

After a moment she opened her purse and dug out the fountain pen Mark had given her for her birthday, the one she used for writing checks. For ten seconds she held it poised over the page. When she began writing, it was in a careful script unrecognizable to anyone accustomed to her usual haphazard scrawl.

Paul Morgan Benedict, September 14, 1918–February 5, 1992. Beloved husband and father. Caring, decent, and infinitely loving, passionate in his interests and passionately interested in others. He could not be more deeply missed.

Replacing the lid on the pen, she read over what she'd written, and was surprised to find the words a blur through eyes brimming with tears.

"C'mon, Benedict," she said aloud, drying her face against her sleeve, "you're gonna smudge the writing."

She took a deep breath and sat back in the chair. She smiled—all right, so it was pretty sentimental, so what? Again, she took the lid off the pen.

Helen Avery Benedict, March 29, 1924–August 19, 1996.
Heaven is a richer place, our home immeasurably poorer.

She read it over, this time with a sense of satisfaction. She knew if her mother could see it she'd be not just pleased but startled. Then, again—what a thought!—maybe she could.

Now she flipped back to where she'd stopped earlier, at the list of lost children. Immediately following was the entry for their father; and soon after, the one for their mother.

Sally Hubbard. November 25, 1654–July 12, 1753 Called to
glory in her 100th year. Her Troubles done, She rests in the
Farthest corner of our new Churchyard, Gazing for Eternity
Upon the Vestry Door.

Sally stared at it, the wheels beginning to turn, rereading the words: *the Farthest corner of our new Churchyard.*

But, no, it couldn't be, her imagination had to be getting the best of her. No question, the churchyard mentioned was Grace Church; of that the timing left little room for doubt. And the first pilfered grave was indeed only a short distance from the vestry door. But the farthest corner of the yard? Not a chance—the cemetery extended a good half acre beyond, with dozens of other graves situated around the perimeter.

Still, before closing the Bible, Sally copied down the entry on a yellow legal pad.

She knew herself too well to expect she'd simply leave it at that.

The medical reporters began arriving in the small auditorium at the FDA's Rockville, Maryland, headquarters a half hour before the start of the meeting. As always, the more aggressive among them grabbed seats in the front where it would be impossible to be ignored by the experts fielding questions; and, more importantly, if the meeting made it onto C-Span, by their editors.

By the time the members of the panel assumed their places at the front table, the reporters had been joined by two hundred or so other interested observers—high-level medical personnel, representatives of biotech outfits, stock market analysts and prominent investors.

Dr. Eric Cooper remained standing at the back of the room, just inside the door, positioned for a quick retreat. His bosses had long ago instructed him never to expose himself, win or lose, to public scrutiny.

There were seven members of the panel, three on either side of the sober, heavyset man in black-rimmed glasses chairing the gathering.

Now the chairman seized the audience's attention with three sharp taps of his index finger on his microphone and peered around the tall stack of paper that someone had unaccountably placed directly before him.

"Good afternoon, ladies and gentlemen," he began in the sort of monotone, aimed at conveying disinterested nonpartisanship, so common to those adept at bureaucratic infighting. "My name is Dr. Whitney Hull, I am the assistant deputy commissioner of the Food and Drug Administration. It has been my privilege to serve as chair of this advisory panel."

Briefly, gazing first to the left, then the right, he introduced his colleagues: the principal FDA regulator on the project; his boss, in charge of the entire cadre of FDA regulators; two independent, outside authorities—professors of medicine, one male and one female, both presumed to be squeaky clean from a conflict-of-interest standpoint, with specialties in infectious diseases and pulmonary medicine; and a pair of investigators from the FDA's Regulatory Affairs Division.

Among these last was Carl Porter. Deputy Commissioner Kennally was elsewhere in the building, monitoring the proceedings via closed-circuit television.

The chairman paused, looking meaningfully around the room, and placed his hand on the stack of papers.

"As you know," he continued, in the same flat voice, "we are here to assess the results of three years of randomized, double-blinded phase-three clinical trials of Alcumine, developed by Cytometrics, Incorporated. This product is designed to ameliorate or reverse the effects of septic shock in critically ill patients in intensive care units. These trials have involved a cohort of two hundred and sixty-one patients, primarily at the University of Iowa under the auspices of Dr. Daniel Brooks. Following my remarks all of us on the panel will be available to entertain your questions."

For all the calculated blandness of the presentation the tension in the room had built almost beyond the breaking point. Like relatives of a defendant awaiting a verdict in a capital case, a number of investors sat literally on the edge of their seats. In the back, hands deep in pockets, Cooper stood immobile, eyes fixed on the points of his shoes, unable to even bring himself to watch.

The chairman paused a moment, drumming his long fingers on the pile of documents. "It is the finding of this panel that the data that has been produced during the course of this trial is reasonable and believable. This data is accepted without dissent."

He stopped again, his eyes briefly scanning the room. "On the basis of this evidence we find that the drug demonstrates no substantial efficacy either in improving the quality of life in septic patients, or in their survivability."

Instantly, there was the hum of competing, whispered voices—shocked, angry, exultant.

"Indeed, the data suggests that in some cases administration of this product may provoke marked deterioration in the clinical condition of such patients."

In the back Cooper merely shook his head. No one noticed him mouth the single word as he turned away. "Bullshit."

The chairman continued in the same vein for several minutes before he spoke the sentence everyone knew was coming. "On the basis of our findings market approval of this agent is denied."

Cooper was long gone by the time he opened the floor to questions.

"You're saying this drug might actually accelerate the shock process in sepsis?" came the first. "Could you be more specific?"

"There appears to be at least some data pointing to that conclusion. In one case, for instance, involving a farmer with a work-related injury, autopsy evidence indicated he was septic as a result of an anaerobic organism. It is likely that with appropriate conservative management—fluid resuscitation and antibiotics—the patient would have survived. Unfortunately, it appears that in attempting to modulate septic shock, the drug in fact modulated the body's natural healing response."

"Are you suggesting there might be grounds for lawsuits here?"

In his office, fourteen floors above, Deputy Commissioner Kennally broke out in a grin.

"I have no comment on that. That is not within our purview."

Melissa Reed took the news far better than her husband. Nothing surprised her about these bastards anymore, she told him—they were determined to stick it to M & R even if it meant screwing desperately ill people in the process.

While McIntyre retired to bed that evening with a blinding headache, she went directly to her study.

The first call she placed was to Raymond Lynch.

"**A**lbany Union Medical College, Department of Anatomy. To whom may I direct your call?"

Hunched over her desk, Lisa hesitated. She'd had no idea what she'd find on the other end of the line when she dialed the number; the first on the list she'd run across at the Life Services Institute.

This whole thing was a shot in the dark. All she had at this point was intriguing questions: What on earth was the telephone number of Edwardstown's police chief doing in the research laboratory in Manchester? What was the meaning of the cryptic notation that followed? But they did give rise to an obvious suspicion. Had Stebben been hired by this outside organization to run background checks on hometown journalists (and longtime adversaries) in anticipation of their visit? If she could prove it, the story would make a big splash locally; the bully cop versus the hard-driving women reporters. It might even cost Stebben his job.

And it would be all hers. This time there was no way Sally Benedict would be able to take credit.

"Actually, I don't have a specific name," she told the operator, with calculated chagrin. "I'm hoping you can tell me."

"Pardon me . . . ?"

"I'm with the Life Services Institute in Manchester, New Hampshire . . . ?" She waited just an instant, but the name elicited no response. "We've been conducting research in coordination with you people."

"Yes . . . ?"

"I'm supposed to get some figures for a colleague who's out of town—he left me your number but neglected to leave a name."

Her disinterest couldn't have been more pointed. "I'd be unable to direct you to your party without more information."

Already, the young reporter was mentally moving on, eyeing the next number on her list. "Thank you, I'll have to get back to you with that."

Department of Anatomy. It was a start—even if it didn't obviously compute. Where was the connection with Stebben?

The next area code listed was 718—one of New York City's outer boroughs—and, since the number ended with three zeroes, it was even less promising.

"Albert Einstein College of Medicine."

"I believe I want the Department of—"

"Speak up!" came the impatient reply.

"Yes, the Department of—"

"I can't HEAR you."

"The Anatomy Depart—"

But she heard the click before she could complete the sentence.

New York City! she thought and, immediately redialing, assumed an air of command. "Give me the Department of Anatomy."

"Anatomy, Dr. Seidenstein's office."

"Is he in?"

"Who is this?"

"I'm with the Life Services Institute. We've had some dealings with Dr. Seidenstein."

"Name?" She sounded skeptical.

"Sheila Adams." The alias was a very private joke; her overbearing tenth-grade homeroom teacher, who'd assured her she'd never amount to anything. "Would he be available?"

"No, *she* is not in."

"I see."

"I'm the doctor's assistant, I make her schedule. I've never heard of you or of this institution of yours. I don't know what you're selling, but I don't appreciate being lied to."

Caught short, Lisa wilted; her charm had never worked nearly so well on women. "Actually, I'm just trying to track down some information. . . ."

But looking up, she spotted Sally coming through the office door and slammed down the receiver. By the time the editor reached her desk, she was earnestly pecking away at her keyboard.

"Back so soon?" asked Lisa.

"You know me, can't stay away."

Lisa snorted—some days lately, Sally hadn't come in at all, issuing orders by phone.

Sally peered over her shoulder at the story on the screen. "Looking good."

"Hey," she said sarcastically, "with a subject like this, how could it miss?"

The story was on pumpkin farming. With an eye toward shoring up the *Weekly*'s finances, Sally had decided to take advantage of the late summer lull to put together a special ad-driven supplement for October to be called "Edwardstown: Autumn Delights." Heavy in yellow and red hues, it would feature just enough legitimate material on trout fishing, hiking, and local sights to draw in restaurateurs and manufacturers of hiking boots.

Unavoidably, most of the writing fell to Lisa—a major new source of irritation in the younger woman's growing catalog of resentments.

"Sally," she said, with sudden intensity, "we've got to talk."

"About pumpkins, I hope."

"It's not right, I've been doing a *lot* more than my share around here. . . ."

Sally nodded. "That's true. I wish I had the budget to give you a raise, but I don't. Maybe next year—if you're still here."

Lisa looked at her in surprise. Though she hadn't hidden the fact she was sending out her resume, never before had it been directly acknowledged.

"I can't blame you for it," noted Sally. "In your place I can't say I wouldn't do the same." She paused. "How's it going?"

No way she was going to admit to Sally, of all people, that to date all there'd been only a couple of interview offers—a copyediting job in Johnstown, Pa., and a slot at the suburban desk in Buffalo. "Okay, it's early."

"You've got talent, Lisa," said Sally, moving off. "You need a recommendation, just ask. . . ."

Well intended as the words were, to Lisa they sounded like condescension. As soon as Sally closed the door to her office, without so much as a moment's forethought, she grabbed the phone and punched in the next number on her list.

"Yep," answered a youngish male voice after a single ring.

"Is this (212) 555-3670?"

"Who wants to know?"

"My name is Lisa Mitchell. I'm trying to reach the Department of Anatomy."

"You got it, Lisa Mitchell. What can I do for you?"

"And you are?"

"Barry Schneider. Think of me as the sad sack around here who has to answer his own phone."

"You're a doctor?"

"That's what my mother likes to tell people. Why, you looking to meet one?"

Lisa could hardly believe her good fortune; *this* was a situation she could handle. "Depends," she replied in kind. "How old are you?"

"Uh-uh, you're the one calling me—you first."

"Twenty-two."

"Twenty-eight. Free for a drink later?"

They both laughed.

Lisa glanced at Sally's closed door. "I'm afraid it'll have to be *much* later—I'm 350 miles away."

"Oh?" He actually sounded disappointed. "Where's that?"

"Someplace you never heard of—Edwardstown, New Hampshire. I'm with a newspaper here."

"Sure, I have, it's up near Union. I went to med school up at the University of Maine, I used to drive through that area."

"Ah. Mind if I ask you something?"

"Shoot."

"What's your connection with the Life Services Institute?"

"With *what*?"

"It's an antiaging research center down in Manchester. I'm working on a story—your number was on a list they've got over there."

"*Really?*" He paused, intrigued. "Who else is on it?"

"As far as I can tell, it's all medical schools. Departments of anatomy."

"I can't see that anything we're doing would interest anyone in that field."

"How long have you been working there?"

"Here?"

"Right."

He paused. "You don't have any idea *where* I am, do you Lisa Mitchell? You're just winging it, aren't you?"

She smiled before answering. "Hey, sometimes a girl gets lucky."

"I'm at Columbia Presbyterian—we're affiliated with Columbia University."

"Doing what, exactly?"

"There are four of us junior guys in the department. We pretty much run the first-year anatomy curriculum."

"Which consists of . . . ?"

"Oh, mainly preparing lectures—there's a whole lot of data that needs to be implanted in those empty brains. Then, there's the standard first-year course in gross dissection, otherwise known as 'bellies and bones.' I get to do lots of cutting." He laughed. "Of course, I'm also the guy that gets stuck with shipping and handling of the merchandise."

"The dead bodies?"

"Please, *specimens*."

"Where do the bodies come from?"

"You are inquisitive, aren't you? Mainly the Midwest. Racine, Wisconsin—the company's called International Medical Services. We prefer our cadavers plain spoken but polite."

She jotted this down on a notepad. "Jeez," she said, with a laugh, "what a topic for our first phone date. Well, Dr. Schneider . . ."

"Barry. Is that what we're having here, a date?"

"Thanks, Barry, you've really helped me out."

"That's it? We're done?"

"Who knows," she said coyly, "I might call again."

"That's not fair—don't I get *your* number?"

"Count on it—I'll be looking for a reason."

Two minutes later she was on the phone to Wisconsin. Everything Schneider had told her checked out. According to a technician for International Medical Services, they functioned essentially as middlemen; each day receiving dozens of fresh corpses from throughout the upper Midwest, carefully repackaging them, and moving them out for next-day delivery to laboratories and medical schools throughout the United States and Canada. The technician also volunteered, in the event it might be of interest to her readers, that they were often able to fulfill special orders, providing customers with victims of particular diseases.

But he was very sorry, he told her—he wanted to be helpful, but he had never heard of the Life Services Institute either.

Even when Sally was a child, her mother's friendship with Ellen Bryson struck her as odd. As the area's leading real estate agent, selling vacation homes to couples from Boston or New York, Ellen was every bit as sophisticated as her clients; hair and makeup in place and done up in Anne Klein, she seemed to belong at Broadway matinees and tony restaurants instead of junior high school musicals and church suppers.

Only now, watching Ellen's stricken look as she gazed about the bare living room, did she understand how strong the bond had been.

"I'd rather not handle the sale personally, if you don't mind," she said softly. "This was always the warmest house in Edwardstown. It's just hard for me to see it this way."

"For me too," said Sally. "I guess I always kind of took it for granted."

Ellen's smile was sympathetic. "Well, it's probably easier from the outside than actually *living* with a saint—as I seem to recall from your adolescence."

Sally smiled. As a close friend of Ellen's daughter Elaine in those years, more than once she loudly proclaimed her preference for the Bryson home over her own.

"What did you do with the furniture?"

"Some of Gram's stuff went to our house and the dining room set's in storage. Otherwise . . . let's just say the Salvation Army owes me big time." She shrugged. "I tell you, clearing this place was like an archaeological dig into my personal history. I couldn't believe how much she'd kept. My first doll! Every report card! My sixth-grade band uniform!"

"I'm not surprised. You were everything to her."

Sally nodded. "Not what I needed—it made me feel even guilt-ier."

"Guilty? What for?"

"I pushed her into that surgery, Ellen!"

"Don't be ridiculous. She told me herself Lee Malen was ada-mant."

"I don't know, I just feel if I'd been there that day, for the opera-tion itself . . ."

"Sally, you *know* that's crazy!"

"So Mark keeps telling me. He really thinks I'm losing my mar-bles." She smiled wistfully. "Speaking of which, can I ask you some-thing? You've done some work with genealogy, haven't you . . . ?"

She nodded. "And you'd be amazed how often I hear that ques-tion from people closing up a childhood home. It's natural to start thinking about family history. Even therapeutic—it energizes some people, helps them get back on their feet."

Sally smiled, slightly embarrassed; always a stiff-upper-lipper, she'd never before thought of herself as *needing* therapy. "I actually spent an hour the other afternoon wandering around the graveyard, trying to pinpoint one of my ancestors' graves."

But Ellen only nodded approvingly. "That's a very good place to start. Any luck?"

She shook her head. "I was trying to guesstimate from a notation I found in the family Bible."

"Well, I hope you're planning to pursue it. How much do you know about these ancestors of yours?"

"Not very much, I'm afraid. Their names, when they lived and died, sometimes their professions."

"There are no relatives who can help out?"

"The only one who's really into it is my aunt Mary down in Florida, and she's on my father's side. I doubt she knows much more about this other bunch than I do." She shrugged. "Any thoughts?"

Ellen smiled. "If you were a real estate person instead of a reporter you wouldn't even have to ask. The county bureau of records is a rat's nest—you'll be amazed at what you can find there."

Though Dr. Cooper shook his hand at the door, it was Melissa Reed, inside the room at the conference table beside her husband, who spoke. "Nice to see you, Dr. Lynch."

He walked in and nodded. "Thanks."

God, how Lynch had despised these people! Their arrogance! Their casual duplicity! For six months he'd been hearing the same song: this was a *bottom line* proposition, they had to see more data, *better* data, before they came through with the promised cash!

In the week since the phone call from Reed, he'd more than once conjured up this scene, imagining himself telling them to go straight to hell. But now that he was here, what he was feeling most of all was . . . intimidated. That was the worst of it; despite everything these people remained their only option.

"We appreciate your coming down on such short notice," said Reed.

"Actually, I have no idea what I'm even doing here."

"You're here because we wanted to see you," snapped McIntyre, who, for all his bravura, looked like he hadn't slept in a week.

His wife shot him a look. "I hope it wasn't too great an inconvenience."

"Well, it does seem to me we could talk just as easily by phone. I'm spending a whole day traveling back and forth when I could be in the lab."

"Apparently, Dr. Lynch, you don't fully appreciate our situation."

"Our goddamn phones aren't secure," said McIntyre. "Probably not yours either."

"I find that hard to believe. I know you took a hit, but—"

"Sure you do. You're used to being ignored up there in the boonies."

"Our concerns are real, Dr. Lynch," added Reed, her voice suddenly hard. "We're fighting for our lives. There are people working to destroy us—people in the government and our own industry. *Do you understand?*"

Lynch looked at her, then nodded slowly.

"They have been encouraged by recent events. Our job is to disappoint them. M & R is going to come back bigger than ever. Whatever it takes."

"That's good to hear," said Lynch, lamely.

Reed looked to her colleagues, then back to the visitor. "You want to know why we brought you here?"

He nodded. "Please."

"Under the circumstances we find ourselves having to downsize—our resources are no longer what they were. Which means we must make some hard choices."

So that was it!

Instantly, whatever confidence Lynch had retained melted away, replaced by rising panic. "Look, I know you haven't seen results as quickly as you'd like."

She held up her hand. "Dr. Lynch, I'll be blunt: we're cutting off funding to all those projects where we feel there is no prospect of a significant, short-term return."

"That's most of the companies we've been backing," said her husband.

"You're not the first manager of a promising enterprise we've seen this week," added Reed. "In fact, you're the last."

"May I say something?" tried Lynch, desperately. "Part of the problem is we've been so badly undercapitalized."

"That's true," agreed Reed, "we accept the responsibility for that. But you should know you weren't singled out."

"I'm not blaming you. But we've tried to stretch every dollar. We've laid off staff, we've bought equipment secondhand—"

"You won't have to do that anymore," Reed cut him off.

"What I'm saying is that we've made tremendous progress, even so—"

"Dr. Lynch, please . . . I'm trying to tell *you* to relax." Reed gave a small smile. "We are putting all our eggs in one basket, and you're it."

Lynch stared at her, scarcely daring to comprehend.

"The contracts are prepared to be signed today. You'll leave here with a check in the amount of two million dollars." She paused. "That's an initial payment. If you can produce the breakthrough Dr. Cooper tells us about, funding will be virtually unlimited."

Lynch turned to Cooper with astonished gratitude, then back to his bosses.

"But," added Reed, "the clock is running, we need it *yesterday*."

"What's your time frame, Dr. Lynch?" demanded McIntyre. "When can we have something?"

He hesitated. "I'd say we could have a drug ready for clinical trials within a year. Of course, at that point the FDA would have to—"

"Never mind that," he snapped. "We're not looking for a perfect product, just a marketable one."

"We plan to start by marketing abroad only," said Reed blandly. "In South America." She paused. "Incidentally, Professor Cooper tells us this research could potentially yield other products unrelated to Alzheimer's. Possibly antiaging drugs. Naturally this agreement will cover these also."

Lynch looked at Cooper in surprise.

"But, again," she continued, "the main issue is timing."

Lynch's head was spinning. "Partly that's beyond our control. As Dr. Cooper has pointed out, before moving to human consumption, we must establish uniform activity throughout the body—"

"We're not interested in technical problems. *When?*"

"We're waiting for vital genetic material that's not yet available."

"How long?!"

He considered momentarily. "Four months, maybe a little less."

"Make it less." She paused. "What about Dr. Foster? He's on the same page as you on all this?"

After all they'd been through, this bounty was almost too much to grasp. "Don't worry, Foster's a few pages ahead of us all."

Sally's regular checkup—weight, blood pressure, urine sample—was every second Tuesday morning at eleven-thirty, and she and Malen had turned it into a quasi-social occasion. After he gave her the standard good news—A-OK, both mom and kid growing normally—they had lunch at the Clover Patch and caught up; and after *that*, she sometimes accompanied him back to the office and hung out, sipping tea and reading magazines in his study, so they could chat between patients.

"So . . ." he asked today, seemingly as an afterthought, "settled on a name yet?"

"Helen. After Mother."

"I was hoping you would!"

"Good, Lee," she joked, genuinely touched, "that was our main consideration." She paused. "I shouldn't tell you this, but you're also running pretty strong in the godfather sweepstakes."

Yet just a few minutes later, alone in his study, a copy of *McCall's* open on her lap, she was intensely sober, as her thoughts wandered once again to the mysteries of her family's past.

Just last night she'd spent a good hour on the phone with Aunt Mary down in St. Petersburg. As she'd expected, Mary had little to add to what she already knew of the Hubbard/Avery clan. But toward the end, when she casually raised Carlton Giles, expecting her to dismiss out of hand Gram's curious remark, after her daughter's memorial service, about some kind of family link, there came instead from the other end of the line a long silence. "Yes," she said, "I seem to recall something about that. Just a rumor, of course—these things aren't to be taken literally. . . ."

"About his being adopted?"

"About that crazy old great-aunt of your mom's *giving up* a baby."

Now, in Malen's study, it struck her that the proof might be right in front of her. A few years back, when she was writing a piece on this extraordinary practice, Malen showed her a treasured piece of memorabilia—the appointment books of his long-ago predecessor, Everett Greiner; a virtually complete record of his nearly forty years serving the Edwardstown area. Leather bound in several volumes, they were in the antique book cabinet just across the room.

In with a patient, Malen would probably be a while—and she knew he kept the key to the cabinet in the jar of paper clips in his rolltop desk, also once Greiner's. Surely he wouldn't mind, it would only take a moment; the record was chronological and she needed only to check out a single date: April 4, 1911—according to Carlton Giles's gravestone, the day he came into the world.

In fact, struggling up from the soft leather couch was more difficult than locating what she wanted, the volume covering 1905–1914, and she judiciously decided to remain on her feet while studying it. Placing it on the desk, she flipped it open and in a matter of seconds found the date in question.

Nothing. No entry for the day at all; the Saturday before Easter, he evidently took it off. "Egg roll on lawn, all present—glorious!" she read the notation for the following day, in his surprisingly neat hand, and smiled.

She was about to replace the book when something occurred to her. Records back then, especially in rural areas like this one, tended to be spotty; not Greiner's, but those of the sort of charitable institution or primitive social service agency that would have handled an adoption. It was not beyond imagining that the date of Giles's adoption had been recorded as his birth date; or even that, lacking formal documentation, someone had simply assigned him a birth date arbitrarily.

To provide for such a possibility, she flipped the book open to the start of the year 1911. Most of the entries were just a line or two; perhaps a quarter had to do with home deliveries. Generally, these listed the names of the parents, the newborn's sex and weight, and a few particulars about the labor or birth. For brevity's sake the most frequently repeated terms were abbreviated: *chl.* for chloroform, *NSVD* for normal spontaneous vaginal delivery, *sb.* for stillbirth.

Clearly, some of the tales recorded in this emotionless shorthand had been unbearably tragic; a number of others made her smile. "Patient irrational," read one, "suffering acute pregnancy dementia"—and she couldn't help but think of how much Mark would love to get his grubby hands on the phrase.

But suddenly, there it was! Or, at least, *seemed* to be. March 4— a month to the day before the official birth date.

Longer than most, this entry was also less precise.

4 Mar, '11: Mother: Miss M. Father: unknown. Called to family home appx. 7:30 P.M., Miss M. in E-twn. for confinement. Difficult labor. NSVD. Healthy boy, 6'14"

The evidence was sketchy, the very definition of inconclusive. But her gut was churning and she had no doubt: it was Susan McKinney, the suffragist who left Edwardstown for New York! Her great-great aunt!

And that baby was Giles!

By the time Malen returned, the book had been back in the

locked case fifteen minutes. Her friend was in good spirits, and the banter between them was as lively as ever.

But something—she didn't know what, exactly—kept her silent about her discovery. Or maybe she did know and couldn't yet face it: after all that had happened these last months, she was no longer sure she could fully trust *anyone*.

The coincidence was a fortunate one for Lisa: not only wasn't Sally around to keep tabs on her, but Tuesday, she remembered, was also Stebben's day off.

As she'd expected, she found the chief in his garden—still gaudy this warm fall day with goldenrod, New England asters, and immense sunflowers—in a pair of baggy coveralls and straw hat, holding a watering can. She was reminded of the illustrations of Mr. McGregor in the old Peter Rabbit book she'd had as a kid.

"Beautiful," she said, coming up behind him.

He turned. "I try. Nice thing about flowers, they never talk back."

Lisa glanced around. "Hard to believe it's been nearly a year since I was last here. It's changed."

"So have you."

"Think I've grown up?"

"Or something." He stood, removed his hat, and wiped his brow. "What can I do you for, little girl?"

"No chitchat today, Chief?" She smiled, more nervous than she let on; never before had she confronted so forceful a figure with potentially damaging information.

"Lisa, I'd be real surprised if this turns out to be a social call."

She looked at the ground, then back at the tanned face, damp with perspiration. "What can you tell me about the Life Services Institute?"

He visibly flinched. "The *what*?"

"It's a research place downstate," she said breezily, emboldened by his reaction. "They seemed to know about *you*."

"Never heard of it."

She showed confused consternation. "Funny, your name was on a list. With your phone number. And the words *check locally*. What do you suppose that could mean?"

"I can't help you, little girl," he said, turning away to examine a cluster of pale-blue phlox.

He remembered the call vividly, of course. Lynch wanted to know if there might be some information somewhere about where old Mrs. Avery's body had been shipped back in the thirties. *For Chrissakes*, he'd told him, *how the hell would he know something like that?! And more: This wasn't part of the deal! They'd gotten their damn stiffs and that should be that!*

If he'd come off as harsh, he wasn't sorry. He was still reeling from the death of that poor boy—and the disappearance of his friend.

Lisa walked around a huge sunflower to face him. "I was just wondering if maybe they had some questions about *us*—Sally Benedict and me."

"Is that it—she sent you here with this nonsense?!"

"She has no idea. This is MY story."

"I don't know who they are, and they sure as hell didn't call me. And if they did, I'd have nothing to tell 'em. I don't inform on people in this community—not even my enemies."

She nodded. "I can quote you on that?"

He glared at her. "What, try and imply something by printing my denial? No, damn you, this is all OFF the record."

She stood there a long moment, not knowing what to say next. "Well, then, I guess I'll just have to keep digging."

"I wouldn't do that. Not everyone handles slander as well as me."

"Why, Chief"—she smiled almost mockingly as she turned away—"I didn't know you still cared. Thanks anyway."

He looked after her as she turned and picked her way through the garden. "You watch yourself," he said, but not loud enough for her to hear.

Sally had planned to wait till after the birth before making the trip to the Bureau of Deeds and Records; Montgomery, the seat of Sussex County, was nearly an hour from Edwardstown on two-lane roads through the foothills of the White Mountains.

But after her discovery in Malen's office she felt a new sense of urgency. She made the trip just two days later.

The bureau was housed in an intimidatingly bleak three-story red brick structure, formerly a hospital, dating to the Victorian era. But inside the place proved to be well lit and surprisingly inviting, and the elderly woman behind the counter actually seemed delighted to hear that Sally was seeking information on the early days of Grace Church in Edwardstown.

"Oh, I've been inside that church, it's absolutely lovely."

"It's our local parish. I've been going since I was a kid."

"You're with the local historical society? We get a lot of those."

"Yes, I am." A spontaneous, pointless lie.

"And when are you due, dear?"

"In a couple of months. I'm about thirty-one weeks now."

"Well, then, I should go down there with you in case something has to be moved. Some of those file boxes are awfully heavy."

Sally felt more than a little foolish trailing down a flight of steps behind her grandmotherly protector; and was grateful, after they'd picked their way through several aisles, to find the one where they stopped free of impediments. On either side, to a height of ten feet, stacks of bound records loomed ominously. A line of gray metal filing cabinets stood at the far end of the aisle.

"Now, then," said the woman, "this is the general area to begin looking." She indicated the bound volumes, on the shelves in no apparent order. "Fortunately, thanks to a grant from the New England Historical Society back in the eighties, we were able to transfer many of our records from that period to microfilm." She indicated the filing cabinets. "Do you know how to use microfilm, dear?"

Only since she was eight years old. "Yes, I do, thanks."

Starting with a reel labeled *Sussex County, 1670–1700,* she quickly saw there was little order to the microfilmed material either. A 1693 marriage certificate followed a document recording an unrelated death four years earlier; which was followed by a bill of sale for a small farm and the particulars of a lawsuit involving ownership of a gristmill.

Still, slowly spooling through the reel, Sally found herself transfixed, transported into the daily doings of that lost world. For much of the afternoon she indulged her curiosity, picking up reels almost at random and threading them into the machine; discovering in each a treasure trove of engaging, amusing, or unexpectedly moving material. Who could've guessed that there had once been notices around here for runaway slaves? Or that a local phrenologist, thought to be highly skilled at diagnosing illnesses via the feel of the bumps on customers' heads, had once charged a nearby medical doctor with quackery?

Several times she was caught by surprise at the appearance of one of her own ancestors. According to a bill of sale dated April 17, 1697, John Willson purchased "one milk cowe with the belle on" for three pounds, eight shillings. A two-line note to a magistrate in Bedford, signed by a local parson, recorded the deaths of Silence and Submit Hubbard; and, with a shudder, Sally grasped that the twins had not been stillborn, after all—they died at two, one day apart, of "the pox."

As the day started to slip away, she picked up her pace, jumping ahead in time, now giving most documents only a cursory glance—scanning them for the words *Edwardstown* or *Grace Church.*

Suddenly she stopped. Before her on the screen was a handwritten bill of sale, dated June 7, 1774.

DAVID MORSE, ESQ. OF EDWARDSTOWN, NEW HAMP-SHIRE hereby grants

TO

GRACE EPISCOPAL CHURCH OF EDWARDSTOWN, NEW HAMPSHIRE, in consideration of the sum of Sixty-Seven Pounds, title and rights to the North Meadow of His Farm, said Meadow lying adjacent to the Existing Churchyard. By a survey conducted by Abner Moore, surveyor, the meadow commences at the stone wall at the edge of the churchyard and runs east 1,120 feet to a Stream; angles north along the Contours of said Stream; and back toward the existing churchyard alongside the property of Mr. John Clark.

Witnessed and Signed This day by: Abner Moore
                                          John Clark

Sally read it over twice. This was not a full answer—the land described was on the north side of the church, and it was the *south* side that interested her. Still, its implications were unmistakable. The original graveyard had been considerably smaller—by this purchase and others, it had *expanded.*

Now she had a specific objective. Did another bill of sale exist for property on the other side?

But instead, ten minutes later, she found something else: a surveyor's rendering—known then, as now, as a "plat"—of the *original* Grace Church property, executed at the time of its purchase in 1738!

Over the past nine months she had walked the cemetery a dozen times, most recently just a few days ago. From the map accompanying the plat she immediately saw how dramatically its very shape had changed.

In her notebook she set down the original dimensions. Tomorrow, with these in hand, she would again walk the yard, just to be sure.

But turning back to the map, she no longer doubted. The first grave violated had indeed once been on the periphery of the yard.

It belonged to her own namesake, Sally Hubbard.

Lynch peered at the capuchin monkey in the cage before him. With its alert brown eyes, furry white beard, and black cowl, it was a hugely appealing creature, every child's fantasy pet—except that it was masturbating wildly, its tiny hand working away piston-like at its tiny penis. On either side others were doing the same.

"Another reason we should be using chimpanzees," noted Lynch wryly.

The *main* reason, of course, was the far closer relationship of chimps to human beings; especially crucial as they worked to perfect a method of gene transfer.

Foster was unamused. "They're looking for instant results—these are easier to handle, easier to cage, and their metabolism's faster. We were damn lucky to grab this batch fresh out of quarantine from Paraguay."

"I suppose it is the best way to begin testing three different delivery systems simultaneously," he conceded.

"The chimps are on order, they'll be here soon enough." Foster indicated a cage housing one of the few females, its occupant passively observing the males through half closed eyes. "I presume we're charting for gender?"

He nodded. "But so far it's had no bearing on the results. Actually, one of the females being treated by intramuscular injection is scheduled to be dosed now. . . ." He paused. "Tran!"—and almost immediately a slight young man in a lab coat, obviously Vietnamese, appeared from the adjoining room.

"Yes, Doctor."

He nodded at the cage before him. "Let's give this little lady her medicine."

Wordlessly, the technician removed from a drawer two pairs of thick rubber gloves. He handed one to Lynch and put on the others himself.

"Tran's been a godsend. If only we'd had this kind of funding a year ago."

"The downside," shot back Foster, "is the bastards feel entitled to keep turning the screws."

Lynch opened the door to the cage. "Okay, Tran, I'm going to need some help."

As the two sets of hands reached toward her, the animal retreated to the farthest corner of her lair and, teeth bared, eyes wide, let out an ear-piercing cry. When they tried to grab her, she abruptly went into attack mode, sinking sharp incisors into Lynch's gloved hand.

"Just relax there," the scientist soothed, lifting her out even as she tried to bury her teeth deeper in the glove, "don't make it harder than it has to be." Then, to Foster: "This is her third treatment. She knows what's coming."

They set the animal on a steel, miniaturized examining table and strapped her down spread-eagle with four-point restraints. "Is the syringe ready, Tran?"

The technician handed it to him. It was little more than two inches in length; which, however, given the creature's size, was the equivalent of a foot in human terms.

"For maximum effectiveness," noted Lynch, "we have to pierce the abdominal musculature and go directly into the peritoneal cavity."

"How many animals have been treated by this method?"

"Eleven," said Lynch, turning back to the task at hand. "More than enough."

When the needle entered its body, the animal, stunned, stopped its thrashing, and appeared to look up at the scientist with beseeching eyes. Only after it was withdrawn did she resume screeching.

"Okay, Tran, put her back."

Returned to her cage, the capuchin was rewarded with a crab apple and Tran was dismissed.

Lynch turned back to Foster. "I wouldn't anticipate much. The gene-transfer results we've had so far with the intramuscular approach don't compare with those produced by the intravenous drip."

Foster nodded. "I was just rereading the dissection data on the animal who went through the intravenous process. The distribution of the protein was impressive."

"Especially considering he had just two treatments before we opened him up. But the animals treated by injection are still showing extremely uneven distribution, even after five and six treatments." He paused. "And there's still nothing encouraging to report on oral delivery?"

"Which is what they're most eager to hear." Foster paused. "The problem seems to be the vector's not acid stable, it gets damaged in the stomach. Tell them to send along some monkeys who've been genetically engineered to produce Maalox."

"Or maybe we should just tell them we've licked it—a nice, soothing placebo instead of the truth."

"I don't give a damn what you tell them, just don't fuck it up!" He eyed him with frank contempt. "Or else you'll have to deal with me."

Sally awoke to find Mark before the bedroom mirror, tying his tie.

"Hi," she said groggily. "What time is it?"

"Late, seven-twenty. You okay?"

"Just really tired. God, I'm *so* ready for this to be over."

He grinned. "I wasn't talking to you."

"What?"

He moved to the bed, kissed her forehead, then addressed her belly. "I was talking to *you*, little one. Are *you* okay this morning?"

Sally laughed. "It's like she's the CEO of my body—others do the work, she gets the attention."

"Getting all set to meet Mom and Pop?"

"Enough, Mark, time to talk grown-up. What've you got going today?"

"Big day—proposals for science-fair projects are due. You?"

With effort she sat up. "Well, there's my breathing exercises, and peeing a lot. And that's just before breakfast. . . ." She smiled. "That's your cue—you're supposed to say, 'I love you just the way you are.' "

"No problem, you get more beautiful to me with every pound. Hell, you could start looking like Pavarotti—"

"Sorry I asked—"

"Like all three tenors rolled into one. I've already gained eight pounds myself in solidarity." He watched as she inched her way to the edge of the bed and swung her feet to the floor. "So, planning a trip back to your place of business?"

"The *Weekly?*" she asked, confused. "Of course."

He grinned. "I meant the cemetery, actually."

"*Not* funny," she said, heart sinking. Every time she tried to talk to him about any of this, the put-downs started flying—always good natured, of course, to give him deniability.

"In poor taste maybe," he said, right in character, "but *definitely* funny. Better dress warm. It's supposed to go down to forty today."

She gave a weak smile. "That's your idea of supportive?"

"Hey, babe, sympathy weight gain is one thing." He gave her a peck on the forehead. "Dr. Spock never said anything about sympathy paranoia."

That afternoon in her office Sally shifted the phone from one shoulder to the other, as she always did when intensely agitated.

"Listen, you're the fourth person I've spoken to at the National Archives in the last twenty minutes. I'm researching a family history and I have what I think is a very simple question: How can I get my hands on *English* records that predate the settlement of this country?"

"I'm sorry, ma'am," said the woman on the other end, with the sort of heartfelt indifference only a bureaucrat can muster, "I wouldn't be able to give you that information over the telephone."

Bullshit, thought Sally, *you'd jump through hoops if I told you I worked for* Time *magazine or the* New York Herald.

"The National Archives is the chief repository for records in this country, isn't it?"

"Yes, we are."

"And you are in the National Archives *Building,* aren't you?"

"We are a very large institution, ma'am, we don't have the answer to every question at our fingertips."

"Don't take this the wrong way," she said, trying to pierce the impersonal shield, "but isn't that your job?"

"We do the best we can, ma'am."

"I'm just asking that someone take a few minutes to look this up for me. You're a supervisor, don't tell me you can't make it happen."

"I suggest," she said curtly, "that you put your request in writing. We'll get back to you within three weeks."

Sally was at a loss. Always she'd been magic working the phones; able, through charm or humor or, if it came to it, coercion to get anything out of anyone. Yet, here she was letting herself get shrugged off by some huffy functionary!

"Ms. Jacovitz, I am *under deadline,* I don't have that kind of time—"

"How did you know my name?"

"Oh, I always like to know to whom I'm speaking. I got it from"—she checked the scrawl on her yellow legal pad—"Mr. Horelick. Who was referred to me by the first person to whom I spoke, Ms. Conrad. Whose name I got from a Ms. Jamison in your Northeast Regional office in Bayonne, New Jersey. At least I do seem to be working my way up the food chain."

"I see," she replied, suddenly wary. "Well, as I say, if you will put your request in writing, I'm sure—"

"Ms. Jacovitz, the only thing I'll put in writing is a fax to John Stanley."

"And who might that be?"

"The ranking member of the House Committee on Governmental Affairs—also the congressman from this district. We go back a long way."

Heavy handed, Sally knew, almost embarrassingly so. But the first rule in these cases was always to get their attention.

"I see. Well, Ms. . . . I didn't get *your* name."

Sally could tell by her tone that she wasn't buying. "Benedict."

". . . Ms. Benedict, I'm a grown woman, not a frightened little girl. I don't *care* about your access to the old boys' network—even if it happens not to be a figment of your imagination. Now, *good-bye.*"

Walking through the front door a couple of hours later, Mark dropped his briefcase with a bang and flung his coat onto a chair.

"How you doing?" he said to his wife, who was lying on the living room couch.

"Okay. You?"

This was more than enough to set him off. "Lousy. I just saw the first batch of proposals for science-fair projects! Not a winner in the bunch. I'm telling you, we could really be embarrassed this year."

He sat down heavily across from her. "I mean, one kid actually proposes something on *astrology*! What's the world coming to?" He sighed. "All right, I shouldn't care so much, the point is to have a good time and all that. But it just *kills* me how many kids try to slide by with these half-baked ideas. If I teach them nothing else, I at least want them to learn respect for the scientific process!"

Through it all Sally lay there, her arm flung over her face. "You mean respect for *logic,* don't you?" she said miserably, as if the comment had been directed at her.

Instantly she had his full attention—and he snapped back to this morning's conversation. Only now did he notice the album of vintage family photographs lying open on the floor alongside the couch.

"Sally, what is it?"

She didn't reply.

Gently, he lifted her arm to reveal red, swollen eyes.

"Please, talk to me."

"I've tried. . . ."

He waited a moment. The sight of the supercompetent woman he had married, nearly eight months pregnant, disheveled and seemingly helpless, was deeply unsettling. He'd had no idea she was this far gone.

"No one will help me—not even the National Archives."

"Help you with what?"

She shook her head. "You're just going to tell me I'm crazy again."

Oh, Christ! "You know I don't mean it that way, Sal, I'm just kidding around." He stroked her hair. "Why don't you run through this theory of yours one more time. You were going through the entries in the Bible, and it seems like there's a pattern . . . ?"

"Don't condescend to me," she snapped, struggling up to a sitting position. "There *is* a pattern. Every other generation lives an incredibly long time."

"Uh-huh . . ."

"At least hundred years. Can I have a tissue?"

He handed her one and she blew hard.

"Every *other* generation?"

"That's possible, isn't it? Scientifically, I mean?"

"I suppose it could be genetically programmed," he allowed. "Identical twins often skip a generation. So do certain diseases— hemophilia, for instance."

"So it *is* possible?"

"Tell me," he said, trying hard not to sound dismissive, "how large a sample are you basing this on?"

"There're thirteen generations listed."

"That means—since you're taking only every other one—you're dealing with six or seven that are supposedly long lived?"

"Seven." She hesitated. "Only, there are a couple of holes along the way. . . ."

"Holes?"

"Two people who didn't live out their natural life spans. One—Josiah Hubbard—died in the Revolutionary War before he was thirty. His granddaughter, Priscilla Avery—my great-great-great-grandmother—was killed in a carriage accident in her early forties."

"So we're down to *five*?" he said, trying to keep his voice neutral. "Sally . . . what you've found is very interesting, but—please don't take this the wrong way—statistically it's meaningless."

"That's why I want to get more information from the National Archives. I want to find out if the pattern goes back before the family's arrival in America—back to England."

He was at a loss; this was such an incredible waste of time and emotional energy. "You'd need, minimum, another six or seven examples. Records probably don't even go back that far."

She dried her eyes with her sleeve. "There's something else. . . ."

"Yes?"

She hesitated. "Remember what Gram said after Mother's service? That remark about Giles being a relative of ours? We *know* Giles was adopted, his own son told me so!"

"Sally, you know Gram's in no condition to—"

"I found some old birth records. At Malen's. There was a child born out of wedlock around the right date—and there have always been rumors about old Susan McKinney, the suffragist, giving up a child for adoption."

He took a moment before replying. "In other words, you're speculating. You're taking Fact A and simply assuming it leads to Fact B."

"Stop it," she snapped, flashing her old fire. "I'm not some kid trying to pass muster with a science-fair proposal. You want facts? At least two of the bodies taken were in that line of relatives! For sure! And I'm telling you maybe all three!"

"And so . . . ? That leads you to what conclusion, exactly?"

"Oh, Jesus!" She threw up her hands. "I don't *know*! I'm not *saying* it's rational." She looked into his eyes beseechingly. "But I just keep thinking my mother was in that line. And so's our baby."

Free for lunch?" asked Sally, first thing Monday morning. "My treat."

Lisa, at her desk, was caught short by the invitation. Their conversations lately had been cordial enough, but with little pretense of friendship on either end.

"I don't think so," she said. "Rough day."

Sally waited a moment before speaking again. She knew this wouldn't be easy, had gone back and forth about it all weekend. But, finally, she had no choice; never in her life had she felt so beleaguered.

At the very least Lisa would *understand*.

"Then why don't you come into my office now? There's something we have to discuss."

Closing the door behind her, Sally motioned Lisa into the folding chair alongside her desk, but remained standing herself. After a nervous moment she plucked up the just-published "Autumn Delights" supplement from her messy desktop.

"I think it turned out pretty well, don't you?"

"I guess." She gave an indifferent shrug. "As long as the advertisers are happy."

"Lisa . . ." She stopped, started again. "You know, we're coming up on the anniversary of the first grave robbing. It was Halloween, remember? The night of our party . . ."

"I remember."

"No party this year. I'm just not up to it—I'm hoping people will understand."

She nodded, waiting.

"I'm thinking"—she came out with it—"we should look at the case again."

"What?!"

"I don't like the idea," added Sally quickly. "It's been"—she searched for the word—"a nightmare. I think about that poor boy and"—she shook her head—"I can't help but feel responsible."

Lisa made no response.

"But I've also run across some new information. It's . . . I don't know, Mark thinks its meaningless."

"What kind of information?"

She took a deep breath. "I think the bodies in those graves, all three of them, were relatives of mine. That just strikes me as one helluva coincidence."

"All *three*?"

Sally explained about her visit to the Bureau of Records and her growing suspicions about Giles. She paused, uncertain. "Or maybe I'm just crazy. Tell me honestly, what do you think?"

Lisa hesitated. In fact, what she was thinking was how this might fit in with what *she* had—and how, given half a chance, her boss would again steal the show.

"Honestly? I think your husband's right. The case is *solved*, it's over."

"But this is *new* stuff," argued Sally, stung. "If I can nail down the Giles case for sure, wouldn't that—"

"Look, you want a yes-girl, talk to Miss Sweetness and Light." She nodded toward the other room and Florence. "I'm telling you it'd be a huge mistake to turn this personal. It would look like some kind of vendetta."

Always a lousy liar, Lisa stood and turned to gaze out the window.

Behind her Sally nodded, suddenly feeling foolish for having raised it at all. "You're probably right."

"Anyway, we're too busy. With you in and out, it's been hard enough just getting out the paper."

Sally paused, then, with a little laugh, edged away from the subject. "Yeah, funny how this life-and-death stuff can interfere with work."

Turning to face her, the wheels turning, Lisa smiled her understanding. "Hey," she said, seemingly seized by inspiration, "if you're not having the party, maybe I'll get away that weekend for some R and R. I've got a friend from college I've been promising to visit."

"Oh? Where's that?"

"New York City."

I'm worried, Steve. I mean, *seriously* worried."

Montera grinned at his friend, seriousness the furthest thing from his mind. "Tell me, Mark, has she used the word *aliens*? Or are we just talking a run-of-the mill Lee Harvey Oswald type conspiracy here?"

"She hasn't said anything like that. Who knows *what* she thinks, it's pretty muddled. . . ." Unconsciously, he glanced around the Clover Leaf, more crowded this chilly, late-fall evening than most, and took another swig of beer. "Look, Steve, I'm trying to give her a wide berth. She's had a rough time lately. . . ."

"You're lying to me, Bowman. But it's a *nice* lie, she'd appreciate it."

"Don't I remember you telling me Cheryl was a pretty edgy during her first pregnancy?"

Montera lifted the skinny red straw from his Scotch and soda. "Here's another one to clutch at." He paused. "What I told you is the woman had a caviar craving that almost broke the bank. And she yelled a little more than normal—her pregnancies had a mouth like Ralph Kramden." For show he winced at the memory. "But, sorry, this takes the cake for hormone-induced loony-tunes. Have you talked to her doctor about this?"

"It's not easy, he's her friend. Anyway, she saw him just last week. He says she's fine."

"Maybe she needs a different kind of doctor."

Had the remark been flip, Mark would have reacted with sharp annoyance—but he saw now Montera was trying to be supportive. Besides, it *had* occurred to him.

"What scares me is we're going to have a baby to deal with, Steve! What if she loses it completely?"

"Nah." He shooed away his friend's concern. "You want some reassurance here? The real thing, not just some bullshit?" He paused meaningfully. "Perspective, my friend. What've you got, another four or five weeks? Just hang on and it'll all be over."

Mark nodded. "I know, it's just so hard."

"It's *all* hard—pregnancy, infancy, the kid starting to walk, the kid starting to fuck with your mind—every stage is all-consuming when you're in the middle of it. Wait'll you have to teach a full schedule of classes after five nights running of no sleep. But it's amazing how quickly you forget once you're on to the next thing."

He looked at him gratefully. "Thanks, Steve, that really does help."

"No problem." He laughed. "Of course, I left out postpartum depression. Let's just hope we don't have to have another one of these talks in a couple of months."

Checking her grandmother's room to make sure she was asleep, Sally quietly made her way into the living room. She was glad she'd urged Mark to go out with his friend. There could be no distractions if she was to do this right.

Settling in on the couch, she took a moment to go over again what she'd say and reached for the phone.

When Sally identified herself, there was a momentary silence. "How did you get this number?"

"Please, don't hang up," she said hurriedly. "I know I owe you an apology. You were just doing your job, there's no reason why you should have to put up with someone like me giving you grief."

In fact, after three calls to her office, increasingly acrimonious on both ends, this woman had not only stopped taking Sally's calls, she'd evidently instructed others to do likewise.

"I asked how you got my home phone number!"

"Believe me, I don't mean any harm. Jacovitz is an unusual name, and I knew you had to live somewhere in the Washington area."

"This is harassment. I want you to leave me alone!"

"Please, I just need a few moments—"

"Good night. I'm hanging up now."

"I'm going to have a baby . . ." interjected Sally, the sudden cry so full of pain, it seemed she was on the verge of hysteria.

But though her desperation was real, its use here was calculated. She knew, or at least thought she did, how this woman ticked.

There was a pause. "A lot of people have babies, Ms. Benedict."

Still, she hadn't hung up. "I don't know why I came on so strong before. That's not me." She paused; then, even more contrite: "Yes, I do—I'm scared to death. . . . It's been a terrible time. I'm out of work."

"You're all by yourself?"

"No, I've got my grandmother."

"Why's getting ahold of these records so important to you?" she said, still hard but softening.

"It sounds . . . crazy. I *know* how busy you must be."

"Go ahead."

She sighed audibly. "My training is as a reporter. But now I'm trying to pick up some cash doing genealogical research for a well-to-do family around here—I'm putting together a book for their daughter's wedding." She stopped. "They're running out of patience. I can't afford to lose this job."

"If I may ask—what about your child's father?"

"Who the hell knows?"

"Tell me about it." She snorted. "I'm a single mother myself."

Bingo!

"But my guess is," continued Jacovitz, "we won't have what you're looking for."

"Oh . . . ?" she said. But along with the disappointment there was sudden anger. Why the hell hadn't this bitch simply told her that the first time?!

"We don't have many records from abroad. And of those we do, many haven't even been filed."

"I see."

"Probably the only place in this country they'd have something like that would be Utah."

"Utah?"

"The Family History Library in Salt Lake City. It's run by the Mormons—the research has something to do with their religious beliefs. Their collection is remarkably extensive."

Sally jotted the words on a scratch pad as she repeated them. "The Family History Library—Salt Lake City." *Strange, hadn't someone else been talking about Salt Lake City lately?*

"I don't know if that does you any good. Some of their material's been computerized, but for the real old stuff, you'd probably have to go there and poke around."

Only early the next day, folding laundry, did it hit her.

Lynch—that guy at the Life Services Institute! Wasn't he from Salt Lake City?!

The chimpanzee kept a watchful eye on Lynch even as he accepted the paper cup from the scientist's outstretched hand. Uncertain, he lifted it to eye level to examine its contents.

"Go on, Hank," urged Lynch, "you'll like it."

The chimp's gaze went from the thick orange liquid to Lynch and back again. After bringing it to his nostrils for a sniff, tentatively, almost delicately, he took a sip.

"AAFFFF!" came the guttural response, his face contorting in rage, his powerful hand crumpling the cup.

"Relax," soothed Lynch, "it's ninety percent apricot juice."

"It doesn't understand you," said Foster caustically.

Seemingly in response Hank grimaced and began pounding the side of his cage with his clenched fists.

After a moment the chimp turned back to Lynch with a defiant stare—an adolescent as stubbornly opinionated as any human of a comparable age. Already he had rejected the drug in combination with a half dozen other beverages, ranging from Coca-Cola to Gatorade to imported beer.

"Try again. All we have to do is get one good dose into him!"

Lynch hesitated, reluctant to risk his colleague's wrath. "It won't work, he doesn't trust me." He shook his head. "The best thing is try again in a few days."

"My *God*!" said Foster in exasperation. "What are we supposed to tell Cooper when he asks to see new data on oral transfer of the gene? That we've only got one goddamn chimp willing to take the stuff?!"

Lynch's slow shrug conveyed his own frustration. "Thank goodness for Champagne Charley."

He turned to the chimp in the adjoining cage. Well into middle age at twenty-six, heavier and far more passive, he observed the other's fury with sad, understanding eyes. It was easy to believe he took his medicine without complaint; he seemed to take life the same way. In fact, he did have an inordinate fondness for cheap champagne, had guzzled down a large foam cup of André laced with the drug in less than a minute.

"I want to perform a biopsy on him," said Foster sharply.

"Another?" said Lynch in surprise. "This will make four in less than three weeks. The last wound isn't even completely healed yet."

"We'll do one every day if we have to. I'm not concerned with a chimpanzee's comfort."

As usual Lynch quickly went through the mental gymnastics that led to assent. The data indicated they were so tantalizingly close now! Where normally the cells of a primate, including those of a human being, will survive in a petri dish no longer than ten days, those cells taken from the capuchins after oral ingestion were still going strong at nearly three and a half months; and the ones from this chimp, much more closely related to man, showed every sign of doing the same; and this after but a single dose! It was staggering, unbelievable—certainly no time for petty qualms.

"Okay, now, Charley," said Lynch, taking the animal in his arms and carrying him to the examining table, "we just have to do this one more time."

When he withdrew a razor and can of shaving cream, the animal shuddered, knowing what it meant, but made no effort to escape.

Lynch began hacking away at the thick hair in the animal's lower back, taking care not to disturb any of the earlier wounds, and in minutes cleared an area two inches square down to the pink skin beneath. Now, quickly, he injected half a cc of Xylocaine with a small needle. It took less than a minute for the anesthetic to take effect.

The biopsy blade was a thin steel cylinder with one razor-sharp edge. In a single stroke he shaved off a translucent layer of skin. The chimp's piercing shriek was more in surprise than pain. There was only the barest trace of blood.

After placing the sample in a petri dish and stitching and bandaging the wound, the scientist deposited the chimp back in his cage. All that remained was to soak the specimen in collagenase solution to dissolve the protein scaffolding that held the cells together, then wash away the debris.

"Done," said Lynch simply. "But he's going to be uncomfortable. I really think this time we should give the poor thing a chance to heal."

For once Foster also appeared satisfied. "Don't feel sorry for it, Lynch," he observed evenly, "it's not such a bad deal. It's getting immortality in return."

Startled by the good looks of the woman who'd arrived at his cramped office an hour earlier, Dr. Barry Schneider was thrilled to find himself equally drawn by her vivacity and unexpected humor.

"I was surprised to hear from you," he said, smiling across the table in the seedy upper Broadway luncheonette that was one of his hangouts. "I thought you'd moved on to other phone conquests."

Lisa took a sip of her vanilla milkshake and smiled back. "You make me sound like a terrible user."

"It's just you did get off pretty fast after I mentioned those corpse merchants out in Wisconsin."

"Don't take it personally. I'm a reporter, it's my job."

And Schneider understood, with a twinge of regret, that this, too, was just a professional encounter. In a tight denim jacket and translucent floral-patterned skirt, this woman was the stuff of fantasy. Maybe, if he was lucky, at least one of his colleagues would happen in and spot him with her.

"Did you get what you wanted from those guys?"

"Actually, I struck out." She shrugged. "No big deal, it comes with the territory—I'm used to rejection."

"You want a piece of can't-miss advice?" He leaned across the table and dropped his voice. "If you're dealing with a heterosexual male, get a fax number first and shoot over a photo. Trust me, it'll help."

She laughed. "God, that's sexist." Skinny and bespectacled, with thinning hair, Schneider wasn't much to look at, but his brains and confidence did lend him a certain appeal. "I'll have to pretend not to be offended."

"So what do you want with me?"

"How much time do you have?"

"I don't know, a couple of hours. It's Friday afternoon, things are pretty slow." He glanced at his watch. "Why don't we head back to my office?"

"Okay," he said, a few minutes later, taking a seat behind his cluttered desk, "hit me with your best shot."

"Wait a sec, I like to know who I'm talking to." She gazed a moment longer at the bulletin board directly behind him: an announcement for a talk he'd given at a medical conference, something about blood vessels in the brain; a photo of himself and several colleagues outside the Pasteur Institute in Paris; a gag greeting card about doctors and overbearing Jewish mothers.

"I should probably add a few diplomas to the mix," he observed.

"It's impressive enough. How long have you worked here?"

"At Columbia Presbyterian? About three years."

"Do you like it?"

"Do I mind living and working in a high-crime neighborhood and occasionally navigating garbage in the streets to be part of one of the top research institutions in the country? Not a bit." He paused. "But you're *still* fishing, aren't you? You're trying to figure out what my number was doing on that list."

He'd hit it on the head. What she'd picked up so far about the Institute in Manchester was at once tantalizing and deeply frustrating. She needed something concrete; either about Stebben's association with the place or—farfetched, but after Sally's weird revelation, a dim possibility—the Institute's link to the grave robbings. Or anything else, for that matter, that might be turned on the printed page into something provocative and attention-grabbing.

The truth is, in her fevered imagination, this story had begun to loom as a potential career maker. After all, the Life Services Institute was big time. Hadn't the place excited the passionate interest of no less an authority than R. Paul Holland?

"Well . . ." She smiled at Schneider. "Can *you* think of why a lab doing antiaging work might be interested in the bodies you work with here?"

"Beats me. I'd love to tell you there's something special about our cadavers, but we just take what they give us."

Smitten as he was, he was also wary. As one of the junior guys around here, saying too much to a reporter could only lead to trouble.

"And they're just used for basic dissection?"

"That's it. Of course, there's been other kinds of research elsewhere in recent years on human remains, but we just—"

"What kind of research?"

This seemed safe enough; it was all in the public record. "Let me ask you one first, Ms. Reporter. What are your plans tomorrow evening?"

She chuckled. "What is this, a quid pro quo?"

"You don't know me. I'll take any edge I can get."

"Me too—you're on." She paused. "You were saying . . . ?"

"For instance, just recently I was reading something in the literature about a group of Biblical scholars in Israel looking into the genetic origin of the ancient Hittites. Were they related to the Israelites, to the Sumerians, *who*? So what they did was extract DNA from the marrow of bones found at a Hittite burial site and compare it with that of other ancient populations. Fascinating stuff—the genetic markers showed the Hittites weren't Semites at all, they were of Indo-European stock."

"They could do something like that after all this time?"

He nodded. "Because the climate left the bones so exceptionally well preserved. It's unlikely they could have pulled it off in many other places."

"Like anywhere in the United States," she observed.

"Well, they did dig up Jesse James's body not long ago in Missouri—ran DNA tests at his family's request to make sure it was really him."

Dimly, Lisa recalled reading about it. "But that isn't a dry climate, is it?"

"No, and the body also wasn't five thousand years old. It makes a difference. But, remember, all these tests are pretty basic. For more meaningful information you really need soft-tissue samples."

She hesitated, thinking back on the conversation with Sally. "Suppose you looked at different members of the same family. Is there anything in particular you might be after?"

"Members of the same family?"

"Their cadavers—from different generations."

"Well . . . obviously, those people would have had some important traits in common. Certain physical attributes, the propensity for certain diseases. Possibly even certain talents and abilities. Why?"

"Just fishing." She flashed him a smile. "What happens to the bodies after you guys are through with them?"

"If the families are interested, the husks get shipped back home for burial. The others, you don't want to know."

"Sure, I do."

"Disposed of in a field out in Staten Island. No grave markers, no nothing—it's pretty sad."

"And the parts you take out?"

"The organs are usually tossed." He laughed. "There are dogs in this neighborhood who know the dissection schedule better than the students—if we don't pack those damn hearts and livers inside five layers of plastic, they're Alpo."

"Usually? What happens to the others?"

He looked at her and slowly shook his head. "There's a facility around here. But sorry, you're a civilian, it's probably off limits."

"Oh, come *on.* . . ."

"Anyway"—he smiled—"I need to keep some secrets to be sure you'll make our date."

Starting with dinner at the River Café and ending with a stroll along windblown South Street Seaport, the evening went better than Schneider had dreamed possible. They moved from small talk to an exchange of their respective romantic histories, to something approaching genuine intimacy.

Around midnight, heading uptown in a cab toward the college friend's apartment where she was to stay, he risked slipping his arm around her; and was surprised when she leaned into him and looked up, eyes closed and lips parted, for a kiss. Before they'd crossed Fourteenth Street, she'd opened her jacket and placed his hands on her breasts. Through the silky blouse and wisp of a bra he could feel her erect nipples against his tentative touch. Her kisses became deeper and she pushed harder against him as his hands began moving over them, squeezing gently.

"I don't know if I'm gonna be able to control myself," he whispered, eyeing the driver in the rearview mirror.

"Good."

Parting her legs slightly, she took his hand and led it to her thigh.

"Stroke me," she murmured. "Very, very lightly."

Her skin was softer than any woman's he'd ever touched. His

hand moved slowly upward, lightly brushing her with his fingertips, as he anticipated the feel of silky underwear. Her legs widened and he heard her breath quicken before he knew for sure. . . .

She wasn't wearing any.

Reaching out her hand, she found the bulge in his pants and massaged him hard through the denim, as she opened her legs wider, placing her other hand over his, pushing it into her crotch.

"Don't stop," she whispered.

He couldn't believe what was happening. He'd never known anyone so totally abandoned.

"Let's go to my place," he got out at last.

Through his jeans she squeezed even harder. "Not yet. I want to see that place first—the one that's off limits."

The facility was in one of the older buildings at the edge of the med school complex, originally home to the entire Department of Anatomy. Flashing his pass at a baffled night guard, Schneider snapped on the lights and led her to a creaky elevator. He pushed the button for the third floor. The room was down a long corridor and through a wooden door marked PRIVATE.

"Hold your nose," warned Schneider, fishing in his pocket for the key to unlock it.

She did, but even before he switched on the light, the odor hit her anyway, so powerful her legs nearly buckled. Yet even more overwhelming was what loomed before her: endless rows of glass containers, floor to ceiling on ancient shelves. Every one contained a preserved body part. An endless array of brains, intestines, lungs, hands, even breasts and penises.

Gazing about, she felt a rising wave of nausea. "What *is* this place?"

"Are you okay? Our own private freak show. We've got two other rooms like it."

"These all come from dissections?"

He nodded. "The oldest date from the mid-nineteenth century."

"Why? What good are they?"

"You have to know the scientific mind. *Anything* can prove valuable, so we hold on to everything of possible use or interest." He looked around the room. "Who knows?—there's a story to each and every one of these. Some represent diseases or deformities that were being studied at a particular moment, some were of interest because of how the patient lived or died. We don't save quite as many anymore as they used to."

"I've seen plenty . . . can we get some fresh air?"

"Right. I can think of lots better things to do myself."

It was almost 3:00 A.M. when Schneider fell back against his pillow, spent. "Enough." He smiled. "I've really gotta get some sleep."

She laughed. "You okay?"

"Never been better." He leaned over and kissed her gently. "You?"

"Yeah"—snuggling against him. "I wish all my assignments went this well."

"How about if you stayed here with me? The rest of the weekend?"

"I'd like that. I'll pick up my bag from Janet's in the morning."

"That's a start—you should know I'll try persuading you to make it longer."

She smiled. "Just find me the right job and I will."

They fell silent. Exhausted as she was, her mind was racing.

"Barry . . ."

"Hmmm?"

"That room with all those body parts—you say it's over a hundred years old?"

"Uhh," he said sleepily, "yeah. . . ."

"Do you know anything about Albany Union Medical College?"
He opened his eyes. "What about it?"

"Do they have a place like that there too?"

"Actually, yeah, they do."

"How about at Albert Einstein? And Cornell?"

"Uh-huh—I think so. But I really wanna get some sleep."

"Okay. Sorry."

Could that be it? Were they trying to get their hands on some old body parts, long ago set aside and forgotten? But whose?

The answer that leapt most immediately was unnerving. Was it possible? Could Sally be right? Was her family, with its propensity for exceptional longevity, really targeted for study?

The notion seemed more plausible with the passing minutes. At last, sure Schneider was out, she swung from the bed and tiptoed into the living room. She found her purse on the floor, where she'd discarded it in the flush of passion, and pulled out her address book. Moving into Schneider's tiny kitchen, she opened it to the home listing she'd copied from Sally's Rolodex.

Should she risk calling at this hour? She hesitated, then, abruptly deciding, snatched the phone from the wall and dialed. It was too important, it couldn't wait.

Adrenaline pumping, she heard it ring once, twice. Then—not the sleepy-angry voice she was steeled for, but a recording. Relieved and disappointed, she mentally composed her message as she listened.

"You haven't yet reached R. Paul Holland. But I do check in. Don't be shy."

Rising from the breakfast table Sunday morning, Sally was suddenly so woozy, she had to grab a chair for support. "Mark, I don't feel too well."

In a nanosecond he was at her side, supporting her, helping her back into her chair. "Take it easy, Sal," he soothed through rising panic, "I'm right here."

"Oh, God," she said, hands going to her temple, "my head's spinning!"

"Just relax, we'll get you to Malen," he said, reaching for the phone. "Just concentrate on breathing easily, in and out. What's his number?"

"Don't bother him, Mark, it's his day off."

He shot her a look and grabbed the phone book.

"Really, I'll be okay. . . ."

"Drop it, Sal. He'll be furious if we *don't* call."

"The guy lives half an hour away and the forecast's for snow."

As he dialed, he glanced out the window at the low, gray sky; true enough, around here even early-season storms could quickly leave the roads impassable. "Then we'd better bring the overnight bag in case you have to stay in the hospital."

* * *

"You're familiar with preeclampsia?" asked Malen pointedly an hour and a half later, after they'd moved from the examining room to his office.

"Oh, Jesus," exclaimed Mark.

Sally was more shaken by her husband's reaction than by the word itself. "What? Tell me!"

"I don't mean to alarm you—the condition occurs in a good five to ten percent of pregnancies. And fortunately your case appears relatively mild. Your blood pressure is only borderline high, one thirty-eight over eighty-five, and there's no undue swelling of the hands or ankles, or evidence of protein in your urine." He paused meaningfully. "But this is a warning sign, Sally, and we have to take it seriously. Preeclampsia can lead to oxygen deprivation for the baby, resulting in damage to the nervous system." He stopped again. "I want you to shut down. Stay at home until she's born."

"What are you talking about? What about work?!"

"Should she stay in bed?" asked Mark.

"For now I don't think that's necessary."

"I say you're *both* overreacting," said Sally, indignant. "I'm fine! I'll just take it a little slower, that's all." She turned defiantly to Malen. "Why not check me into the hospital *now* on the off chance there's an emergency?"

"That's an option. If it gets appreciably worse, I will."

Two hours later, after he'd dropped off Sally at home, Mark was back.

"What did you tell her?" asked Malen.

"That I needed to run to the hardware store, pick up some stuff for a woodworking project. She always tunes out."

He smiled—"So would I"—but immediately grew serious. "I

asked you back because I'm going to need your help. This condition has to be very closely monitored."

He nodded. "I know that."

"I'll be coming by at least every couple of days from now on. But if there's anything unusual—blurred vision, abdominal pain, even excessive irritability—you let me know. Because it's for damn sure she won't." Unexpectedly, he grinned. "Though I guess with Sally and irritability, it might be hard to tell."

Once again Mark found himself put off by the guy's insufferable smugness. "I really don't think she'd do anything to jeopardize the baby."

"Not intentionally—it's that crazy grin-and-bear-it attitude of hers."

"Trust me, she's not nearly as tough as she seems."

Malen snorted. "You probably never saw her run the four forty back in high school. I used to go to all her meets with her dad. . . ."

"As a matter of fact I did."

"Sometimes even when she wasn't the fastest she'd win on pure will. Sally could give *lessons* in toughness."

Mark stood there a long moment, the annoyance rising. Where the hell did Malen come off presuming he knew Sally better than he did? "Speaking of before my time, what's with you and Paul Holland?"

He looked liked he'd been slapped across the face. "What do you mean?"

"I happened to see you two together—it was the day he made that job offer to Sal. I was driving by the hospital and you were walking him to his car. Looked pretty chummy." He paused. "I was surprised, Sally can't stand the guy."

"I hope you didn't tell her, it might upset her."

"No. *I* know her well enough to know that." He stared at him levelly, still awaiting his answer.

"He and I might be doing something together. A book on the life of a modern country doctor. But we have to keep it under wraps."

"Oh? Why would that be such a secret?"

"You know this town. Even with pseudonyms, how do you think people around here will feel about seeing their medical secrets revealed in print?"

Mark nodded. Though the explanation was plausible enough, it avoided a more central truth. He knew damn well that the doctor's real interest in such a project was the possibility it offered at associating with Holland and his big-shot friends. For that, star-fucker that he was, he'd betray his neighbors here in Edwardstown.

"Let's be straight with one another," added Malen, as if reading his thoughts. "You don't like me."

"Not much."

He tried a smile. "Maybe that's my fault. I admit it, there was a time I thought Sally would've been happier with some Ivy League type."

"Someone like Paul Holland," he spat out.

"Please understand, I only wanted what was best for her."

"Malen," shot back Mark, his control beginning to give way, "you don't have a clue what's best for her. What the hell do you know about a loving relationship?! I teach kids older than some of your girlfriends." He shook his head bitterly. "Sally and I are partners. Do you even understand what that means? When you underestimate me, asshole, you underestimate her."

"Look, what I want to tell you is that I'm sorry. I was wrong."

"Don't try to placate me, I don't want to hear it."

"Mark, I don't care if you like me. The point is, I really need your cooperation now."

"Relax, I'm not going to do anything to hurt my wife and child."

"I'm not just talking about her physical condition," he said meaningfully. "I think we both know she hasn't been herself lately."

Mark looked at him in surprise, wondering how much the doctor knew. Was he aware of her growing paranoia? Of her sudden, over-whelming fixation on this library in Salt Lake City?

"So again"—Malen extended his hand—"I really have to have that promise."

Hesitantly, Mark took it. Like it or not, for the moment this guy was his closest ally. "I'll keep you posted," he agreed softly.

Spread out on an autopsy table meant for human beings, the old chimp was a heart-wrenching sight.

The scientists still had not determined the precise cause of death, just knew that once it took hold, it had run its course with remarkable speed. Less than eight hours after Charley refused his morning ration of fruit, he was bleeding profusely from both nostrils. An hour more and he was on the floor of his cage, writhing in agony, arms tight around his belly.

His cries of pain were especially piteous given his normally stoic nature. But the scientists, taking careful notes, were not tempted to intervene.

By nightfall he was no longer fighting it; curled into a fetal ball, he moaned softly in the corner of his cage. He died a few minutes before midnight.

Now, scalpel in hand, Lynch leaned in close. To the naked eye all the internal organs appeared healthy, but he quickly located the problem by touch. The small intestine, usually softly pliable, was stiff and unyielding, less like foam rubber than the kind in tires. Slitting the organ open, he found thousands of mushroomlike nodules growing from the inner wall toward the center, effectively cutting off the passage of digested material.

"Epithelial hyperplasia," he confirmed.

"Good," said Foster, with a conviction reflecting his need to recast this setback as minor. "That suggests the problem is almost surely not with the efficacy of the drug itself, but with the delivery strategy."

Indeed, Charley—the only one of the twelve chimps to suffer such a fate—was also the only one who'd been dosed with the drug orally.

Lynch nodded uncertainly, peeling off a rubber glove. "Absolutely, this kind of thing happens in the development stage of most successful drugs." He looked down at the dead chimp. "I'll have Tran dispose of it."

"No!" Foster's look was intense, even savage. "Do it yourself. No one else needs to know."

"Of course."

"If anything," added Foster, "we've established that oral administration works *too* well. After all, if a single dose can stimulate such a massive *over*expression of the protein in this organ . . ." His voice trailed off. "Of course, we'll know more when we move up to a human model."

Lynch couldn't hide his expression of surprise. "You plan to run human trials?"

"I didn't say that," he said, his expression impassive. "We obviously will have to be judicious. At the moment I have just one human subject in mind."

Holland didn't get home from his weekend place in Amagansett till late Sunday night, and it was only the next morning that he bothered to check his messages.

"Mr. Holland . . . My name is Lisa Mitchell and I'm calling at some ungodly hour Saturday night. You don't know me . . ."

The young woman's voice pulsed with barely contained excitement and, only half listening, he at first thought she was a fan. Then he heard what she was saying.

". . . but I work with a friend of yours, Sally Benedict at the Edwardstown Weekly. *By the way, I'm a great admirer of your work. Anyway . . ."*

She paused, apparently wanting to get what was to come next just right.

"I'm calling about the piece you wrote a while back on the Life Services Institute—about certain facts I've discovered. I'm just here in New York for the weekend at"—she took a moment, evidently searching out the number—*"555-5623. This is quite important. I would certainly never bother you otherwise."*

Glancing at the bedside clock—8:54—he played the message again. Then he dialed the number.

An amiable male voice answered.

"Who's this?" asked Holland.

"Who's *this*?"

"Is there a Lisa Mitchell there?"

"Could be. Who should I tell her is calling?"

"Tell her I'm returning *her* call."

There was a muffled exchange in the background, then the voice from the tape was on the line—only this time more guarded. "This is Lisa Mitchell. Hold on, please."

He heard her say something to her friend, then she was back on. "Why don't I call you back in fifteen minutes?"

"Damn her," muttered Sally walking through the *Weekly*'s front door. She stamped the snow off her boots "Typical!"

Florence, the only other person already in the office, was surprised; an hour before, when she'd reported the crisis to the editor by phone, she'd seemed to take it in stride.

"What a pain getting here!" she explained. "Seven blocks and I got stuck twice! We're definitely due for another editorial on snow-removal problems!"

"Well," said Florence, characteristically upbeat, "at least it's stopped."

"For now. It's supposed to start again tonight." She paused. "I shouldn't even be here, Florence. Doctor's orders."

"Why? What's wrong?!"

"Nothing major, I'm just supposed to ease off for a while. I was hoping I could manage things by phone and fax." Sighing, she took off her coat and maneuvered herself into Lisa's chair. "All right, tell me about this lurch she left us in."

"It's just that I got in this morning and there was the message from Lisa. No explanation, no forwarding number, only that she wouldn't be back for a couple more days."

"What's the problem, isn't this issue about ready to go?"

As managing editor Florence each Monday oversaw the closing of that week's issue, then sent the mechanicals off to the printer in Montpelier early Tuesday; ensuring the finished product was ready for distribution the following morning.

"I thought so too. But then . . ."

Florence took a mock-up of the issue's front page from her desk and pointed to a space below the fold. "This is the slot for Lisa's tree story . . . ?"

"So?" The article in question was about a new ordinance under consideration by town trustees prohibiting the destruction of trees bordering on village land without specific authorization.

"She told me last week she was done with the reporting and was almost finished writing. Only, when I went to retrieve the file from her computer . . ." She indicated a block of text on Lisa's computer screen.

At a glance Sally saw it constituted only the merest beginnings of the story:

> Are Edwardstown's trees a treasured resource that should fall under the village's protection? Or should individuals keep the right to cut down stately oaks and elms on private property even if such destruction detracts from the overall beauty of our . . .

"That's it," said Florence. "It just suddenly ends like that—unless she has another file somewhere I can't find or some notes on the story."

She took a deep breath. "Oh, boy . . ."

Florence was obviously expecting her to take the situation in hand, as she always had; rereporting the story over a couple of hours, then dashing out the requisite five hundred words. But all at once the prospect seemed overwhelming. All she wanted now was to be back in her own home.

"Isn't there something else we can run in that slot?"

"I don't know, Sally. It's a news slot—nothing else is timely."

She sat there a moment, unable to focus on the problem. Abruptly, from nowhere, the dizziness was back—not nearly so intense as before, but sending her anxiety level through the roof. *Was it the preeclampsia or merely the task before her?*

"I'm sorry, Florence, please forgive me. I've got to get home."

The older woman looked at her in alarm. "Are you okay, Sally?"

"Fine." She flashed what she hoped was an encouraging smile. "Just do the best you can here."

"Mr. Holland?" said Lisa, picking up the phone on the first ring.

"Ms. Mitchell?"

After all this time in the boonies the thought that it was R. Paul Holland on the other end of the line was intensely heady. She laughed easily. "Sorry to pull the cloak-and-dagger stuff so early in the morning. It's okay, I'm alone now."

"I was surprised to find you at all. Your message said you'd be leaving town."

"I decided to extend my visit a couple of days."

After all, when would she ever again find herself with another such chance?

"That message you left was quite intriguing."

"It was meant to be."

Holland had run into far more than his share of eager-beaver scammers over the years, but rarely one who sounded so charmingly guileless. Which made him even warier.

"You say you're a friend of Sally Benedict?"

"A colleague, yes."

"How is she?"

"*Big* is the word that comes to mind. Very pregnant."

"Ah," he said, wondering if there might be more to be gleaned there. "About this matter you mentioned . . ." He paused. "Where are you now?"

She gave him Schneider's Upper West Side address.

"I've got a magazine deadline hanging over me, but we probably should talk. Would you mind coming down here? I'm at 415 East Fiftieth Street, it's just off Beekman Place." Better, he reasoned, not to risk being seen with this girl.

She jotted it down. "When?"

"For lunch—say, around one? It's a town house. Just ring the bell."

"Maybe I could bring along sandwiches or something—it might be more convenient."

Holland paused. *She was as interested in not being seen together as he was!* "I'll order in," he said pleasantly. "Actually, any chance you could make it noon?"

Town house.

Lisa wasn't at all surprised to hear Holland say he lived in one. The very concept—the word itself!—bespoke the dizzying heights of influence and celebrity to which she herself longed to one day ascend.

Her first impression was sharp disappointment. The building at the address scrawled on the paper in her hand, midway down a short block that dead-ended in a cul de sac, was anything but imposing; three narrow, nondescript stories in weathered brick.

She approached it through a cold, steady drizzle, protected by an umbrella bought on a nearby street corner. The only other soul within view was a white-clad nanny, waiting hopefully for a cab beneath the awning of the building opposite.

"Well," said Holland, "right on time—I always appreciate that. Come in. Dry off."

"Thanks."

Again, she was surprised. The great journalist was thinner than he appeared in photos and far more haggard.

She stepped into the entryway. This was more like it: a gleaming black-and-white parquet floor, a small chandelier overhead, an antique gilded mirror hanging over a mahogany umbrella stand.

"Nice place."

"It is. Unfortunately, I'm only renting." He shook out her umbrella and stuck it in the stand.

He was surprised also, startled even. The woman before him was drop-dead gorgeous. "Planning to stay?" he asked, indicating the overnight bag slung over her shoulder.

She smiled, flattered. "I'll be heading back to Edwardstown—I was due at work this morning."

"Ahh, that's the way all my luck's been running lately."

"So," he asked, ten minutes later, delicately hoisting a chunk of lemon chicken with his chopsticks, "you enjoy working with Sally?"

"It has its moments." She paused, then impulsively added, "A few, anyway."

"Is that a no?" he asked, intrigued.

"We're just different. Frankly, I'll never understand how anyone could give up this"—her glance took in not just the apartment, but urban life itself—"for *that*."

"You think she ever regrets it?"

"Who knows? She sure rubs my nose plenty in this glorious past of hers."

"Really?" he asked, surprised and secretly pleased by the obvious animosity.

Lisa set down her plate. "I can't tell you how I've *dreamed* of the moment where I tell her she can screw her job. It would probably kill her to know I'm sitting here right now with you."

He smiled—it was hard not to like this girl. "Is that why you're in town? You're looking for a job?"

"Partly." She flushed slightly at the admission and shifted in her chair, aware he was studying her.

"This magazine piece you're writing . . ." she spoke up, to break the silence. "Are you allowed to tell me what it's about?"

"Scientific fraud—mainly plagiarism."

"Sounds fascinating."

"Harrowing, is what it is—a cancer on the industry." He paused dramatically, an old hand at impressing with the force of his moral authority. "But the sad truth is you find the same kind of thing in every business that attracts talented, highly motivated people—including yours and mine."

Surprised and flattered to be seen as a colleague, Lisa nodded soberly. "Yes, Mr. Holland, I can see that."

"*Please* don't call me that, it makes me feel so old. It's Paul." He smiled. "In any case, that's why one can't afford to get a reputation for sloppiness. In the end our integrity is all we have."

Lisa nodded; she hadn't expected the conversation to get to the point so quickly.

"That's why, speaking personally, I'm always grateful to a fellow journalist kind enough to alert me to even minor oversights in my reporting."

"I was afraid you'd think I was arrogant."

"You *should* be arrogant—if you don't have that to build on, you'll *never* get serious respect." He leaned forward. "Now tell me about this discovery of yours."

"I don't want to give the wrong impression," she said, suddenly fearing she'd oversold herself to get in the door. "It's just I've run across a couple of things that might be interesting. . . ."

His eyes continued to bore into her.

"Not that it even means anything. I mean, you wrote so posi-

tively about these people. It's hard to believe you might've missed
something that I found. . . ."

"Hold the flattery, Lisa. For instance?"

She took a deep breath and let it out. "You never mentioned that
they might be using human body parts in their research."

"No, I didn't," he said, nonplused. "Do you have information
they are?"

"They've been calling university anatomy departments all over
the place—places with anatomical collections that go back before the
turn of the century."

Holland nodded noncommittally. "Well, that is interesting—I
never pretended I saw everything. Still, given the nature of their research, that would certainly seem an entirely legitimate course of
action."

"But why *old* body parts? Why would they be interested in people who died eighty or a hundred years ago?"

"You tell me," he said, bemused. "It sounds like you've got some
kind of theory brewing."

She hesitated. "I know this sounds crazy. But did you know
there've been some grave robbings in our area . . . ?"

"In Edwardstown?" He paused. "Yes, I think I did hear something about that. Are you *really* suggesting some kind of link?"

"It's just an idea. But there's evidence that the bodies are all from
the same family. Sally's, as a matter of fact."

"Jesus, that's one helluva charge!" He looked incredulous.
"We're talking about the same people? The scientists from the Life
Services Institute?"

"It's just, I don't know, it's a theory," she retreated. "Maybe not
even that. But what's interesting—what got me thinking there could
be a connection—is that all those people lived an incredibly long
time."

"Didn't they catch the ones who did it? The grave robbers?"

"That's true." She nodded, wondering fleetingly how he knew.

"Only, one of them killed himself without ever confessing—no note or anything. And the other one took off." She shrugged. "He's just sort of a weakling, he could've been bullied into saying anything." She paused. "Besides, couldn't they have done it *for* someone?"

Almost imperceptibly he raised an eyebrow. "I'm sorry, Lisa, I've got to tell you it strikes me as pretty far fetched." Rising to his feet, he started back toward the kitchen. "Any interest in dessert? I've got some terrific mango sherbet."

"I know it sounds crazy," she called after him, her opportunity seeming literally to slip away, "but I thought maybe *you* might make more of it."

It took him a couple of minutes to return with the bowls. "*Me?*" Sitting back down, he smiled. "I'm the one who wrote so positively about these guys, remember? If even a tenth of your crazy theory pans out, I'll spend years wiping egg from my face."

"Not if *you* break the story yourself." She paused; at least that had gotten his attention. "You'll get everything I have. If there's anything to the story, you'll reek of integrity."

"And if I don't take it on, you'll pursue it anyway, right . . . ?"

She looked away a moment, then back at him. "I'm not interested in embarrassing you. But if you were looking for someone to help you out, I'd certainly be open to an arrangement. No one knows the territory better."

"You're suggesting the *Herald* bring you on as a researcher?"

"The title doesn't matter to me, all I'm looking for is a shot."

He leaned back and folded his arms. "Well, you've certainly got persistence and drive. That's a helluva good start."

"So I keep telling people—it's nice to finally be believed."

"All right," he decided with a nod, "what the hell, I'll take a flyer. Crazier things have happened. I'll set it up." He paused, looked at her intently. "But this is my ass on the line—I need to be absolutely sure I can count on your discretion. Who else knows about this?"

"No one."

"Sally?"

She shook her head; no way she was going to blow it now by mentioning her nemesis had suspicions of her own. "Everything I've picked up I've kept to myself."

"What about the guy who answered the phone?"

"A friend. He's not even in the business."

He sat there for a long moment, fingertips pressed together in a church steeple, thinking it through. "You're planning to return to Edwardstown this afternoon?"

She nodded and glanced at her watch. "My car's in a lot around the corner. I'm hoping to make it back by eight-thirty or nine tonight."

"Good. Which would put you in Manchester when, around seven?"

She looked stunned. "You want me to stop at the Institute?"

"Why not?—let's not pussyfoot around. I want you to ask Dr. Lynch directly if they've graduated to using human tissue in their research. Because this all comes as news to me."

"But, I mean . . ."

He nodded. "I understand. It can be unpleasant when someone objects to the tenor of your questions. But that comes with the territory, Lisa. Frankly, one of the things I want to see is what you're made of." He smiled, reaching inside his jacket pocket for his address book. "Don't worry, I'll start you off with a safety net."

"Dr. Lynch?" he was saying a moment later, and she noted that his phone voice was as full of easy confidence as Sinatra in his prime. "Paul Holland of the *Herald*—hope I'm not catching you at a bad time." He waited a couple of beats. "Listen, I'm sending someone to see you, just a courtesy call." He paused, winked at her. "My new assistant. Actually, I think you know her already—Lisa Mitchell, she's been with a weekly up in your area, a terrific young reporter. . . ."

By the time he hung up, she was already in her coat. "Thanks. I won't let you down."

"Welcome to the big leagues, Lisa."

He walked her to the door. "Call me as soon as you get back home, don't worry about the time."

"I will. Thank you."

He gave her arm a squeeze and opened the door.

The rain was coming down harder now. "Oh, my umbrella!" she said, and retrieved it before stepping outside.

He watched as she started off, again remarking to himself on how attractive she was.

"Hey," he called out, "drive carefully."

The rain started changing to snow about three hours out of New York, just past Providence. Light at first, and picturesque against the still-colorful trees, soon it was coming down so hard the traffic could no longer chew it up. By the time she made the Massachusetts–New Hampshire border, Interstate 93 was a broad river of white.

As darkness fell, visibility down to almost nothing, few cars were doing better than twenty. Too thick for headlights to pierce, the cottony flakes reflected glare back at drivers.

But Lisa's bug managed to maintain a steady forty-five, staying in the left lane behind a monster semi with, she gratefully surmised, a speed-addled madman behind the wheel.

She was late to the most important appointment of her professional life. The scientists were expecting her. And, more to the point, R. Paul Holland waited for her report.

Never had she so regretted resisting the impulse to spring for a cellular phone!

Still, she made it to her exit, just north of Manchester, little more than an hour past her goal. The Institute was several miles from the interstate, off a two-lane road north of the city. To her surprise and relief, for she was wearing loafers, the long drive leading up to the imposing brick structure had already been plowed, and she was able to pull to within fifteen feet of the front door.

The plow-equipped Range Rover that had done the job stood at the side, idling, set to go again. As she cut her engine, its driver, a short, thick man in a heavy down jacket, came hurrying toward her through the snow, hands in pockets, an umbrella tucked under his arm.

Before she'd even gotten out, he'd opened it for her.

"Thanks," she said, and stepped quickly from the car. Only now did she realize how bitterly cold it was. "I really wasn't ready for this kind of weather."

"Well, hurry inside. We'll get something nice and warm into you."

The man was just a couple of inches taller than she was, and turning to him in the entryway she saw his blue eyes, moist with cold, were reassuringly kind.

"You're a brave girl to be out alone on a night like this."

"It's no big deal." She smiled. "I've got an appointment with Dr. Lynch, he should be expecting me. . . ."

"Oh, surely," he said, nodding to the left.

As she turned in that direction, a rag was suddenly over her mouth and nose, the powerful hand pressing down with incredible force. Startled, for an instant she didn't even react. The odor was intense, sickly sweet, overpowering. Now she began writhing, kicking at him, even as, from some classroom deep in her past, it began to register. Chloroform! But already the neural impulses in her midbrain were shutting down and the world started to go dark.

A moment later, Van Ost had her in his arms, carrying her down a flight of stairs to the basement lab. He noted with satisfaction that there was not so much as a bruise.

The silver cylinder was empty, the walls of its inner chamber thickly coated with ice. A fresh sheet had been laid on the bottom. It was only a couple of hours since the removal of Stagg's body.

"Set her down carefully," instructed Foster.

Beside him Lynch was expressionless. Though he wanted to accept Foster's assurances that Stagg would understand, he couldn't escape the thought they'd violated a sacred trust.

Now, studying the girl, her eyes closed, breathing easily, he observed, "She looks like Sleeping Beauty."

Foster closed the lid and cast him a withering look. "Try Snow White."

You know what?" exclaimed Mark, examining the *Weekly*'s front page with surprise. "You don't *need* Lisa!"

Sally smiled. "Nice save, huh?"

"Florence did this completely on her own?"

"I gave her the ball and she ran with it." She paused, trying to summon up the image. "Or something."

What the managing editor had done was delve into the photo file and come up with shots of three of the town's most majestic trees. These she ran huge—across the entire front page above the fold—as a kind of visual essay, using a few pertinent lines from Lisa's unfinished effort as an extended caption.

"The question is what we'll do for the next issue," observed Sally.

"Relax, Lisa will be back. She's probably been job hunting down there, and is too embarrassed to let anyone know."

"Screw her embarrassment! What about us?"

Mark put his hand on her shoulder. "No one's arguing. Just watch the blood pressure."

"I mean, Christ, it's been three days since she left that message! She doesn't even have the decency to call?"

But, in fact, this outburst was camouflage for a deepening sense of apprehension. She knew, even if Mark didn't, that this was totally out of character for Lisa. Spoiled and demanding as she was, she was also a pro. Always, in the past, when she made a commitment, she had followed through.

"She'll be back," he repeated.

"I'm sure you're right."

"And if she's not . . ." He blithely waved the paper, as if this were the only thing that mattered. "When are you going to start showing some faith in Florence?"

Sally was alone at the kitchen table, relaxing over toast and jam and tea.

God, how she'd come to hate tea! She'd never imagined she could so crave a good, strong cup of java in the morning! Just one more reason she longed for this pregnancy to be over!

As soon as the phone rang, she snatched up the receiver.

"Sally Benedict?"

She didn't recognize the voice. "Who's this?"

"My name's Barry Schneider." He paused a moment, hoping it would ring a bell. "I'm a friend of Lisa Mitchell."

She tensed. "Do you know where she is?"

"Oh," he said, disappointed, "I was hoping you could tell me."

"She hasn't been here in more than a week, Mr. Schneider—the last we knew she was heading to New York."

"*Dr.* Schneider," he corrected self-consciously, "—just in case my mother's listening in." He laughed. "I know that, I was with her in New York. In fact, I wouldn't let her out of my sight."

Sally had less than no interest in this guy's version of repartee. "Until when?"

"She was at my place Monday morning when I left for work. I get back, and there's just a note saying she'll be in touch."

"So you're involved with Lisa romantically?"

"I hope so—with overtones of the professional." He laughed softly, without conviction. "You've trained her well—she never stops grilling me."

"Grilling you? About what?"

"You name it—surgery, genetics, creative use of cadavers . . ."

Sally was only glad he wasn't there to see her expression. *Genetics!* she wrote on her notepad. *Cadavers!!!* "Go on," she said evenly.

"You know her better than I do," he said, the veneer of self-assurance gone. "You think she may have just been using me?"

"I don't know. Tell me everything."

Late that afternoon when Stebben appeared at her door, Sally wasn't entirely surprised.

"Can I come in?" Stebben's face was pink with cold and he was blowing smoke.

"What for?" she said stiffly.

"Is Mark here?" He leaned around her, trying to peer inside.

"No, he's still at school. Science-fair stuff."

Though he'd only known since lunchtime, the chief looked like he hadn't slept in days. He'd been so dreading this scene, he very nearly passed on the assignment to Simmons.

But, no, there was no way around it, he had to do it himself, in person. Already he was armed with a story for when she asked about the delay. As long as investigators were gathering evidence, he'd tell her, he'd had to remain at the scene.

If she asked about anything else . . . He didn't know, he'd wing it.

Maybe she'd see how much he himself was hurting. After all, he'd never imagined it would be like this! Not for an instant! All he'd done was grab the chance to pick up some extra bucks, enlist a couple of kids for a harmless prank.

It wasn't his fault. He loved this town, it was his whole life!

Hadn't he even tried to warn her?

Stebben realized he hadn't seen Sally Benedict in a while. "Pretty soon now, huh?" he said.

The attempt at empathy was so unnatural, it instantly removed any lingering doubt. "Something's happened," said Sally, not a question.

Still, he hesitated. "When do you think Mark might be back?" He'd counted on his presence as a calming influence and a buffer.

"Damn you, just let it out!"

He briefly averted his eyes, then looked into hers. "I'm afraid Lisa had an accident. I was just over there. . . . She didn't"—he hesitated—"*survive.*"

For a long moment her expression was blank. No way she was going to give Stebben even a fleeting glimpse of what she was feeling. She blinked a few times, like someone caught unawares by a flash camera. "What kind of accident?" she asked, with a reporter's equanimity.

"They found her car off on a little side road, half buried in a drift. That little VW of hers."

"Where?"

"About forty minutes from here, off 113A—a little south of Craterville. She must've pulled off the highway in the storm and got lost."

Sally nodded. Way the hell out in the middle of nowhere. "Have they determined the cause of death?"

"Exposure. It's not official yet—the body's at the coroner's in Montgomery." He looked away, thinking, *Jesus, it's like she's discussing a stranger!* "It's quite a shock. She was a good kid."

"She froze to death?"

"The storm must've caught her by surprise. All she had with her was lightweight clothes. The temperature was down in the single digits." He paused, felt compelled to absolve himself of even a whiff of responsibility. "I'm not involved with the investigation, it's under state jurisdiction." He stopped again. "I hope you know how sorry I am."

She nodded. "Someone will have to talk to her family." For the first time her voice wavered slightly. "I'd really rather it not be me, if you don't mind. I'm sure Florence can find you a number in the office file."

"All right."

There was a momentary silence. She sensed the facade about to crumble entirely.

"You okay, Sally? Maybe you ought to lie down or something."

"Don't worry about me."

He nodded and started backing away. "Well, I'd better get on it. But, please, anything at all I can do, I want you to—"

But already she had closed the door behind her.

Mark charged through the front door half an hour later, calling her name.

"I'm up here."

He bounded up the stairs and stopped at the bedroom door, breathing hard.

"Sally, something awful's happened. I wanted you to hear it from me first. . . ."

"I know," she replied with exaggerated calm. "Stebben was already here."

Before her on the bed was a pile of laundry that she was methodically sorting, making small neat stacks of socks, underwear, blouses.

Mark stood, uncertain for a moment. This eerie calm was even more inappropriate than the tears and rages to which she'd subjected him in recent weeks. He tentatively approached, arms wide, and slowly she moved into his embrace. "Oh, God, Sal, it's so awful!"

Now, over her shoulder, he noticed beside the laundry pile a half-filled suitcase.

"What are you doing?"

"Packing. I'm going to Salt Lake City. I have to know, Mark."

"Know *what*?!"

Pulling away, she resumed packing with the same preternatural calm, selecting a sweater and putting it in her suitcase.

"Sit down, Sally. We have to talk, you're too upset to think straight!"

She ignored him. If anyone was going to be accused of hysteria around here, it wasn't her.

"Will you STOP that?!" He snatched the clothes from her hand. "You're not going anywhere, Sally! This was an *accident*!"

She picked up a different sweater. "All those stolen bodies were from my family, Mark. . . ." She launched into the now-familiar litany. "Every one!"

"We don't even know that for sure, Sally!"

"Mother dies suddenly. Now Lisa. And Lynch *worked* in Salt Lake City. . . ."

Even more than the tortured logic it was her purposefulness that was so unnerving. He put his hands on her shoulders and looked into her eyes, appealing to whatever remnant of reason remained. "Sally, have you given a single thought to how dangerous this is to the pregnancy . . . to the *baby*?"

"I'm PROTECTING the baby!"

"No, Sally—I AM!" Suddenly, despite himself, he was shouting. "What the hell's wrong with you? You think you're the only one under pressure around here? The only one affected by what's happened?! There is NO connection between those things! Lisa died of NATURAL CAUSES, same as your mom! The grave robbings were SOLVED!" He turned away from her, breathing hard, trying to regain some semblance of control. "Goddamn it, this is *Edwardstown* we're talking about!"

"I'm sorry, Mark, *I* will NOT just sit around doing nothing," she said, walking past him toward the bathroom. Reappearing a moment later, she flung her prenatal vitamins into the bag.

"Forget it, Sally, I won't allow it! And neither will Malen!!"

She zipped the bag, and spoke with finality. "The flight's at six-twenty out of Burlington. I'll leave tonight and stay at a motel near the airport."

Malen must have flown—he was over within a quarter hour of getting Mark's call. He had his bag with him.

"I don't know what to do," Mark told him. "I really think this has pushed her over the edge!"

"Where is she?"

"Still in the bedroom."

The doctor remained impressively unperturbed. "Wait here."

"Well?" said Mark, seizing the doctor's arm when he emerged from the bedroom twenty minutes later.

"I gave her an injection. Ativan, a very mild sedative."

"That's it?"

"We also talked it out. I think we're okay."

"She's not going?"

He shook his head. "I made her understand how completely irresponsible that would be from a medical standpoint."

"Thank God!" He exhaled audibly. "If you only knew how much I appreciate this!"

"I promised her I'd get you to go instead."

"*What*?!"

Malen gave him a look that conveyed at once helplessness and profound understanding. "Just do it and hurry back. Don't worry, she'll be safe in my hands."

Mark got the next shock when he dragged himself to the counter at Burlington International Airport just past dawn. The ticket Sally had reserved came to $1,287—triple what it would have cost had this particular bit of insanity kicked in in time for the Super Saver rate!

Exhausted as he was after less than three hours sleep and an hour-and-a-half drive through an icy drizzle, he still couldn't doze off. During the entire first leg of the trip, two and a half hours to Cincinnati, the thought kept rattling around in his consciousness: almost nine hundred extra bucks pointlessly subtracted from the baby's college fund!

It was as if he no longer knew this person! Would she even remember to alert the school he wouldn't be showing up? Or should he blow *another* twenty bucks, or whatever the hell it cost, calling himself from the plane?!

But, no, he realized, of course she'd remember. That was partly what made it so maddening: when she had to, at work or in a social situation, she still seemed normal. Were he to try describing her private behavior to people who knew her socially, they'd think *he* was the delusional one!

"Is something wrong, sir? You don't seem to have touched your breakfast."

He glanced down at the plastic tray, then up at the stewardess. Damn right something was wrong—*shouldn't all that money buy something more than a granite minibagel and lumpy, overcooked eggs?* "Thanks, no. I'm just not very hungry."

It wasn't until after he'd changed planes in Cincinnati that he pulled from his briefcase the revised and updated science-fair material he was supposed to have reviewed last night.

Laura Diamond's report charting the geologic record of the Edwardstown area seemed in good shape, a nice balance of serious science and community spirit. His response to young Steve Merritt's effort—an electronic "scarecrow," intended to replicate the screech of chicken hawk—was more complex. The contraption didn't work; even the most gullible crows on his family's farm were scared off only for a few minutes. Still, the originality of the attempt was heartening and so was the scrupulousness with which he'd abided by the first rule of scientific inquiry: respect the data. Though it didn't help make his case, perhaps even made him appear slightly foolish, the boy had resisted the temptation to fudge it even a little.

Making a notation on the top page of Steve's report, Mark allowed himself his first smile of the day. *Got any photos of the crows ignoring this thing? We'll do "Before" and "After" shots when you unveil the new improved model next year!*

Now he turned to the most ambitious effort of the bunch—a research project by Elaine Seggerman on the obstacles confronting scientists in the ongoing effort to restore full flavor to the hardier tomatoes created by genetic manipulation. As she summarized the problem in her introduction, the reason tomatoes rot is well understood: because they produce an enzyme that triggers the breakdown of carbohydrates in the cell wall. Unfortunately, that same enzyme appears linked to what's regarded as succulent, sun-ripened tomato flavor. The challenge, never more than partially successful, has been to partially block the enzyme's function without paying any consequences.

Mischievously, the girl had moved beyond reporting to informed speculation of her own, concluding that the effort to produce hardiness without the sacrifice of flavor was almost surely doomed to remain "fruitless." Why? Because although scientists working at profit-driven labs would never admit it, maybe even to themselves, nature's scheme was flawless, full of masterfully hidden, self-protective biological safeguards. Tantalizingly close as human beings come, they will never succeed in bettering it.

Good! wrote Mark in a bold hand. *Excellent analysis!*—then, remembering where he was and why, his spirits plummeted.

"I'm sorry, sir," said the pretty young woman behind the Hertz desk at Salt Lake City International Airport, "there seems to be a problem. I'm showing you've reached your limit on your credit card."

"That's not possible! Can you try it again?"

She did.

"I'm genuinely sorry, sir," she said, seeming to mean it. "Do you have another card you can use?"

Christ! She'd used it to pay for the ticket!

"I don't," he said. "You don't take checks, do you?"

"No, sir, I'm afraid not."

And of course he'd have the same trouble at his hotel!

He made a conscious choice not to jump over that cliff until he got to it.

"Is there a bus that goes into town?"

In her sleep Sally reached toward the other side of the bed. When her husband wasn't there, her eyes opened.

Still only half awake, she saw Mark's flannel pajama bottoms flung on the chair by the window, the damp towel hanging on the doorknob, dust particles dancing in the flat, early winter light.

Then she realized. The bedside clock showed 7:35. He was already in the air.

She lingered in bed for another twenty minutes, then took a leisurely shower.

It was over breakfast with Gram—fresh squeezed orange juice and oatmeal—that she first felt it—a sensation unlike any she'd ever experienced before. Though not painful, it was impossible to ignore.

Even her grandmother noticed. "What's wrong, Sally? Is it . . . time?"

The possibility was too horrible even to contemplate—she still had a month to go. "No, Gram," she said, reaching out to give her arm a reassuring squeeze. "Just a touch of gas."

But within half an hour there came faint stirrings of nausea. Though she knew she should call Malen, instead she took a couple of tablespoons of Maalox and returned to bed. Almost immediately she felt better and soon drifted off to sleep.

*   *   *

The pleasant, bespectacled young man beside Mark on the bus seemed to know everything about the Family History Library. Of course he did, he cheerfully offered, he was a Mormon himself, and the purpose of the place was spiritual.

"We do family history research because the Church teaches that family life continues beyond the grave. If we the living make covenants on their behalf, even ancestors who've been dead hundreds of years will receive the blessings of eternal family union." He paused, then added blithely, "To do this, obviously, we've got to figure out who they were."

"So the Church began accumulating files of genealogical records?"

He nodded. "From all over the world. They started more than a hundred years ago. They say they've got some kind of record on two billion people. And now, thanks to computers, the records are expanding by another hundred or so million every year."

Mark was fascinated; the concept was staggering. "You've done this yourself? Searched for your ancestors?"

"Oh, all of our people are accounted for. But sometimes I'll go there just to rummage around."

"The eventual object is to get something on . . . *everyone*?"

"That'd be great, wouldn't it? But, no, that's impossible. There have supposedly been something like seventy billion human beings on earth, but there's only a record of maybe a tenth of them."

Mark sat in silence for a moment, looking out the window. The morning was crisp and incredibly clear. Ahead he could make out the city's skyline, and the crescent of snowcapped mountains beyond. From photographs he recognized the outline of the imposing Mormon Tabernacle.

"We've traced our own family all the way back to the fifteenth century," his seatmate added.

"Really?"

"My ancestors were German and Dutch. The early records of both the Lutheran and Dutch Reformed churches are pretty good."

"How about the records from England?"

"Oh, they're excellent. Probably more complete than from anywhere else in the world."

The library, it turned out, was in the heart of downtown, part of a vast complex on West Temple Street that also included the Tabernacle and the office building that was the Church's international headquarters.

Inside, from the high-tech lighting to the microfiche work stations strategically placed at intervals amid the shelves, it was indistinguishable from many other such state-of-the-art research facilities—except for the cadre of young volunteer guides patiently waiting alongside the reception desk.

Within seconds a clean-scrubbed young Oriental man—Korean, he guessed—was at his side. "Can I help you?" he asked in a heavy accent.

"I'm trying to trace my wife's family . . . they came here from England."

The young man nodded briskly. "You have a name, a date, or place of birth?"

He pulled a folded sheet of paper from his inside jacket pocket. "John Willson—that's with a double *l*. Mildenhall Parish, Suffolk. May twentieth, 1637. He was her first relative in this country."

"All *right*," he exclaimed. "Then we are in business."

He quickly led the visitor down a long corridor, then turned down another. From the place names affixed to the shelves Mark realized they were in the section for the British Isles. "I do not think what you want will be on microfilm," he said. "For most English counties—*shires*, they were called—what we have from that period are bound copies of early records. You say the place is called Mildenhall?"

"Mildenhall Parish."

They stopped and the young man began scanning the shelf. "Here," he announced, standing on tiptoe to withdraw a volume.

SUFFOLK, read the notation on the binding, MIF–MIN.

He led Mark over to a carrel. "First, you find your village, then you look for your date." He paused. "These people made it easy. In Church of England records events are usually listed chronologically. The local minister just wrote them down as they occurred."

The section of the book on Mildenhall Parish, covering nearly four hundred years, comprised eighty-five pages—endless lists of names and events. With the birth date in hand the volunteer found what Mark was after with astonishing speed.

As he read the entry, Mark was surprised to find himself seized by real excitement.

> *20 May, 1637. Born to Richard Willson, farmer, a son, baptized this day John.*

"He was baptized the same day he was born?"

"That is how they sometimes did it back then," observed the young man. "It's because so many babies died."

"Why isn't the mother listed?"

"That was often the case. To find her name we should look for the entry recording Richard Willson's marriage."

Less than five minutes later they found it.

> *4 May, 1634. Richard Willson, yeoman, betrothed in this church to Sarah Whitney, daughter of John, yeoman.*

"You see?" said the volunteer. "Simple." He nodded and started moving off. "If you need more help, just ask for it."

This was just a start, of course: what Sally was so desperate to know was how long these people lived. So he now jumped back twenty or so years to ferret out Richard and Sarah's births—1611 and 1616 respectively, as it turned out; then he moved forward in time, hunting for the record of their deaths.

Already, curiously, he was feeling a kinship with these ancient in-laws, and it was with a certain sorrow that he located Richard's with ease. He had perished—*dyed accidentally by a blowe to his head,* as the notation quaintly had it—at the age of thirty-seven, roughly average for that time and place.

But finding Sarah's end proved harder. After a quarter hour trying he decided that in his fatigue he'd inadvertently passed it by. "Shit," he muttered to himself. Or maybe, it occurred to him, she'd remarried and died under another name. Or even moved from her native village.

Damn you, Sally! You're NEVER gonna stop owing me for this!

He was about to start over when he turned a page and the name jumped out at him.

November 17, 1721. Today died the widowe Sarah Willson, welle beloved, in the fulleness of her years. 105 years, 7 months, and 12 dayes.

Hearing the doorbell ring while she slept, Sally actually incorporated the sound into a dream. She was at her old newspaper in Philadelphia, and flinging open the office door at the sound, she found Mark, toting an oversized network news camera. Though apparently working for a rival news organization, he was to accompany her on a big story. She knew she had to be wary, protective of her exclusive.

The second ring, longer and more persistent, brought her to consciousness. For a long moment she lay there, taking stock. No, it was okay, she didn't feel it.

Now she heard her grandmother, moving laboriously through

the living room with her cane; and after an eternity, the sound of the door opening.

Words were exchanged, indistinct but unmistakable. It was Malen.

The knock on her door came almost immediately.

"Sally . . . ?"

Malen opened it and peered in. "What's up?" she asked sleepily, covers drawn almost to her chin.

He stepped into the room. "Just checking in. How's it going?"

She was aware of his glance finding the Maalox on the bedside table and was furious at herself for leaving it there.

"I'm fine, just a little tired."

"Nothing else? No queasiness?"

"I felt a little something before, but it went away."

"What sort of 'little something'?"

"It's nothing, Lee."

"Well, I'd like to take a look, just in case. Why don't you get dressed and I'll run you down to the office?"

It was not a request but a statement of an intention.

"I really don't think we have to do that."

He took a seat on the edge of the bed and snapped open his bag. "We'll start here, then," he said, taking out the blood-pressure cuff.

"C'mon, Lee, I just had a little heartburn, it's gone now."

"You think you could sit up?" He held up the cuff. "Humor me."

Slowly, she drew herself up and extended her arm. Attaching the cuff, he saw she looked pallid.

"Tell me more about these pains of yours."

"Nothing to tell."

But even as she said it, the feeling was suddenly back—only much sharper now. She winced slightly.

"What's going on? Tell me exactly what you're feeling."

"It's nothing, it'll pass."

On the gauge before him her blood pressure read one sixty over ninety.

"All right, Sally," he said authoritatively, "we're going to the office. I want to do a pelvic exam."

She'd never seen him like this before. Where was his warmth? Why was he bullying her?

"Is your bag packed?"

She nodded, panic stricken. "Why?"

He looked at her closely and spoke with exaggerated calm. "Because I think you're in labor."

"Can't we wait for Mark?"

"Sally, get dressed and let's get out of here."

"Who else will be there? At the hospital?"

"Who'll *be* there?" he repeated in exasperation. "I don't know, I don't have a duty roster in my pocket."

"I don't want Dr. Crocker anywhere near me. Or Dr. Downs!"

It took him an instant to understand—of course, her mother! "I'll try, that's all I can do. You need help getting out of bed?"

She remained where she was, frantically reviewing her options. Was there another hospital she could get to?—Madison was little more than an hour away. But under what pretext? If she could just get to a phone, maybe . . . !

She heard it before she felt it, a rush of liquid between her legs. Her reaction was involuntary. "Oh, my GOD!!"

Malen was aware of it too. "Just stay calm, it's okay."

"I think my water broke."

Her nightgown and the mattress beneath her were soaked, traces of stain appearing even on the cover above.

"Enough, Sally. From now on you are going to do *exactly* what I tell you."

Even four hours later Mark resisted the evidence before him. Surely there was some other explanation. There HAD to be.

Yet his resolve was fading. By now he'd gone back nearly two hundred and seventy years farther—eleven generations, into the early fifteenth century, moving beyond the Church of England records to the even older ones kept by local landed gentry—and it was nothing short of uncanny. Every second generation was astonishingly long lived. Hundreds of years before modern medicine, when even the most basic hygiene was unheard of, these people were living into their late nineties and beyond!

Just as she had predicted.

Was it possible? Had there really been a genetic mutation that gave this family such fantastic powers of survival?!

He'd mastered the drill by now, flipping the pages faster and faster, flying back through the decades.

The very possibility was mind boggling. Things like this just didn't happen. Stumbling upon such a magical quirk of nature was akin to hitting a ten-million-to-one shot in the lottery—no, hitting it ten weeks in a row!

Nor, here, was it just a matter of pure science. Maybe his wife, in her paranoid fantasies, saw such a thing as a threat, but Mark knew better. Even the most gifted molecular biologists couldn't hijack a genetic mutation. Hell, just this morning he'd been reminded they couldn't even get this razzle-dazzle genetics stuff to work right on *fruit*.

No, should this prove out, Mark recognized it for what it would truly be: an extraordinary, awe-inspiring blessing. Their own child would actually be *programmed* for a long and healthy life!

His fatigue and hunger were gone now. All that mattered was ferreting out data that would further support or—suddenly he didn't even want to think it—demolish the theory.

But he never for a moment expected what he found. The mutation's source.

Mary Whitby, 1297–1396.

Before her, Mark saw, the pattern did not exist. Neither of her parents lived past forty; and, more meaningfully, neither did her maternal grandparents. Nor, continuing back another hundred years, were any of *their* ancestors especially long lived.

Clearly within the DNA of this single, unremarkable woman, something astonishing and inexplicable occurred. Where in other families comparable genetic aberrations would produce centuries of heartbreak by a predisposition to sickle-cell anemia, or Tay-Sachs disease, or Huntington's chorea, or early-onset Alzheimer's, or innumerable other inherited maladies, Mary Whitby's heirs hit the jackpot.

"Okay," Mark reined himself in, whispering the words aloud, "let's see if we can nail this sucker down."

The idea was simplicity itself: if Mary had other children in addition to Sally's direct ancestor, the mutation should have been passed down in those lines also.

Hurriedly, for by now it was late afternoon, Mark began moving forward again; launching this new search in 1297, the year of Mary's birth.

Oddly, the book opened to the page immediately, seemingly of its own volition. He smiled at his luck—then saw it wasn't luck at all. There was a sliver of paper in the crack halfway down.

He flicked it out, and moved on, the fact barely registering; there was too much to do.

Yes, indeed, there was a sister—Jane Whitby, born two years after Mary's more direct forebear! Rushing ahead, he located Jane's children, then theirs; and the two generations that followed.

It was true! There was no longer the slightest question. This line, too, had inherited the longevity gene!

Mark sat back in his chair, exhilaration washing over him.

He reached for the huge volume, still open on the desk before him, to return it to its shelf—and noticed the second sliver of paper.

He picked it up, placed it beside the first marker. They were of the same stock.

Checking the open page, he saw again it was the one listing the death of Jane Whitby's great-great-granddaughter, the first in this second line to exceed the age of one hundred.

Okay, thought Mark by force of habit, *what the fuck is going on here?*

But for once the impulse to reason it out was overwhelmed by something far more primitive. No, a pair of book markers wasn't proof—not the kind he usually insisted upon. But this wasn't just some meaningless academic exercise.

As he stared at the page, a single thought took hold.

Someone had been here before him.

Someone else knew.

Slamming the book shut, Mark was on his feet, briskly walking, then trotting, toward the exit.

How many times had he dismissed Sally's lunatic ravings about their child being in that line?!

In the hall he grabbed the first pay phone in a long bank and dialed collect.

Gram answered on the first ring and, to his surprise, readily accepted the call. Thank God this was one of her lucid days.

"Listen, Martha, I have to speak to Sally."

"She's not here."

"Where is she?"

"I've been waiting here all day by the darn phone. She's having the baby."

"How long do you think it'll be?" asked Sally in the labor room, making the question almost nonchalant.

"Hard to say—you're still only four centimeters dilated," said Malen, pleased at her newfound calm. "Do I take care of you, or what?—Crocker and Downs won't come anywhere near this place."

"Thanks. Sorry I lost it before."

He smiled. "Of course, it helps they're both off duty."

She nodded. "It's harder than I thought going through this without Mark."

But she'd forced herself to accept it. *Everything will be fine*, she kept thinking, *I'm safe here. These people are my FRIENDS!*

Still, despite herself, another thought kept intruding: *Maybe there's still time. It's only a little past six o'clock—and weren't first labors usually long?*

"Any chance it's false labor?"

"Sally, your water broke."

"Right." She managed a smile. "There is that."

Even as she said it, she could feel another wave of pain rising, rising, till it began to crowd out all else. They were coming regularly now, every five or six minutes.

As she gripped the sides of the bed hard beneath the covers, her expression scarcely changed.

Beside Malen, Barbara Walker looked from her face to the printout reading from the fetal monitor belted across her midsection, then back again. According to the printout this contraction should have been the most intense yet.

"Doctor . . ."

Sally watched as together they examined the sheet.

"Well," he said to Sally, masking his own confusion, "we always knew you were tough. . . ."

Barbara shook her head appreciatively. "Hey, we got Ms. Macho here! But don't be shy, the doctor'll be glad to give you something to speed things up."

"That's okay," she said quickly. "You know me—a natural girl from way back."

Ostentatiously, her eyes roamed the labor room, unlit and dim as the daylight faded between half-drawn curtains. "I'm pretty tired. Think there's a chance in a thousand I might be able to get some sleep?"

"*Sleep?* While you're in labor?" Barbara chuckled. "I guess there's a first for everything."

"It's not a bad idea to try testing," said Malen. "We could be in for a long night." He started from the room. "I'll check back in a little while."

"Go easy on him," said the nurse, with bemused confidentiality. "He's nervous as a cat himself. This is as close as he'll ever come to a grandchild of his own."

"I'd gladly change places with him."

Barbara wiped the perspiration from her forehead. "I know this isn't how you imagined it. But don't worry, I'll be here for you."

She smiled gratefully. "I don't want to keep you either."

"Relax, we have no other customers. It's between you and a back issue of *People* magazine."

"Actually, I'd *rather* be alone awhile. I won't be able to relax."

"Sure thing." The nurse gave her hand a squeeze. "You need me, just holler. Remember, Sally, this is no time to be foolishly brave."

Mark sprinted the block and a half from the library to a taxi stand and headed for the airport, cursing himself for his unaccustomed lack of foresight: booked to depart at midday tomorrow, he hadn't even bothered to look into earlier flights with connections to Burlington. Still, there had to be *something* that would get him there fast.

No good. The woman at the Delta desk told him the only direct connection, leaving in two hours, was a red-eye, and it involved a three-and-a-half-hour layover in Cincinnati. With the time change it wouldn't have him home before midmorning.

But, if he hurried, there was a lightly booked flight leaving in twelve minutes. It connected with another that could get him into Boston's Logan around midnight. The first Boston-Burlington flight was also tomorrow morning, but he'd sweat that later. What mattered was to get moving.

He made it onto the plane just before they bolted the door. Taking a third-row seat on the aisle, he snatched up the phone embedded in the seat ahead of him and found his list of key phone numbers in his wallet.

"Sir, you can't use the phone now."

"Why not?"

The young male steward flashed a programmed smile. "I'm sorry, we'll be taking off momentarily. FAA regulations."

He lied. It was ten excruciating moments before they were airborne.

Even as the plane was ascending, Mark ran his credit card through the slot. Instead of a dial tone he got a recorded advisory to try again. "Oh, fuck!" he muttered, remembering—loudly enough for the woman across the aisle to shoot him a dirty look. He tried the card again and got the same recording.

"Excuse me!!"

Halfway up the aisle, the same steward wheeled to face him.

"I've got a problem here!"

Annoyed, he made no effort to hide it. "We're very busy right now, sir."

"My credit card's overloaded. Do you know if I can make a collect call? Or charge it to my home number?"

"No, I don't."

"My wife is in labor! I have to reach her!"

"I really can't help you with that right now, sir."

"Damn it, *I NEED to reach her*!"

"I'm *sorry*, sir," he said, and continued up the aisle.

Instantly, Mark was on his feet, trailing after. "I want to talk to the captain!"

The young man barely suppressed a smile. "The *captain*?"

"Then your supervisor, goddamn it!"

The head flight attendant, an older woman, was far more sympathetic. "I understand, sir," she reassured him, "we've had other passengers in the same situation. But I'm afraid without a credit card . . ."

"Please, *someone*, I need help!" he was suddenly shouting over her. Up and down the aisle, stunned faces turned his way.

"Sir," said the stewardess, "I *must* ask you to return to your seat."

Ignoring her, he whipped off his watch—a cheap Timex. "My wife's in labor, I have to call her. But my card's maxed out."

There was a moment's pause. Then, to his relief, someone was actually waving a card in the air—a middle-aged black woman in a business suit, one row up and across the aisle.

"I've been there. Go ahead, make your call."

With a surging gratitude he offered her the watch.

"That's really not necessary."

"Please, take it."

She smiled and handed the precious bit of plastic across the aisle. "Just call your wife."

The phone on the stand beside Sally's bed was the kind still found only occasionally in older hotels and hospitals; lacking a dialing apparatus, it allowed patients to place outgoing calls only during certain hours, via an operator. Since she'd already picked up the heavy receiver and found dead air, Sally was startled when it suddenly began jangling.

She cut off the sound in midring and held the receiver to her ear.

"Hello . . . ?" came the voice, at once so familiar and a million miles away. "Is someone there?"

"Mark?" she asked with hushed urgency.

"Sally?!"

"Where are you?"

Hunched over in his seat, he spoke softly. "On my way back."

"Really? *When?*"

Her excited relief heightened his anxiety. "It'll be a while, I just left. Are you all right, Sal—is there a lot of pain?"

"I'm okay," she lied. "Contractions about every four minutes."

"That means you've still got some time. Who's there with you?"

"Right now, no one. I'm in the labor room. Lee Malen and Barbara Walker are outside."

"They taking good care of my girl? Monitoring you pretty closely?"

"Yeah." She paused. "What about the library?"

"I was there all day," he said, with all the calm at his command. "Fascinating place."

"Nothing to it, right? My hyperactive imagination getting the best of me . . ."

He hesitated—"Probably"—then instantly regretted the cryptic dodge.

"What do you mean?"

"You were right," he said, upbeat, "your family's got some unbelievable genes."

But she knew the nonchalance was a ruse. "What else?"

"That's all I can say for sure."

"Oh, God, here comes a contraction!"

"Hang on, Sally," he encouraged, "hang on. . . ."

In response there was only a gasp, followed by the rapid, shallow breathing they called "the dog pant."

"That's it, baby," he said soothingly, "just the way we practiced." Unconsciously, scarcely aware of his surroundings, Mark rose from his seat and started toward the front of the plane; then reversed himself and headed toward the back. "Short breaths. One-two-three-four, one-two-three-four."

"It's peaked, it's getting a little better."

"Good. Now take a deep, cleansing breath."

She exhaled loudly.

"You're doing fine, Sal. You're doing great."

"What do you mean 'probably'?" she picked up, but suddenly heard approaching footsteps in the hall.

"Just talk to me," she said hurriedly. "What do I need to know?"

Momentarily he was confused when he heard her cry of pain—it was too soon for another contraction. Then, in the background, he was aware of a new voice, surprised and questioning.

"It's Mark," he heard Sally gasp. "In Utah. Helping me with my breathing . . ."

Listening as she went into the dog pant, he understood this was a performance for the benefit of the other person in the room.

"You listening, Sally? Give me three short breaths if the answer's yes."

Immediately, they came.

"I think you're okay, do you understand? Just be strong."

In response there was only a questioning silence, and he knew he couldn't leave it at that.

"I want you to play it safe—stay alert, don't let them give you anything. Try to hang on as long as you can. I'll make some calls to get someone up there with you."

There was a pause—then the three short breaths.

"This looks like a pretty bad one," came the other voice suddenly, closer now—Barbara Walker! "Is the breathing helping?"

In the room Sally watched as the nurse took up the paper spooling from the printer linked to the fetal monitor. Holding the paper close to read it in the dim light, she was momentarily bewildered—it showed no contraction at all.

"It's better now," said Sally. "It's fading."

Moving beside her, Walker said gently, "May I speak to him?"

Reluctantly, Sally surrendered the receiver.

"Mark, this is Barbara Walker. I know your intentions are good, but I think this is pretty stressful for her. Why don't you call Dr. Malen's line and leave a forwarding number? One of us will get back to you."

He hesitated—and before he could answer the line went dead.

Mark rushed back down the aisle.

"Please," he said, "I need to make a couple more calls."

* * *

In the room Sally watched as Barbara pulled the jack from the wall and looped the cord around the phone. "I understand," she said sympathetically, walking toward the door. "But the doctor was very clear. No more disturbances."

With friends for an early dinner that evening at a new Italian place in Soho, Holland was in the middle of an amusing story about incompetence at the upper levels of the NIH when the pager in the holster at his waist began to vibrate. Stopping literally in midsentence—"Excuse me"—he glanced down. Top of the line, the SkyTel display screen could run a message several lines long. But now there were but three words.

Come tonight.—Lynch

With a tight, apologetic smile, he rose to his feet. "Sorry, a call I've been expecting."

The first call from Edwardstown Community Hospital had come in the early afternoon, and there had been updates every twenty minutes or so since. Lynch took the calls at the desk in the library, Foster listening in at an extension from what used to be Stagg's chair. Each message was the same: no problems, things were proceeding well.

But between calls Lynch stayed on his feet, alternately pacing and standing at the window, staring down the snowy front drive.

"What the hell are you looking at?" demanded Foster finally.

"I don't know."

"Holland won't be here till God knows when—if he makes it at all. There are six thousand damn books in this room. Grab one and park your ass in a chair."

"I'm not sure if I'm up for reading right now."

"What do you want to do, *talk*? Have a *personal* conversation to pass the time?"

He shook his head, knowing Foster was mocking him.

"Well, then, why don't we talk about the weather? That seems to be a big topic around here."

Silence.

"Do you ski, Lynch?"

"No," he replied tentatively. "Do you?"

"Why would I do that? Would it get us one fucking centimeter closer to the goal?!"

"I'm sorry," allowed Lynch, "I guess I'm just a little nervous."

"Don't be." Foster nodded with certainty. "We've waited this long. What's a few more hours?"

Chief Stebben zipped his leather jacket up another couple of notches, as high as it would go.

Christ, a man could freeze his pecker off! What the hell was he DOING here?

But, no, he knew. Though Mark Bowman's call had come at a bad time—fourth quarter of a good PAC-10 game on ESPN—he instantly had his full attention. The guy was scared—*terrified!*—and Stebben didn't feel in any position to reassure him.

Should he start the motor back up to get some heat going? But, no, that was insane—sleepy as he was, out here, miles from anywhere, that would be asking for it. More than once, on crisp mornings after nights exactly like this one, he'd personally helped remove bodies from cars, their engines still idling. Hey, no problem, those poor bastards were getting plenty of sleep now.

If nothing else, at least the cold would keep him alert.

Carol hadn't wanted him to go. It was no time for one of these wild goose chases, she said—and besides, *Sally Benedict*? After all she'd done to *him*?! Of course she had a point—but in a funny way, for Stebben that's what cinched it. Her hubby had made it clear he was calling as a last resort; if Sally knew, he said, she wouldn't allow it. Well, screw that! Sally Benedict didn't know him, never had! Okay, he'd made a few mistakes in his time, maybe looked the other way about things he shouldn't have. But how the hell had it come to this?! That someone in his community afraid for her life would be even *more* afraid to let him know?!!

The question was how to proceed. No way he could march into the hospital—she'd start screaming bloody murder.

Then, abruptly, he knew, the idea hitting him even before the cruiser was out of the driveway. If there was anything to it, after all, he knew what route they'd take: County Route 112 through the wooded slopes south of Mt. Waumbeck, a little-known shortcut that knocked twenty minutes off the trip from Manchester to Edwards-town.

Why shouldn't he know?—he'd sent off a map marking the road himself, just a few days before the first grave robbing.

She'd expected the pain, was as ready for it as she could possibly be. But what Sally hadn't counted on was that the contractions would leave her so spent. Only now did she realize that nature intended that every precious moment between be used to gather up strength for the next onslaught.

But that was impossible now. Even before the agony of the last one had fully abated, she unhooked the fetal monitor and was struggling to sit up. Swinging her feet to the floor, she managed to stand—then, as the room began moving in a slow circle, had to seize the bed's side rail for balance. She took a long moment, legs apart, as much squatting as standing, then slowly made her way to the door.

At best, she had three minutes.

Opening it a crack, peering into the well-lit hallway, she saw that the plastic chairs lining the wall opposite were empty. An instant later she knew why: Barbara Walker could be heard at one of the pay phones around the corner, her voice hushed, but agitated and impatient.

Quickly, Sally was out of the room and scuttling down the hall in the other direction.

She'd been here dozens of times over the years on both professional and personal business, and knew exactly where she was going.

Turning a corner past the deserted nurse's station, she glanced at the wall clock. 12:07. Her timing couldn't be worse: it would probably be another six hours before any of the daytime staff returned.

The stairwell leading down a flight to the back exit was just around another corner and to the right. If she could make it outside . . . And then . . . what? She hadn't thought it out! Look for a passing car? Give birth in the woods like some Indian woman? She hadn't even brought a blanket.

But for now, all that mattered was escape!

Reaching the door, she gently pushed down on the metal bar to open it—and was startled when it held fast. She hadn't even considered the possibility—this door was never locked. She tried again, this time putting her shoulder against the door.

"Goddamn it!" she whispered. *"GodDAMN it!"*

She knew by now she had no more than a minute. Quickly, she began retracing her steps—then, at the nurse's station, she stopped. Posted on the bulletin board behind the desk was what looked to be the duty roster.

Suddenly the wave hit, this time completely without warning. Fighting it, she seized the desk, then sank into the office chair behind. As it peaked, the pain blotted out all else. Head back, eyes closed, mouth open in a silent cry, she dug her nails into the padded armrests and drove her legs hard against the floor, sending the chair shooting backward into a file cabinet.

A few hundred feet away Barbara Walker thought she heard something. But there was nothing to be done. For now, her full focus was on Steve Montera.

"Look, this wasn't *my* idea," Montera was saying with a smile.

"Frankly, I didn't even enjoy being here all that much when it was *my* kid."

Standing before the open elevator door, blocking his way, Walker smiled back. "I remember."

"But when a friend asks you to check up on his wife . . ."

"She's doing fine, Steve, hanging right in there."

"Can't I see her?" He paused. "She's been, you know, a little *off* lately."

"You know better than that—the woman's in labor. It's the *last* thing she wants."

Montera chuckled. "That makes two of us. Still . . ."

"Steve, you're a better friend than I'll ever be. Now go home and get some sleep. She's doing Mark proud."

The pain had left her eyes full of tears. She brushed them dry with her arm. It was half a minute before she was able to hoist herself back to her feet and focus on the duty roster.

Young Judith Marsh was supposed to have been on duty tonight, not Barbara Walker! But a line had been drawn through Marsh's name, and Barbara's penciled in instead.

Her first reaction was curiously muted. Clearly, such switches were routine.

It was only after a moment that she understood she was starting to give up! The impulse to denial was overwhelming. Somehow, she had to summon up the strength to resist it.

Spotting a tray bearing a couple of pairs of scissors, a roll of gauze, and a scalpel, she snatched up the gleaming instrument and stuck it in the pocket of her robe, before continuing down the hall.

Reaching the corner, she peered around and saw the chairs outside her room were still empty. But now, in the distance, she heard voices.

Could it really be? Montera?!

"Help me!" she screamed, starting down the hallway as fast as she could manage. "Please help me!"

As the elevator doors slowly closed, Montera watched the nurse turn away. "Gotta run," she called back coolly. "*That's* the sound of a woman in heavy labor."

When Mark's flight from Chicago touched down at Boston's Logan Airport at twenty-five past midnight, he was the first passenger off. Dashing through the near-deserted terminal, already largely shut down for the night, he emerged into the frigid night and ran to the taxi stand.

"Where to?" snapped the dispatcher.

"New Hampshire," he managed, breathless.

"*New Hampshire?* How far north?"

"A little past Berlin."

"You gotta be kidding me!"

"Please" he called, pulling out his checkbook, "my wife's having a baby."

He waved it at the first driver in line, an Indian or Pakistani, watching through the window of his beat-up Mercury. "I'll pay anything!"

"How far is this place?" asked the driver pleasantly.

"I don't know, maybe two and a half hours."

"Try *four* and a half," said the dispatcher acidly. "Straight up 93, then on Route 3 nearly to Canada!"

"Certainly, yes. Get in."

"Thank you so much," said Mark, collapsing into the backseat as the cab pulled away. "Really, I can't tell you what this means to me."

"Indeed, you can—I've got seven myself! No doubt you want me to hurry."

"Please, if you could."

There was almost no traffic this time of night, but the roads were still icy. Trying to shut out that along with the rest, he closed his eyes as the accelerating car rattled with the strain.

"Do not worry, my friend," was the last thing he heard as he started to drift off. "For sure, I will get you there."

Stebben knew this desolate road well. Two narrow lanes twisting through a heavily wooded pass, it was treacherous even under the best of circumstances. Since the storm it was nearly impassable; the deep freeze having transformed the single lane left behind by a plow to a solid strip of ice.

The chief was certain there'd be no unexpected traffic tonight. He himself had posted signs at both ends warning off would-be intrepid motorists.

Only one driver, he was sure, would ignore them.

Stebben had chosen this spot carefully: a straightaway half a mile long, appearing suddenly after a series of harrowingly sharp curves. The curves would slow him down. Parked at the midpoint of the straightaway, the cruiser would stop him cold. There was no way around him. The roadbed was raised here, dropping fifteen feet on either side into the woods.

Just in case, his vintage .38 Smith & Wesson was in his holster, and the department's Remington .223 rifle was within easy reach on the rack behind him. Now, again, he patted the rifle and a phrase came to mind: *The whites of their eyes.* But in his nineteen years on the force he'd never fired either weapon in anger.

Already he'd been here in the blackness nearly an hour. Twice, he'd volated his own rule by turning on the engine to warm himself. Now he was aware of his stomach rumbling. Why the hell hadn't he at least thought to bring along a snack? A couple of those Hostess minipies, maybe, or some chocolate doughnuts from the 7-Eleven.

Worse, he had to pee. *Bad.*

"Ah, shit," he said aloud and, adjusting the earmuffs beneath his cop's hat, opened the door and slip-slided his way to the front of the car. He had to take off his gloves to open his fly, and it was so damn cold, it took longer than usual for the thing to start working. In the still blackness he couldn't even see where it was going.

Suddenly, over the sound of piss on ice, he heard the other vehicle approaching. At first he thought it was still quite a ways off, but just an instant later the Range Rover's distinctive yellow fog lights flashed around a curve in the middle distance.

Less than a mile away, he was coming *fast.*

Stebben slipped running back to the car. Landing hard on his hands and knees, he struggled up; then almost fell again as he yanked open the door. Behind the wheel he reached for the rifle.

Already the sonovabitch was hitting the last curve before the straightaway.

Rifle in hand, heart pounding, Stebben rolled down the window.

Ten seconds more and the Range Rover was on the slick straightaway, doing seventy-five, heedless of what lay ahead.

"Take this, asshole," Stebben muttered, and simultaneously flicked on his brights, his siren, and flasher.

"Oh, Jesus!" shouted Lynch, in the passenger seat, shielding his eyes.

Stunned, Van Ost took nearly a full second to react. Though the Range Rover had four-wheel antilocks, at this speed, on this surface, they only helped him hold the road.

Leaning out the window now, the rifle against the side view mirror for support, Stebben watched the distance between them close in mute horror. It wasn't until they were within fifty yards that he fired, the shot crashing through the windshield between them.

Focused on the obstacle ahead, Van Ost was oblivious. At the last moment, desperately trying to miss him, he swerved sharply to the right. But he still hit the cruiser just past the driver's side headlight, slamming the smaller car backward over the embankment to the left, where it flipped onto its hood, as the Range Rover careened over the embankment opposite, flattening bushes and small trees before plowing into a massive oak.

Stebben was dead on impact. Lynch, unconscious and bleeding profusely, did not last the hour.

Miraculously, beside him, Van Ost had suffered only a concussion and several broken ribs. But he was pinned inside the vehicle and, the windshield gone, exposed to the elements; and no one would come upon the wreck for hours.

Ushered into the Institute's spacious library, Holland realized it was the first time he'd been in this room since the day he met Stagg.

He was more than a little surprised to find Foster sitting in the old man's chair.

"One-ten," he said, checking his watch. "You made good time."

"I caught the last flight out of LaGuardia. Where's Dr. Lynch?"

"Asleep. He asked me to wait up for you."

"He wanted me up here immediately. Tonight."

Foster rose to his feet. "We just thought it was something that couldn't wait."

Holland watched him, fascinated. Foster seemed a transformed man, as suddenly decisive as he'd always been painfully reticent.

"Do you drink champagne?" he asked.

"Is there something to celebrate?"

"Come with me."

Holland followed as Foster briskly led him from the room, down a corridor, and around a corner.

"I really don't know how you guys navigate this place," offered Holland, by way of conversation.

But already Foster was turning into a room. He flicked on the light—a lab Holland had never seen before.

"This is where we've done some of our best work," said Foster, walking into an adjacent storage area. Holland heard the opening and closing of a refrigerator door and the scientist returned with a pair of slides.

These he placed side by side in microscopes on a lab table, turned on a powerful overhead light, and with a wave of his hand invited the journalist to examine them.

"Biopsy samples?" asked Holland, peering at the first. It showed healthy cells, growing in a regular, mosaiclike pattern, the dark nucleus within each a near-perfect oval.

"Very good, Mr. Holland. You really do know your stuff."

"Human?"

"Close—chimpanzee."

Intrigued, Holland then moved on to the second sample. Here there was mayhem; the cells irregular in shape and size, their nuclei disintegrating.

"It looks like one of your chimps has about had it," he remarked.

Foster nodded. "You're right, the sample reflects extremely advanced age."

"And the other is younger. . . ."

He looked at him meaningfully. "No, Mr. Holland, that's the point—it's the same animal. The healthy sample was obtained two months *after* the first—following a single treatment with the drug."

It took Holland an instant to fully grasp the meaning. "You've nailed it?!"

He allowed himself a small smile. "No one else knows yet. We're calling it Terminase."

Holland looked like he was about to hug him. "My God, if I were you I'd be bouncing off the walls!" He thrust out a hand. "Congratulations!"

He shook it. "So . . . champagne?"

"Absolutely!"

Foster again disappeared into the back room, this time returning with a bottle of André.

"It's not exactly my usual brand," laughed the journalist.

"It's a private joke, actually—it's what we used to slip the drug to the chimp." He paused. "Of course, you're free to choose your own poison."

"Excuse me?"

"Or you can take it straight—as both Dr. Lynch and I did."

Only now did he see that in his other hand the scientist held a vial of colorless liquid. "You've tested the drug on *yourselves*?"

"And you'll be the third. As promised." He held aloft the vial. "Twenty milliliters. When it's marketed, a dose like this will cost upwards of twenty-five thousand dollars."

"Tonight?" asked Holland in a sudden panic. *"Now?"*

"The truth is, I envy you. Given your condition, your results will constitute the real breakthrough. We fully expect that whatever damage has already been done to your nervous system will be reversed in a matter of months."

Always a coward, Holland felt faint. But he couldn't allow himself to hesitate. Never again would he be handed so stunning an opportunity.

"I'll take it with the champagne," he said, and watched as Foster carefully mixed the liquids in a plastic cup.

The contractions were coming on top of each other now, and this was the worst one yet—a jagged knife slowly turning in her gut. She breathed rapidly through open lips, her cheeks puffing with every exhalation until, at its peak, she clutched the bedsheets, arched her back, and cried out against the white-hot pain.

Watching, the nurse stood over her, arms folded.

"Oh, God," said Sally, a moment later, face bright with perspiration. "That was a bad one."

Sally reached out a hand. "Hold my hand, Barbara. Please."

"You're doing just fine," she said, taking it, but there wasn't even the pretense of warmth. "It won't be much longer."

"Thanks for everything," offered Sally, desperate to reestablish the bond. "I can't tell you how much it means to me."

She nodded. "That's what I'm here for."

In fact, this was their longest exchange in the nearly five hours since the nurse had caught her out of bed. Irate, Walker had not even responded to Sally's frantic claim that she'd just been trying to go to the bathroom. And she hadn't let her out of sight since.

Now the nurse moved around the bed to check the fetal monitor's tracer sheet. "As a matter of fact, I think it's about time to get the doctor now."

Already, the next wave was upon her. "No," she managed, with a ludicrous try at nonchalance, "I'm sure it'll still be a while."

Ignoring her, Walker moved briskly to the door and flung it open. "Dr. Malen!!"

In seconds Malen was in the room, bleary eyed, his white jacket not yet completely buttoned.

Walker drew him to the side and indicated the printout. "It looks like she's in transition. Contractions are strong and lasting more than a minute."

"How far apart?"

"A minute and a half."

The doctor watched her struggling against this latest contraction and knelt beside the bed. "You're pretty far along now, Sal. I'm gonna give you the old once-over."

She grimaced, biting her lower lip, unhearing, as he moved down to the foot of the bed.

"Right," he said calmly to the nurse, "let's get her into the delivery room."

Only now, the pain abating, did she focus on his words. "Not yet! I'm not ready!"

"But the baby is. You're fully effaced and nine centimeters dilated."

"She's resisted every step of the way," said Walker, unclamping the front locks that transformed the labor bed into a gurney.

"Well, now it's zero hour," said Malen, positioning himself at the front of the bed. He nodded at Walker, behind. "Let's do it."

They'd moved the gurney out the door and into the hallway when Walker cried out. "Watch it!"

Wheeling, Malen saw the nurse was flat against the wall as, still on her back, Sally slashed at her with a scalpel.

"Just keep away from me!!" she said with the remorseless determination of the truly mad. "Don't touch me!"

"Jesus Christ! Put that down, Sally! You're going to hurt yourself!"

"I swear to God, Lee, don't come any closer!"

Her face bright red, her features twisted, she seemed utterly possessed.

"What should we do, Doctor?!"

"Just wait."

For he could see that even now, a new contraction was taking hold.

"All right, Sally," he said with quiet authority, "give me the scalpel."

"Stay away," she repeated, grimacing.

But now, closing her eyes, she momentarily went rigid. In no time he'd grabbed her wrist and was working the scalpel free. "Quick," he shouted at the nurse, "get her in four-point restraints and let's do what we have to do!"

"I'll cooperate, Lee," she gasped. "I promise."

"Damn right you will!"

Another minute and she was immobilized on the delivery room table, her feet in the stirrups. She gazed around, wild eyed, at the high-tech surroundings: the various monitors and blinding overhead lights, the "crash cart" loaded with emergency drugs. Focusing on the wall clock, she saw it showed 5:32.

"Now, PUSH, Sally," ordered Malen, with the onset of the next contraction, "I want you to STOP fighting it!"

She ostentatiously gritted her teeth and made grunting noises.

"HARD!!"

"She's still holding back," noted Walker.

He glared at her. "Goddamn you, Sally! Do what I tell you!!"

"I'm trying."

"Like HELL you are! Don't you know you're putting your baby at risk?!"

She made no reply. Already she could feel the next wave starting to build. But his terrifying warning cut right through the pain. *Fuck you, Malen, you'll say ANYTHING!*

"Should we put her out, Doctor?"

He hesitated, then nodded at the crash cart. "Get a syringe ready. Succinylcholine."

As the contraction eased, Sally saw that Walker already held the syringe, predrawn for crisis situations, at the ready.

"I don't want to do this," Malen was saying, "but you're leaving me no choice." Then, to Walker: "Prepare an IV line. I'll also need a mask and an intubation set."

Sally turned away, hope all but gone. "All right," she said softly, "I'll do what you want."

"Are we doing a C-section, Doctor?"

Malen hesitated, unsure. "I don't know. Maybe it won't be necessary."

He leaned close to Sally. "I need to know you mean it. Like it or not, this baby's *coming*. Nature's tougher even than you."

"I said I'll cooperate," she repeated softly.

The next contraction was so intense that, closing her eyes, she could actually see the pain, kaleidoscopic, changing shape and color, going from white, to orange, to brilliant red. It was like she was being slowly ripped in two.

"Go on, Sally, push," urged Malen. "Only you can make it stop."

It only took another five minutes.

"There it is," she dimly heard Malen, exultant. "There's the head! C'mon, Sally, push! Do it! Just a couple more!"

She summoned forth a strength it seemed impossible she still had, so absorbed by the effort she was oblivious to her own screams.

For an instant she felt only the sudden, wondrous absence of pain.

Now, cutting through the fog, came Malen's familiar laugh. "See that, Sal, nothing to it. You've got yourself a beautiful little girl."

He gently lifted her for her mother to see. Tiny and hairless, still slick with vernix, she was remarkably unperturbed; indeed, seemed to gaze about at this new world with genuine curiosity.

Sally reached out for her, the powerful, contradictory emotions surging: ecstasy and uncertainty, a growing sense of relief warring with deep mistrust and suspicion. "Let me hold her!"

"Whoa, mind if we cut the umbilical cord first?"

"Please! My baby!!"

With practiced efficiency Malen double-clamped the cord and snipped it. "Now, then," he said, smiling into the newborn's eyes, "let's spruce you up to meet this crazy mommy of yours."

"GIVE ME MY BABY!"

"Okay, okay," he said, handing her over, "we'll towel her off later."

Sally clutched her close, arms around her defensively, shielding her from the others' view. "Oh, God, look at her!"

It was nearly a minute before she risked laying her down on the pillow beside her and ran her pinkie across the tiny cheek and lips. "Hello, darling Helen. Welcome to the world."

"Barbara," asked Malen, "did you catch the exact time of birth?"

"Five forty-six."

He looked up at the wall clock, which showed 5:49. "Good— wouldn't want to screw up her astrological chart. Why don't you fill out the form while we take care of the afterbirth?"

"What about clearing the child's ears and nasal passages?"

"No!" interjected Sally, instantly back on alert, "she stays with me!"

"No problem," agreed Malen. "That can wait a few minutes."

"Doctor, you know it's standard operating procedure."

"I won't tell if you don't, Barbara. God knows we haven't gone by the book on anything else tonight."

"Dr. Malen, we are responsible for this child's well-being—"

"That's *it*," he cut her off. "I'd *appreciate* it if you'd please fill out that form. There are some blank ones in my top drawer."

Sally watched in tense silence as the nurse left the room. She felt far safer with both present.

Malen turned back to her. "Now, think you have one more good push in you?"

"Can the baby stay with me?"

"Why not? And this time I can even help you push."

She kept a protective arm over the baby as he moved to the table and placed his hands on her abdomen. Gently he began applying pressure, helping her expel the afterbirth.

"Well," he said, smiling, as he heard the door behind him open, "at least *that* part was uneventful. But we still have a lot of work to do on your attitude—don't you think, Barbara?"

But the figure who entered the room, gowned and masked, wear-

ing a surgical cap and gloves and even shoe covers, was unrecognizable.

"Excuse me, Doctor . . . ?" asked Malen, confused.

"I'd like to examine the child, if I could," he said, ignoring the
question but elaborately polite.

"No!" shouted Sally.

"And you would be . . . ?"

"My name's McCall, I'm from Madison General. We got a call
from the father asking that someone look in on this child."

"It's okay now," said Sally. "Everything's fine."

"Excellent. If I can just have a look . . ."

Already she was edging off the table, the baby in her arms.

"You're frightening her, Doctor," said Malen curtly. "I really
must ask you to leave."

"I have a job to do, I've come quite a ways."

Her soreness and exhaustion abruptly gone, in seconds she was
in the far corner of the room, shielding the child with her body and
eyeing the door. "Keep him away!"

"That's *enough*," said Malen, sharply.

Eyes on Sally, he continued slowly forward. "It will only take a
minute."

Malen stepped in front of him, blocking his path. "Thank you,
Doctor, but these are my patients. *Both* of them."

"No, Doctor!" he said, and from within his gown produced a
gun. "No more!"

Incongruously, Malen smiled.

"Stand back," he snapped, caught short by the reaction, "this
isn't a joke!"

"A twenty-two? It sure looks like one."

The gunman himself seemed startled by the crack of the gun. He
looked on in silence as Malen reeled backward and sank to the floor.

The bullet had shattered his clavicle and collapsed a lung. As he
lay there, laboring to breathe, blood started to foam at the corners of

his mouth, Sally made a sudden move for the door. But, recovering quickly, the gunman stepped over the prostrate form and cut off her angle.

Suddenly, the baby started to howl.

"I promise I won't hurt her," he said, edging closer.

Sally moved around the table, using it as a buffer. He circled around, stalking, as if they were children playing indoor tag.

"I promise, I won't hurt her," he repeated.

She said nothing, kept moving.

"Try to understand, this is important! Vital!"

Suddenly, her legs started to buckle and she had to reach for the end of the table to keep from falling, the baby nearly slipping from her grasp. "Keep away!"

The man stopped, terrified by what he'd just seen. "Careful!"

Sally instantly picked up the fear. "Keep away," she said again—and now backed away from the table toward the window ledge.

"Just hand me the child," he urged, following, his tone almost seductive, "and it will all be over."

She reached the ledge and grasped it for support, looking like she was starting to swoon. "Please," she said, her voice notably fainter, "just leave us alone."

"It's going to be all right," he said soothingly, inching forward, "no one's going to hurt the child. . . ."

All at once, she started to totter, her hand slipping from the ledge.

Rushing forward, lunging for the baby, he never saw the syringe—the one left unused earlier—flashing upward from waist level. It entered his abdomen beneath his rib cage and slightly to the left, the drug shooting directly into the left ventricle of his heart.

For an instant he was disoriented, then saw the words on the label of the syringe embedded in his chest, *Succinylcholine, 20 mg,* and understood. Already his blood pressure was plummeting as his heart rate slowed, the electrical impulses that drive the muscles misfiring.

Foster looked at her, his eyes full of pained surprise, as the color drained from his face and he toppled to the floor.

Sally watched in mute horror, the adrenaline pumping so hard she was unaware of the sound she'd been awaiting so long: the ding of the elevator.

Mark heard a baby crying as he bolted from the elevator and down the hall. The first thing he saw on flinging open the door was Foster, faceup and glassy eyed on the floor, a tiny bloodstain on his gown by the syringe; then his wife, slumped on the table with their howling child still in her arms.

"Jesus, no!" he gasped. "Sally!"

"We're all right," she said. "Help Lee."

Across the room Malen managed to slowly raise himself up on one elbow.

Mark rushed to his side. "My God, what's happened here?!"

"A tough delivery." Though Malen's breathing was labored, his smile was intact. "But we got through it."

In her first party dress and a headband festooned with fairy roses, two-month-old Helen stared wide eyed at the throng as her father cruised her through the living room in his arms.

"Quite the little party animal, aren't you?" cooed Steve Montera, following with a camcorder.

Lee Malen, his arm in a sling, smiled at them from the couch. "Just tell her not to forget who this party's for."

Montera turned the camera his way. "Ooops, sounds like the doc wants to remind us again of his heroism. Then, again, if you're gonna get shot, a hospital *is* the place to do it."

"The battling co-godfathers!" observed Sally, setting down a plate of hot hors d'oeuvres, "I just hope this isn't a preview of the next twenty years. Actually, Lee, we're celebrating lots of things."

In fact, though they'd delayed it until Malen was out of the hospital, the party's timing seemed perfect; for only now was the town itself beginning to recover from the gruesome episode.

To the rest of the world the story was a two-day wonder, soon overshadowed by the next eruption of violent mayhem in some other community. Afterward, few news outlets even bothered to follow up that M & R Associates had shut down its American operation, relo-

cating to Brazil; or that the renovated factory building on the out-
skirts of Manchester, formerly home to the Life Services Institute,
was on the block. Even in her own circle only Sally seemed to notice
that Holland suffered no repercussions for having missed the story of
the Institute's secret project. Known for taking care of its own, the
august *Herald* continued to feature his byline as prominently as ever.

But the night's terrible events shook this small, isolated town to
its very foundations. Few in Edwardstown were startled to learn of
the naked amorality of Lynch and Foster; it was understood that, in
other places, the ruthlessly ambitious did horrible things almost as a
matter of course. But Barbara Walker was one of their own. At one
time or another almost everyone in town had been in her care. Even
though she was caught that night on the Mass Pike after an APB,
some refused to believe she was involved at all until she plead guilty
to attempted kidnapping.

Malen, at least, helped redeem the town's sense of itself—along,
of course, with Chief Stebben. And if some harbored suspicions
about Stebben's role in events leading to that night, no one was
inclined to voice them now. The *Weekly* had even undertaken a cam-
paign to mount a plaque celebrating the chief outside police headquarters.

"Hey," called Sally, leading Florence by the hand in front of
Montera's camera, "how about getting the god*mother* for posterity?"

"Oh, really, no," demurred Florence, hand to her face as the
camcorder turned her way, "I always get so tongue tied."

"Right—and you told me you couldn't run the paper either."

Florence shrugged this away. "That's different, I'm just keeping
the job warm for you."

"Uh-uh, I've never been happier, only having a weekly column to
worry about. . . ." She looked around, her eyes finding her daughter. "And plenty of material to fill it."

"How about a toast?" chimed in Mark. "Everybody get some champagne!"

Though this early February afternoon it was nearly as cold in New York as in Edwardstown, the heat in Paul Holland's East Side home was turned way down. Holland always worked best this way, it helped him think.

Supposedly fiction, the work in progress was actually a thinly veiled account of his own involvement with the project—and he fully expected it to make him more money than he'd earned in twenty years of journalism.

But even more, the book loomed as his ticket to immortality. It was recognition insurance, the guarantee that he'd receive full credit for his role in helping promote, finance—and test—what would soon be recognized as the greatest research breakthrough of the age. He remained in close touch with Eric Cooper, now working in São Paulo in a lab sponsored by M & R to refine the drug's delivery system; and Holland was planning the book's release to coincide with the sensation certain to be touched off by the first reports of the coming medical miracle.

Today, though, the writing was going badly. Awakening with severe stomach cramps, he'd had to drag himself to his computer, and even in the chilly room, he found himself sweating profusely. Hard as he tried to focus, the words just wouldn't come. In over four hours he'd managed only a few paragraphs.

Turning back to the screen, he reread them yet again, reaching for a glass of seltzer water. Suddenly, he froze.

There was a drop of blood on his keyboard.

Now, as he watched, there came another. Touching his face, he felt it coming from both nostrils.

"My God!" he said softly, and ran to the bathroom. The blood was pouring out, uncontrollable.

In horror, a washcloth to his face, he retreated to his bed and called his doctor, but got only the service.

Now, all at once, the abdominal pains grew so severe, he reflexively grabbed a pillow and clutched it hard against his midsection, drawing himself into a fetal position.

Lying there, softly moaning, he was a pitiable sight—if there had been anyone else to see it.

"Well," said Sally, eyes glowing, as she gazed around the room at her friends, "I guess it's my turn." She paused. "What can I say? I've done lots of things in my life people consider incredibly interesting and exciting." She held up her glass, and smiled. "To our Helen. Who would've guessed that having a child would be the greatest adventure of all?"